HYBRID'S SECRETS

Book One

LINDA TRAINOR

authorHOUSE®

AuthorHouse™
1663 Liberty Drive
Bloomington, IN 47403
www.authorhouse.com
Phone: 1 (800) 839-8640

Published by AuthorHouse 03/10/2016

ISBN: 978-1-5049-8203-0 (sc)
ISBN: 978-1-5049-8204-7 (e)

Print information available on the last page.

Any people depicted in stock imagery provided by Thinkstock are models, and such images are being used for illustrative purposes only. Certain stock imagery © Thinkstock.

This book is printed on acid-free paper.

CHAPTER ONE

HE RAIN-SMELLED LIKE ACID as it came down around me, the feel of water falling down my face stung to a point that I wanted to scream. My flesh burnt as the rain flow down with each step I took. I gritted my mouth and teeth as the feel of acid stinging my skin and eyes, it wasn't as bad as it used to be, but the pain was still intense. Yet, I kept on walking toward the one path that would lead me to where I needed to be. I couldn't see the path to well; the grass was so tall that my feet were even hidden beneath the grass that I stomp on. The grass was so tall that I felt as if I was in a forest and knew I was in my neighborhood my community was not that far from where I was heading. I knew I was tired from going to work, it was one of those days that my job at the website news, I couldn't leave for three nights and days, my stomach growled as I had not eaten much during the days and nights I stayed at the website. I knew the website news didn't pay well, $50 a day or more $ 50. Dollars a news that was not record yet, not hourly. I had stayed there among the other people who were struggling to make enough money to feed their family or their own responsibilities. I had made enough money to buy a slice of bread that cost Fifty dollars. Yet fifty dollars was all I had gotten from that website news job.

Yet, I still held on to it, there is no other job that would take me. I had worked for the website sense I was in my early teenage years, now, I am not sure how old I am. That last account of my age was a guess, just like many other things were in my life. I remember I was too young when my parents died and my sister and I had to survive somehow, even though we only had each other and our parent's home to live in.

However, it was our home and there were things at our home that was important to us, like the fact that our parents had left the home for us, so we could have some kind of shelter. As I thought quietly about my sister back at my or our home, I felt weak as my legs started to buckle under my weight, I knew I was hungry and my stomach had made it clear, the rumble inside and the pain that drove me to keep on moving almost blinded me in my effort to continue on. My hunger grew stronger and louder as I took in the sight of the sight of where I was heading. The building was old with bricks missing and a roof that keeps on peeling off with little wind to blow on it. My shoes flop on the ground sounded odd as sticks and tall grass stumbled in each path I went. On each side of my view were other hidden buildings that were once lived in and are now covered with trees and tall grass that hidden the homes. Windows were broken with another tree inside of it that stretched out its branches upward. It looked like hands trying to reach for help. But there is no help for anyone.

The sky seemed to open as the acid rain fell down hard around me, the sight of just one large cloud following me made me feel bad. I took a breath and hope that it wasn't a bad sign. The acid rain kept on falling and stinging those that was following me with the same reasoning as I had to find food. The acid in the rain was making the grass and trees turn brown and yet the ground seemed to simmer as if it were on fire.

I could feel the steam beneath my feet as kept on walking. My mind was not on the pain as much as it was on my sister who was waiting for me to come home with something for her to eat. My sister was the only reason I wanted to stay alive, we were family she needed me and I needed her to keep on living. My sister would smile at me and I would just do whatever she wanted me to do. Sometimes we would tell each other stories or would just sleep together to keep each other warm at night. But she is my sister and I love her more than anything. I kept on walking toward that one place that would at least have food, it was the storage house or building that the government had open up on certain days or month to let us have food. The costs of the food in the stores were too high for anyone that could even afford, let alone anyone who even had money either. Most of the time people would just hunt for food or steal them. Some would just die alone. My sister and I survived our parent's death; we lived through many nights and days without food or water, but then we also had Mr. Farmer who came to us many times to feed us and give us some hope. We survived through diseases that the wealthy could afford for the cure, yes; the government had a cure for all diseases, but only for the wealthy, and the powerful officials were the only one that were allowed to have the cures.

The government had taken the choice of who lives and who dies; we just live and watch the rich get greedier and more powerful. Right now, I had to get to that store that had bread-food inside. I know I only had fifty dollars on me and I could only get a slice of bread. However, it was food just the same. I got sight of the building and found many others had the same idea and felt the need to eat in great numbers. They like me looked like the living dead that our parents had told us when we were bad. People that could not die, but were already dead, the feeling of being deprive from food shelter or medical attention was like being dead but not dead. People eyes sunken dull without life or reason to even live, but still fighting to live.

I reached the storage store as I pushed and pulled my body forward through the large group of people that were struggling to get in too. I was inside the store that was not clean or would ever be clean, the smell of old urine and rotted food made my nose twitch at the smell around me. The sound of my shoes flopping on the cool tile floor sounded strange as it echoed around the store.

There were people already running through the store trying find something that they could afford to pay with the little bit of money they had. As I noticed in front of the store, the cashiers were standing up close to the computers stand, their faces showing worn out and depleted of strength and the same as everyone else, hungrier. The line that led out of the store and start at the cashiers, some of the cashiers were complaining about the hours and the time that they had to leave. The store owner shouted at them that they had to work until all the food was gone. If they kept on complaining, he would make sure that they get less pay.

The shouting grew more as the line of people started to shove closer to the cashiers as the cashiers tried to leave their stations. I had to ignore the shouts and screams, as I knew I came here for one thing that I knew I had enough money to buy.

One slice of bread was all I could afford for my sister right now and it was all I could think of. She was important to me; we grew up as one, until I got a job at the website news. It wasn't much of a job, but it was all I could get for each report I could mustard quickly on the site before anyone could. I was lucky at least I knew how to read and write it gave me a more advantage over some other reporters that worked there that only knew a few words and not more than that. I had to know how to read better and use a computer. My parents believed that reading and writing was very important to both my sister and I. Brooke was the oldest out the two of us, but I was healthier than she was. Therefore, I was the one to get a job to feed us. Yet, the job didn't pay enough. A matter of fact no job paid enough for any one that need food and shelter. Life was hard struggling to just to survive. Each day I hoped that Brooke would still be alive. Shouts and screams were getting louder. I heard the overhead com announced that the cashiers were working free. The government had ordered all cashiers to be working free; no one is to receive any kind of payment. The announcer said. Then the sound of broken glass came close to my hearing range as I heard screams of people crashing through glass that was in front of the store windows as some of the people storm through cashier's line. A riot broke out in front of the store, more people scramble to either get out or get in the store, I heard shouts or something that sound like the police firing off guns at the crowd. I walked a little faster through the stores lanes of foods that were sitting on shelves rusted and dirty with some dent in each can. Fruits and fresh vegetables were stack on the shelves rotted decay with bugs eating off the food. Can goods scatter everywhere on shelves some open dry a nose peeked out of one of the cans, I knew it was a mouse.

The sound of the cart was making clanging bumps on the uneven floor of the store. The store was only open a few times for anyone that need food. I was anxious to see both the food and to get what I could afford; I knew I had only enough money for that slice of bread I was buying. I still was nervous and comprehension of my surrounding. Yet the sound of struggles in the front made me stop to look around me, I had to be aware of what was going on around me at all times, you just never know if someone would be behind you and kill you too. I could hear carts pushing hard on the tile floor as uneven floors made then lurch hard against the floors path. Cans falling down on metal clanged hard, loud around me as I kept on walking slowly. Then out of nowhere, someone had pushed a cart down my way empty and waiting for me. I took it without questions, then started to put food in my cart as the sound of more shouts and scream rose, I knew that the police would be here soon. I had to work fast if I was going to steal any food from here. It was my chance to bring more food to the community and my sister (if she was still alive). As I went down the lane, I took everything off the shelves and into my cart. Meats were at the back of the store, I grabbed more than I thought with one loaded armful into the cart. Then I ran to the side of the store hoping that no one saw me yet loading more fruit and vegetables in the cart too. I never thought that I could move so fast. However, I had put more into the cart as it felled up to the point that I might not be able to move the cart out of the store. I stopped close to the pharmacy I had a feeling that inside I would find something to save my sister. I heard the sounds of people screaming, others storming the storefront windows large glass pane. The sound of the window crashing open glass broke as it shattered all around people as they scramble from the falling glass. Steve could hear people screaming and some moaning aloud from the front of the stores windows that must've have stabbed them from the fallen glass.

Then the sound of people trampling in a stampede of other people pushing and fighting police officers that were call to control the crowd were push underneath their feet. I could see more people underneath many feet, some fought to get out from underneath feet, but more died as the floor turn from brown dirt to red bright blood that soak the dirt. More guns going off with more police shouting out orders that no one heard or just ignored. The ground turned a bright red as it glistened on the grass and in puddles. The blood that flood feed the grass with its thick red liquid. The blood was from those that fell in front of the store trying to get in, but the police fought with the people trying to get in the store. The results were a storm of hundreds of those fighting to get to the food inside and those that fought to get out. The police tried to control the people from getting in. but the police could not control them as the crowd went wild and the police went under the feet of the people that fought to get in the store. The sight made me wince as I continue to move closer to the pharmacy that might have the one thing that might save my sister life.

Brooke was a diabetic that depend on insulin, it was something that the government had the cure, the fact that Brooke and others like us were denied of any kind of help or the cure was the government need to kill all those poor people that live in the out skirts of the city. I had to watch my sister die slowly for year's sense she was showing signs

of the diseases. We couldn't even receive insulin to save her. Coming
home I felt pain and fear from knowing that she might me dead, Brook
pale face and Skelton like body wasting away, a slow death that I knew I
would have to face someday. I feared that if I could get her help it might
be too late and she would one day die and I would find her. My mind
wondered at the pharmacy and if it had any insulin in the refrigerator.
I jump over the pharmacy door then looked into the refrigerator and
found ten vials of insulin. I grabbed them and put them in my pocket
and left fast back to my cart that was in front of the pharmacy.

The sound of glass breaking then children and women screaming
out as thunder of feet raced through the broken door outside. The sound
of people screaming as a light beam glowed with a high intensity that
almost blinded me. I knew who it was and they were killing innocent
people that only wanted to have food and drink. Their death was the
only thing that the government believed in. I cannot remember if the
police ever took anyone in their compound for anything they wanted
to pin something on alive.

I had to work fast; those sounds were people being either killed
or rushed out the front doors with the police right behind them. He
knew it wouldn't be long for the police to rush inside of the store and
kill those that were taken any food. The cart made its clangs sound as it
went through lanes of food in cans and in boxes. I had just let the food
fall into my cart with my arms straight across the shelves knocking
everything in sight into my cart. I could feel my heart beating faster
as I kept on moving though the lanes and finding myself in the back
of the store, the taste of salted sour sweat running down my face and
stinging my eyes hurt, but I kept on going, my mind was on one thing
my sister. Frozen meat of all kinds stack on cold bins waiting for me to
grab all I can get into my cart. Then I watched as those that had been
in the back of the store move toward the back door of the store, they
were doing the same thing that I had done in the store, stealing foods
because it was the only way to stay alive. Everyone in the store was
attempting the same thing that Steve was doing with carts and yet the
cart that he had made too much noise. Steve still could hear those at
the front of the store screaming and yelling as the enforcers beat those
that would not obey them. Steve watched others moving toward the
door that led out of the store storage area. I had to follow them and let
them led me out of the store with my cart clanging along in the alley, I

knew the alley would lead back to my home. The storage that held the cold food been dark as I enter the area, the smell of old meat flagged my nose with a stench that drove me almost back in the store, I knew I had to keep moving and out as fast I could go. The street or alley I had exit into from the back of the store was dark and the pavement was not all that level, grass and weeds that spring out from the uneven ground hid any one coming out of the alleyway. I knew it would be hard for any enforcer to find me or anyone else. As I kept on walking toward my home, I thought about my sister and her illness. She was sick for so long that I could not remember when she ever felt good. She was all I had in my poor life. I can't really remember ever seeing her feeling good ever. I would continually compare other girls to my sister. Yeah, and no one could take her place in my heart. Then I saw something that looked like a light that open and close got my attention fast as I kept on moving, I hit another door that open up; I found the alley that led straight to my street and my community.

I had to get home fast; I had not seen my sister in a few days and hope that she was still alive. The rain was coming down fast now, the acid was still stinging my face and arms, but I had to get home with the food in this cart. The grass scratching and hurting his body, bugs new and large were biting at his legs and shoes as Steve kept on moving toward where his community would be soon. Food, he was finally going to have meal that would fell his stomach. Bread, cheese with two slices of onion, and tomatoes with some meat on it sound too good as my stomach complaint again as I thought of the meal. That sounded too good to be true, it would happen; he had the food in the cart. He would make it before the police catch him; he wasn't far from his community.

Then he saw the great divide from his community a large wall of woods and forest and trees that grew tall and wild there were also some places where his great-great-great-grandparents had built to keep people and things out from the place that his family took as theirs-homes that people they had called friends and brothers for some reason that Steve and his friends that live in the community. Everyone in the community help each other with either food or something they had learned to do to help each other. Steve was the only one that knew how to work on computers and know if anyone was hacking any information that was important. Steve seemed to see some light was shining around the great wall around the place. Homes tore from trees bursting out of windows and roofs were scattered in side of the walls blockage, grass tall as the trees and weeds. Across the way was more homes empty that were surround with trees growing in them like forest claiming what was theirs again. He couldn't stop until he got to front of the community doors. The doors were flushed to the wood base, no one could tell where the doors were, but he knew where the doors were and how to get them open. If he were right about who was on watch this night, it would be one of his best friends, Jack.

Jack stood on the top of the wall that looked down, the part that he stood on was hidden by branches of a large tree, the platform was called a lookout tower that was built by everyone greatest parent centuries ago, now the sight was better as the tree's branches hide anyone on the platform from sight of those that might come to destroy them in the community. Jack dark skin blended with the night sky, his eyes dark as the night even with his skin became unnoticed to those that hunt all those that walk in the darkness. Humans were innocent survive differently now some hunt other humans and then there are those that do other things that Steve and Jack shiver at the thought. The sound of birds screeching out its warning to everyone walking below as it flew over our head.

Jack moved slowly around the staircase that was built many centuries ago. His head looked down below with his long pipe that he had made into a weapon that could shoot out metal balls that hurt enough to give warnings to any one that thinks to come in the community without permission. Jack's features were more on the wild side, his hair dark as his skin was full of tangles of dry mud and leaves. His face long, but small around his chin. His mouth was wide, but his lips were white in color from dryness that pledged as very little water clean and clear was to be found around the community or any other places like it. His lips cracked in places that made Jack licked his lips with his dry tongue. Jack was a thin man that bones grew out of his dark skin that made his look like a skeleton walking.

I yelled up the secret words as if I was starting a conversation with Jack and waited for him to open the door for me. *Coming home, I am coming home.*

Jack looked down and knew who it was at once as the familiar voice echoed upward toward him. Jack opened the door wide as the feel of the old chain rope burned his feeble hands and fingers as he pulled the chain up ward toward him. Chain clanged as the chain hit the sides of the walls wheel that pulled the wooden door open for Steve.

Steve father had called it a pulley of some sort. The chain rope was crank through a wheel that hooked to another chain rope that connected to the door that raised the door up to a point that an adult could go through it easy. Many of times, the wheel would be stuck and we could not get the door to rise. But today the door opened up easy and I got inside of the community that was home to those that help in providing for many that lived there. I could only do so much, but we all shared the food, clothes or anything else we could. I got in with the cart that was full of food of all kinds. The cart bump along the grassy path back that led to one of the homes that people took as their own.

Many of the houses along my street had no running water or electricity, we had to depend on either Mr. Farmer's home (that has both) or we just waited for the rain to come in order to bath. That was when many of us would run out into the natural shower then we washed the best way we could. No one had ever own any kind of body wash, so we did what we could with what we had. Jack jump to the trees that had small landing that connected to the walls edge walkway across the frames walls. Jack had help with the building of the landing and of the stairs that ran down the trees large trunk.

The wood was easy to find, as many of the homes around here would never miss any of the wood inside. Either many of the owners had died by diseases or the police had killed them. It really didn't matter the homes were impossible to live in, although some of the homes had some occupants in them. Yet the People had no electric or running water, the homes were just a means to keep out of the elements of weather or the police.

Jack ran down the stairs of the trees case and came up behind me as I clanged along the path. In the distance, I could make out a home that had brightness and warmth bleeding out of its interior and on to the outside world. Mr. Farmer lived in the house that had electric and water; he also had a working hologram vision that only worked before nightfall. I knew I got to his home in time to watch the only news cast that was on.

The government had so much control over everything that those that had hologram vision had to watch what the government wanted them to watch and not want anyone else wanted, the news shows were controlled to a point that no one really knew what was real and what was not. No actors, no music that my grandparents had once told me about was ever heard or seen. I got close enough to see my own home across the street from Mr. Farmer was waiting outside of his house with Max and his woman Susan (who was holding their baby girl), then I saw someone that I hoped I would never see, John. Everyone knew about John hunting down children and adults for food. Most people that was as poor as we were hunted dogs or some small animal around the neighborhood. Nevertheless, no one else hunted humans for food, it was one of the rules that Mr. Farmer and my great grandparents had agreed not to do or have. John was just one of those people that ignored the rule that was law here. Everyone around had to stand guard whenever John was around or close by. We somehow knew he was the one when one of the children or people became missing. I turned to look back at my house and hoped that Brooke would come out running toward me at any moment.

The house was dark and silent. Still I waited for some sign that she was inside of the house. I shook my head low as I concluded that she must have died sometime when I was working downtown at the website news. I had lost her, my sister that was everything to me. We were soul mates in way that brothers and sister who survived life's turmoil and tortures of hungrier and thirst. My heart was pounding in my small chest I could feel my skin stretch out as my heart beat so fast I thought it would just fall out of my chest. I had to get control of my emotion before John could see my pain. I hoped he didn't prey on her, I hope he didn't kill her; if he did I would kill him. Moreover, I think no one would be missing him if I did.

The birds were starting to come out from hiding after the rain fell around us. (Chuckle) Well at least they know when the rain was safe to drink or not. I guess we humans are the dumbest animals around. I could feel the cold breeze flowing down my neck or maybe it was just a fact that I was scared of knowing about my sister's faint and hoping that John didn't eat her. I held my head up to look at the bastard in the eye and just hope he would say something to invoke me to kill him, but he just stared at me with a blank face and dull eyes. He had more meat on him, no bones showing around all that muscles and good teeth. Many of us didn't have teeth or were still losing our teeth many of us hadn't eaten good food. Food was scarce. Whatever we could find or hunt was taken as enough food for all of us. Now as I dread my legs to move even closer to Mr. Farmer's home the feel of death invaded my soul, coldness seep in my bones as I shook and tremble my way toward the others that were waiting for me. My lungs stung as I took in the acid air in my chest, I had to lower my head to take some kind of control of legs and body. Force was one thing I knew and that of my sister faith. I heard some dogs in the far distance barking then a growl, again a bark, yelp of the dogs owns fate. Someone or something had attack the dog it could have been human hunting the dog for food or another animal. I took a breath and coughed hard as I the feel of sharp sting guide down my throat, tears dropped across my cheeks stung my cheek and lips. I couldn't recall why I was crying, but then when did anyone cried about things they could not control.

The government controls our everyday life, and yet we have to fight for food and others just to survive in this world. Rich and powerful had everything, healthcare, food, shelters, education. The government only pushed us to work in order for us to give them more and us less to survive. It was and is the only life we have ever known.

Yet, my eyes were wet with salted tears mix with the rains acid. I could almost smell my own flesh burn from the rains poison liquid. I turn back at Mr. Farmer with hope that Brooke would be alive, even though I knew that it was just hope and not reality. Mr. Farmer couldn't look at me in the eye that was one indication that told me Brooke was dead. Silence was all around as I tried to control my emotion about my sister faith.

So where did you bury my sister? Or did you or anyone have taken her to one of the empty houses far behind the community that we use for the rituals? Did she suffer any or was she already dead when you all found her? Steve asked, he had too many question, but he was both scared and relief. His sister was sick for long. That maybe it was best she was gone.

John stood there listening to us talk as I asked the one question that scared me right now. So is my sister dead or what? I asked them as they just looked at me and then at John. I turn to John with a fear and then with angrier as I thought of Brooke being eaten by this horrible man that calls himself a human. He was more monster than anything I know. Nightmares had always haunted children during the day as well as at night. Mostly children would hunt for food at night and stay close by homes that they knew were good or safe.

Now my nightmare of this wicked evil man more monster than human might have eaten her, a nightmare I had lived to close by to even think otherwise. Shiver of fear gather in my bones and in my thoughts of what happen to Brooke.

No, I did not kill your sister or ate her; they wouldn't tell me where they buried her. I can't even say if they burnt her body or not. These so-called righteous human are hopeless when it comes to hungrier. Damn it all, you all know that the government wants us to just give up and die. They only let us know what store will open up that has food and the selection of food varies when no one has any money. Therefore, if we even think about the food it is just a fucking dream. So you do whatever to survive and yeah I eat others like us, I want to be the survivor and not any stupid person who is just sitting back and wait for death. No not me, motherfucker I will survive no matter what. John said with one breath toward me.

I shook my head slowly then I waited for him to leave before I decide to do something that unusually wasn't me. John just stared at all of us with one huff of his large shoulders that showed no bones sticking out like ours he left us alone. I think he got the message that we do not tell him a damn thing about no one and that was final. He stormed away from us with his heavy body and his long spear that he used to kill people. I hoped he would be the one under that spear. But I knew better than to think about something that won't happen. John marched away in the darkness as we all watched him carefully; we knew he was just waiting for one of us to let it slip about any one that had died reasonably. We kept quiet and knew that any words were in silence. I could not wait to eat something, I thought about Brooke, but knew she would want me to eat and I would for her I would eat.

Hey Jack, did you lock the gate really good? I couldn't tell if the police saw me or not when I left the store with all this. I told them as I pulled the cart closer to Mr. Farmers home. The hologram was on in Mr. Farmer living room as I heard the news show on that only reported what the government wanted the people to hear or see. The show never showed how the poor in the worst part of town was doing. It was all the same thing every time it came on. Our top leader's children had just finished school and would soon be able to take over the job of governing the people. It made me sick to my stomach those in government had been top so-called leaders for more than I can remember. Susan went in the house with her baby in her arms; Max (Susan's mate who was a little too old for her, but they loved each other and that's what counted) came down from the top of the house's step to help me with the food in my cart. Jack grabbed some of the food and ran up the steps with his hands full of fruit and vegetables.

I noticed that some of the food was rotten and not fresh as I thought it was. But I knew to that, we could cut off the bad parts and still eat the good parts. I then grab one of the meats and cheese to smell them. I had to know that the meat was okay still. I wanted a sandwich in a bad way. My stomach was rumbling like the thunder over our heads. It was then I also saw some kids fighting close by with something by one of the homes by us. I yelled at them to come over and help us if they wanted any of this food. The kids stop fighting and came over quickly toward us with their arms open wide to help us. I took out three large loafs of bread that I had taken and promised them I would let them have the bread with some meat too if they helped. Their small bodies were like skeletons walking but not dead. Their faces sunken close to the skull like leather, I could almost see the brain pulsing beneath the thin skin. My heart felt pain for their lives, as I knew they barely were able to find food. I didn't mind sharing the food with them. They were children that no one wanted and no one cared about. But I cared and I knew what it was like to be one of them. Finding food was a luxury in itself as all of us fought to find enough to live. Right now, I had enough food for them and for us. After we had put all the food away, I was still stun by Booker's death and being alone in a world that thought nothing of the poor situation in life.

Steve, we uh, found Brooke lying on the kitchen floor, she wasn't breathing, and those damn rats and mice had a field day eating her. Booker's arms and legs had large gaping holes with blood draining out slowly. We think the rats were drinking her blood and she just died. We can't say when she died, but we took her body and put her in a house that had seemed not too infested and let the house burn down with her. She wasn't it seemed not in pain or suffered. Therefore, Steve, she was alright. No one took her and ate her. Susan said as she moved her baby around her lap. Jack went to sit next to Steve left side of an old faded out blue (I think) couch that had its cushion torn with gaping holes everywhere. But we still sat on the thing that was uncomfortable. Mr. Farmer's windows hide behind large blankets to block any signs of the outside world's invasions of life. The blanket was dirty and smelled of spoiled death past done. I coughed again with the back of my hand I cough and coughed hard. The smell of dry air mix with acid made me cough hard now. I need some air, but the air around us now was full of acid rain and dry dust. I was still eating the last bit of my meal when Jack ate his large sandwich that had questionable meat and veggies on it. I question Jack sandwich choice. In my mind I thought the sandwich was strange, but everyone is different I guess. Jack sandwich looked strange, but he did eat it and well I ate my sandwich with one bread with choices of rare meat that was still dirty from the ground I found the meat on, but I was hungry so I ate it.

Both of us were hungry, just like everyone else here in the living room of Mr. Farmer's house. The children that were still outside had gathered close to the porch that was Mr. Farmer home, they waited for what we could spare of the food for them. I had given them some bread with enough meat and cheese, but Susan had suggested giving the children something else too. Jack went down the stairs were we had put the food in either four freezers that Mr. Farmer owned. The freezers that Mr. Farmer had in his basement worked great, he had at least four large freezers that almost touched the ceiling of his basement. Jack turned the lights on with one flick of his fingers against the wall of the stairs. The light was fair to see down, but as he descended, the stair's the light faded, as he looked hard at the bottom of the basement floor. The floor was cover with dust and filth, a mouse scattered across the floor as Jack felt his feet landed on the cool ground. Jack shoes were old and had a thin liner inside of the shoes, he had put the liner in so he could have some comfort, and the rubber soles were worn out so badly that Jack could almost feel the ground underneath his bare feet. The shoes were not really good and the shoes did not protect Jack from the cold grounds he walked on. Jack stood still as he waited for something to happen, but nothing sounded or flashed at him. Mr. Farmer and he had installed a simple system to go off if anyone came down the stairs without the right code to stop the loud siren and the bright light. Jack knew just about everything about electronic and machines. He built the system to use the sun as a resource for its energy to last as long as the sun still shines. Slowly Jack stood up straight, and then the alarm went off with the lights bright and blinding the light struck his eyes fast as Jack movement was like the breeze blowing in. Jack had to cover his eyes with a cloth that he uses for just this purpose. His voice smooth and soft as he called out the code that would disarm the system, *Lizzbeebr,* as he walked over to one of the freezers that was in front of him. Jack open the freezer, then looked for the one thing that he knew Steve had gotten from the store. A box of cold color ice sticks ready for the children delighted them, as Jack smile at the sight he was to see in the children faces. Ice sticks were one of the favorites of the children that came to Mr. Farmer home almost every night. No one knew where the children came from or who they were; Jack and the others only knew that these children were hungry and thirsty. Often the children would come over to Mr. Farmer just to see if they could get any food or drink that was clean and fresh. No one around would hesitate to help the children with their needs. As far as Jack was concern about the children, they were important as the means to keep human race alive. Jack grabbed the ice sticks in his skinny boney hands, and then marched back up the stairs. Jack stopped at the top to reboot the system back on with the other code to boot it up. (Babes) was reboot (words) closed the system altogether.

The kitchen that Mr. Farmer had in his house was not very big, but the kitchen had a working stove that connected to the surface of the counters underneath cabinets. The doors of the cabinets were hardly on its hinges, most of the other cabinets hinges hung loose of its frames, where empty shelves stood open for anyone to see.

The floor wasn't even level right as Jack walked along the uneven floor toward the area where everyone was sitting in the front room. No one had said anything as Jack went straight outside to where the children were at waiting for more food. Jack noticed that the youngest wasn't around anymore for some reason, he wasn't sure he wanted to know, but something inside of him told him that the worst happen to the little one. Jack mother had never told him why the government had treated the poorest like this or why food was so scarce for them all. All Jack knew was the innocent children were dying from hungrier and thirst, disease played the biggest part for the children and adults. Yet, the government had only thought of themselves and not the people. Jack had watched many children suffer in the past years he had survived, but he had asked why he didn't ever die; the answers were the same as it was to day. No one could figure that one out the why or how of it all lived. Jack couldn't guess how old he was, he knew he was young, but how young or even when he was born. He knew his mother gave birth to him, but birthdays were just another day. His mother would say a day is another day to live no need to count life through years no need to use months or days to count, as long as you live each day you wake up.

No one ask about any one's age we only knew we had to fight to live. So did these children in front of him holding the ice sticks in their small skinny hands with sunken eyes that sunk deep in their skulls? Jack heart wanted to scream out the injustices but he couldn't think whom he would scream out to. Jack was glad that Steve gotten so much food from the store, Steve told them that the store was being thrash by both the police and the people who were storming in and out of the stores. Steve got lucky as he stole so much before he was even caught, but he was never caught and brought the food back to Mr. Farmers only house that could keep the food fresh and ready for anyone to use or eat. Jack sat back down after he had finished passing the ice stick out to the children, their faces made him feel good inside.

Mr. Farmer stood over Steve as he sat down on the couch next to Susan and her baby as they talked about Brooke. Steve looked up at Mr. Farmer as he thought it strange that Mr. Farmer would just stand there in silent looking at him.

Steve, are you going back in town to work sense your sister had died? I thought you might be able to find a shirt that might fit from your father. You both seem to wear the same size shirt. Maybe if you look for one up at your attic you might find one of his shirts. Mr. Farmer asked me.

I couldn't understand why he would ask something like that about my shirt I have on, it isn't as if I have new ones somewhere tugged in some hiding place. Yeah, the shirt I have on right now has stains and holes under the armpits and some of the button were missing too. But for me to go up in my parent's attic to find a shirt, that was strange. I had to think for a moment and looked back at my house across the street through the open door. I could see my house dark and forbidding as bumps rose across my skin. I want to know why all of a sudden you want me to find a new shirt, especially up in my family attic. I can't remember if that attic even has any of my father's shirts.

Well I see it this way son, if you are going into town with a shirt that smells and has torn pieces all over, I wouldn't let you back in the website newsroom. No one wants to smell how bad you are. Not only that you may get a better chance with something new that might get attention and better money. I'm just thinking about you now and how your sister would react if you came home with that smell that is gagging me to a choking hold. So I am asking you if you want me to help you find a shirt that belonged to your father at one time. I know that you don't have light in that old house, but I got something that might work just as good as if you even have lights. So come on and let's get busy. Mr. Farmer said, as he pointed toward my house. I got up and then looked at Susan and her baby. Who is going to protect Susan if that asshole John comes back? I asked. Max went over toward Susan and whisper in her ear. Then Susan went in the back hallway in Mr. Farmer home. I heard a door slam shut hard and then another sound of something heavy moving against the door. It was then I knew she had gone in the room that had no windows and no way could anyone get in the room. Jack stood up with his make shift laser gun type and nod to us. He was going to watch over the house and Susan. I knew Max was coming with us. I could not figure Mr. Farmer interest in my family attic. I had never wanted to go up there. All I ever wanted was to find something for Brooke.

But never thought of that attic that held nothing or any memories of my parents, still I would check out what we could find. Maybe Mr. Farmer knows something that he isn't telling us. On the other hand, maybe my parents or someone else that grew up with my parents knew something that was in that attic. Curiosity stole my thoughts as I went out the door with both Max and Mr. Farmer behind me. Why are you two following me back to my house?

The only thing I am going to try to find is a shirt and nothing else. So why are you two following me again? I asked him. Max smiled at me. Max teeth rotted with the smell of old garbage, I knew he ate very little and gave most of his food to Susan and their baby. Max is very protective of Susan and their baby girl. Steve rolled his head as he kept on walking away from Mr. Farmer home.

I felt the silent wind that blew through my head and made me wonder if I was walking into something, I don't want to. All I want was to survive if that is possible in this world, a world that put the poor, the innocent fighting every day to hunt, to live. No joy, no laughter, only hunting for food, finding safe place to sleep if possible without fighting mice and rats, roaches and other unknown animals that would start eating any one that thinks they would be safe inside homes that may look safe, but then again the sight of those homes may be deceiving. I hated to think about the children and what would happen to them when they found an empty house.

As we enter my dark house that I had shared with my sister, I paused at that thought, when I remember she was not home anymore, she would never be home, she would never be sick ever again. I had to take a breath just to stop my heart from pounding out of my chest. The pain of never seeing her or holding her was great; I had to control my emotion before I broke down in more pain. People and children die every moment that life goes on. It is something we should be use too, but I still feel the pain of losing her. Alone, I am alone and no one will ever be here for me. Mr. Farmer held his left hand up as he shined a light from something metal in his hands wave around my house in a light beam that shine out shadows that were cast out from us. The rats ran from the beam that bounced off walls and places that was empty of seats. My feet hit the wall as I turned to my left, the feel of pain hammer out as I grab my feet and held it for a while. But Mr. Farmer still held his light beam outward against my walls. I should have paid more attention to where I was going and not watching the shadows following us. I felt the wall for something I knew did not work most of the time, but I still tried. Sometimes I could get my lights in my home to work, but not very often. I tried the switch a few times until I felt the sting of current in the walls. The light came on, that was a relief at least for a while until we are finished.

The door to the attic was stiff and sometimes it just would not work. I never had been up in the attic, but I knew it was there, I just wasn't interested in going up in my parents' attic. Now I need to know what was up in the attic that Mr. Farmer wants me so badly to go in there.

I tried to pull the door hard, but the knob did not want to move any which way. The door that led up to the attic was in the hallway across from one of the bedrooms that Brooke and I shared together.

Don't get me wrong with incest and shit. She was the only family I had; we depended on each other a great deal. Neither one of us dated or even had interest any one or anyone had interest in us. So yeah, we loved each, but we never had sex or anything like that. We just had each other and no one else in our lives. Now though, I don't even know her now. I felt kind of sad, then again, I felt relieved that she had died, because she had that damn disease that was slowly killing her and now it had her. If the government wasn't so hard on the poor struggling to stay alive, she might have been able to get that damn vaccine that would have cured her. She would have been alive right now. But no poor person that was uneducated or dressed in rags, live with rats, mice, roached and such would be getting any medical help. We the poor was not worthy of the government help in anything. We were the useless human beginnings and the government had no use for us. So many of us die with that fact of life, a life of fighting just to live another day. I looked up at the darkness inside of my home with sigh and then with a cough.

Max came over toward us with his own light show with that smart ass grin of his, Max just pulled harder on the attic door with all his might. I could never understand where in the hell he got the fucking strength, Max was skinny, with hardly any meat on his skin, but he was stronger than any one I knew. I heard the door move a little with a grunt and moan, but then I went to help Max tried harder to open the door. The door open fast as dust flew out with the mice scurried out of the darkness. I had to stomp on two or more mice, just to keep them from running up my body. I felt a chill run down the back of my spine bones as the skin on my arms seemed to rise with the chill. Something I had never felt before, yet it felt as if I was being warn, I shook my head clear again with that feeling came over me. Then I knew something was not right, I could not fathom the feelings, but just knew it was something I had to listen too. Look, maybe we should not go up there for just a shirt, it isn't worth it if something up there might hurt us. I said as I tried to back out of their way.

Look Steve, your parents and their great-great parents has something very important up there that might help us if it is what I think it is. So let us get to it. Mr. Farmer said as he flashed his light up the staircase. I looked up from where I stood behind both Max and Mr. Farmer. What was up there that Mr. Farmer was talking about, that got my attention, although my skin started to chill again as I walked behind them and up those dark stairs that led to who knew what? My legs were shaking as if they were nothing but leaves from a tree. I held on to the sides of the walls that led up into my parent's attic, shadows seemed to be coming to life as the three of us walked up in silence and yet the light that both Max and Mr. Farmer held made the shadows glow larger than the true ones that held the dark figures to life. I had to take a gulp of dusty air in my weak lungs, and then coughed hard with gagging waves. Rush of heat bit into our faces as we reached the top of the staircase. I found no windows that would show somewhat of light from the stars, but a deep darkness that smelled like dust, mildew, and mold. I coughed as I gagged at the same time; the air was dry as the smell blend with the air that made all three of them coughed.

Mr. Farmer pointed his light over the walls carefully as he looked around for something I could see or knew what it was he was looking for. Wwwhat are y-yy-ou looking for I said as more bumps came across my arms and back. I could feel the hair on my neck grow straight up with chills spiking.

I know my great grandfather had said something about Jameson and attics. I could figure it out when I was a kid— I can't remember how old I was, but I never forgot something else he said or rather showed me, then told me never turn your friends away when the time is right. Friends the only friends I had were the ones my family were involve with every day. That was the Jameson, the Wrights, Camtons, and the Northerns. I had watched those friends grow up, marry, have children, die. But the Northern left the community before their children had even grown up for me to play with. But—but there is something—just something I need or was it supposed to know. Though I—uh think it has something to do with your folk's attic. A switch— switch –no windows—need more lights to see what I can't remember, but something in the back of my head is nagging me. Mr. Farmer said in a confusion tone as he turned both ways to look at the walls.

What happen to Jameson and Wrights, Camtons? I asked as my voice became apparent that I was confused as memories of them all that had once lived here in the community and now are just plain gone. No death, only gone like my own parents had done. I shook my head as webs crowded my thoughts. I couldn't believe that maybe they were alive or maybe they died by the hands of the police government control. Then I heard Max laughing at something. I watched him touch the attic walls as his light cast its shine on something strange.

Max walked closer in the dark attic touching shadows he was casting with his light, a chuckle and moan as he stepped on something that sound like a thud. Max dropped his light as he went to grab his foot. Damn it all, motherfucker, shit fuck, my damn foot hurts badly. I hope I didn't break the damn thing again. The light fell close to something I never saw before. It looked like a small girl with curly blonde hair and dark eyes, body was covered with a faded cloth that seemed to have something around the small neck and down its gown I guess that is what it is called. I never had seen any girl wear something like that. I had seen some girls wear faded robs with fancy necklines or light colors that matched the sky or earth. But this color of gown on this small girl was very different. I noticed Max staring at the small girl with confusion and puzzlement in his eyes. Hey, what would happen if I held the small girl? It can't be real man, no girl is this that small, Max said as he bent down to pick the thing up off the floor. A faded sound came out of the thing that looked like a small girl, Max jump as he dropped the thing to the floor, that was when Mr. Farmer found a switch near the staircase that we had come from. The light was bright enough that it spread over the whole room of the attic. We stood in awe and confusion of what was around us. Small and big girls of different sizes and colors skin, color hair and eyes, they were sitting on cushions with soft fancy things that went around the cushions. I saw something that reminded me of Jacks mobile we found when we were kids. It had black round things on each side of its body; I think there were four of them. But these here are small enough for someone to hold on to and make them move I found out as I held one in my hands. Max went back to that doll (Mr. Farmer told us what the thing were called) and felt the dolls hair that was curly and blond. The doll made that sound again, but this time I think everyone was ready. A smile came over Max face as he shook it and found out from Mr. Farmer that when he was young, his grandmother had told him that she had something like this when she was a little girl. It's called a baby doll, it's for little girls to play with, and these things with wheels and metal bodies are call cars and it's for little boys to play with. Then I heard footsteps running up the stairs to my attic. A small dirty girl face peeked up to see what was going on. Susan wanted me to check on everyone up here, so here

I am, but wwhat isss that? She asked as she looked around the room. The dolls (as Mr. Farmer told what they were called) stood still as if they were waiting for someone to hold them. The girl that came up to them, stretched out her small arms to see if the things were real. Their called dolls and you can hold one if you want to. I told her. She grabbed the tall doll off a stand that had long black hair and blue glass like eyes staring at her. The girl just held the doll in her arms like a baby. The face was soft with green and gold dress on them. Mr. Farmer had told us that each of the dolls what were they wearing dresses or gowns. Then we watched the little girl sit on a strange looking chair with the legs curved under each part of what was a leg. The girl stood up fast as the chair rocked back and forth. Her eyes went wide with shock and awed as she circled her arms around the dolls body. Mr. Farmer laughed at the sight. That chair is called a rocking chair and I remember my great grandfather rocking in one of them when I was small kid. I promise this doll would not hurt you. Go ahead and hold the doll. Just sit in it with your baby doll, and rock her. Mr. Farmer told her with a smile. The little girl sat down on the chair carefully as it tilts back and then forth with her weight and her feet. The sound of the rocker going back and forth was a gentle sound that made us feel good inside, something that we couldn't describe.

Look, we are looking for something small, not a doll, car, or any of these different toys here around us. But something small that –I can't remember what it is. But it is something small that is the only thing I can remember. Our parents and that of our great parents and that of our ancestors before them were all involved in something my family held in secret and only told down the line that is until you were born and I had a chance to recall something that was to important. I just wish I could have recalled it before Brooke died. But maybe there was a reason for Brooke death. Look, we really need to look around for something that is not a toy, but something different and small. Mr. Farmer said as he rubbed his chin with his left hand and looked around hard. Then we saw something against one wall that had blankets of different colors and sizes with different designs, some had flowers. The blankets flowers and designs were faded, but there were still some designs that they could see and figure out. The smell of mildew and mold came from the blankets that sat on a long brown box that look like a square wood. Steve slowly walked over to where the blankets were. The box seemed to draw Steve attention and his curiosity, as he got closer to the box. Steve rubbed his hands over the smooth flat surface of the box, Steve wonder what was inside of the box, he knew at least he thought he knew that it couldn't be more blankets or toys. It had to be something else, but what? Clothes could be. Maybe something he could use at the website news, something that would help ease pain for the poor and the ones that would die by the police hands by the government orders. Steve smiled at the thought. Then he moved his hands away from the box, another thought rose in his mind. What if the information would bring the police here, and then everyone he knew, he grew up with were like brothers and sisters, most of all those children that come around their homes begging for food would be killed without any reasons. Steve took a breath as he kept on thinking of a way finding out what was inside of the box and how to deal with anything that was inside of it. Max and Mr. Farmer started to take the blankets off the box gently.

Let see if what I am trying to remember is inside of this chest-box. Mr. Farmer said as he picked up three blankets with a grunt. These blankets are heavy and they stink like hell. Mr. Farmer finished as he dropped one of the blankets with a thud. The sound wasn't soft like it should have been for blankets. Mr. Farmer looked puzzle as if a thought came back to him. Steve turn back to the chest box that Mr. Farmer had called the box. Two leather straps touching another straps that was under the box holding the lid closed tightly, but Steve noticed that the straps were old and brittle as he pulled the straps apart with ease. The box, brown in color with nicks on each side of the corners gave the sight more understanding as Steve imaged that the mice had eaten a path inside of the box. Maybe the damn mice had eaten whatever was inside too? Steve thought as he opened the lid wider. Steve was stun when he found six metal boxes in a row across and six deep. Then Steve noticed that there were more metal boxes-eighteen in all across and in the middle of them. Steve counted. But there were more underneath each of the boxes, six each underneath the six across. They were dull and black from years of being inside of the box. The cool flat metal was smooth against Steve hands as he picked one of the metal boxes up from its stack of other metal boxes under it. Steve kept on looking for something that would open the boxes. Steve couldn't find any kind of opening that would help him. The metal boxes seem like they had no opening at all around them. The box seemed to have no opening to where Steve could find. The seam was rust around with silver that blended with the boxes old colors. Steve studied each box he had picked up out of the brown box that held them.

Mr. Farmer kept on looking at the blankets as if the blankets spellbound him. What was inside of the box that kept them intrigued? Something not right with these blankets and Mr. Farmer was intent with finding what his family and that of the others too had driven deep in their minds to find.

Max took one of the blankets and thought about his Susan and their baby. These blankets would keep them warm at night and would help them during day too. But which one would Susan like? There were so many different color and sizes of blankets. Max found one with strange looking animals that looked in a funny way half humans and half animals. The landscape seemed to be full with hidden buildings hiding behind forest full of trees, bushes that grew out of those buildings as if they were normal. In four corners were people with children around them and two strange people dressed in gowns of blue leading them away from the forest of hidden buildings. Then he picked up a light blue blanket with lines breaking up in different parts with roads rising up off the lines in heaps as trees block paths and streams along the lines. A mobile of some sort was paint in two different spots of the blankets. Max couldn't understand why those blankets had those strange designs on them. Then he picked up another blanket that was gray and white with a blue path with white lines spread out with forest growing close to the path and on large gray hills with white tops. It seemed familiar, but strange at the same time. Yet the sight was calming and peaceful. Max tugged the blankets under his arms and looked at the others. Every one of the blankets had something on them; it was strange and yet somehow interesting to look at. It was like looking at a story on the vision screen at Mr. Farmer home at night. But whoever made the blankets made them with something that might be important. Max decided to take all of the blankets and put them together, Max wanted to know if these blankets had some secret that stretched on them, some kind of meaning that was for them. He had to find out before it drove him nuts.

Steve sat on the floor becoming very irritable with the square metal boxes that he could not open. Steve sat back against something else that he didn't want to know and really didn't care right now.

Mr. Farmer watched Max with the blankets and then Mr. Farmer knew at once that those blankets were maps to some place they had to go. Some place that was very important and yet it Mr. Farmer couldn't recall what it was. It was as if his or her parents had put something in everyone's sub concussion mind. That his had started after Brook's death. It was as if Brooke was some kind of key that open his mind to something very important it was strange and yet, it felt right too. Mr. Farmer wanted to shake his head to clear it, but found the metal boxes that lay inside of that chest and those blankets were more than clues; they were the answers to what was puzzling him. Mr. Farmer took one of the metal boxes and then he put it down close to one of the empty spaces on the floor. As he did that, he asked Max to take the first blanket and find out if there is some way to hang them up. I think they might be maps to places that we are to going. First, we need to get these metal boxes open fast. Mr. Farmer said as he studied the box slowly. Steve took a breath and let it out in one huff as he got up off the floor, his hands, and arms flopping at his side as he looked at Mr. Farmer with one of the boxes that he was trying to figure out to open. Steve noticed something under the box as Mr. Farmer turned it repeatedly, but then Steve put his index finger and his middle finger on the box long line that seal the box together. Then Steve noticed a strange looking symbol underneath the box that Steve hadn't noticed before. The symbol looked almost like a fingerprint something not very big, but something to look at more closely. Steve picked up another box from the brown chest box, and then he turned the metal box over his lap and just put his index finger on the symbol out of curiosity, the metal box made a strange sound like scraping metal against metal. Then the box glowed around the symbol a small bright light got bigger as it ate up the metal box and let loose a shriek of soft scrapping again. Steve eyes went wide as he watched the metal box dissolve within the light and finally the cool metal that sat on Steve lap was open up. Steve noticed as he looked inside of the metal box that there were at least hundreds or more square things, the sight of the small square metal took Steve breath as he realized what they might be. But what was inside of them was another mystery. The light that came out of the metal box went off when Steve took out one of the squares metal things as he exam the things carefully in his hands. Mr. Farmer turned to look at what Steve had done and what he had taken out of the metal boxes. These were what Mr. Farmer was looking for. They each held something that would or could take down the government easy. Mr. Farmer knew too that Jack was a genus when it came to anything electronic or mechanical. These things were for more advance computers and Jack knew everything about computers inside out.

Max went over to the little girl that had the doll in her arms; she was still rocking the dolls to sleep. Max bent down carefully and looked at her in the eyes. Can you go back down stairs and get a man named Jack up here. Max asked her. She turned to look at Max and nodded yes, but then she looked at her doll and then at me. Her eyes spoke of sadness and thirst hungrier was all she knew, but this doll spoke to her as a friend she will never be alone.

You can keep her and if any of those other kids want any of these toys up here, they have to help us, Alright. I told her with a small smile. I was nervous and anxious too. I wanted to know what was inside of these computer things and how it can involve us in any way. The little girl ran down the stair with the doll in her arms and the stale air whipping around her thin hair, her feet pound the stairs fast. The next thing we knew a loud crash with a thud of wood falling apart somewhere down below us.

I don't know what they are or how to use them on a computer, but we all know that Jack would know and he would know how to use them on a computer.

I got up off the floor to look more closely at the blankets with the strange symbols all over them. Each of the blankets were of darker or lighter colors with something that looked like a map of some place that none of us ever seen or been to. I took a breath as I listen to both Mr. Farmer and Max take one to. Our hearts pounded heavy in our chest, as we seem to come to some kind of realization of all we might have taken in here. I wished there was a window that I could see out of and not a blank wall where a window should be. But the walls around us seem—wait a minute, I think there is more to this room than what we seem to see. I felt as if I knew something about those toys and these blankets, and the square things for the computers, a connection of some sort. I realized as I got up off the floor. Then the sound of heavy and small footsteps running through my house with voices coming from below, it was strange that I could hear all of this up here. There was no way that sound could be carried up here with all the walls sealed up and the flight of stairs were so heavy with solid wood thick against each side of the walls coming up.

The sounds grew closer as the children ran up to see what toys were and how they could help in order to get one of those toys. Mr. Farmer watched the children take whatever toys they felt they liked. Steve went straight to one of the young boys that found a small soft old stuff animal that reminded Steve of a strange dog without a tail and short snout. It was strange with its dark brown fur and shiny eyes of brown looking at nothing, but the boy held it tight in his arms against his chest. The sight of the children up in the attic playing with the toys made all three men smile. Max whistle for the children stop and listen to them. Jack watched the children talk and laugh as they sat down with the strange things that he heard Steve call toys.

Jack walked closer to where Steve and the others stood in a corner of the attic looking at the children. So what is it that is so important that I had to leave Susan and her baby unprotected back at your house? Jack said as he pointed to Mr. Farmer as he spoke.

We need to know if you can identify these small square things as something for a computer or not. Mr. Farmer told him as he handed Jack one of the open boxes that Steve open up with his index finger. It seemed that Steve and Mr. Farmer had found out that Steve finger was the only one that opened the strange metal boxes Mr. Farmer and Max had tried to use their fingers but nothing happen. So Steve was the only one that the boxes opened up too. Mr. Farmer had come to some kind of conclusion about the two facts that might be evident true.

One: Brooke death had triggered a memory that was deep in Mr. Farmer mind that he didn't even know for sure was real.

Two: Steve was the only one that could open up a metal box that looked as if there was no way of opening it up, but then Steve index finger had the metal box open with ease.

Those finding made Mr. Farmer remember again to everyone here's past family. None of these people even knew their mothers or father very well, yet there was a connection to them.

Jack pick one of the square things up in boney like fingers as they shook a bit with each turn of the thing that Jack studied carefully. His eyes stern and concentrated on the object as he turned it repeatedly over in his palm, his face flat with firm with thought hard, a study, Jack long shaggy hair falling in his eyes as he swung his head back so his hair would fall behind his back. Yet he never took his eyes off the thing in his hands.

It looks – (Jack smack his lips together as he thought carefully with the next words) like some kind of hard drive, but it is too big for that or maybe it is a hard drive that is very old. I mean real old. I had seen one almost like this one; I put it in one of my older model computers back in the heap of my place. I might be able to open up one of them see what is in them. I'll tell you later on tonight or tomorrow before you go to work Steve. Jack said as he left with two or three of those small square things.

Oh? Uh—Jack I think there might be about a few hundred in each metal box's, I counted six deep across and three with six deep underneath them on two side. So, I think total either is 160 or may be more of these things. We're not sure about either the amount of the things or what they are. So can you decipher how to use these things? Steve asked him.

Yeah I think I could find out, as I said I think I got a computer that would work with these things. If I am right about my suspicion of these things— I might be able to tell you with in a day or sooner. Jack then told them that the metal boxes needed to be at Mr. Farmer house now. So Max and Jack picked up the large brown leather type box that held the metal ones inside down the stairs slowly. Steve and Mr. Farmer took the blankets down too over to Mr. Farmer home across the street. The children followed us down the stairs and back to Mr. Farmer house each of them holding on to toys that they picked out.

CHAPTER TWO

———◆———

THE CHILDREN PLAYED WITH their new things in the lawn of Mr. Farmer's house with voices that were mere whisper of sounds of something of happiness. Susan came out the house with her baby in her arms as the babe slept. So what have you found that was so important that you had to take Max and Jack from me. I was total alone; I almost decide to go up those damn stairs to find out. Susan said.

Well in a way I glad you didn't, but then again you might find something up there for our little bit. Max said as he helped pull the chest up the stairs that led in Mr. Farmer house. Darkness covered sky with the faded stars that burnt bright in the sky.

The moon was round with its glow shining like a forgotten blub fading in a deep black silk night. The birds in their silent voices letting the world know of its warning of danger.

I had to stop in my tracks with the blankets as I noticed the soundless night. A faded rain dripped its acid sting on my face as I winced from the sting and the smell of flesh burning. My legs still weak from only eaten one sandwich, I knew it wasn't enough to keep my legs and stomach from going underneath me. I could almost feel the ground coming to meet me. I was weak, yet I had enough strength to get the blankets inside with no word to anyone.

Susan told us as we got inside that Jack was gone with four metal boxes in his arms. He said he would get back to us as soon as he could find out what was inside of those things.

I relaxed on the sofa as soon as I got the blankets on the floor.

Susan, you're good at making images on a flat board right. We all seen your paintings and drawings, so can you help us.

29

Yes, sort of I guess. What kind of picture you want me to do? Susan asked as she sat back down on the big chair that was overly stuff and faded of colors.

Well we got some blankets that have something like maps or types of pictures that sort of looks like maps. But anyways we need you, so if you can put the maps on something that we could carry. It has to be small on something, we need to be able to know that we could pull it out fast, but be hidden in something that no one would be able to find it. We don't want anyone that may want to know where we are going. I mean we may or might be going away from here soon. I don't know when or how we going, but I know it will be soon. Mr. Farmer asked Susan.

Susan nodded yes and put the baby down on the chair with one of the blankets that was on the floor. You want me to make something that would be small enough to hide these maps or whatever they are call am I right. Hmmm. Let me think and look around. Susan thought aloud. Right then the baby started to cry, Susan and Max (who just walked in) ran to the baby fast as they sat down on the floor next to the chair where the baby was laying. Max can you find me something to change the baby bottom. Susan asked as she untied the cloth that was used for the baby diaper. The smell of baby waste made other smells a bit more pleasant. Max went into Mr. Farmer bathroom and looked for something for Susan to use to clean the mess up. I ran my hands into the closet that Mr. Farmer used for his towels and washrags. I found one rag with enough holes and piece missing on edges. I looked it over then thought about the maps. Hmm something about the washrags ran through his mind as he turned on the water for the rags wetness. Then he got back to the sitting room where everyone was sitting around the baby waiting for the washrags. Steve saw Max tearing up a fade white sheet that Mr. Farmer gave him for the baby.

Susan, can you put the maps on diapers you use for the baby or not. I mean diapers can be different in colors or shapes right. No one would ever know that the baby was wearing a map. I asked her. She looked at me at first with puzzlement, then her smile wide as she put the new diaper on her baby girl body.

Let me look at the sheets and the blankets too. May be I could use the blankets as a diaper or something that would keep the diaper dry. But I could use that idea; yeah it's a really good idea.

How long would it take you to work on the map? I asked her as Mr. Farmer took the dirty one back in the bathroom to clean it.

I don't know how long it would take, but Max would help me if I need it. So when I get started on them I will let you all know by then I could also tell you when I can be finished I send Max to tell you all. So Max how are we going to take these blankets back to our place. Susan asked him.

Hmm wait a minute. Max said as he went outside with one of the blankets and then yelled at the children.

The children stopped playing with their new toys and looked at Max.

We need some help with something and we got food and these blankets too. So if you all could help me take these blankets back to my home, after Susan takes the pictures off of the blankets and into something else, we can give you all the blankets for helping us. So can you or would you help us. Max said to them.

The children all six of them looked up and nodded yes to Max as they each took one blanket in their arms. The feel of the blankets thick cover warmed each cheek that was sunken from lack of food that each child needed.

Max and Susan left Mr. Farmer house in the darkness of silence with a small baby girl wrapped in blanket that had animals mixed with human parts. The scene was a faded one on the blanket, but then again if you knew it was there, then you could almost see it. I knew that Max and Susan home was not that far away, a few houses down from the corner that was once a street and now nothing but a forest of forgotten places. The community had decided before I was even thought of to let the trees and forest take over that part of street, but lay any traps to keep the police and government official out of their homes and away from those that the government wants. I had only seen predators that hunt down other humans for food go through the forest. Some say that those that come through not always get out. One way or the other eventually they would be killed. If I know them well, Susan and Max would let those children in their home to sleep. Susan had a knack of letting children inside of their home for safety reason, but then again, she loved them all no matter what.

I looked at Mr. Farmer with a puzzle thought of what he had said earlier about leaving or something like that. So Farmer can you tell why you said something about leaving in a hurry. What is so important that we have to leave soon? I asked him. Mr. Farmer just looked at with one of his know it all grins that spread across his old face that made me laugh at times. But, now I just wonder what he really was thinking.

Steve if I am right about what I know, then I think you might be the next clue that would lead us to save the children from our government's disaster to end the human race! Mr. Farmer told Steve.

Clue? What do you mean clue? How—can I be a clue and be the one who would save the children from our government? Look you lost me a long time ago when you insisted that we go to my parent's attic. Now with —you know what you said. Steve said as he felt the pain grow stronger in his head.

The throb of his head was making him dizzy, weak, he just hoped he wasn't going to vomit. Steve put his head down on his hands as he shook his head back and forth.

I just know this much about those things and the blankets. My great grandparents and your ancestors and something to with our genes, and what they had put in our subconscious minds— I mean what was put in them unknowingly. I ca—n't explain it I mean I can't say how the thought of where to go for those things or how I just know things. But they did and I know that you are the one that would either save the children or be part of it. So question of how do I know that we are going to leave this place, it's the same answer as I said before. I cannot explain it. I just know and I cannot say the how or why of it. My mind is like a tunnel that seeks an end, a light that may not be insight. But I know that it is just that, I know. Mr. Farmer said as he rubbed his neck. He started to have pain shooting through his neck light as if someone took a sharp-needles then shoot him downward along his spine. Mr. Farmer had to shake off the pain with one twist of his neck and rubbing his neck, the side of his back.

You're back again. Steve asked him as he looked around for something other than going home to that silent nightmare of losing his sister.

If you want to stay here for the night, you can. I got another bed set up across from my room. The bed is not all neat or smelling great. But it is a place to lay your head down. Mr. Farmer said as he sat down on the large over stuff chair that Susan used to change the baby diapers.

I think I am going to see if I can eat something first, my stomach is acting up and my head is doing the same thing. So if you don't mind me I am going to eat something. Steve got up and went back into the back room that was a kitchen of sorts. Mr. Farmer had an old type refrigerator that was tall and fat with white surface around it, handles that had rust, and faded silver on the top of the refrigerator was the freezer and the bottom was the refrigerator. Steve couldn't understand why he had it. Steve that Mr. Farmer never put food in them. But he had them just as he had this strange black thing next to the refrigerator the tops of the black thing lit up bright, but it was also hot to touch. Steve knew that Mr. Farmer used the thing for something.

Steve knew where the basement door was hidden, and he knew that only certain people in the community knew about the freezers too, but only those that knew were allowed down stairs in Mr. Farmer's basement. The basement was dark with a faint smell of old rotten food and mildew that hung around wet damp places. Mice moved fast along the floor as they scramble across the floor looking for food. Steve had to stop on the middle of the stair when he heard the sounds of the mice running fast along the basement floor. He took a breath as he searched the walls for any kind of switch that might turn on some light for him. Steve took a deep breath with each step he took going down the basement steps of Mr. Farmers house, he was careful as he knew too that the switch on the walls came on sometimes without touching them and times he had to find them too. Steve feet met the uneven floor of the basement as he went straight for the one freezer he knew had cold meat that was uncooked. Yet Steve stomach made another complain that sent Steve close to the floor. Both of Steve hands held tight around his stomach as the wave came again with more of Steve moans. Oh, fuck in shit. I have to find something fast that I can eat without cooking it. But what do I feel like eating right now. I got to one of the many freezers that were down here in the basement. My legs were weak as my knees felt like a feather off a bird, my head spinning like a fast whirlwind. I had to eat and sit down; maybe I will stay here for the night after all. I knew I needed to sleep and be ready to go to work in the morning. Right now with Brooke's death, I wasn't sure if I would even come back here. But then again with things that

I still don't know what they were and the things were at Jack house to be processed. May be I will stay until Jack could tell me what the shit were they. My head spin with everything imaginable that went through my mind as I thought about those things and my job. Hmm if I knew, what they were and why they were in my parent's attic, mmay be I could use them for something that would bring in more money and more hope here in the community. I took out some small flat square frost thing that I thought was meat of some kind. I smell it and tried to open it up better, the frost made it hard for me to see what kind it was, so I tried to peel off the clear seal and get some idea of what it is. As I clean away the frost from its package, I notice that the meat was thin and had tint of red on it. I thought of how to cook the thing. As I turn to go back upstairs I had to stop, then listen as I heard silence and then more steps coming from outside. The sound of running feet scrambling against the wet grass, then thudding up the front steps of Mr. Farmer home. Steve heard like a faded echo of sound coming down the basement walls. Steve went on ahead up the basement steps with each thought of who had just walked in Mr. Farmer house.

I'm not going to believe what I had just found out about these shit things. The information is out of my league, but I can't even think straight either. Well fuck me you know, I can't still believe some of the shit I found out. If the shit is all-true about our past government and shit, well we have to do something to stop those bastards right now or we are in shit fuck. Jack said as his heart beating so fast after he had found out what he heard and seen. Those damn small square metal like wires and shit were hard drives that were full of information that he had never seen, heard or anything.

Jack had taken some of the metal boxes open back to his place that was once his parents and now his. His place was full of different metal and electrical wires-poles-things that he used in his home. His door was a metal flat wall that had a doorknob that was more like a knob of metal pole stuck inside of a hole in the center. Its hinges were nail or screwed on with joints that were buried inside of firm heavy metal plate that was Jack walls around the small place. Jack had a memory of his parents, it was the last time he had seen them. They were standing right there close to the door of the home. His mother's smile at Jack as she pointed to the computers, Jack son, you have to remember that one day those computers that you and your father had saved and fix might one day will save you. So son be careful what you use in them and be aware that the government has ways of spying on people easily with computers. So use your common sense first (that is your instinct), then wager all out comes of what would happen if things were done a certain way. So be care son, only trust Mr. Farmer, Steve, and his sister, Max. Those that you call friends are the ones you must trust only and care for. And Jack, we love you very much. Jack smile sadly, as he recalled a memory that he had pushed back in his mind came out like a fog voice of whispers and moan. His mother voice had always been there when he needed to hear her!

Jack look at the only windows he had in his home they were like holes round with round type flat metal that matched the holes perfect to close the windows when it rained or when he needed to be safe. Jack sat on cushion that had been Mr. Farmers seats at his home at one time, they were worn out and yet Jack sat on them here in his own home. Lately the room seemed empty of anything that could be on the walls and yet the walls had metal panels that help in with the electrics in some strange way, but the facts that his walls were of metal and gave his computers a better connection.

Jack had taught Steven everything he knew about computers, the ins and outs of how the computers work and how to disable one if necessary. Now with five different styles of computers, that dated from different time period over the centuries was sitting right next to Jack newer one he had fixed. The hard drives that Steve found in his attic would work on either computer's he had at his place. Jack mind was spinning as he installed each small chip's into his hard drives and waited for something to happen. Jack could see and feel his hands shake with both fear and with excitement as he waited for the drive to open up. Jack computers had programs that could decipher codes and use hologram pictures when it needed too. Jack other computers that were around him had other programs that were old and not used any more, but he used them when he needed to find something that the government would not be able to hack in. Jack voice was the one key that open the drive and any programs he needed to use. Jack sat back in his chair that had wheels on the legs.

His home wasn't like anyone home, one bedroom with a blankets on the floor for his bed like everyone else, but Jack home was made of metals and wires, most of it was all electrical, computers took most of the sitting room. His father had made a tunnel in the hallway for cases of police or hunters like John. The tunnel led straight to Mr. Farmer's backyard within a few minutes. Jack took a breath as he watched the screen come on, the sight was very impressive, and a large strange room seemed to appear close to Jack seat. He could feel the place in his bones as the hologram came closer to him. Jack had to take a breath deep in his lungs and then a gulp of air. The sight was nothing he ever seen in his life. The community was all he knew and thought he would probably die here too or maybe not as Jack watch and listen.

The first drive was a museum that had a voice that he did not know. But he was stun as the person speaking had told a sort of story about men dressed strange with strange things they held in their arms as they walked in a strange way into forest and fought other men that dressed almost the same. The museum voice was back telling them why they were fighting and each side had someone that led them unto a battle. Jack saw that the vision screen showed that the voice had stop close to a glass box, the paper seemed faded as it lay inside the box, Jack notice that there were many names written on paper. The voice said those that had written the paper were the ones that fought to bring our people the right to establish their freedom to govern themselves in their own homes and the right to work to provide the necessary needs for basic life. Who in hell was British? The voice went on with more things that it showed on the screen; another type of freedom paper was in sight. Too much Jack could not understand. But something inside of him told him that these chips were very important. Jack made his computer repeat what he had just listen to half way down his brain. Jack took a gulp as he finally understood about the papers and why these strange men fighting against another factors of men. Those papers were the foundation of everyone's rights for freedom of speech, freedom to choose where to live, work, etc. that Jack realized wasn't just for the rich and powerful, but for the poor right to live, work get education, to vote. Everything he was ever told growing up was all lies that was handed down for what, how many years, centuries that people like him had to obey, had to learn that they were nothing and would never be anything but expendable to the government own use. Yeah, Jack had seen people missing, but he thought that John or one of the cannibals hunted the missing humans around the community, he never thought if it was the police or not. Just the same, they were missing and no one knew where they went. These chips, these things that he calls hard drives had more to say about the past government that should have been in use today. Our rights were taken away easily by ignorance by uneducated adults and those that really didn't care about what happens. Something went wrong somewhere back in the past. The program of these hard drives these small devices that held information of both the past and how the government was formed and how it came to be was too important Jack realized could indeed take the government down.

But then again as Jack thought as listen more of the chips and watched the screen unfold many different events past.

Then another hard drive kicked in as Jack had put three of the things that Steve found in metal boxes up in his attic. The voice in this one was different from the last drive he listened too. This one was about something called civil war-north and south. Again, Jack became intrigued with the story of how the north won and how black slaves won freedom! After the one story ended, Jack heard about the World War I and then the second one. It sounded too much to understand, but understand he did as Jack compared the story to many of the riots and the freedom fighters that were fighting the government and those people who were missing. Jack looked at the fourth chip with some hesitation to listen to it. Jack thought about Steve, Mr. Farmer who had insistent that we all had to be involve in Steve parent's attic. Now he knew why, but what can all these chips do, how can it save anyone with just this knowledge? Yet somehow, Mr. Farmer knew and he wasn't going to share his own knowledge of the chips or why of it. Still Jack had to go back with what he knew about the chips and just see what Mr. Farmer has to say.

Now Jack stood in front of Mr. Farmer with caution and out of breath as he ran as fast as his weak body could take him back to this place.

Calm down Jack and tell what you witness on those hard drives. I need to know before I can say anything. My mind is in a spin of voices and certain words that keep on repeating over in my head. So tell me what you had seen and heard and maybe we can solve this mystery or not. Mr. Farmer said as he patted Jack back and took him inside of his house. The smell of heat burning in the back sent Mr. Farmer off in a hurry as he walked in the kitchen.

Linda Trainor

Steve was trying to cook the frozen meat on the stove without a pan and the sight of Steve trying to touch the meat and the top burner made Mr. Farmer chuckle with the sight.

Mr. Farmer took down one of his pan that he had hidden in one of the cabinets behind the stove. Let me take care of that Steve. Go and sit down with Jack in the front room. This meat is enough for both of you... I cook it just for both of you. Now get out of my kitchen. Mr. Farmer took Steve burnt hands and put the meat in the pan with the burner still on. As Mr. Farmer watched Steve go in the front room, he thought of the meat, it was one food; those boys need more than just meat. Potatoes was a starch, hmm, yeah green beans a vegetable. Mr. Farmer took two potatoes down from a bag that was stuff in cabinet at the far end of the kitchen.

The green beans had been in a tin can that had a pull up lid. The food would be ready in a few minutes if he cooked them right.

Steve sat down on the sofa that was closer to the kitchen door. The food started to smell good, his stomach was aching with hunger, and Then Steve looked at Jack and knew his best friend was just as hungry as he was.

So what did you discovered about those hard drives isn't that what you call them. Did they have anything that was important I could use at the website. Steve asked him. Steve hands were clench together as sweat and nerviness of everything around seem to fall into his world.

I don't know if any of this shit I found out could even be real or not. But it all sounded real and sure, I think if we knew where some of the things that they were talking about and found them, maybe could go and find the shit and show the government the things were true facts and not some fucking game. I don't know. I need to ask Mr. Farmer if he heard of constitution, declaration of independents, laws that protected everyone rights that involve that rule of whatever it is.

Mr. Farmer heard what Jack had just said, and again something of a distance memory hidden deep in his subconscious mind came up with reasons, understanding of the hard drives that Jack took.

Mr. Farmer walked in the front room two plates for Jack and Steve. I heard some of the things you had told Steve about and wanted to know more of what you had found out. I can tell you both that constitution and declaration of independents is the very base of our rights, even

38

though the paper it was written on is missing and with that our proof. What you had witness and heard are the most important facts that would take down the governments control over us all. That and other things that would be on the chips in each of the metal boxes we have here. Then again, I thought about those papers and the possibility that those papers were gone or stolen. The papers that were used during the 1770's or earlier than that are nothing but faded words and brittle. We need something stronger that holds those same words together and push the damn things up against the government's ass. Mr. Farmer said with a gasp of air as he sat down next to Steve. Mr. Farmer hands shook as he laid his hands on his laps and his head tilt back against the wall behind him.

I am hearing so many voices that they seem to scream at me with light and colors mixed together in waves that I cannot keep up with all of it. I—I am not sure of everything, but then again I am not sure if the drives are false either. Mr. Farmer felt his heart beat fast as if the beating of his heart was going to burst out of his shirt. Jack do you still have that strange looking mobile that has wheels around it and its front has that long nose with the grills and lights that work. Mr. Farmer remembered that Jack had found something strange looking thing that almost looked like a tanker mobile that the police use to catch people and take them somewhere and never come back. So he figured that if this thing was as large as the tanker mobile, they could use it for escapes from here. Something had told him he would need that thing soon. Look Jack that mobile you put together from scrapes you found in your parent's heap of old and I mean very old things that I can't even know what they are. Didn't you say that some of the shit in the heap dated far back that you could tell anyone how old the shit was in the heap. I just know as big as that thing is, we might need it fast and soon. Can we start putting things inside of it soon? Mr. Farmer asked Jack. Jack was eating the meat and potatoes as if he was in a hurry to leave. But he hesitated to listen to Mr. Farmer words.

Okay you said that about a paper I told Steve about has something to with freedom fighters is that right. Jack asked Mr. Farmer as he ate his meal.

Yes, and it has everything to with us as the people, as humans. We have rights to all that every Senators and Congressmen and the leader of all the nations has taken away from us and use those rights to their own persons. We need to be prepared at any time now for one of the opposing element to try to kill us and take these chips to be destroyed. We cannot let that happen. So be very careful who you talk to about the chips and Steve when you go to the website news, please do the story in a way that police would not know it is true and we have the prove of all the lies we were told for so many years, centuries to be right. Mr. Farmer said with all his strength he put in his words.

I had to look at both Mr. Farmer and Jack to be sure I heard him. I felt a chill go down my spine again. This time Mr. Farmer set my chills down my spine as I ate my meal slowly. I can't think of a story that would do both lie to the police and then tell my website readers the truth behind my story. Can you give me some sort of a start Mr. Farmer? I asked him as I finished off my meal, now my throat need to be quenched with something wet. I had gotten up to put my plate away and get me some water or something. I knew I had taken some bottle water from the store with all that groceries too. As I went in the kitchen, I felt their eyes on me. It was as if they thought I was going to do something important or I don't know it felt strange. I grab a cup from one of the cabinet, and then just looked at it with some kind of strange feeling as if the cup was something I never seen before. But I did see a cup before and I had used one too. I couldn't shake the strangeness of it. Then I coughed as I went to the large refrigerator that had clean water without the acid in it. I never asked how Mr. Farmer knew how to get the clean water that didn't have the smell of acid. Right now, I didn't really care, my throat was dry, and I need something to wet it badly. I pour the water in the cup then drank it dry; the water-felt good in my throat as well as it went down my stomach. I felt better now after I ate and drank something. It was odd that I felt full and not a bit hungry still. I went back to the front room; Jack fell silent as I came in to sit down next to Mr. Farmer. Their eyes glued to me as if they had never seen me. I rubbed my hands together, the air I noticed was stale, had a tint of mildew. The light in Mr. Farmer home was not so bright so shadows were more apparent against the walls. I had felt my arms prickle with bumps. So what now? Hmm did I do something wrong or what? I asked them as I looked back at them. I had to rest my head in my hands as I thought of what was going on.

Steve, we need to do things here while you are at your job in town. So we thought or I thought it best that your story should be about a man that found something that took him back in the past with strange things called cars that use gas instead of rays from the sun.

It has to have although in a small way you have to mention about something with freedom and something with fighters. Don't put them together as one word, but put together in different format. Understand what I am telling you is very important. I want you to be careful. Mr. Farmer said. Then he turned his head around to look at the night sky through his front door that was still open. I noticed the sky was getting lighter, yet, the darkness that was night faded with the morning sun rising over the trees that were reaching high over homes, the community that was home too. I knew I was too late to go to any kind of bed. But my body was fighting me for sleep. Maybe I can doze off on the trans-mobile back to the city. My lean up against the wall behind the sofa I was sitting on. My hair felt like it would get glue on the wall years of not able to clean a wall or even dust off something seem like a dream of sorts. Webs clinging to corner masked in brilliant design present the room with beauty and grace. I got up off the sofa with sturdy legs walked around the room with no words spoken. Jack looked up at Steve with some thought. Steve you are the only one who could open the metal boxes. Your parents were the ones who kept the boxes and those toys that the children are playing with up in an attic that door was closed, hidden behind something heavy (that was what Mr. Farmer had told me). Then you somehow knew where the door was without any problem to go searching for it. I knew this much about our parents, they died when we were too young, so it couldn't be anything that our parents put in our minds. If it wasn't for Mr. Farmer feeding us and watching over us, we would have died fighting just to survive. I think we would have been dead. But then all this, I mean all that has happen in a short time. How did you remember that attic door? How did you know about the imprint under the metal box to be a key? I know that there are things that I never thought I knew about and then I just did or knew. Jack rubbed his long black tangle hair that looked like braids old and unmanageable. Jack face went pale black with dark rings under his eyes that showed lack of sleep. His body long skinny with bones hard and more shown than that of his skin. Any movement made Jack look like a walking dead. His eyes fixed on all of my movements as I paced around the room in a nervous reaction to all his questions. He was right about our parent's death and that we were too young to remember things. But I did remember pits of my grandparents and a small, a very small part of my great grandfather. But other than that, I remember very little about them. How old am I really, sometimes I feel as though I am in my forty's and then again as I watched those children I feel very young? I asked myself, but I didn't realize that I spoke aloud. Jack and Mr. Farmer gave me a strange look as I looked back at them.

Alright what is the problem now, did I do something I should not have done or what. I don't have a shitty answer for any of you about why I know things and not really know how I do it. So that is it right, you wanted that answer. Well I gave you one and now without sleep, I am getting the hell away for one day and bring home some money or something of that score. I left as I could not think of how I knew or why I knew things like that attic door, but then Mr. Farmer was the one who was remembering more than he was. So why were they giving him the question that should have been for Mr. Farmer not him. The years of running the streets to find food and clothes just to survive, was a blur yet as faded, as it was one thing was clear, Mr. Farmer had been there for both him and his sister and that of Jack when his parents had never come from a job, just like his own parents. Bits and parts of his mother face and his father voice came at times when he really needed him. His life was full of discovery and learning as Mr. Farmer had kept everything Steve and Jack done around the community as a learning experience. The day when Jack found that strange thing that was too big for Steve even could image something could be. To many round wheel to count, the seats stuffing torn out with another strange thin wheel close to the window rested strangely on the seats. The walls around the inside of the strange mobile had wires with metal pieces sticking out with colors faded, but Steve and Jack was able to know the colors. As they kept on looking around the front seats for anything that would help them identify the thing, Jack went farther behind the seats with a laugh that Steve had never heard from anyone before went through fast in back of the seat, a long cover old mildew with dirt and smell of old decay hung between the seats. Steve swung it away from his face as he faced Jack a puzzle rode across his face as Jack kept on laughing at nothing.

What the hell, are you doing acting like a fool? Steve asked him.

Steve, look at this little thing, it moves with this funny grass around it. It doesn't have a head and the thing moves back and forth and around. Jack said with a laugh again. I just stared at him with more confusion. I looked at the thing that seem to look a little like a human with only its lower parts. Strange, I thought at the time. But Jack took it up to his home.

What are you going to do with it? I asked him.

I think I am going to give it to my mom. Dad would have a big laugh. Jack said as he got up off the floor of the thing. Something strange was hanging over Jack head as he got up. I reached over Jack small head to look at the thing that jingled like small metals touching. The shapes were ragged with brown rust that made the things weak in form. Yet, they still made a metal sound when it was swinging against each other.

What is that you're holding? I can I look at it? Jack said as he put the metal things in his torn out pocket that he swore that he had never lost a thing in those pockets for as long as he had the pants (which was a total of one day).

If I recalled right that day, Jack father had been looking for his young son among the large heap of metals of both old and that new. Jack came out of the metal thing through one of the windows as he noticed that Steve was standing straight at someone or something. Jack turned around found his father standing close to Steve and him. Oh, hi dad. Uh, look what we found in the deep heap. I think it's some kind of mobile car. I found something funny for mom. What to see it, it doesn't have a head. But I think she might still like it for laughs. Jack said as he looked up at his father. Jack father had a stern face that showed little emotion or care. The sight, the memory faded in a distance of one face, Jack's face looking at me now with that same excitement of finding something big. I took a gulp of air that stun my lungs as I tried to shake another thought away from a cobweb of spiders that seem to just want to cling to my mind. I am not the enemy here, we all grew up as a family in this community, went through hell of death, disease, hungrier, thirst, fighting the damn police at one time or another. So why ask me something I don't know. What about Mr. Farmer, how did you know about the attic? I never told anyone about it or want was up there. But you seem to know quite a bit of it. A matter

43

of fact you know more than I do. How did you know about it, and what all those toys were too? I pointed out to Mr. Farmer with a stern face.

Mr. Farmer just looked at me with a puzzle face of confusion and dismay of what I had accused him. He took a breath as if it pained him to even try, but with that face of uncertainty showed on Mr. Farmer face as he turned to another aspect. His own determination of really not knowing how he knew about the attic, and yet he did know more than he was sure of. Mr. Farmer shook his head as more confusion seemed to vanish off his mind.

All I know is what my mind is letting out; I am not sure how I know or —well anything really. Right now, I just know things that I cannot deny that I even know what I am saying or what I know, it just comes to me like some kind of fog that opens up with knowledge that — I did not even know I –don't really understand any of this. But – it's just that it – I just know it alright. So if you want to know something, I don't give a shit right now. I took care of both of you after your parents had died and left you boys alone like those children out there. When you were hungry, I feed you both, when you both need some rest I let you two sleep in a real bed with a bath and warm cloths, clean and not a torn. So if you two are going to do the 100 question of why? Don't, just don't question it, just take it, and believe it to be true. Steve I know that you are special and what is inside of you I can't know for sure if what it is right now. So take my word, and know this, you are supposed to be our protection. But why are you and what makes you so special? I don't know, I really don't know. But I am going to listen and obey those voices in my head carefully with some caution. I don't want to stir us in a conclusion with the police or anyone else that wants us. Mr. Farmer became upset with Steve and Jack as they watched him wrestle with his thoughts and his words.

All right, we need to calm down and stop fighting with each other. We don't know a shit about anything, but these hard drives have some stuff that we don't understand, and yet we understand enough about things that tell us it is important that we take them to someone who may help us. Maybe we were chosen to be the heroes of the past and now the present or future of those children outside. We need to make a chosen of how we are going to do it and when we are going to do it. So I think we made it clear to each other. Steve, I think Mr. Farmer was right about some sort of story with some clues of what we have, but don't going telling the police what it is. We don't want anyone to be killed because of what we found. So be careful of how you state your words-story. Next step is after or during your time at work; we are going to prepare to move when we need to. Jack can get that mobile thing running for us. Max and I can drag the portable ice-box that I have stashed in a far corner and put the thing in Jack mobile. We will put as much food as we can in it. I know it is pretty heavy and big, but we need as much food as we can bring. Clothes, med's, everything we can thing of we need to put it in that thing of Jack's. So let us get moving-wait Jack do you have a portable computer that we could use for those hard drives we found? Mr. Farmer asked him. Jack stood up in his seat and nodded yes, then moved to get out of the house fast. He wanted to get the big mobile ready for the big move if they need to do so. All three men agreed with the plan. Jack went back to his heap home to look for a portable computer that would take the hard drives. Steve went in the back bedroom to go to sleep for a few hours before he took off to work. The next trans-mobile to come close to the community's doors was some time in morning. No one had any type of clock or any kind of time piece that told anyone of time of day. It really didn't even matter if someone had a time peace anyways, no one could read or write, or even count, no could even recognize what a number or letter looked like either.

So Steve was sure of when the trans-mobile was to arrive. Instinct was the only thing he had to give him knowledge of time or situation that could be dangerous.

Steve knew he had to get some sleep; his head was spinning with everything that had happen last night and this morning. The only thing that Steve knew about Mr. Farmer home was it always felt safe. Cobwebs hung over the ceiling walls of each corner like a laced cloth hiding something that was not there. No one noticed or cared about what was on walls of people's homes. It was just a building to stay safe in for the moment and time. Life was not pretty or safe; it was full of danger and mysteries. Death was an open invitation to end all sufferings that those who live around the community in such way as Steve and his friends had for too long of life. Now Steve thought, maybe he was the answer or maybe it was all of his friends put together to save those people that are still living the lie the government has been telling them for centuries, or more. That made Steve smile and then wonder more about how they are going to pull it off. Could these the papers they found save the human race or would it put them in danger? He knew too that they had to take the chance and go with it. Steve stretched his arms high over his head and let out a yawn then climbed in bed that was not all good clean. But it was a bed just the same, more than what he was sleeping in when his sister was alive. They slept on the floor together with only a blanket and one pillow that was more rags than what he was using now. The lumps were hard and pointy as Steve felt the needles climbing on his back. Steve didn't mind it, as he just wanted to sleep forever in something than that of the floor. Steve got in the bed as soon as his eyes closed his mind wondered off in a bright dream of animals and humans mixing in a way of confusion and excitement.

The forest covered many of the homes that had once been there now fell back into the wilderness where many people and some animals taken for themselves. The air was clean with birds flying high over paths and forest trees that stretched out toward the bright night that glowed with the star's that shine down along their paths. Something or someone had howled in the night as bird's large flew over heads. Steve felt calmness, felt as if he was one of the night creatures running along the path that lead to nothing, but there was something, he couldn't see it. Something important was in the darkness, but his eyes red glow saw nothing but darkness ahead. Then someone touched him with cold pointy hands that felt like bones scraping his shoulders. Again, the pointy cold hands touched him harder as the hands pushed Steve more into the bed.

What the fuck? Steve sat up in the bed with a start; his eyes still closed, but awake from a dream of something he could not understand. Slowly Steve open his eyes as vision blur and unfocused as he stared at something dark with something on his head that Steve as could not see well, as the sight came clear with Steve right hand rubbing both of his eyes, it was Jack standing over Steve bed. Jack long haggy dirty hair hanging over his face made Jack look like something from a nightmare. I had to shake my head to clear my head of the sight I was seeing.

Are you awake yet man? We need to get your ass out of this bed and get your ass to work man. I found more damn shit I didn't even know about. I can tell you about it when you get your ass up and get to the kitchen table. Mr. Farmer got more shit too. So, let's get up pretty boy, Time to make some money for us, we don't have time for sleep right now. I didn't get any damn sleep because of the damn shit you all found up in that damn attic of your fucking parents. I'm still wondering right now if my own did some shit like this up somewhere in my own hiding places that my parents had. Come on mother-fucker. We need you to do your shit at the website. We don't have time for shit. Jack said as he went in one of the closet in the room. What the fuck are you trying find. I don't have any clothes here. Actually man, I haven't shit for clothes. What are you doing in there? I said as I `stretched out my arms high over my head. I need to pop my arms and my back, as my back had been known to grow stiff.

Look Mr. Farmer asked me to look in this closet for something important. He said we might need it for you. So don't shit me right now. I don't have time now to make my words right. Jack kept on searching in the closet, his long pointy fingers touching the rough surface of the closet walls made a loud scratchy sound that Steve held his mouth close tight. The pain was invisible, but there still. Then something came open as Jack pushed with all his might against the wall as it moved inside of the wall. Somehow, the closet opened up to another room that was in total darkness. Jack slowly put his head inside of the closet to feel if there was any kind of light switch against the walls. As if Jack was pulled inside the walls, a light came on above the ceiling of the small room. Damn shit and fuck me hard, I can't find no light switch, but damn it if the lights came on by themselves. Steve get your ass over here and tell me if this room isn't no bigger than a kid. I can't raise my fucking head straight up. The ceiling is low or something. Hmm strange fuck, I think, no shit thing but wait a damn minute man. I think I found something and it isn't no toys or food. But maybe it can help me with some of my computers and those fucking hard drives. I got messages or stories out of some the drives I had used in one of my old computers, I know from reading or more listening to those damn fucking hard drives have more than what I had seen or heard. So maybe this would work. Jack said as he pulled on something that seem to be heavy for him to pull by himself. Steve crawled low on the ground to help Jack pull the large black metal box that had some round colored lights on top of it. The bottom of the black metal box, seem to have buttons or switches to touch for some reason.

Oh, my fucking shit of life, I think I know what this is? We are ready for papa to take it home. Shit man of a dream. I know what this is and it isn't no fucking computer, it is a hologram fucking vision computer. Come home to me my sweet love child. We are ready to go home. Jack said with one of his almost toothless grins and his dull eyes that looked kind of strange. It almost had some shine in them. I got up off the floor with a painful pull of my knees to stand up slowly. I had to hold on to the wall that was next to closet where Jack was kissing that metal box. I stretched out my arms, and then felt the popping noise that came with my weak bones as I stretched harder over my head. I had to get ready for work and find out what was going on. I thought about Brooke, but knew she was dead; I knew she was in a better place than here and now. She was at a better place than I was right now. I took a breath as I stride with some hope of something good to come out of her death. I need some food, something to eat along the way to the mobile stop. I just hoped that mobile had some clean air. That thought made me laugh as if it were the only thing I was worried about right now yeah a great threat to the common people struggling to survive. The smell of food stirred my stomach to a growl, then I walked a little faster as my hungrier grew more as I came in the kitchen. Mr. Farmer was at the strange metal table that had what he called burners and one large thing he called a pan. I slowly walked over to sit on a chair that lost its backing. Mr. Farmer had only two chairs and Steve took the one that had four legs and let Jack who had followed him into the kitchen. Jack had taken the chair that had only three legs left and was against the wall for support.

Jack gave Steve a funny look as he licked his lips with a smacking sound as he rubbed his stomach as if just rubbing the stomach would settle it down. Farmer I got that thing out of the closet, did you know man that thing is a vision screen with some kind of computer enhancement that might help us with those drives you all have found. So what's in that pan of yours? Jack asked as he rubbed his hands together. Jack had to push his hair away from his face so he could eat what Mr. Farmer silently put in front of our seats. The food looked good, yellow mix with cheese that I had gotten from the store last night was stir in the yellow mix, the smell made my mouth water as I started to pick the food up with my fingers and Mr. Farmer had smacked my hands away from the plate of food. I watched him as I rubbed my hands together looking at him with disbelief of what he had just done. I knew my face showed some puzzlement as I looked at him. Mr. Farmer went back to the place where he had just finish cooking and took another pan off the burner, slowly he walked over to us and pour something that had meat with white thick liquid covering the meat.

The smell was too much for my stomach, I had to eat now, or I couldn't go to work. My head was spinning from all the food in front of me and in front of Jack too. I knew they might have heard my stomach rumbling loud. I took a gulp of stale air and let my eyes close too just let the scent roam over my nose, then breath in the smell of the food in my lungs. I open my mouth, as the taste lingered in my open mouth. My throat dry, my stomach complained as I waited for someone to say time to eat. I could feel wetness, moister gather along my tongue in a silent argument with my stomach.

Mr. Farmer cleared his throat as he scooted another chair that sat in a corner of the kitchen far end toward the table that Jack and I were sitting down to eat. I didn't notice that the table had three plates with eggs, and something that Farmer called sausage and biscuits and gravy. I ready didn't care what the food was call; I just wanted to eat it.

Jack I forgot the juice in the old box, can you get us some yellow juice please. Mr. Farmer asked Jack. Jack got up from his three-leg chair and opened the old box (that was what we called the refrigerator) that had food that need to be cold. Then Jack came back with the orange juice. I had orange juice only once and that was when Brooke and I were just small kids when our parents were alive. Now the juice was in front of me, in a glass cup that I didn't know I even had. My heart started to pound heavy in my chest fast and hard. I almost couldn't catch my breath, my lungs going dry painful as my head spin with hungrier that ate up my stomach.

Steve picked up your fork if you are going to eat any of the food. Mr. Farmer told me as I slowly pick the metal thing that had four long spokes that I drove in my eggs and shovel the food fast in my mouth. With my mouth full, Jack had to ask me a question. I just looked at him as I chewed the food that was in my mouth. As I tried to swallow carefully, the food was good, my mouth didn't want me to swallow, but my stomach was complaining more as I slowly let the food down my throat, the feeling of heaven and content was flushed over my face as I closed my eyes, a moan rose out of my throat. I fought the urge to swallow and then talk to Jack about whatever he had asked me. I was to concern about the food on my plate than what he was saying. Holy shit if he didn't want his food, then I will gladly take it too. I was that hungry and that was all I thought about right now. Jack gave me a funny look as he picked up the fork and started to eat, his hands and fingers were unsteady as they tremble picking up the food and putting it in his mouth. I had slowly savior the food in my mouth and wondered if Jack felt the same way with the food. I swallowed the food in my mouth, yet my eyes seem to close on each swallow forced down my throat. The dryness of my throat rebelled against the food. But my sense drank up the smell and the taste of the food. Yeah eating the meal had sent me into ecstasy. I took a swallow of the juice that Mr. Farmer had on his table. I went into a mind straight up to heaven fast. The taste of the yellow juice went down my throat to satisfy my dry throat. I hung my head back as the liquid went down. The taste was more than I had ever thought it would be. Yeah, I had water that only flowed down either, from the sky, or in puddles or streams, I had found along my paths coming home. My lips parched and cracked from not drinking so much were now wet with relief. I wanted more food and drink, but thought I should reframe from asking. The store had brought more food than I thought, but we had stored more in the basement from past stores that had the same results from yesterday riots. That was the best food I had ever tasted in my life. I told Mr. Farmer as I looked at him. Mr. Farmer was still eating his morning meal when I looked at him. I smiled and up to stretch my arms and legs. The kitchen wasn't very big. But the size wasn't important; it was the food and friendship that made it important to everyone that came to Mr. Farmer home. Steve came to realize that it really wasn't just the food or friendship or Mr. Farmer, it was a fact that they were family in many ways, sworn to protect each other without words to justify any oath. They just did naturally, as any family would and more, they help each other in any kind of form. I walked back in the room I had slept in and went back to the bed with one question that plagued me. Why? Just why us? What could we do to save anyone? He still had to find a story that would lead them to the freedom fighters. Steve needed a clean shirt and not like the dirty shirt, he had on right now. I couldn't tell what color shirt I was wearing right now, but knew I had to find something else to wear. I was curious about that closet that Jack had open up from the far end of it. First, I need as some kind of light to look inside of it. I think I still had that light thing from last night around the room somewhere. I kept on looking around until I recalled where the damn thing was. Underneath the bed was where I had drop the thing before I had fallen asleep. The smell of old urine and shit rose up to my nose as I bend down to pick the light thing up. I started to cough and gag on the smell, my hand, and fingers rubbing and covering my nose and face. As I got off the floor with the light thing in my hands, I shine the bright light over the closet in all directions. The shine around the closet, but only shadows of nothing was seen, No clothes, no anything. Confusion set in my brain as I kept on looking around the closet for something I wasn't sure of was going to be anything that would help us or I don't know something like the disc we had found in the attic. I knew I need a shirt, but then I didn't really know what I wanted again. As the light flicked back and forth from one corner to the next I saw something a little higher over my head, it was flat, but it stood with something shadow like stood over the flat thing. I put my fingers over it slowly as I thought the thing would like disappeared before I took it. The softness of the thing made me think that it might be a shirt after all. I shook the soft material off the corner closet shelves. I kept on feeling round the material for anything else hidden. I couldn't feel anything around the shelves inside of the closet or felt any kind of level that would open the closet more. The shelves were dusty and litter with dirt, the dust flowed down over my head, and I cough and gagged, as the dust and dirt seem to fly around me in the room. I pulled the material away then back away from the closet. The cloth was old faded with long torn sleeves, dirty with dust soak in the material. I wasn't sure what color it was, so I shook the shirt around the room I slept in, coughing and gagging as the realization of the odor that was coming off the shirt. More than just mildew or mold, black fungus spread over the shirt with some kind of decay scent. I threw the damn thing back in the closet with a loud slam of that closet door and watched as the damn thing went back open again. Fucking shit door bounce fucking damn shit. I had to get out of the room and just leave with what I had. I knew the mobile bus would pick me up soon if I could get to the mobile stop on time. I started back toward where we all sat last night or was it early this morning. The front door slammed close hard as it banged against the frame of the doorway.

The morning air reeked of old piss mixed with fetus of what ever had done it. I coughed harder as I took the smell and air into my lungs. At least I felt better after eating something this morning. I stretched my arms high over my head; the walk wasn't as far as last nights' cart made it feel. The birds rested on branches that broke through windows of house old and abandoned from more years that I could even remember. I wanted to look back at my own home that I grew up in, but I knew Brooke would not be there anymore. Somehow, I felt as if I had abandoned her somewhat. I had let her die alone without me. Breath damn it, you had to work and get food for the community. Now stupid you got more responsibility with a story to reach the damn freedom fighters if possible. I had to many what ifs rolling in my head. Hmm I said as I search my pockets for money I knew I had pinned somewhere inside of them. I found it as I open a crack of the walls door to get outside of the community homes. The wall closed behind me with a crack of wood slamming against each other. (Thud) the sound loud and clear that I had left the safety and my sisters' body somewhere inside of the place I called home. The sun rose over the tall trees that crowded the path of homes that stood across from where I waited for the mobile bus.

Then from a distance I heard the sound of swoosh and humming of metal and air coming close to where I stood. I could see the strange mobile getting close to me. The sight of the old bus with its broken windows and its fading light inside of the bus made it apparent that the bus was too old and not of any use to anyone but the driver. The mobile bus stopped in front of me, I waited for the doors to open up as I step up the steps that were not that steady as each step moved. The doors slide into the bus sides easy as the two metal pieces let the door slide into it with only a whisper of screech and grind. I step in with as I pause to look around for any one I knew. No one around in the bus I ever knew any ways, I let the bus driver scan my hands as I put the money in the slot close to him. I went to the back, my head bent low as the ceiling of the bus was lower than my height. I wasn't that tall and yet the damn ceiling was still too low for me.

I sat down close to the window as the mobile bus jerk back and forth with another screech of the air-compressor jerked more protest when it tried to move forward more. I watched others wrestle with seats that were torn or broken to a point that no one could even sit down on; I had to search for my own seat. The driver had long dirty hair that tangled in knots behind his head. His face was small round with a nose that seem to slope at a point, his eyes dark with circles over lapping each other, he didn't smile, but chewed his lips as he touched buttons and laid his hand on the flat controls that steered the bus around. The flat controls turned red to stop the bus and green to get the bus going. No wheels like the thing that Jack found to make it move. In the distance, I could hear a motor rip with rumbles of the ground shaking as the large clingy thing that we all call a bus coming closer to where I was waiting. Lights on the bus were dull and lifeless. I enter the bus as it stopped in front of me with some uncertainty of how this day was going to end or even start, the smell hits me deep in my nostril as I knew what it was and why. The odors rose up from those that could not afford to bath lingered in the air around everyone on the bus. Many people could not afford the cost of having water from the government own company. The odor heavy around me, gagged me with fits of coughing and choking. I know I should be used to the smell as all of my friends were in the same boat. Then something took my attention although. Something that smell like clean air, forest green and new, spices of that smell drew me to look around, my head scratchy and falling out in places I couldn't see, but knew the spot where there. I rubbed my head as I looked around the bus; people of all kinds were sitting around seats that were broken. I noticed someone standing close to the drivers control panel; he was tall with curly yellow hair. He had his hair in a ponytail strap around with a brown leather band. His clothes were clean and fresh as he stood up to his height. I figure he was half-Max height of 6ft or more, I wasn't sure. Then he turned to look around at everyone on the bus. His eyes bright with intelligent blue as the dreams of the sky once color. He was broad shoulder; I could guess he had muscles with ripples flowing down every inch of his body. I struggled with the thought of seeing this individual man in a way that was not right. But I had to shake that thought off. I could never sleep with a man in intimate way without being paid. But this man seemed nice, as he smiled toward me, I could feel him staring at me as if he wanted to say something but couldn't. his teeth straight and white with something strange that I could not well I thought I saw fangs, but that could not be. I was both scared and confused at the same time. Then he moved closer to where I was sitting, his smile reached my sight like a candle at night. My teeth weren't straight or bright clean or even as full as this man's were. Black broken chipped in many places; I was more ashamed at my teeth sight. Then I knew too that everyone around me had the same type of loss of teeth. No matter how old we were, everyone had teeth problems. Yeah my mom would always tell me that if we could own just one toothbrush, maybe we all would not have broken and decay teeth. Yet, no one had a toothbrush or knew how to use one. My heart started to pound out in a rhythm of thuds and thumps as the man got closer to my seat. I coughed as I turned around to look out the window. Then I felt him sitting down next to me. Was he a cop that just happen to get on the bus looking for someone or something to —I don't know, I just knew that he was cute or handsome if you want to go there. My heart pounded hard in my chest as I felt him sit next to me. Was he going to arrest me for something I didn't do or what I did do? I was nervous, the sweat came in small tear like down my forehead and underneath my arms. I became twitchy and antsy in my seat. I turned my head to look around me slowly, the man just smiled at me with his straight teeth shining. I took a gulp and let my head just nod at him.

Are you going to town too mate? He asked me.

Yeah, I am going to work. I said low in my throat.

Where do ye work? He asked me again with that smile that could melt an ice storm.

Uh—uh website news. I write stories about people and things for them. I guess I am alright in all. I said as I rubbed my palms on my pants. My hands were sweating like no tomorrow.

Are ye nervous, look mate I am not an informer, I can't tell what I do, but I am on ye side of things. I know you are hungry for food, shelter and things that all those damn rich fuckers have. It is not fair that they have and all these people here on this bus and those that hide, but are starving for the things that rich, powerful have. My name is Mike or some call me (he lower his voice in Steve ears) some other name I can't tell ye right now. But mate, I got wind last night on the com-vision world net. Ye think that they might be ones that maybe looking for peace? Look I know it is you with the information I need. But you don't trust anyone outside of the community. Yes, I know about where you live. Hmm Mr. Farmer is a good friend to trust and so are Jack and Max. Each of you is very important to the cause. But I have to know if you are willing to trust me a total stranger and yet a part of the fight against the government.

I looked at him with suspect ion and mistrust. How can he know about the community? Or about anyone that lives there. I felt something telling me not to trust this man, but then again I had another feeling that I need to trust him. A feeling of confusion and mistrust from experience I guess. He was not one of us and I was sure that he wasn't one of freedom fighters. My skin was crawling with distrust and held something that said to run as far from this man. My mind went to puzzlement and caution with each word I spoke to him.

I really don't know what you are talking about or who you are talking about, plus I don't talk to stranger that I feel I shouldn't. So if you don't mine I need to focus on my job. I said and turned back to the window. I heard him inhale a breath and then a chuckle of sort came out of him like pebbles underneath my shoes.

I don't blame ye for not trusting me, I wouldn't either. So, just let me do this I will wait for the right time to make myself clear. He said as he got up and left me alone. The bus finally stops at the start of the towns limit. The bus never goes directly in the town, but stops as close to the town as possible. I got off with one leap from the stairs of the bus and ran down two dark alleys that lead to where I need to be. Tall buildings with no windows to keep the element of weather out, in the distance dogs and people fighting to retain each other for food. In the distances, someone was shouting out something at someone or something, the loud scream sound (a girl perhaps) it was high pitch and Screech out. I couldn't tell who won the battle, but children close by ran through the streets with large sticks in their hands banging on walls of buildings that were empty of people. Steve could hear dogs barking, snarls and growls, snapping teeth could almost hear the children fright as they fought with the dogs for the same reasons. Steve had to shake off the fear of what was happening around him, he had to keep on moving to his job. Buildings large with only people words whispering out from behind dark corners from empty buildings, the sound of Steve shoes scuffing against the ground made an echo in the alley that led to the building where he worked. Steve coughed, and then felt something that was not right. Steve rubbed his arm as if a chill road up and down his arms and back. Someone was watching him. He didn't see the person around, but the feeling was there. The thought of that man on the mobile bus made Steve wonder if what he said was true or was he the one watching him.

CHAPTER THREE

HE PLACE WAS CROWDED with people inside of the website newsrooms. In each corner sat a desk made of either wood or metal that was stack with rocks or boxes of some kind to keep the tables up right. Computers with vision screen sat on top of them or beside of them. Chairs were whatever anyone could find to use as a chair. In the center of the rooms had more computers-vision screen with communication-vision that were or could be used by anyone that knew how to use waited for them. Each of the people that were waiting to use one of the computers for some job related news that would bring them some kind of money to help their growing families there would not be much for them as money, but what we get is a lot more than being hungry every night. I had never used one of those before, but to see one was good I guess? I wasn't sure if we were even allowed to use a communication-vision. Looking at the computers that I had never used before set my interest on a higher level. A cradle of thin wire laid flat next to the computer screen that was black and totally in the center of the desk table. The hard drives, that help the screen to broadcast any statements or news was the size of my small fist. I sat down close to the computer main broad and thought of how my story would start out first. My neck was stiff with tension and stress as my mind started out with one word(escape) I wanted to escape away from everything that happen within the few hours I felt was confusion, frustrating, nothing made sense. Then something just reminded me of my grandfather that I barely knew, and yet, I recalled a story he told me about his younger years during the early times when he was 10 years old. His mother had plenty of food and holidays were of family gathers. Children played with toys of all sorts. Steve remembered how happy his parents were with what little they had, but still happy. The government had control over everyone's jobs and everyone's money, but the government could not take individuals happiness. It was then when Steve noticed more whispers of other things that made Steve skin crawl. A shake of his shoulders that lead down to his arms as the hair stood on end.

Steve went back to his story and tried to concentrate on what he was doing. His thought waved back and forth from what he and his friends found in his parent's attic back at his home. Then he would think about that strange man that was on the bus with him. Steve mind went wild with all that had happened in the short few days he had left to go home from work. Now Steve wasn't sure if he wanted to go back home or not. As he typed his by line over some of the already top front top news, his words became confusion and puzzle, his fingers moved fast over the keys that lay under his hands and fingers. His mind seemed to be controlling his fingers, his mind swept over the layout as it came over the screen. A story about his grandfather's father in a time of people helping people to survive, as he wrote the by line, a red light glowed over the screen. Steve stop writing as his story told of how his great grandfather had gone to a store that had food that was fresh and clean. Steve grandfather had money as many people had jobs and homes that had fresh water and electricity, each home had beds and furniture that was clean and sturdy. Animals small or large were pets to play with and enjoy. Everyone enjoyed life that was good and free from the darkness that was so common to Steve. Steve finished with the idea playing in his reader's mind of how his great grandfather went to work each day as freedom stole in his soul deep inside of him. Yeah Steve planted a more in anyone that was reading it. The red light came on again. Steve went back to the red light and found his mail that gave him a decision of how his story was read. Anyone responding to his story would be on the red light page. More than one had told him that the story was a good one. They are waiting for the next page to give them what happen to Steve great-grandfather meeting his wife. A story with some codes that Steve hoped the freedom fighters would get soon and not the police. Then again, the codes he sent out were not that good. He just sent out hints of things that Steve hope would look or read like a code. Rubbing his hands together as he stared at the outline of his story and hope the story was good. Redder glow showed over the screen as a word came up across his page. What happen to the grandfather and his girlfriend? Did they get married or are you going to wait to write another part? Another part might be a good idea. Maybe he would get lucky and be able to keep on with the story, and then maybe one of freedom fighters would catch the code by then. Rubbing his face and then just letting the story flow out of his fingers and mind felt as if someone else was doing the writing. Steve finished for the day and the night as he slowly stood up and went over to his boss room. The area was now full of people running to find a computer to do some kind of work for the website news. As I turned to look around and stretched my arms high over my shoulder, someone had brushed by me as I look up at the ceiling to think where I was going to sleep tonight. The way I see everyone here right now, my mind told me that I should just go back home. But then again another nagging thought sneak in my mind like an itch that would not leave me. Who was that man on the bus, and how long would it take the police to chase on to my community. My head shook with a chill that ran down my bones. I closed my eyes as I felt another brush against my back again. I moved away from my computer and let my story stay on screen as is. Got up off my seat and started to walk over to my boss. I wanted or need to know about my story and the impact that it made or would have made. I look at the computer again then found that many people were turning to my story as a red light blink on and off to let me know that some people where reading my story line. It seemed that time was holding still and again I felt as if times was going too fast to at the same time that those were reading my story. I had written other stories before and had little reaction, but now I could see that the numbers of those that were responding to it. Red glow kept the story on high alert as more red lights ran across my screen with messages. I smiled as I went across the small line that was crowded with boxes or broken chairs that were occupy with other people struggling too with the site. Steve felt the heat of the room mingle with the sweat of others that worked around Steve on other computers. The odors of bodies unkempt unwashed gagged Steve as he coughed.

I just about feel the tension and excitement as many fought for the computers that worked or the chairs that were good. I started to get a little comprehension of what was really going on around me, fear, confusion mixed with excitement I could not understand swam around my stomach and head, as I got closer to my boss. He wasn't a tall man, or a fat man with balding head, no he was just a man with short gray hair and thin long face that showed years of both worry and fear of what to expect from the police and his people. His nose was small with a round end that made him look like a kid at times. Skin wrinkled around his mouth and his eyes told me again that he was older than he told anyone he was. His body leaning against the wall to his office was pack with more people that were shouting at him. I had to step back a few behind other people. Words spoken about someone making up a story about freedom was giving a false idea that wasn't real. I knew that the story was mine and I left the bylines alone on the computer to absorb on the internet as I tried to talk to my boss. The way everyone was getting upset, I knew I should just shut up and not say it was my lines.

My boss looked straight at me with his grey sad eyes and his heavy bushy brows that pop up at the sight of me standing behind other people talking or arguing of something simple and not making a lot of sense. Some of them telling our boss that the story should die fast or someone would call the police on the website newsroom. Shout of disagreements with some fist fling around the room among those that had disagreed with my story. I stood there not far from them listening and deciding what to do. I needed to talk to my boss, but the sound of everyone shouting and some screaming out things I couldn't hear or understand. I just watched, my stomach rumbling with hungrier, my throat dry with fear of what would happen next. I decide to turn off my computer, so walking toward the computer I went into shock, as that man that was on the bus stood over the computer I was working on smile at me. He just stood there waiting for me to get over there I guess. My legs frozen on a path that was all wrong. I knew I had no choice but to confront the man. My breath came out ragged as I started to move again toward, but my legs and feet would not obey me as I stumbled and shook with both fear and with the unknown. Would this strange man be my downfall or would he help us? Who was he and why all of a sudden show up to help us with a cause I really don't know. But I do in so many other reasons. I cleared my throat with a cough that was quiet, but heard only to me.

I took in that rare smell of things I had never had, but knew it could only be good, fresh green grass with a hint of forest old but grown, something else that I could not describe tickle my nose. I took a deep breath to inhale the smell in my lungs and memory. He just stood looking at something or me as if he wanted to eat me up like that. I shook with fear and with some thought of how he found me. Would the police be here soon, because of him or was he here for something else? I was too confused to even think straight. I slowly walked toward him with my head held high and my fist ready to fight if I had to. Somehow, I felt both distrust toward the man and this weird feeling of safety, I couldn't shake it, and that was what scared me the most about him.

Well are we the one staring oat nothing or are ye staring me? Do I have something on me face? Or do come to realize that I am ye friend and want to help ye. What can I do to help ye believe me? Mike said as he smiled at Steve shock and confusion. He couldn't believe that this small frame of young man was to be part of his pride. Hmm can it only be an illusion or something? Maybe if the kid would eat more or something like that he would be worth the effort to train. Why make any effort if he was this small, he would not make it to the first trail without killing himself or someone else? Yet, Mike knew his Uncle was right about many things and this maybe one of them that he could not see. Mike took a breath and let it out slow as he took in the odor of unclean bodies around him. Their smell was of feces and urine with a stench of mold around their clothes as they came pass him and around him. At first mike wanted to gag and then he just took small breathing intakes until he had control over his feelings of gagging and coughing hard. Mike knew too that Steve was going to have one hell of a bath before they even trained. He couldn't or would not work with someone with that bad odor. Slowly mike put covered his mouth as he coughed a little without making a scene. Steve didn't want to gag in front of all the people who work with him and were trying to make some sort of living, although Money was or is the root of all evil and yet money was the only way to keep on living. Without one or the other life would not exist for a purpose or reason to keep on living. Mike didn't like any of that. But he had to carry on with his Uncles blessings. Mike cleared his throat again, as he tried to make Steve listen to him. Look mate, I know ye may not believe me about me knowing Mr. Farmer and your friends, but I know them well and I know your parents too. They were great people that I respect honestly. I grief too when I discovered their bodies close to me home, my uncle and I gave them a proper burial on our property. I could not get to any of you all in the community because of their death. I do nay want to bring the police or any other government official close to any of you. So I kept away, and made contact with Mr. William Farmer not too long ago. My own parents had given me the right code to contact Mr. Farmer. Jack had been on the code line of the fighters. I had coded Jack to let Mr. Farmer know I am waiting and watching out for all of you here close to the government rule. My Un—look this place is not the greatest to talk about who I am, but you have to believe me. Moreover, I know about the hard drive your parents had hidden for centuries, because of my own family had done the same with me. I grew up with not knowing things until me teenage years and it was pure hell after they died too. So please listen to me and let me help you and your friends because it is time for your destiny to be full fell. We are the same and you need to sense it, do not fight the feel that is deep inside of you. Mike said as he pulled me away from the shouts that broke off with a sudden sound of pop with the smell of something burning. I looked back as Mike pulled me harder toward the closet that was lock with a missing nob; Steve found that where the nod had been, was only a whole cover with a thin paper that was easy to open. Yet, you could still see the whole were the nob was once. The front door of the office broke out of the hinges that barely held it up came crashing down on top of other reporter that were on computer near the front door. Their screams were silent as the police came in their guns ready to strike anyone around them that got in their way, the green light that came out of the guns shot out and sent those around them gone they all disappeared. I couldn't stop from screaming myself as I was being tugged and pulled by Mike's large hands and arms toward a wall that was closed. Computers around us exploded with each firing of the police guns that kept on going off without any words or sound coming from the police closed faces that was metal and protected the police faces from anyone that might have the same weapons as they have. The sight of their bright metal gray suits made Steve shake with more fear of what was going on around him. His boss fell to the floor as a red glow covered his old body that was trembling with death. Did he lead them here (the police)? Where they after my story or did my story bring the police here? Maybe those that were upset about were right. His story about a past life that was all his grandfather untold life story had made the government enforcers active to come here to the website news room headquarters and kill everyone that was in sight.

Mike pulled harder on Steve arm as he knew where the hidden room was in this place. It was once part of the freedom fighter's newsroom itself many centuries ago. His Uncle had told him where the hidden room was and how to escape the police fast. Mike slam in the wall that swung open with feel of his heated body against it. Desk or table were turn over as those that fought the police with whatever they could find to defend swung with the fierce need to stay alive. Steve could feel his own heart beat fast as it thundered against his ribs. His chest hurting as the feel of his heart beat. Steve face felt wet as sweat came down hard over his face and nose as it stung his eyes. Blur was more of his sight right now as all he felt was that hand squeezing his arms hard. The pain coming from both his arm and his eyes as kept up with mike punishing running to another room that Steve was sure wasn't there. The wall opened up into darkness as Mike struggled to pull Steve closer against his solid chest. Mike own heart was beating a rhythm that made him gasp. Mike breathing became heavy in his lungs that matched the feel of his own heart beating the same rhythm. He had to close his eyes to force the pain that shot through his body as he felt Steve head rest against his chest. The smell of Steve unclean body took Mike breath as he struggled again to keep the gagging from escaping him. Steve we need to be quiet, we do nay know if they could hear us or not. Mike whisper in Steve ear. The feel of the dark hair of Steve tickled Mike nose as silent plea of not scratching or sneezing was all Mike could mustard in his mind.

The feel of the walls rough with edges of wood splintering off its own walls inside of the hidden place. Steve and Mike could only hear silent behind the door. Mike knew better to stay hidden. His feet felt something sharp hit his old shoes, his eyes could see in the dark without trouble, his talent was to protect Steve and his friends from the government police and the government period. A talent that he knew was hidden in Steve too. He could sense the same in Steve, but Steve was not alpha, but a fighter, a strong fighter if he could just eat right and more for his body and soul to come out alive. Something was on the floor that felt sharp and then again, it was flat as he kept on looking at it. Steve can ye see the floor close to me shoes on me left side. I think I found some kind of level on the floor. I am not sure but I think there is a hidden staircase that would lead us straight to the street. We need to try to open the floor slowly. Mike whisper in Steve said.

Steve gave Mike a dirty look as he stared down the floor of the hidden room. Steve wasn't sure if his eyes were adjusted right to dark as he kept on looking down at, Mike left shoe for something that wasn't there. And yet, somehow knew that the floor would open up under his feet. Steve slowly bent down trying not to make a sound as he touched the metal thing that was almost under Mike feet. The feel of the metal thing was both smooth and then again the edge rusted as flakes old and rusty calking off whenever anyone touched the metal. The smell of mold metal-stung Steve lung, Steve hated to leave the warmth, strength of Mike chest. Mike made Steve feel safe in an odd way. Steve was becoming more confused as he thought about how it felt when Mike held him. Yeah? Steve thought, he had slept with women for money or food, he even slept with men at a time, and it was more out of desperation than anything else was. But never had he felt something close to weird to describe and yet it felt like something that he would not want to say or could not say aloud. One thing he noticed that his lower part of his body (in between his legs) was getting to tight and he did not want to think about it. Come on Steve the guy is built like a hard solid tree, with branches that could kill anyone that would get in his way. Someone like him would be more interest in someone more like him, someone who had money and power to even up his own persona.

So think Steve, he said something in the way of fighters and freedom too. But he also knew a lot about community that made me want to fight him. Yeah, right and be killed in the process. Damn it all, but Steve still had tingles and a hard on that fuck would not listen to a damn fuck what he had tried to control. But his fucking thing would not listen to him. Steve pulled harder on the metal thing as it finally opened up to a staircase that was old, dark, here where no sounds coming down the darkness below them. Mike held his breath as he silently tugged on Steve arm as they took the staircase slowly. Be of care Steve, we do nae want the police finding us. I think your broadcast of your grandfather's life and that it portrays a man that has freedom and a job that pays well enough to support a wife and children shows that ye were using a code to contact the freedom fighters and ye did. Mike said quietly as he finally reached the bottom stairs.

I had to feel the walls in order to know where I was going even though Mike kept on tugging my arm, the feeling I felt as if I was falling down the stairs grew with each step we took going downward. My eyes could see, or just adjust to the darkness in a way. However, I noticed that Mike moved in the dark as if he owned it without any kind of hesitation. Mike was sure with every step he took going down as if he could see in the dark. Our feet not giving away any thought of the police coming behind us, I turned to see if they had found the secret wall that went open not too long ago. The sounds now were silent from the police killing spree of all those that had worked with me in the website news. Now I believe I was the both the cause of their death and the reason why they died violently.

If I would have known, I would never had sent out that story over the website. But ignorance is a part of our life lessons that we learn from and we will continue to learn from until we die. I took a hard breath as my lungs grew heavy, the pounding against my chest started to drive my head aching with some dizziness as I tried to look at Mike face. The sight of him standing close to me started to become a blur. My eyes were unfocused my head beating with my heart at the same time. I could feel my legs unsteady as my stomach decide to take a celebrated reason to let loose this morning breakfast on the flat empty floor that was more concrete than wooden. I figured that sense the main floor of the website was on the first floor, it was obvious that this basement was down here, an area close, and not in use or ever had been. No one really had ever been here that I knew of. No sounds of humans creeping around down here, only something small in a low distance, maybe at the end of the area's walls. But still close enough for us to hear it moving around.

Mike looked at Steve with confusion as he watched the young man bent over the floor and let out all the food he had eaten in the short time of 48 hours. Mike smell was keen and strong as the Steve nausea rose up around with the smell of mildew and mold. There was another smell, but he just shook his head slowly as if he was knotting no.

Mike tried harder not to gag, but the coughing and smell made it a lost cause. We "cough" "gag" need to keep as quiet as possible. Those damn police are still looking for the one that send those stories about freedom. We cannae let them know it was you or we both would die without question. We need to stay alive as long as we can, for the sake of the human race and others that need us. Mike said with each word he spoke he had taken a breath to control his gagging and his coughing. Mike was to use to living close to forest and jungles that let him roam in a form of freedom, but he was also fighting hard to keep children that were missing along the jungles edges safe and alive. He knew the government were involved with the missing children and still are involve with many things that were missing or found dead. When his Uncle Northern told Mike, it was time for him to find or seek out Steve now and the others too. It was time for the fighters to open war against the government, but then again Mike knew that would not be now or tomorrow, maybe soon, but that soon. It was more confusing than really thinking right. The air down the basement of the website news was full of other smells of feces and urine that blend with the already mildew and mold. Mike stomach was already in bind as it tried to rebel with pain and with rejection of his earlier meal. That meal was the last time he had eaten with his Uncle Northern and his cousin Jab. Jab had another mission to do and it was dangerous as the one Mike was doing right now, they both knew that their meeting was in another few months from now. Right now Mike wasn't sure if either one of them would even live long enough to be there at that meeting. Mike breath came out in a slow whisper of ease as smell air that was not foul, the feel of the air moving slow around the basement that seemed closed off to anyone that wanted to use the basement for something. Steve you need to stay close to me, we don't know what's down here. Mike said. Then he felt it the aura of the area grew with each of his sight that gathered around him, he grew more lethal. Deep down Mike, chest a roar and loud rumble grew inside of him that made him tremble with need that was more danger to others than anything else was. His sense storm around him as he kept his footing silence as each step seem to stop before he felt the hard slippery ground of the basement. The basement floor was cover with moss and mushrooms that made the mildew hard to breathe without coughing or gagging. The air grew heavy with the smell of stale Urine that was old and still lingered around.

Steve walked slowly around the basement floor, his shoes flopping down with each step he took. Steve heard only his shoes moving in that flopping way, the smell from the ground rose over his nose as he recognized each smell of mildew and mold that was mixed in the grass.

But there was something else that smell of death, and of old urine and feces, but Steve also smelled something else that he could not describe. Steve started to cough as he followed Mike in the dark. His eyesight was not that good, but Steve had figure that somehow Mike eyes were a lot better than his were. Mike stop suddenly in front of Steve, something made Mike hold still like a brick wall. His head tilt a little on his side as Steve tried to listen carefully at what Mike heard. However, it was fate a small scramble of tiny feet running along the ground with no other sounds. Steve still didn't move, he waited for Mike to do something first. Mike chest rose slow and then exhale fast, he didn't move, but looked down at Steve holding still as he was. Then slowly both men walked again toward the area where they felt the air that tickle slowly toward them. Steve never knew about the any secret passages that lead this low in the website before. The sight of not seeing was not anything new, but being below the building he was working in was new. Mike banged on something on a wall that was in front of Steve and Mike. Mike knew that there was a hidden door that would lead them out of the building, but where was it and how would he get them out. Mike felt the wall for some shallow sound that would tell him that the wall had the hidden door behind the walls. Mike fist large bulging with strength as he kept on pounding on the door. The silent around them disturb from Mike continue pounding and the doors thundering its own protest as the door broke open half way.

The air came out of the doors entrance that Mike had finally broken open, the smell that invade their noses was of old urine and feces that I wasn't sure was good to breath. The sounds of police shouting out words that were muffle by the sound of the Transport-Mobiles hissing as the mobile hummed above the ground.

The sight of more police storming other homes, other buildings that were housed by people, people that were innocent and yet, being killed rapidly. Both Steve and Mike watched as more police, enforcers hunted down more innocent people in other buildings around them as they escape from the mass destruction around them, Steve knew that the only purpose the police have within the human world was to maintain its strength against anyone that threatens the government rules and laws. There are those in government that use their powers to rule those that are underneath them in ways that only one word to the police and the individual or family would disappear. Steve had always suspect that was how his father and mother had just disappeared, then he wasn't too sure how or who killed or even if they were dead or not. He only knew that he had to be responsible for Brooke and he tried very hard to help her when she needed it. He worked day in and out for the website news and that of solacing his body to other people that had more money he needed for the community. He really didn't care how he got the money, only he got it and took the money home for the others in the community, especially for Brooke. Now Brooke is gone and never come back ever again. Steve thought about his friends and his responsibility for the community's needs. So Steve figured he would still have to work, but what work, the website news, and everyone else that he knew that worked there were all dead. Steve took a breath and coughed. Mike turned to look at Steve as he glared at him, his face a mask of hidden emotion that only his eyes could tell. Steve knew Mike was upset with him for coughing. The police didn't even notice that they were being watched by Steve as he watched the police storm the building he and his co-workers worked and are now gone, Steve could not tell or know if any of them even lived. Steve could feel his heart pounding hard as he watched the excitement of the police hunting someone or something. Then again, Steve thought about it and somehow knew that the person they were after had to be him and maybe even Mike. How would Mike know that Steve was the one that sent that story over the news web and included the message in the story about freedom and fighters too? A cold shiver rode through Steve spine and down his arms, sweat creep up his brow and under his armpits. Mike slowly came out side of the basement and motion for me to follow him. The night sky came in a shock as Steve was hoping that it was morning and not night still. Steve knew he had come here in the early morning. But it was dark now and not the early morning sun haze flowed down like a blanket that was hot, humid, wet at times. It didn't matter though, it was hot humid and sweat was beaming down his face, Steve looked at Mike face, he saw that his was not effected and he was calm and wet only by his shirt that was a tad open by the neck line. Steve watched carefully as the police moved away from the scene, with their mobiles rising with a humming sound that vibrated and made what trees that grew in buildings and outside too swish with the sound of the mobile taking off. The breeze whistled and shattered the leaves and branches that reached out toward the sky disappear along with the mobiles that rose higher over the ground. Screams and shouts of pain ran out of the remaining parts of buildings that were still standing. Steve felt debris falling around from buildings that the enforcers had burnt or blew up scattered around them as they fled. A breath of air shadowed the fog that Steve mind was playing right now. Was he in shock from all that was happening around him? Yes, he was as his mind play out the events of the last few days or was it hours sense he came home a night or two ago.

The fog seemed to fall away as he thought about everything that had happen in the few hours that he came into the website news building. The confusion and puzzlement of how he got to where he was now had almost made his want to run as fast as he could. But where would he go? Should he just go back to the community and his friends or should he — no Steve wasn't a coward. But what was he if he wanted to run and then not run at the same time? He was definitely scared out of his mind and knew somehow that he should listen to Mike and do as he says. The fog of confusion was wavering in and out of focus and Steve needed to be somewhere or something. A shake of his head and the feel of Mikes strong arms wrap around Steve smaller body felt comforting and he wanted to stay just like that. Safe, secure and something Steve could not define what else he felt. Steve looked at Mike with a question in his eyes as he kept quiet watching him move silently. It seemed to Steve that Mike feet was not even touching the ground, Mike seem to float over the ground silent with each step he took.

Steve looked down at his own feet and noticed that one of his flip-flop shoes were missing from his feet. He must have lost it not long ago in the basement somewhere. Steve bent down to take off his other shoe on his left foot and just let his feet be free of its bind. The ground was cool to Steve feet as he rested them down next to Mike firm flat feet that looked big, long (although, Mike wore shoes that were like new, Steve could not see any holes or any place that would have been torn). Ignoring the small broken debris of bricks and glass that remain what was left of the buildings around Steve sights cluttered the ground underneath his feet stun and pinched his feet as he tried to the mimic Mike movements. The sounds of cries of pain was all around them as they kept on moving away from the sights of buildings falling down with people screaming out for help. Mike couldn't do a thing to help them. Those that survive from the police raid to find them were only a few that would be lost to the cause that would have been thousands or more to what would have been salvation. Mike worn out shoes silently felt the cold ground wet grass that grew out of the old concrete of hidden past. His mind tried to progress what was going on under his feet, but he kept on walking and hoping that Steve stayed quiet with his own shoes that flop on the ground loud and clear.

Mike stop as he looked up and down the path that lead to another alley. Mike had to make sure that they were safe and no police were around. The sounds of people whispering and some shouting danger in buildings that were surrounding them in all direction in the alley, the only sound that echoes off were their shoes as they continued to walk down the alley path. Mike looked carefully around them as he listened for anything that would tell him of the dangers that may wait for them a behind each corner of alley or buildings that may hide any government police.

Mike could feel Steve body casting a chill that caught Mike's own back, mike wanted to shake the feeling away, but he couldn't. Mike mind was on getting them as far away as possible from here. The city was cesspool of government spies and police control. Nothing that Mike wanted to tangle with right now, he only knew that he had to get Steve to a safe place. His uncle lived not too far from here and he would help them, if only Mike could get out of this shit. Sweat glisten down Mike brow as he felt the wetness come down his nose that was large with a round point. Mike took his left arm and hand to wipe the sweat off his face. The feel of the sweat dripping in his eyes stun, made his eyes go blur. Mike had to squeeze his eyes close to keep the pain from hurting more and then again, he wanted to readjust his sight too. The sting of the sweat hurt still as he slowly opened his eyes. Mike wiped again his brow to keep the sweat from stinging his eyes again. The alley had to have a way out, an end with a path that was— yeah, there it is right around the corner of this brick building that has little to be of any shelter. The sound of children screaming a warning of where the food was being hunted down made my skin crawl. Feet running toward them as Mike stop to just look or watch them pass. Mike could hear Steve heavy breathing as Steve stood behind him close. The breath stale, heavy with rotted teeth and food that Mike could not tell what it was that Steve had eaten. Steve needed a good brush and someone that could fix his teeth or remove them. Then again Steve need his teeth, his teeth was part of the reason Steve was special. Then again, that foul smell made it unbearable to be close enough to Steve. Mike look up at the sky that was clouded now with dark shallow clouds, the clouds told him in an odd way that it was going to rain soon. The smell of acid mixed with salt and stale air crowded Mike lungs. Yeah the rain was coming and it was heavy with acid. Mike stop close to the far side of the alley. Mike could hear the children shouts as they came closer to the opening. A loud crackling sound stormed across another street, the city came alive again with shouts and screams as the smell of burnt flesh met with the light breeze that seem to just kiss Mike face like a gentle hand caressing a lover's face. Steve had to cover his nose, the smell of rotted flesh linger in the air was strong. Mike slowly motion Steve to walk across the street slowly toward the darkness part of the alley's pathway. Steve nodded as he started across the street. The only light that was shining was partly peeking out from the dark clouds that hide the stars. The moon reflected off the sunglow from the morning side of the world was Steve thoughts as he looked up and then straight ahead for some kind of light to show him that he would be safe. His breath heaving hard in his chest, Steve coughed and gagged as his feet touched the alley Mike had told him to get too. Steve hand touched the surface of the walls that were cold and rough against his hands. The alley ground was cover in moss and grass that was wet with mildew that rose up to Steve nose. Mike walked in a fast paste as he reached Steve side. His breath coming in slowly and steady, and yet he could feel his heart beat fast in his chest felt as if he was coming apart. Steve could smell Mike body again; the smell sent Steve in a comfort form of Mike present. It was both odd and—Steve couldn't quite find the right word to describe the feeling. Steve took a breath with a gulp of stale air that was still mix with acid and burnt flesh. Steve wondered if the smell of burnt flesh was coming from the website news building or the one next to it that the police had evaded and set on fire. That was the only thing Steve could explain the smell of burnt flesh. Mike s eyes were stein, his brow arched with a point downward crinkled along the sides of his eyes; his nose now sniffing like a dog would toward Steve face. Steve throat ached with dryness as he tried to say something, but the words would not come out.

Steve wasn't sure what was going on with Mike, but he knew that something was not quite right with him, those eyes of Mike was making Steve shake all over. Was that it, Mike was going to eat him or kill him. Steve had been set-up and Mike was going to get the disc and all his friends.

How can he save them from Mike? If Mike wanted to he could rip Steve in two, Mike was built hard with muscle Steve could almost see through the clothes Mike wore and Mikes weighted a lot more than he did. Mike was bigger and stronger than Steve was. Mike looked up and then back through the alley with one long step inside of the darkness that was covered with trees and more bushes and vines that grew around each of the buildings they were close too. Each step Mike made it was silent along the grass. Steve just stood against the wall without moving a muscle toward where Mike had disappeared into the darkness. Silently Steve moved away from the wall and just stared into the darkness and tried to see if he could see Mike or something. Steve felt the ground vibrate under his feet as he held on the vines that clung to the walls the building he was next too. The feel of the vines that clung to the walls felt wet as he gasped how slippery the walls seemed to be. Somehow Steve knew Mike could drive without any problem as he road against the walls wetness. His hand slipped off the hold of the vine, his feet missing some solid surface that wasn't wet and moist.

Steve had ditch his shoes back to where his job had once stood and now he stood on moist ground bare feet. The sound grew louder as it came in view of Steve sight as another strange thing happen with the sound, a light bright and round shining toward Steve, it made Steve quake with fear. His mouth went open as he slipped a little on the grass and found himself almost kissing the floor as something hard cold slam close toward Steve, its bright light blinding Steve sight as he tried to see who or what was causing the thunder to rumble underneath his already weak legs and body. But that damn light made it almost impossible to see anything. Steve stumble more as the sound came closer to him, his legs gave out, his hands slippery from the wet vines that he tried to hang on from falling gave way with his legs as he fell knee first on the wet grass and stones. Then the sound was almost down to a growl in front of him. He was still shaking from the loud thunder the thing made, and then it stopped all together as Mike got off the thing that had wheels of some sort and the thing Mike sat on was metal with two pipes blowing out smoke behind Mike seat. Mike held on two out stretched metal bars with long wires that was connected to another handlebar that was smaller and underneath both bars on each outstretched part of the thing. Mike noticed that Steve was kneeling down on the floor of the alley entrance, Steve face was sweating with dirt dripping down his face as he looked up at Mike tall statue looking down at him. His face blank with any kind of emotion that would tell Steve how he felt or what he was going to do. Steve took a breath that was haggard with sprits of coughs and gags. Wh—at is th-th-that? Steve asked Mike as he tried to get off the ground by holding on to the wall again. Steve wiped the sweat off his face with the back of his left arm as he stood up and looked straight at Mike.

This machine is called a motorcycle, a very old motorcycle. I found it you might say at me great Uncle James had hidden the machine for centuries or more, I can't say how old it is. But I learned how to drive the machine when I was not even 10 years yet. But I worked hard every day to learn how to ride the thing. My great Uncle calls this thing motorcycle or bike. I have worked on it so I could be able to get not just one person on the bike, but at least two people. It is a big bike and I had modified the bike throughout my years with my great Uncle James. So get on the bike behind me and let's go to yer community and meet with Mr. Farmer and the others. I think they might be waiting for us. Mike said as he turned the handlebars and stomp on something to make the bike roar to life. I was scared to death to get on the bike he had called it. The feeling of something that sounded like thunder from the sky made my ears hurt as well as shakes my legs to a rhythm that I was not comfortable. Then some warmth seemed to rise up my legs as I straddle back of the bikes seat. I settle my feet down close to the flat like metal plate that Mike had point to put my feet on. Mike hands grab hold of the bars that were stretched out in front of him, Mike grip the bars in twist and turns as his feet kept on kicking another flat like plate that was kind of loose. The sound of the bike roar vibrated the ground and Steve seat. I had to grab hold of Mike waist to keep from falling off the bikes seats. Mike shirt had mud and other untold filth that started to smell. The sweat dripped down Steve face and into his eyes, the feel of his vision blurred as the taste of the sweat touched his lips. Steve tasted the sweat that tasted like salt water mixed with blood. Steve thought he might have some injury that he didn't realized he had. The wind blew through both of the men faces as they speed down the trail of patches of both dirt and grass that grew over the once cement streets and sidewalks. Buildings stood on either side of their ride through town with windows broken and some without walls or doors. The night air was cloudy, blanketing the night sky with clouds covering the bright stars'. The only light that shone to where they were going and gave Steve some direction of where they were at. His hair blown away from his face stung, as it whipped against his cheeks. His ears felt the wind whistle, Steve had to wince as the pains cold sting touched his ears repeatedly. How can Mike ride this thing with the wind blowing in his face and in his ears? Doesn't the wind hurt him? Steve thought as he watched them pass people running and screaming as flames rose high over the building that once was the website news building. Some of the people ran out with flames engulfing their bodies and yet they were running as fast they could with both the pain of the burns and the fact they thought if they could just run the fire would be gone and so would the pain. Steve nodded his head as if he was trying to clear everything in his sight like a bad dream. But the vision and the sight would not leave, nor would the smell of burnt flesh or the sound of many people death screams. The police came in sight as Mike drove the motorcycle through the rough parts of fallen bricks and parts of the buildings that were still on fire around them. The sirens were nothing but loud voices from the police that were behind the controls. They command that Mike and Steve stop at once or they would have to shoot with intent to kill. Mike ignored them and pound though debris and bodies left to rot around the other injured people. No one wanted to help anyone that was burnt or barely alive. They were afraid of the police violent action. Children scrambling to find food or shelter from the fierce force of the police action to kill anyone that might have information the police need. The sounds of the people around Steve was muffled as Mike motorcycle roared out of debris and death that seem to just lay in the streets path as they left. Another sound woke Mike's stern concentration of driving his bike out of the city as fast as he could. The police were behind him and above him as their Tran mobile levitated over their heads. The sound of the air-mobiles had been silent in flight, only sound was a humming that vibrated the air around them. Mike took a gulp of air as he realized they might be caught if didn't do something fast. He had to do something that would get rid of those damn mobiles. The air was stale with hints of more rain coming, the ground was hard with debris fling and falling down from buildings burning around them. The police were getting closer as they flew above the buildings and tried to turn sideways into the alleys. Bushes tall block paths that Mike tried to go through, but the bike stall at one point. Something solid hard and cold rough on edges that Steve held with his left hand as Mike tried to move the bike into the alley without a sound from the bikes motor. Silent was all around them, no sound of people screaming for help, no birds out in the darkness hunting for food. Nothing at all that would tell them that life was around them. Mike looked back at Steve as he noticed that Steve wasn't on the bike. Mike thoughts were not on who-what-was coming after them. Only that they needed to get out of this town without the police following them. Steve ye need to stay with me and the bike. We need to find a way out of the alley of bushes. They feel as if they have thorns on them. Be careful if ye touch one. We do nay need to leave blood for the police to us to catch us. Mike said as he tried to move the large bush that was still in his way.

Wait a minute I think I know some way out. Steve said as he recalled the alley they were in. Steve kept on touching the large green bush that wasn't a bush, but something metal even though vines and a bush had grown over the sight Steve still could feel the metals coolness. And, yet, Steve knew that there was something that he could—move and—they would be—under the ground. Yes, the metal had a round black button that blend in with the greenery. Mike watched as the metal open up to a slide like tunnel. Mike couldn't see anything in the tunnel. But the police were getting closer to them. No way out, but down. Mike knew that this was the only alley that he could not go though and be on another street. So now, he had to make a choice that he could not decide. Steve got back on the bike behind Mike, then yelled at Mike to go on. The bike will make it down, you don't have a choice. If we get caught, the community and the rest of the world will be in danger. Mike said then thought about his words, they were in danger and it was up to him to keep Steve and the others safe. Mike thought about Steve friends that were more than that they were his family. Mike knew to the danger had bothered Steve too the concern was events in Steve eyes and his attitude.

Steve knew that his friends were always there when he needed them the most and he was there for them too. Something Mike wished he had during his own childhood. Again, He was glad for his Uncle's help in learning so many things that he had no time to wish for something he could never have. He was part of the freedom fighters weapon that was secret to only a few to know.

Now that Steve found those things that would take the government to their knees and maybe just maybe, wipe the government officials completely. It was a dangerous risk, but Steve had those important things that had information that would make them scream. Yeah, they were, wait a minute, did Steve open up a passage that might lead them out of the city? That bush and those vines must have hidden something metal that had a passage built in it for a reason. The relief of finding that made Mike bow his head with thanks to who ever made them. Mike took a gulp of air and let his mind clear so he could concentrate on going down that tunnel. Mike bike bright light beam down the tunnel like the sun coming down across a sky. The weight of Steve behind so fast made the bike unsteady as he fought to control more. The tunnel was as dark, or more so than that of outside. As they went down ward with the bike making screaming sound like something metal had eaten someone alive. The sound was high pitch with a roar of loud vibrating thunder underneath both men seats. Then a bump that told them that they had finally come to a flat level and not a slide angle downward. Mike stopped the bike to listen and smell around where they were. He wanted to make sure that the police did not follow them, as Mike looked up to where they had come down from, he noticed that the door or hatch turn down with the metal bush sealing them inside like a tomb. Somehow, Mike knew that there was a reason for what had happened the thought was there and without a complaint he knew he had to do whatever to stay alive for Steve and the others. They were safe from the police and from anyone else that wanted them. Steve got off the bike slowly as his legs wobbled from the ride down, the smell of mold and stale wetness was hard on Steve breathing as he coughed again and again. His eyes grew large as he found he could see a little in the darkness around them. The ground was muddy with peddles of stone and rocks under his bare feet. He had lost his shoes after left the building that housed his job at the website news and now was all gone with those that worked with him there. A lump form in his throat as he remembered all that happen. So many innocent people had died because of him and those damn things he found in his parent's attic were to blame.

How can those small things that only had stories and some other things that he had no idea was about in them be so important. Steve looked at Mike for something he could not figure out. But the sight of the man with the broad shoulders and blonde that curled under his neck like a lion's hair around his face gave Steve hints of what kind of man Mike was and is. Mike face shown no emotion that Steve could see in the dark, but watching him sniff the air made Steve cough again hard. What are you doing? The air is polluted down here the tunnels hold waste! Human waste! I know because it was one of the places that the police won't go down. Too many people had used this area for their body waste. Toilets are for the rich and powerful, we here and around use the sewers to put our waste in. So, if you think you are standing in mud, think again friend. Its shit and more shit with piss all around in puddles. I know how to get out of here and I know my direction around town better than most. You have no idea how many times I had to hide from the police sense I came here years ago. So follow me. You might as well know that I can't be sure if the cops could hear your motorbike or not down here. I would be safer to just walk the damn thing any ways (I thought again I knew no matter what I would always be in danger because of the police, government). Steve said as he saw that Mike had a puzzle look on his face as well as one look of you got to be joking face. It was kind of comical in a way, his eyes stern and puzzle as both his brow are pull together. Mike had never been in this part of town apparently. So Steve was the one to show Mike the how's and the when and why of things and how to get them out of this. Yeah, Mike might be strong and smart about something's, but not in Steve world, he wasn't. This Steve world with all the shit, and piss was all around them right now was just a part of things that Steve lived with. Then there is the fact that just running from the police was an everyday life and so was the everyday of never knowing when there was food and if the food was not going to either make them sick or kill them. A giggle escape Steve throat as he thought about Mike. Rich kid meeting real world, might die, might live if he listened. Then again he was one strange person with his bike that roared like thunder. That wasn't all that made him strange, he knew everything about Steve friends and Mr. Farmer. It was almost enough to make Steve terrified of Mike. Steve shivered as if he was cold, Steve could hear his legs shake like bones bumping against each other. The sound echoed against the long dark tunnel that was both solid bricks mixed with metal and dark green that was wet.

How are we going to find a way out of here? All I can smell is shit and old piss. How –can— you stand this smell. I know that ye live poorly, but this? Mike said as he wrinkled his nose and made another sour like face.

Steve giggle more as a twinkle bright in his brown eyes glowed like amber in the darkness. Mike smile at the sight as he found some evidence that he was right about Steve being different. Steve didn't know what his parents had done. How he would be the one to save many of thousands of people and those like them from the government control of everyday life. Hmm. How old did Steve say he was? Steve wasn't sure and Mike thinks he could find out how old he is by way of doing some asking. Hmm. Yeah, Mike thought about his uncle next and how much power he had. Mike nodded to himself after he thought about his uncle Thomas and if he could talk to the man. A shake of Mike head brought him back to the present, and where he was!

Steve looked at him after he controlled his laugh. Steve bowed his head for a second and then looked up at Mike long tall body. Steve smiled at the sight of Mike confusion and then with two of his fingers Steve snapped. Look and just listen to my direction and we will be out of here in no time. I promise that you will not get lost or fall in the shit lake. Steve said with a wide grin that showed off his dimples.

Mike took a breath and gagged from the harsh smell of the tunnels ground. The smell of waste rose higher as the heat and the cool air mixed to make the shit even worst. Mike almost wanted to faint from the smell. Mike got back on his bike with Steve sitting behind him. Mike kicked his petal that started his bike, his legs tremble from the roar that spun out of the metal beast that Mike called his motorcycle. Steve own legs shook underneath him as they turned into the darkness.

CHAPTER FOUR

MIKE KNEW HIS BIKE would be full of shit and the smell might not come off of either the bike or him. Echoes bounced off around where Mike was riding hard and fast. Mike could feel his heart pounding against his chest with the sound of his bikes roars and tremble beneath his legs as the motorcycle carried him farther into the waste tunnels that Steve told him were called more sewers of sorts. Steve tight grip around his waist didn't bother Mike it was the signals that they had planned on how Steve would tell him how to get out. Steve right hands pulled twice for turn right and his left hand tugged once for left turn. Both hands were tugged hard told him to stop. Right –left-stop, confusion and puzzlement on how did Steve know about this and why was he so sure of how to get out. Yes, Mike knew or Steve told him one way or another that this was one of his hidden ways of getting out of the city when the police was after you. But how could he stand the smell. After a few hours it seemed to pass by, (I felt as if it was forever down here) the smell of fresh acid air wavered downward toward Mike face. Somehow, a sight of end of the tunnel would end soon and they were getting close to get out. Yes, thank god for the outside pollution Steve tugged Mike left side of his shirt. Mike turn left at a tall a vine tree that had something darker than green and smell stale old, the sight of the dark green moss spread out around the tall tree that Mike had realized was round. Somehow, Mike knew it really wasn't a tree or large bush, but something else that held the ceiling above them. Then as they rode through, Mike also realized that there was many of those large round trees were holding up where all around them as they went through labyrinth of shit and piss and of other unknown things on the ground. Steve tugged again harder on his left side of his shirt. Mike turned the bike around toward the left of the round tree like and found himself facing a solid wall of dark smelly shit that covered from the bottom to the ceiling. Mike had to stop his bike and waited for Steve to tug his shirt, but all he felt was Steve rumble of something that sounded like a curse or worst.

Steve couldn't believe that the path that was used by so many people to get away from the police had been covered with shit. Now what or how are they getting out of here? Steve knew that Mike might not like what he or they would have to do in order to get out. Then again, they didn't really have a choice. They need to get out here. Steve thought of how long would the police figure out how to get down here. Somehow, Steve knew the police would figure out how to get down somehow.

Steve got off Mikes motorbike and walk up to the wall, took a breath as he tried to determine where actually the opening was. Steve raised his hands over the wall without touching it. Steve was hoping he might be able to feel some draft of wind or air coming from the wall.

What are ye doing Steve? I can tell ye I smell fresh air coming from here in small pockets. But I canna tell where the air is coming from the wall actually. Mike said as he sat on his bike watching Steve move his hand over the pale of shit wall.

Will all I can say is if I don't feel air touching my hands, then we got a longer ride out of here. This is where the wide opening is that would have taken us closer to the street that would have lead us home and out of the city.

Look we got another area I know about, it's a short cut. it is one area that is the government police would never be at they are afraid of the place and we— Steve couldn't finish his sentence when Mike interrupt him talking.

Ye are telling me that ye donna think that we could get out this way and ye know of another opening? Mike asked Steve before Steve could even finish his sentence.

Yeah, I know another place, but as I was trying to tell you, the place is more dangerous, with the police might be waiting for us back there, (Steve pointed back at where they had come from). They might be waiting for us at that point too. So — Steve stop talking as he looked at Mike studying him carefully.

How close is that opening to ye community? Mike asked as he rubbed his chin with a thought of how they were going to get out of this mess. Mike lowered his head as his hair fell in his eyes to hide his glowing eyes that wanted to just change into the nightmare that plagued him all his life.

Well it's a lot farther away and could take us —maybe another hour or more, the opening comes out close to the main police headquarters. I think or maybe I — don't know how far it is for sure to my home in the community.

I do know that the police will be right there when we get out the place we are going to. But the path I am talking about well the opening, it leads straight to one of the police headquarters—it's at least I am not sure how far, but I know I took it one time or maybe twice. Well any ways I got home within a day and a half. But —but I wasn't running from the police. So we should go through the shit hill and —Steve thought he heard something, Steve watched Mikes face as he realized that Mike had heard the same thing. The sound was like a humming roar that vibrated the walls of shit. Steve looked at Mike and knew that they were thinking the same thing. The sound was a police mobile that was not too far from where we were. I knew Mike might be able to feel or hear my heart beat fast in my chest, fear was one thing I found made my heart beat to a faster rate that sometimes made me almost faint. Sweat started to drip around my face as I looked at Mike.

Do not get off this bike by any reason. Now I need to smell something fast. We need to smell the right exit to leave this shit-piss sewer. Mike said as he turned the handle of the bike and looked up at the pile of shit that was in front of us. Then he turned the bike around in the puddle of shit and piss that was all around us. Then the police airmobile came in view of our turn that lead us into the darkness that was almost too dark to even see in front of us. But the light that glowed off the police mobile was enough for them to see where they were going. But it wasn't in the shit that was in front of us. I held on Mike's chest like I was going to die in the next two minutes. I slammed my head in to mike back as if I was hiding from the police. But I knew that they could see me clearly. The puddles slashed high as the back wheels dug into the air that spit out over my back and head. But Mike was in a mode that I couldn't see, and then I knew he was not just scared of getting caught, but he was in a rage of getting us out. The sound of

Mike heart beat in a thundering pound that shook my own hands in the grip I had around him. His breath coming out in huffs of smoking air I felt warm and yet deadly.

The mobile was in sight of the two riders on the strange thing that had wheels spinning on the earth in front of them. They were to hold the two and wait for farther command from headquarters. Then again, the damn thing was fast and more mobile than they were. But the police inside knew they could not stop until they have those two on the strange thing. No one in the airmobile wanted to die. The thoughts of not getting the two important civilians that were escaping them became more dangerous of losing their own lives. The airmobile was divided in four halves with each police officers seated close to one of the control panels. A large glass window wrap around the airmobile top with a thin metal rod that was flat but curved from back to front of each policeman that was sitting down near a panel that glowed like a holiday tree with bright lights that covered each branch. The inside of the policeman's mobile was more white with glowing panels that made the men glow with each color of the flat lights that glowed under their hands as they moved. The rod was part of a divider that kept each policeman at his seat moving each hands in a fast motion that only they could have noticed their own hands moving over the panels. As each officer watched the strange thing move away from them with a roar that vibrated the air around them. The sight of the back wheel-spinning fast as the puddle of muck splashing upward close to their grand window shield almost made them winch from the slash. Angrier drove the police to drive faster as curses and words that were not heard shot out toward Mike and Steve strange thing. One of the police man had touched a yellow panel that switched on a beam that glowed the tunnels sewer light it was daylight.

Mike thought about that light beaming off the police mobile that hovered behind them in the chase, that light had two good and one bad thing about it.

One: they could see what is in front of them and behind them as they drove off fast away from their pursuers.

Two: they were able to find a way out that total darkness could not (even thou Mike could see alright in the dark, it still had its limits)

The one bad thing about the light was that the police could see everything they did and went too. Damn good and damn bad at the same damn time? Mike thought to himself.

Steve felt as if he was holding his breath as he buried his face deeper in Mike's back. Then he looked behind him, the police had gotten closer and not to close that Mike's bike was able to spin out another puddle of shit on their windows. The tunnels darkness forgotten as Steve realized that the police bright beam bounced off shadows that spinout around them as they rode by. Steve wasn't sure about how far the other passage ways was, but he was sure it wasn't the way Mike was going in circles. He could have sworn that they had passed the shit wall twice. Now Steve grab hold on Mike as his breath took a gulp that shock the hell out of Steve. Steve thought he felt something soft inside of his pants. Oh, shit that's what it was, he had shit in his pants. Mike forced the bike to ride on its hind wheels as the front wheel rode high in the air. The sound of more thunder struck louder as Mike spin the bike in a circle and went straight toward the Mobile that was in front of them.

The police watched in horror as the thing came toward them. Each officer covered a blue panel that glowed brighter as the two riders on the strange thing came right straight at them with the thing standing on it back wheel like legs. The mobile separated the police as three pods and not one mobile. The sound inside of the mobile separating as three was nothing but a swish and the glass panel that separated them apart. One of the pods struck against one of the vines that hide a wall of hard brick of concrete that was old and ready to fall. The sound of the wall tumbling down around him brought a sudden fear to the policeman that he pulled his hands off the panels and the pod explored against the wall in a ball of flames. Steve noticed the heat that came off the pod's explosive as passed by. The flames and heat spread along the wall in a path that followed Mike and Steve getaway. Steve recognized where they were going as the area became thicker and more pungent, and yet Steve saw the slide that Mike and Steve took in plunge with the bike into the puddle of shit. But the slide was not right, it was off somehow. Mike stopped close to the slide and looked up at the opening and knew that his bike would not be able go up the slide. The pods came out of the flames light a nightmare Steve thought as he watched them shooting out a red beam that Steve knew was a laser that could kill them. Mike saw it too as he turned the bike around toward them again with as Steve threw some shit at the police windows. Then Steve grabbed more shit off the ground and swung it straight at the beams as they passed. Steve pick up the fucking shit and through it at the beams. We need to wipe the fucking red shit out. Mike said as he made the bike roar again in one place as he counted silently for him to size up his next move. Steve found a large shoe next to the bike. Steve got off the bike, and shoved the shoe full of shit and mud, slug the crap high over his head. The shit struck pods wide windows as some of the shit slide down to laser red beam and cut it in half. The beam hesitated with its flashes of red and then the beam went out completely. Mike sent the back of the wheels (of his bike) spin up some of the shit up on the other pods laser beam. Both pods almost crashed into each other, but that moment the pods spin out of range and flu off in opposite directions of the tunnel.

Mike knew he had to move faster if he was going to escape from those impossible men that could have him if they were smart enough. But, luck may be on his side as he realized that the cops mobile was sideways on the walls as it skidded and scape on the walls that had shit covering the walls sight. The smell of burnt shit mixed with old piss and mildew made every breath deadly. Yet, he had Steve had breath the foul air in their lungs. How much poison would it take from down here to kill them or until the cops finally get a hold of them, either-way they would die. Steve had said that he had taken this route before, and he hadn't died from this smell that Mike knew that this smell was poison. He had to get back to where that wall that Steve said was a path behind the walls layer of shit and mud. Steve tugged on Mike shirt again to point out the cops on both side getting closer to them. Mike yelled at Steve to hold on tighter, he was going to do something fast. Mike swerve his bike on both sides of the walls as the smelly shit rose up again to blind both pods on both sides. Steve felt the shit splash against his back, the cool and sticky stuff made his back feel clammy and icky. Steve could feel the motor from the bike vibrate more between his legs. His legs tickled as the vibration continue as Mike drove the bike wild through puddles or slim pond (as many people call it.).

Then Steve saw the wall of shit again, but this time Mike had stop a few yards away. Mike noticed that the police pods were still too close for his own comfort. Mike had to do something fast but what? Mike backed the motorbike away from the wall, then started down the tunnel that lead to another path, another area of escape that might, just might not be all that safe for them. Mike took a breath and let it out slowly through his nose. The rumble of his bike speed blew through with a roar that made Mike face stung as his eyes bleed from the winds that kiss his face and his eyes. Steve tugged left on Mike shirt as he felt the wind nip him too as he looked for that one hole in the wall that told him that he was close to the other path. Mike skid his bike into a sharp turn on his left. Then he heard what he knew that the pods where closer than he thought. He had to do something, his fingers moved to the one smooth handle of the bikes, cool to his touch as he thought of the changes he made to his bikes motor and its computer parts that no one could even see, unless they were driving the thing. Mike really didn't want to use the devices that were hidden. Mike was afraid that if he used any of the things that he had made on the bike, he might either hurt or kill someone that was innocent or even Steve if he got in the way. They were close as Mike felt another tug on his left side as Mike took another sharp turn and then he saw the large hole or two more openings that were as dark as the tunnel, but the paths were nothing like the slide they took to get down here. The path were large holes in walls or were they vines that hidden the path. It didn't matter, Mike knew that there was an opening that he felt or sense was there.

The feel of the motor underneath him felt good as he ripped the handle bars tight as he turned them hard to the left. The pipe that spill out behind them, blew out a large flame that heated a set vines on fire. Mike held the bike in such a way that the pipes that blew out of its tail blew out not smoke, but flames that in lit the vines that grew around the shit and waste in a way that he had decide had to be the path out of the of hell. Mike shot through the vines and found that he and Steve landed in pure darkness. A little light that glowed from a large round building had twenty or more pods that were light blue almost white with one-word enforcement sat around outside of the building. It made Mike a little nervous or maybe real nervous at the sight. They rode even faster toward the deep darkness that Mike could tell that it had up rooted concrete, with grass and trees growing alone the pathway that Mike knew he had to take. Steve knew they were on the right track toward his community, but would they make it on time. Mike and Steve both knew that those cops that had followed them inside of the tunnel was still in there. Mike heard some humming like what the pods made when they were close. Sweat beat down nose and eyes stung as he watched the enforcers in pods hum out of the round station. Steve, do ye know any other route we could go to get rid of the cops?

Steve thought about it and then he remembered one path, one turn that no one really wanted or even knew about. Steve tugged ten times of Mike left side of his shirt then pulled hard on his right shirt. Mike hoped he knew what Steve was trying to tell him to do. But then as he found that there was a tall tree on his left standing right in front of the streets path way, Mike turn left and left again at the next tall tree that was not far from the first tree. Another tree came up in front of him on his left and Mike turn left and kept on turning left until he counted ten left turns from the trees and one sharp right that lead him to a short edge of a neighborhood that broke off in a hidden valley or neighborhood that once was old or great on hills. For some reason the homes and houses had fallen in down a large valley that sunk more with each year or years passed. The ledge became more of a cliff or side mountain or large hill, I couldn't really tell the difference. Even though, looking downward along the passageway that lead to or close to my neighborhood made me think of how all had come about here. I had thought of how far I was up and how low it was to going home. I knew the area around us had once been great homes, for some time the homes and area had sunken more down into a craven and made it easier for those that lived in the lower range. Years or centuries many of the homes had fallen roofs and homes grew trees that grew tall with bushes scattered around more trees fallen walls, fallen fences that if you look could almost see underneath parts of the grounds. At one point, the ledge was once part of the ground and now a cliff was there instead of hard ground. Steve had thought the cliff was made centuries ago and now he could only see on it had to have clasped from something centuries ago and now could only see a large rock's around that dirt covered them as the cliff's edge and rocks stood downward like stairs leading them down to their doom. And yet it was the only place he knew that would take him closer to where Steve community was.

He knew how to get there within a few hours, but Mike's bike could not fit down the path that was narrow, sharp. Steve face was wet with sweat and grime, his long black hair tangle with leaves and small twigs.

Mike looked down at the edge of the cliff as he twisted the handlebars hard, the sound of the motor rumbling echoed though both his soul and that of the valley around them. The vibration trembled under his legs, then made him stumble and sway from the sight of the valley below them. Steve had to grab hold of Mike arms as he noticed how Mike was swaying.

Take a breath man, it isn't that hard to get down. I know the path in this darkness of night better than you think. Steve said as he too noticed how many lights were still on down below them. Somehow, Steve knew that those lights were not from houses or homes. The lights were glowing like stars, blinking off and on. Someone or more people were using fire station to eat their meals close to where they live. Steve hoped none of them where like John that everyone knew who ate other humans, no matter who they were (children, adults or animals), it didn't matter to him, more to worry about in the darkness for them to survive? Steve huffed air out his nose, looked at Mike.

Ye know I will not give me bike up for no one. Let me see where the path leads and I shall walk me bike down the path first and see if there is any way I may be able to ride it down. Mike said as he still looked down at the valley below them. Well I don't think you can —it's tricky and I would not trust the paths. Its –it's to —to uh– it has rocks and pebbles and maybe a tree or two or maybe a brush too. You just can't trust the path footings. I had done the path during the daytime, but never at night. This is weird though. I could have sworn that when I left Mr. Farmer house this morning it was still daylight, this –night is too strange to me. I guess when I went to work or got up the sun was at the middle of day or something like that. I do not have a watch nor can I tell time anyways. Steve said to nothing but air. Steve went over to where he thought the path lead down to with his hands shaking with both fear and hungrier. Steve stomach started to rumble loudly, his head started to feel a little dizzy, light headed. Steve shook his head slowly as he tried to get some kind of control over his dizziness. Then he took a deep breath as he fought his weakness. The feelings were not new to Steve, he had worked and lived many days without food, only sips of water he would find around his job. But now, Steve knew his job, website news was over, gone, never to come back. Everyone he had worked with and for, are dead. His heart felt weak as everything in the short time of a few days passed came tumbling down. Then he just watched Mike struggle with his bike down the narrow path. Steve felt the rocks and pebbles beneath his feet as he tried not to fall with unsteady legs. His mind kept on repeating events that had taken place within the few days pasted. Steve noticed that Mike was having trouble walking too with his motorbike. Steve just hoped that Mike would not lose his bike, even though the bike was bigger than the path they were walking down on. The wind kicked up over our heads blowing our hairs high over our faces, I could feel the sting from my long hair whipping against my cheek making me flinch some as we continued down the path.

Mike head turn to look upward back to where they had started from to see if any of the cops had found their passages way. But only stars brightly blinked toward them, but then the stars had gotten brighter and larger. SHIT. Fucking shit! The cops, the fucking enforcers are right up there with their bright lights beaming around to find us. Shit fuck. Steve is there a cave or something closer we could hide in or not. Mike asked as he thought. Mike knew how much he had installed in his bikes upgrade and how much he had wished he would have put in and not just let the appearance show it had none. A computer on each side of the handlebars came with sequence of turns to make the bike either pipes on each side blew out more flames than any kind of weapons the enforcers had. Then there was that pedal near the backside on his left that he did not use, but knew some how he would need it. That one side had more in pact or force that would make the whole side of the top ledge that the cops were now looking down at them come down in flames with the sky going total light. Yet, Mike had to hesitate and make the right decision; if he shot, the cops up there with one of his weapons there might repercussion from the backfire of his own weapon and that would not be good. Steve ye need to move ahead of me, I give you the flashlight that tis in me seats storage of me bike. Mike said as he thought fast on how he was going to save them the best he could. He had only one chance of firing off that one of his jet missiles and he need Steve to be as far ahead of him so he could do it without getting any one of them injured. Mike watched how Steve struggled to move over to the side of the walls of the paths. Steve hands grip tight on the dirt as he tried to move around Mike bike to be in the front of it. Steve mind was on the same wave link, to survive and not let the enforcers get them. They were worse than those cops; when it came to torture or just kill anyone they felt like killing, it didn't matter if they were a child or someone old. They just like to kill and watch the innocent die slowly. I struggled to get around Mike bike and be in front of him and not behind like he told me too. Steve look up at Mike as fear seep in my bones, I knew Mike felt the same.

Then I saw something in his blue eyes that just glow another color. My hair on my neck stood up as a chill ran down. I lean back against the wall of the pathways edges. I had to think, the air around me blew hard cold, and yet, I sweat as if I was hot. I had no coat, only a shirt that was both rip and torn in places that show little skin and bones. But the shirt was the only thing I found in my parent's attic that fit me. That attic was something else as I recalled how we also found the toys and those hard drive, that were small and in a square like metal box that seem at the time impossible to open up. But we did finally open the metal boxes and found those hard drives that was when everything went in a spiral of dizziness and confusion. I still am confused and a lot of dizzy.

Mike turn the handles bars once and kicked start the bike as he pushed some sort of button under the seat that I had been sitting earlier. Then I heard something click and snap, the smell of something burning and then something went off from the pipes that blew out smoke and flames, shot out something long, skinny, metal like with a nose that was pointy, there were two of them that came out of the pipes on both sides of bike. I watched as the metal things silently went over the top of the edge we had just come down from. Then explosion was bright with heat that smear down us. Mike yelled at me to get my ass on the bike fast. I did as he told me too. I felt the heat burn at me back, but the sound of the cop's mobile going off like a bomb was more than what I had ever seen or heard. Metal or whatever they used to build them, was like a scream as the metal thing went off and glasses breaking, shattering around us like rain. Mike kicked harder for the bike to move down the path. The motorbike rumbled loud like thunder, the ground shook with its motor vibrating underneath its wheels as we took off. I still held the flashlight that was inside of the seat, and thought about giving it back to Mike, but how, mike was driving the bike and I had to hold on tight. I had put the flashlight in my front pockets and hope it would not interfere with Mike driving. The bike drove down the narrow path that would lead us to or close to where we need to be, the path was rocky as hell as we came down faster than I imaged. I wanted to look back at the sight of the top of the edge that looked down at the valley we were head to. Something told me not to and I just buried my face in Mike back as I held on tight. Then Mike just stopped then turned around in his seat to shake me off him.

What the shit, why did we stop and what is wrong with you? I asked Mike as he looked at me with his glowing blue eyes that shine like one of the stars. It was both creepy and amazing at the same time. I kept on wondering why his eyes were like that and my eyes were just dull and normal. What was he and why again did he wanted me and my friends? We need to get over that small stream. There is houses and a street not far from here. I don't know how far, I can't count, but I know what numbers look like. I can tell you when to turn like I did back in the tunnel, but we need to get over that stream. I told Mike as he nodded to me. I held on tight again as I felt him move the bike backwards with his feet, then turn the handles bars hard, the sound of thunder and the feel of the vibration trembling under my seat, then the bike came down faster than I had ever felt or seen before. The feel of the wind kissing my face and neck, stung as we leap over the stream that I had thought was small. The stream had gotten larger from the last rainfall we must have had. I held my breath hard as we soared over the streams loud rush of water. The trees were hidden behind the darkness that open up to them like the sky stars behind the clouds. Branches stretched out their arms to the sky in hopes to gasp a drop of water from above. We made it, we really made it, the feel of the bump from landing, jarred my head against Mike back as I rested there. The feel of his back was warm, but he was shaking like I was. We had just survived one escape from another in just a few hours apart, one from the police and the other from the enforcers. I couldn't really tell how many of the enforcers followed us from their headquarters, but knew we had enough following us that my own heart rate was giving me pain and making me weak.

We rode in silence for a few hours I guessed, Mike was hard on the bikes turns as we got close to kissing the paths uneven road that came up off the ground in gulps of dirt and hard rocks. My head bobbed up and down as the bike rode fast over each rock.

We stop again after I guess another few hours. But it was the sight that stopped my heart. At the end of the neighbor that we had to go through to get to my own area, we saw a blaze of fire that made everything around us bright as daylight. We could see people standing close to the flames with large sticks or something like that waiting for someone or something. I couldn't really tell what it was. My mind confused as it already was, just got more scrambled with the sight. The breeze from the fire blew heavy toward our faces as I caught the smell of flesh burning. Then I knew what it was or why the flames were so high and bright. The signal of death was enough for me to remember my sister that had died not too long ago. My heart broke again as the pain of knowing that she would not be at home to greet me ever again. I had lost my best friend, my soul, and heart of wanting to live. I watched as more people came with more bodies of those that couldn't survive the hungrier, the thirst the everyday need to just live. Mike we need to leave. This is where one of the other communities bring their dead to be burned. We can't bury them like the rich can in grave yards or in one of those buildings they have. We burn ours, so that if they died of something like a disease or something like that, then everyone around would be safe from it. Come on, we need to let these people do what is important to us.

We need to get to my home like you said, my friends are in danger and if we don't get there soon, we may not be able to free them. So let's go. I said as I kicked the back of the bikes wheels hard with the keel of my feet. Mike said nothing as we rode by, I saw Mike's face as he turned to look at the flames and the people. He had a tears streaming down his face. He was crying for them I think. I couldn't image why he was doing that. He didn't know anyone there, I sure as hell didn't either. But I guess it was sad. All I knew about those flames were, the lost lives that just gave up. No one grieved or felt any lost when the bodies came. It was just a relief that those people had died and no longer need to endure the everyday torture of hungrier and thirst, the threat by our governments continues of not letting food or the right food come into the zones of the unneeded or the unwanted. Mike kept on with the paste of riding hard, fast into the darkness and the unknown that seemed to be following us. Death was around us and we knew that the living only had limited time on this earth. But, Mike would not stop again until we got to my home, my friends.

I felt the sun coming up behind me as the warmth touched my back I felt something else sadness of not knowing what life will bring, another day of hungrier, another day to fight just too live, just survive. Dawn is here, we got a better chance of seeing where we are going. I thought as Mike kept on driving hard though each turn and bumps we encountered. Trees and brushes stood either side of the paths that we took as well as in the middle of the pathways we rode. I had to remember hard which way to turn without being on the main roadway that would put us in sight of any enforcers or cops. Birds flew over our heads in large numbers; they were larger in size as I noticed them closer over us. Their wings were color in multiple colors of red, yellow, blue, white, and black. Their beaks red, white pointy with a hook like. The feet or claws were large with sharp needle points that could shed anyone that came up on them to pieces. I had seen one of those birds attack a small child for food. It was not good, and it haunted me at the time for years. Brooke helped me get over the sight and memory of it for some years as I grew up. We had always depended on each other for support and survival. Now –she gone, dead, one of those that were put in the lasting flame of the dead back where we had come from, the homes, the houses that no longer held people but used for the dead last place of resting. My sister dead, it was both a relief that she had died, because of her illness. We were too poor to get the cure, but her death was the cure the only cure that Steve knew. Steve was relief too that Brooke would never feel hungry or thirsty again. But he would always miss her.

CHAPTER FIVE

COULD SEE SOME PLACES I recognized that would tell me I was getting close to home. building's that stood high with open roofs wide with larger trees that grew out of them, its branches long and naked from its battle with the acid rain eating off its green clothes, the branches pulled out of windows empty of glass, forgotten home that must have been nice one time or another.

We passed by many houses and woods that covered places that once stood as homes. Then I saw the walls that covered streets and neighborhoods that were called communities. The walls were made out of hard wood, layered with more woods against each other with no division of space, line up across and around certain homes or houses that had not fallen, but stood stronger than time itself. With that knowledge of the area's outer structure, Steve knew that the walls were stretching around other homes that were empty of any humans living in them, wrapping around its long perimeter for another hundred or more either stone walls from the homes or wooden walls that double on its self to keep it secure.

We rode passed the wooden walls and came to the end that held a large tree that were so large that it took up most of walls structures as part of the walls entrance.

The branches were just as strong and large as the tree as it stretched outward and up with hidden places of where another wall that blended with the trees green leaves and branches made up a guard's nest. A place for someone to keep watch of the neighborhoods people to keep them safe and to yell out any warning of any kind of attack that would harm or kill anyone here in the community's homes. I knew where I was, it was home, my community, my safe heaven. Mr. Farmer would have a large meal waiting for me when I got in, that was something I just knew about him. Jack would be up on the guard nest waiting for anyone that knew the secret words to say to him that he and the person would know only. STOP! Mike we need to stop here. I know who is up in the guard nest. I can get us in. I said as Mike stop his bike right in front of the walls.

Jack, its Steve, can't blame you can't be you. Got to be me. I tried those words, nothing, not a sound or movement up the tree. I kept on looking upward staring at the tree that blew lightly against the leaves. The sun was almost at its highest point in the sky it must be close to midday. I couldn't believe the night or the few days past sense I got home that one day. I just couldn't remember when that day was. Everything seemed like a fog of a dream that was too confusing. My mind just didn't want to process the days of all the events. It was still confusing and hard on my heart. But I had to continue on fighting to live and now I had to do it for my friends. Silence from the nest, I had to think of the other passwords that might work. We had more than one and more than four passwords. One of them should work I hope. I kicked some rocks with my feet as I thought about what to say next. Nothing came to my mind, my stomach although growl loud. I looked up at Mike, then, shook my head slowly. Uh... Jack, Jack he had no fat, Mat, Mat, he had a cat, Susie, Susie had a woozy. Then I watched the nest that was above us and the door that was almost invisible moved. You could almost hear the wheels and pulley move as the door came open. I knew somehow, we were not in the front of the wall, but the back. Mr. Farmer home was more than a few homes away from here. We walk close to Jacks place of old metal sheets that had wheels of pure dark, black wheels. Some of the metal had rooms with seats and things that made them move. Jack and I would play in the metal heaps that Jack father would call them when Jack and I were kids. I remember finding one large, very large thing that was big enough for us to sleep behind the large seat up front. The thing had ten black very large wheels that held the thing up kind of high, but the black things were flat against round metal. We climb up and inside of the thing with ease. Inside of the thing was a wide-open face with a rusted old nose like that stuck out. Two opening that were large in size the opening was big enough for us to get in easily. We discovered that in the back of the where we had come in from was large with things like old seats that flat on the ground. But that was just part of what we had found in the metal thing, we had found jangling thing that was rusty and curved to the size of another hole that was in the panel part of the front window (I figure the large wide thing was once). There was also a part of a wheel that fit in another hole that was near the hole, we took the rusty jangle thing and put that in the hole, then we took the wheel and put that in the next. All of it fit perfect we one exception the jangle thing broke. We played in it for a little while, but then we stop as Jack had figure something about the big metal thing with wheels. Jack finally had the jangle thing out of the hole and took back with him. The next I found out about what Jack did, was he had made the big metal thing work. The sound of rumbles and the feel of the thing moving slowly in the metal heap, where the large thing that Jack had called it a big truck, would help them some day. I could never understand what he meant by that. But now, I think I do.

The door opened slowly as we came into where I had lived most of my life. I felt something that had always told me something was wrong. My neck felt tight with a chill running up and down my spine. There was no sound, no one came out of their homes or shelters to see who was there. Mike got on his bike and motion for me to get back on the bike with him. The bike roared with its tail blowing out smoke and flames, the front of the bike came up on it back wheels and we took off toward the front of where I really lived. That was where my friends where too. Jack heap was close by as we noticed something smoking from the deep side of the metal heap. The smoke was a dark cloud like coming up from somewhere inside. I hope Jack wasn't there or hurt. We kept on going by homes that no one had come out to see us. I figured again that the homes were empty and the only ones living in the homes where rats, and mice and some other creatures that I could not say. The air was clear today as we kept on going and then I smell something familiar mold, fire that rose up from a house or homes, yes, I see the end of the neighborhood that was mine, but some one's home was on fire, there was people standing around with men, many men wearing dark clothes and round hats. Closer we came, the more I knew who they were. Mike stop farther away enough that we still could see those men, then Mike found one of the homes with a large building and went in. Jack was standing inside watching Mike and me as he motioned for us to stay quiet. I whisper what happen and how did the damn fucking enforcer got here?

They came by way of air, asshole. They think we got you hidden and someone that is one of the freedom fighters. A rebel that had them running I guess for years it seems. I had to laugh inside as I couldn't image who that guy was. Hi Mike my man. It's been too long sense I seen you. How are you man? I remember the last time you had made that enforcer quarters light up the sky as if it was day light. That was a sight. Yeah, you are one mean dude. Jack said as he and Mike swat hands and gave each other fist shakes. Jack grin with a shake of his head, then turn to look at me with his concern and his confusion. Jack rubbed his chin with his left fingers and lowered his head down as if he was looking at something on the ground. Look these assholes are looking for you both and Mr. Farmer and Max hide those cases that had all those hard drive shit. We sort of thought that when you left to go to work, we needed to put them somewhere safe at least somewhere that no one but us would know. So we knew we couldn't let damn enforcer find them either. Mr. Farmer said that if they found the hard drives —well many of the fighters would not live and many of us would die too. It's bad and dangerous and we are in a lot of trouble. Jack said as he looked up at us.

How did they know to come here to find us? I asked him as I tried to understand what he was saying. An-d well Jack I don't remember seeing Mike or know him either at any time. So when did you all meet him and when did he know our parents? I asked him as I stood there just looking at the distance of where my house used to be and now it was up in flames.

We were kids back when Mike had come down here with our parents and his to, we all sat down close to the derby house that feed us chicken and hamburgers. Your sister ate a long thing with ketchup and you and I ate hamburgers. Our folks had been talking in whispers as we ate. I remember watching them as we all sat down on the curve. Of course that was the last time we all saw our parents and Mike too. But, then again, Mike was taller and he had this-weird-odd-looking thing that roared like a mini thundercloud that had speed was nothing but a blur as he ripped out of the parking lot on two wheels, it was something else to see. Jack shook his head as recalled the time when our parents were alive. I didn't know that they were involved with the freedom fighters until then. Jack said again as he looked up at me with those knowing eyes that spoke of years of growing and learning with each other. It was at that moment when they heard a shot coming from houses where the enforcers had stood close to Mr. Farmer and the others. All three men swung around their heads as they peeked at what was happening out there. Jack head lowed toward more of the ground as Steve and then Mike head came above Jacks head.

Someone was on the ground and the enforcers had their weapons out. Their weapon was long like a pipe with the end they held square, the square part had green and blue lights that told them how much force to use on any one. Steve felt his body stiffen with fear. The sight of the dead man just lying there had taken Steve already pale face that looked grey, a look of death of its own. Steve pulled away as he thought of whom that person had been and why the enforcers had killed that man. Jack, who was that...... I mean whooo was that, I don't recognize him. I asked Jack as I looked at Mike with some help in my eyes.

I think it's John or one of his cannibal's hunters. They think the enforcers are here to take some of their prey away. This morning they came-you know the hunters looking for kids or anything one that just don't belong here for food back at their own hood. But when they talk about the enforcers getting closer to their place they said that they were looking for someone with long blonde hair and rode a strange thing that shook the ground and made the sound of thunder. I knew who that was and kept quiet. I ran back to my heap after that. It wasn't long when the damn enforcers came in with their hover mobiles and landed right close to your house. I was sweating at first and then remembered that we took the hard drives out of there and put them away safely. But those damn shit fucking hunters still came back in four with their packs full of body parts fling out of them with their weapons high over their shoulders. They were set on fighting those fucking ass enforcers for the sake of properties. Mr. Farmer and Max stood back away from the fight. As all three men stayed hidden from view, but watched as more hunters came through the forest that blended in with the neighborhood that separated the cannibals and Steve common sense neighborhood.

Can ye get some kind of vehicle together and get it ready for a long drive out of here Jack? Mike asked Jack as he looked straight at the enforcers and then at Mr. Farmer. He knew that it was time for the move and it would not be safe. But the hunters were giving the enforcers more trouble than what they were supposed come here for in the first place. And that. Was. Good. Mike thought. Mike moved back inside of that building with a frown as he thought about the next step to this entire calamity. They had to work fast and quietly. Jack looked at Steve and then smile wide as a memory came over his face. Jack remember his father calling it a tractor and trailer, it was special in an odd way. It was large and could hold more than just them and Mike's bike. Mr. Farmer had asked Jack months ago if he could find more ice boxes to put in the trailer and start putting taking the food from the basement of his home. Jack done that within the few months Mr. Farmer had asked him to do. I got the right machine to out the enforcers and cops air mobiles and still hide us safely. Jack said as he tugged on my arm. I turn to look at him, my head shaking as I knew what trailer and tractor he was talking about. The tractor was the one Jack and I had found. Steve recalled.

Mike took a breath, as he knew what they were thinking and tried hard not to respond. Things are going to be really bad and they may not live though what will happen to them. Mike just didn't want them to die now, not until they get those damn fucking hard drive that have all the information the fighters. With That information on the hard drives it could cripple government in such a way that — Mike couldn't hope or think about it. That thought was just that a thought, first thing first, they needed to get away from the enforcers and stay alive. Jack looked at Mike with one word. When. Jack said as he motioned toward his place farther up from where Mike and Steve came from. Mike had to think and look back at the sight of enforcers, and the hunters argue and it seemed wrong.

Then something told Mike that they need to get down and stay farther inside of the building they were in. Mike was grateful for the shadows and darkness that the building had. It helped them as they waited and watched what the enforcers were doing with the hunters. A breeze swam through the building and kissed each of their faces with the smell of death penetrating the winds air. Steve tried to fight the cough that plagued him whenever he was home or close to home. Somehow he figured that his cough was more than just a cough, it was a sign of something more, and a warning or just that he was getting sick too. Look I can get to my place without being seen, Max showed me some systems under our neighborhood that had passage ways from one end of our street to the other end. I can get that thing here by late tonight, but those damn enforcers got to go first or we are not going to see the next day. Jack said as he swung his hands to his sides.

I knew he was nervous and anxious as Mike and I were. Things had to turn our way or no way, there has to be a solution, a plan something that would get the damn enforcers off our scent and us on our way to whatever. I kept on thinking with frustration and confusion about everything; I was ready to scream? But I had to stay calm and in control of my emotion if that was possible. I paced in the farthest part of the building shadows as all this was just driving me mad.

Mike looked at me with his eyes narrow with tense and the same frustration as I was having, but then he turned to look at Jack, his left hand landing on Jack shoulder and nodded to him. If you can make sure that thing you said ye have, then bring to life and here for us. I know how to get us out and away from the enforcers and cops when we get out of here. But we need to get out tonight soon. Jack moved fast as he found the hole in the ground close to the building, without any words, Jack jump down through the hole and ran toward the end of the neighborhood where his place was.

Mike held his breath as he wiped his hands on his pants, the sweat seemed to be heavy now. Mike was nervous and upset about the damn fucking enforcers.

Things just wasn't going the way he wanted. The freedom fighters were depending on him to find Steve and these misfits' friends of his. But they were just important as Steve and the damn hard drives. Mold mixed with the smell of old dead grass blend underneath Mike feet as he paced back and forth rose up to kiss his nose. The smell made him think about home, his home back in Scotland and the greater part of Britain's isle. He missed the open fields, the forgotten homes there were old with animals free to live and survive like him inside any of those homes. Trees grew into forest inside and outside around homes and empty places that once were stores and government offices. Now the places were nothing but part of the forest that is growing fast over buildings and places. Roads were just as bad there as they are here, Mike thought again. Staring at the walls of the building, Mike thought of the gray concrete cracked in places that were also breaking apart in pieces, crumbling down around them.

Steve moved near the front of the building shuffling his feet as he came closer to the opening. Hey, the hunters are in the enforcer's faces. I think they are challenging them. Hey I know one of them. I mean one of the hunters. That is—John—yeah that is John. I don't like him, but I don't know, I don't know. I think in a way I think maybe John is helping us by distracting the enforcers away from us. I can't say for sure. But Steve stop mid-sentence as a shot was heard from behind two large trees. His eyes blurry, but Steve knew who was who by way of the color of their cloths or the weapons they used. And yet, Steve had to wince his eyes to look better. More hunters came out with guns firing off fast as they hit enforcers before they could even move to their airmobile.

Mr. Farmer had enough of those stupid hunters, the only good thing about them they were side swapping the mother-fucker enforcers. At least he had time before the enforcers came to move most of the food out and store them in Jack big mobile that had those strange wheels. Mr. Farmer had also put the hard drives in hiding place that only the few would know. A smile rose across Mr. Farmers face as he thought how hard those stupid enforcers tried to talk him and Max into telling them where the drives were.

Max had taken everything he could and the children could get out of that attic of Steve home. With those toys that were connected to the hard drives and the freedom fighters. He just knew it somehow. Max went back in the house as he thought of Susan and his baby girl. He hoped they were safe down in the sewer closer to Jack place. The children ran in the sewer as if it was nothing but an everyday adventure. His heart beat faster as he knew the time was coming to leave this place and burn every home around them. Not one home would be standing after or before they leave. But his fear for both of the girls that took his heart, stolen his soul, he would not want any of those thing back although. Susan and their daughter gave him hope, a reason to live, to keep on doing what is right. Max had never been outside of the community, he just never wanted or was interested in leaving for anything. Things he found for Susan and their little girl was always around here. Now Mr. Farmer said if they stayed, the enforcers and the cops would kill both Susan and the baby without any remorse or regret. They would use Susan and the baby to insure Max would tell them where Steve and the hard drives were. They could not afford that kind of risk to anyone. Beside Mr. Farmer was right, Max did not want to see Susan and the baby killed. He cared too much for that to happen. What kind of father or husband would let that happen to his only family? When he heard the shots and the hunter's shouts with the enforcers, the time was now and they had to work fast.

Steve house was the first to blow up, Max had discovered many years ago that underneath each home had pipes that had some kind of gas going though. The smell made Max head dizzy and weak, but he knew losing the first pipe under Steve home would be a domino chance of all the other homes blow up like the sun. The sound was loud and the smell was bad. Max brought Mr. Farmer and the rest of the cloths and food down in the tunnels sewer line behind Mr. Farmers other building room. No one had paid any attention to them as they left the argument go on between the hunters and the enforcers. It was the best distraction they could have hoped for right now. Max just hoped Steve would show up soon or – Max couldn't or wouldn't think about that. His long shaggy hair tangled, never seen combs or been washed, but he had pulled it back away from his face and down his back. The clothes he found up in Steve attic were the best for both him and Susan. Mr. Farmer called the one he wore a dress. However, Max didn't care! The thing gave him more freedom to move than a pant that kept on falling off him.

Both Max and Mr. Farmer head went up fast as they heard one of the hovers rose up unsteady in the air. Then the popping noise of the guns came upward with a crack and then another pop. The aircraft flew wobbly as the enforcers tried to stay up in the air to leave. Then another pop came and the enforcers airmobile blew up in one fast glow that almost blinded them as Max and Mr. Farmer climb down into the sewer lines.

Jack came back when he heard someone yell house. That was one of the check-points that told Jack that all the homes were unsteady with gas, the homes would blow up fast if Jack didn't get to Mike and Steve. As Jack got closer to the sewer near the building where he had left them, he heard the sound of the bikes motor roar away from the fighting up front. The motorbike rumbled and vibrated under Mike's legs as he squeezed on tight, he felt his blood rush hot as his heart raced with the bikes speed. The wind blew kisses as he and Steve passed each tree and bush that were on either side of him as they passed by.

Somehow, Mike felt the feel of those hunters still battling the enforcers for territory of the community. Maybe they had a chance to escape and get to the agreed place to meet with the freedom fighters. The chances were right now good. Everything around them seemed to go into a blurring stage as Mike and Steve speed off closer to Jack heap place. The sight of the smoke and fire that rose high over the metal gave a scent of burnt rust. Another sound came from behind Mike, a rumble of tremors shook the bikes wheels as they spin back and forth around each turn and path. The sound blasted hard, more homes, buildings started to fall down around Mike as he put more speed on the bikes drive to get to Jack place. Roofs, walls were falling down in front of Mike, Steve and all around them. Mike heart beat too fast to get control of his body change that would make it impossible to drive, to get Steve out of this alive. No sound other people screaming or running out of any of the empty houses, no dogs running to chase down any one either. It was all too strange for Mike's feelings or his instinct. A large wall of steel blocked the way to escape anyone that might have been behind them. Mike tried to back his bike up to take another look around. Mike wanted to see if there was (or any chance he might not have seen before) anywhere else that he might have missed when he rode passed or not have seen to help their escape. Steve took a breath and coughed as he got off the bike and touched Mike shoulders as he turned to look at the wall. We need to go into that wall fast, I know you think we might hit the thing hard and get hurt or something. Believe me, we would not feel a thing. Steve said as he moved back on the bike, Steve had a grin on his face as he put his legs over the bikes seat that was close to the motor.

Mike nodded his head as he realized that maybe there was some trigger that would get the wall up over their heads? Mike pulled the back farther back with Steve sitting behind him, holding on to Mike shirt that had torn more during their escapes and chase though the city and forest.

Steve can ye do something to me hair, tis a bother right now to me vision, can ye pull the length behind me head? Thank ye. Mike said as push with his hands his hair back away from his face. Steve looked around for something to hold Mike hair, he knew that Mike had a band of some kind to hold the first time they meet, but the band must have gotten off somewhere during their struggle to stay alive. It didn't matter right now, Steve need something to tie Mike hair back away from his face. Steve looked down at the grounds dirt and debris that was still flying around them from the houses that were blowing up. It wasn't long before the one they were close to was going to go up next. A small round red band was hanging on a small broken branch that lay next to Steve feet, Steve picked the red thing up and held Mike hair back with it and then tied the band around tightly. Mike kicked the bikes paddle hard with his shoe and then rolled the bars on the handle tightly, the bike screamed in protest as he back the bike again slowly, then let the bike go with more speed and more power that Steve breath was caught in his lungs. The feel of the bike vibration shook Steve teeth and body as he felt the power thunder under him wildly. Then the bike came forward with speed and power, the blur was there as the wall steel rusted brown and gray came up close to Steve sight. The wall fell back with thud of the bikes back wheels. Then the wall came back up behind them as they landed hard on the ground. Mike looked back and saw that the wall was up and still standing as if they just went through the wall without touching it. Mike smiled as he thought of those enforcers blowing up and maybe the other ones were gone too. They had a chance to escape and maybe reach the freedom fighters soon. Mike go slow now around the heap of metal and steel. Jack has the place full of traps. We need to move very slowly toward the smoke and fire. I think Jack has his place set up for something. We need to stay away from anything that looks covered up or stack in a pile like (in the center I mean). Mike turn twice left and then once right and missed, just missed a pile of metal doors rusted and stack on each other like a tree. The bike swerved many times on edges of those stacks and missed them by inches, but the last one neither Steve nor Mike saw it sitting in the middle of the path they were going. A small snap, then a wide rope swung up wide around the area they were speeding through in a web-like net came up fast with one swish and bang. Mike had just missed the net as he drove around a corner and up two hoods that were old rusty, discolored, but still high over the ground. Mike flew high over the hoods like a jet speeding over other heaps of metals that stack high for many centuries or years of neglect. Steve felt airborne, almost like a bird or one of those hovercraft boards that he had seen in the city many times. The taste of the rust rose up in the air like dust giving Steve another seizer of coughing and gagging, some of the rust –dust went in Steve eyes. Steve felt the sting and the pain from the dust that gathered in his eyes. He couldn't rub his eyes without letting go of Mikes shirt and falling off the bike. Steve knew he need to do something, the pain in his eyes was killing him, so he buried his face deep in Mike back and rub hard against mike shirt. It still didn't relieve his eyes from the pain and the dust that was still in them. Oh fuck, I can't get the fucking shit out of my eyes. Steve shouted at no one as both of them kept on moving on the ground with a thud of both of the wheels that landed hard. Steve head wobbled up and down against Mike shirt. Jack metal house was in view as Steve looked up with his eyes hurting and winch hard as the pain came over his eyes. Yeah, he could see the metal house, but, it was a blur that was even more painful to open his eyes to see. Mike stop the bike as he heard the sound of something loud roar more over his own bikes motors.

A hush like air coming out of a metal pipe puff up made a thick hard crackling sound of metal shaking against each other, then the sound of another hush like sound and a rumble of sorts as the thing back up and came forward toward where Mike and Steve stood with the bike. Steve smile as he realized what was coming and that Jack had finally fits that old truck thing that used some kind of fuel that could be used to sit things on fire if needed. Mike waited for whoever was driving the big thing that stood right in front of him. The truck was bigger than anything Mike had ever seen in his life. It was like looking at a giant of something from out of space, but the thing had ten wheels or more in the front with a nose that was square with a metal grill that shook as the truck rattled on with the motor making more sounds of hush and crackle. The only thing that they could see out of the truck large window was only darkness and the driver seat had no light that was on so they could see, it hidden them safely. The door on the side came open with a clang and Mike saw some one's feet land on the long flat bar that strip along the trucks path of its body. The foot was Jack black boot and his blue jeans that rip on the sides to let the boot fit on his legs right. Jack jump off the side bar and let his eyes meet Mike and Steve own eyes too. The smile that came over Jack and that of the two young men was a sight. Jack didn't have much teeth left as he ate little and worked harder to keep the truck and the other things he had made to help them work for this day. His teeth decay and became brittle as years of low nutrient food that would have saved his teeth.

Jack had to struggle to survive by stealing food from storage stores that open up once a month or once every four to three months. Anytime the storage stores open up, it was by the government order. It was one of the government way of helping those poor innocent humans in places that they no longer wanted or needed. Jack had decided that if he wanted to eat, he would at least steal something to eat he thought. Now Mr. Farmer had always stored food, but had been a wee bit careful to how much a kid could have or eat and yet, he did feed him on many occasions. Jack went to bed many nights with a not a full stomach, but his stomach wasn't empty either. He still was losing his teeth early in life and really didn't care right now. Jack watched Mike and Steve as they walked over with that damn freak of a bike. Uh... we will put that thing in the back of the trailer and well I guess you both can go too in the back with the others. Jack said as he seemed to walk slowly with a hint of wobble legs. Steve thought for a moment and then it occurred to him that Jack had or may not have been eating much lately. His stance was long and slow as Jack came closer to Steve and Mike. Look you both need to get in the back of this trailer and put the bike in there too. I got a ramp that I used for the freezer and the other shit that we need to take with us. Jack said as he motioned to us to move a little faster.

The ramp was then pull downward from the trailers open back door the sound of metal slamming down on the grounds solid concrete and grass lead Mike up with his bike pushing hard into the large dark back of the trailer.

Steve couldn't see anyone inside of the trailers back, but knew Susan and the baby was there with Max waiting for him to get in. Mr. Farmer was there too with his freezers full of food and the hard drivers should be somewhere in there too. Steve felt the cool metal under his feet that was bare from any kind of shoe. The sound of his feet walking made a flip flap as Steve got closer to the back of the trailer. There in the darkness that had a dim light that was almost impossible to see at the opening of the trailer, but getting closer the light was small, but enough for Mr. Farmer and Susan and Max to see them. Mr. Farmer came close to Mike with a hint of a huff and a bout time you got here attitude to Mike wondering eyes at everyone around him.

We need to understand that this will not be a safe, but deadly, dangerous venture we are all headed toward, the police-aka enforcers-government officials will do everything in their power to stop us and kill. They will not want us alive at any cost. We are expendable and very much unwanted alive. We can say that they would find out about the hard drives we are carrying in here. So be aware that we may get killed hiding and fighting these asses that call themselves leaders for the people. We all know that they are not or ever was for the people. We need to trust only those that are here and now, anyone else we need to be aware of being part of the government spies. Now let me reintroduce something's that I might not have said or remembered well. The freedom fighters could be anyone and no one, they could be a child or a very old person, and they could be anyone or anything that we do not know. So be very careful who you speak to and how much you tell them and what you tell them. Mr. Farmer said as he let out his breath from his nose as his chest rise up and down (like a rising tide in the ocean shores). Mr. Farmer walked on back close to the freezer as he had put one of his comfortable chairs (that was in his home and now is in the trailer) against one of the walls. Susan waved her left hand against her thin black hair that fell in her face away and stared at her small baby that rested in her arms. The breath was sweet and gentle as Susan felt the babes breathing touched her face. Susan smiled low as she watched the sleeping baby. Max rose from his own seat and came close to where Mike stood looking at everyone sitting down.

We-we-took some of the children that where still-hunting for food around our community. I—I didn't want John take them for his own food collection. We need the children to live and learn that — we will protect them. They (the children) are our future that may or may not be good. It all depends on them and us to (well) insure that promise. I think Mr. Farmer is right on what he said and we all have special things we do or learned from years of surviving around our community. I —think our parents had something to do with the learning in some ways too. That is my parents had me going in sewers underneath streets and homes sense I could remember, I know how to put the water lines into homes without the government even knowing it was me that done it. I also know how to find pipes that hold gas that are still working in some area's that is a plus for us. Max said as he rubbed Susan head gentle like. Max still wore that long gown like of faded brown and green on, his legs hairy skinny like sticks held him close and strong for Susan own head as she rested her head on his legs.

Mike took a breath a small chuckle escaped his lips that were full of mischief and promises of something that no one would even understand. Ye are well of ye own demise of the future that is not written, but tis known is nay good either. I agree with the children being here. I would have taken them too with us if I had known of them. So Max ye have done good on that. I know of each of ye talents of things that would help us with our escapes and our fights that we do nay know of yet and then we do know tis will come to us sooner or later. Mike put his bike deeper in the back between two large freezers that stood against each wall on either side of the trailers large inside. Looking at us all.

His walk was sure and arrogant that spoke a lot of things to Steve as he watched him move. Steve just walked over toward Max and Susan with his small steps and unsure of his weakness bring him down. He needed to eat and have something cool down his throat. His body was screaming at him with howls and growls of protest that he was sure were loud and clear to anyone around him. Steve went to sit down on the floor next to Susan.

You want something to eat Steve? Susan asked him. Max moved toward an open box that sat down next to Mike long legs that stretched out on the floor. Mike head down against his chest as his eyes drop down closed and fell asleep fast against his bike and the other freezer and the box that sat across from him. Max scooted the box closer to him and pulled out a bag of bread and jar of peanut butter then he looked for a flat knife to use to spread the butter on two slices of bread for Steve. Max gave the sandwich to Steve who sat on his right side. Steve took the sandwich from Max and took a bite out of it with his eyes closed to the favor of the butter and peanut. Then I heard Max pulling out something that clanged when he took it out. Max handed me a cool tin can that was cool and wet as I took it and open the lid to drink out of the can. The drink was cold as it went down my throat, it squelched my thirst and felt good in my stomach as both the sandwich and the drink settle in my stomach. My stomach was still growling as I burp after words. The children were talking quietly, the sounds of whispers and some coughing, I knew they were talking about the fighters that we were going to meet soon or maybe later. I hope the children had taken all the toys that were in my parent's attic down and were now with them. I looked back at them and grin, as I watched two little girls holding the dolls with the long brown and blonde hair. The dolls dresses were yellow faded colors. And yet, the two girls held on to the dolls like they were the most important things to them. I bowed my head and just let them be with the dolls. The boy's (five) had the cars and small bears in their arms. The older boys and girls were scared to touch the other toys that lay on the floor of the trailer. I lean my head back on the freezer corner and let my eyes close.

CHAPTER SIX

 R. WESTERN WAS NERVOUS and anxious to get this meeting over with senator Righous here in the Restaurant. The place was nice if you liked walls circling your table that divided each table with privacy. Mr. Western figured the walls were good. Many important people come here for just that, the privacy when they eat and were able to talk without anyone listening in their conversion. Mr. Western knew who came to this restaurant and what they were cable of, life inside or outside of the congress or even some low Senators had disappeared because of things they found out and tried to go up against the high leader Castle.

High leader Castle had been and still is the leader of the congress and Senator Government of the people for more than 400 or more years. How Mr. Western couldn't figure that out, no one could live that long, and yet—somehow— Castle had. But then again, Mr. Western thought about cloning. It was possible that when the first high leader (or President back then he was called) had put his sperm and those of his wife eggs frozen in a way that when the leader found out he was going to die. He let the scientist do their thing and split the leader's genes his sperm to recreate more of him so that he could live in a way for many years to come. How did Castle mind or even his thoughts on many things emerge with his clones that had to be individuals not a repeat of who he was or is still? How could he know how to have the same thoughts and feelings of each clone that was made through out the centuries sense he found out to live forever without dying of having anyone know what he was really? Deception and hiding truths about people lives and controlling everyone's words or actions seemed impossible. But he has with his own way of staying alive by passing or using his own genes his own DNA that would in able him to stay alive forever without again no one knowing who or what he really is or was.

Mr. Western shook his head with disbelief mentally. He had to focus on Mr. Righous and what the leader had to say now about the new law that was going to come. Mr. Western had to take a swallow and hoped that someone had changed the leaders mind or something that. A waiter walked in booth and asked what he wanted to drink and perhaps to order the food now awhile he was waiting for his company to come. Mr. Western touch the table that was flat with bright round colors of yellow and blue, red, white, green. The white showed different drinks of different colors, some were heavy drinks with alcohol that was made out rare vintage of grape or something. Restaurants have a hard time getting the drinks that are both out lawed by the government and yet it is the government that controls and receives the drinks in restaurants and in their homes. What else that was out law and against a law that was more secret or known more to those people that have more links to the government and those that either work or live within the limits of government control. Then there are those people that are so poor that no one even bothers to even think about them. They are the ones that Mr. Western was more concern about. Mr. Western touched a red round glowing button like form that brought up a list of different foods and desserts. Mr. Western looked again at the list of drinks and selected the white dry wine. Both the food and the drink appeared on his table like magic. The food smelled good as Mr. Western watched the steam rise up from plate that had cut potatoes with slices of green onions and red peppers, spices that made Mr. Western mouth water as he took a deep breath to receive the scents in his memory. On the side of the potatoes was a small square thick steak that was medium rare. The meal was just as the way he had always liked it, Mr. Western rubbed his stomach as he heard that damn thing making a growling sound. Mr. Western ate slowly as each bite, each taste lingered in his mouth like heaven. He really didn't want to swallow the food down to his stomach, but the damn thing was making noises. Food was a rich man hope and dream at times. Mr. Western knew too many people that were poor had only a small amount of food and if that much, the food was mostly old and rotted. That thought made him wonder how he could eat this wonderful food and not just hide the food in one of his pockets in his suite. He had tried many times to bring something edible that was worth eating, something that was not rotted or spoiled to those poor people in the farthest part of the government outreach. He had been stop one time or another, but because of his statist as a government official many of the police and enforcers had let him go by with the foods. Now he just hoped that he could do something more for them and not watch those poor people die more each day, each week, it has to stop. Mr. Western took another bite as he sat back in his seat, Mr. Righous came in quietly with a waiter behind him, and slowly Mr. Righous sat down and took one of the flat boards that the waiter gave Mr. Righous. The board was thin with not much of a back, but the board lit up like a rainbow of different colors sprang up to light Mr. Righous face in different colors. Mr. Righous face was round with a nose that came to a small point, his eyes stern with more concentration on what he was looking at. Several different style of food came up from the lights that shine with some foods that had aromas that filled the air around both men. Mr. Righous was satisfied with his first choice of the meals he seen. A plate with a leg of chicken roasted in garlic and potatoes diced in a cream and chives with green peas on the side. Mr. Righous choice of drink was a dark rich liquid that rose with a small cloud of steam from a small cup, the smell lingered and blend with the food making it smell even richer, stronger. Mr. Righous didn't say a word as he ate and drink his food and lean back in his seat. I couldn't say what I wanted to ask him, but knew he would answer me without a word from my lips.

As Mr. Righous, wipe his mouth with a clean white napkin and sat the napkin down on his lap as he turned to look at me. His eyes brown dull with age as the knowledge of what we do in our lives more exhaustion. Mr. Righous lean back in his seat as he looked at me carefully, then he pulled out a flat note pad that looked like he had put in some information in it. The notepad was small square computer, the size of my two-year daughter palm of her hands. Mr. Righous notepad was clear and was able to hide the pad within his mobile glasses that he had taken off when he gotten in the restaurant. His glasses were as wide as his own eyes and fit easily over his eyes with no bridge over his nose to hold them in place. Mr. Righous had to adjust the glasses to fit over each part of his eyes socket in a way that no one really could tell if he was wearing one. Genius on the part of our scientist and inventors to government officials only, I got one myself, but not because I need the glasses to see. But, so I can be able to go into any form of government meetings or find out about something that I need to know fast. I cleared my throat as I put down my own napkin to read what he had written to me. A warning about what we were to discuss and talk about. I shook a little as the warning was clear to my eyes and I could feel the air around us deepen to a dull stale state of fear. The warning said: We have been watching all your action, be advice of who you are seeking out and that we can disarm you and those that you are attending. Be aware of any moves you make and that of others you are with, they will be exterminated with you. Do not think to alarm anyone that is involved with the government that would put your sentence more forward faster than you would want it.

The warning ended without stating who made it, and yet, I knew who it was that gave that warning to us and why. I could feel my blood drain out of my face as the weakness settled in my legs and my stomach felt the food trying to empty out of my throat. I had to get control of my body function. I closed my eyes as I tried to see who the warning came from, but knew I would not see who it was, but somehow I knew, I just knew it had to be the leader, our President, our master. No one could threaten anyone like he could, but how did he find out about what we were planning. It was enough for me to get scared even to go to the rest room to pee.

Jeremy how are we going to get the children into market safely? We know that the place that houses the children can get a little tricky. But we need to get the enforcers to place those children in the right place for the sale to start. I said slowly, I knew the government had plans to sale these children on a market for the rich and powerful to have for anything they want to use them. Neither I nor Jeremy are truly sure for how the government was going when it came to children. But we needed to talk in a safe mode and not let anything leak out that might be heard on either side of us. Everything was possible when it came to our leader mind and his self-control for everyone and everything that lives. I had to keep my eyes closed as I thought each word carefully as each one came out of my mind and thoughts. My stomach was still upset, I still felt weak. However, I need this conference with Mr. Righous or Jeremy I called him sometimes. We need a plan, but couldn't talk or even think about what we need to do or say. That was just how the government wanted us to feel, scared to death. I had to look around slowly as I lean back toward the table and at Mr. Righous. I wanted to ask him about the new law and how are we going to go about our visits to the poor and to our contacts to others. But I knew if I spoke to him about this, we might be heard somehow by the government. I started to tap on the table and knew that if he had any kind of teaching by our parents, he would figure out what I was telling him. I just hope he was not a mole by the government. I hope my tapping would give him some reason to show what he was or was not. I had to take the chance of finding out. One tap and then a slide of my fingers across the table told him I wanted to talk. I watched his eyes as I kept on tapping the table with the same question.

Mr. Righous eyes looked at me fast and back down on the table and then at me. He grabbed the neck of his shirt and pulled on it with a nodded and a shake of his head. I watched him pick up his drink and drank fast, then `put his drink down. His fingers tapped out twice and slide left to right with both hands.

No, we cannot even talk here or anywhere about anything. I lean back and nodded yes, then knew he was scared to even try.

We could tap our discussion and retrieve any information we could use. I had tap fast and slid my fingers and palm across the table in hopes he would return the same thing. But I was interrupt with a slap on my hands by Jeremy's own hand hard and firm. I felt the pain expand down my arms as the shock that came from it. I lean back in my seat and rested my head back on the wall that had been around us with its privacy shield that came down as we sat. But then again was it so private that outsiders like the government would know what we were talking about, would they know enough about our defiance? I had to think and think fast. I nodded my head at him and decide I had to leave now, I could feel more than just fear coming from Mr. Righous, a warning of sorts and the feel of danger if I stayed here with him. Somehow, he had been found out, my best friend, we were both in danger as we sat there looking around us as if we were looking for someone else. I was nervous and scared for my family and my friend's family, they were human not hybrid. My wife needs me. But this was not in my plan for them. Look Jeremy, we need that building for the sale of those children next week and not a day later. Do you understand me? The leader had told us that those children would be the ones to do jobs easier in the mines on Mars small caves that hold the metal and the other components we need to keep our weapons and our stand against those damn freedom assholes who want to destroy us all. They are the enemy and we are the ones including our families that they want to destroy. We need to stop them fast or else we are going to be the ones dead. I shook my head as I hope anyone listening would know I was not the traitor and marked for death with Mr. Rigouts family.

I step out of the restaurant with weak legs and tried to calm myself enough that no one would know what I had just found out. It was not good and the fear would show on me if I just let it. I ran to the side of the building, and then let food I had eaten come up close to a large metal like dumpster that was rusted and old. The food came up fast with my knees trying to do the falling to the ground with the food. I swung my head up, took a breath, worked hard to keep more down, held on to the side of the metal thing and let the air clear my head. I walked over to my mobile that was parked close to the restaurant a half a street away. I had to get word to someone, but who and how? I watched from behind me as Mr. Righous got in his car and the enforcers were not far from his mobile. But I knew something about Jeremy; he had put something in that car that would take out a block with him in the seat. That was when I saw him smile at me with a nodded, I saw the enforcers try to pull Jeremy out, but it was too late. The car blew up like a bomb that I had never seen or heard go off like that a sound that thunder hard shook the earth with trembles that made my legs grow weak as I ran to my mobile. I drove it close to the side and cried for the friend I knew I had. I had to call my wife by mind and not by any other device; I knew that our mind link would come in handy if it all came down to this, and this was way too dangerous for us to use anything else.

Marie-Jane was a good wife with secrets that no one but he knew about. Her long blonde hair with black streaks thick may look strange to some people, but the sight made Mr. Western stop breathing. She was too beautiful for his eyes to look at her for long periods of time, and yet, I talk to her with our connection – mind to mind-heart to heart.

Mary love, we are in danger, can you get to Joan, and the kids, Jeremy will not be coming home, and we need to get Joan and the kids out of here fast. I need you to be discreet and careful of any enforcers that are close to her home or ours. I could feel her mind scream out the pain of losing one of her best friend's husband. It was more than I wanted to feel from her. But she was getting scared to.

Jimmy, Joan and her kids are here with me, but I can contact the system we are working with and they could help us get everyone out. I think I should go too. If they see us together the government will follow us and try to kill all of us. Get a hold of my Cousin and let him know that the place we are to meet is being breach. Danger? Danger? We are in danger. Jimmy please be careful. I love you in life and in death I would love even then. Mary Jane said with her sweet melody like voice that sung like a bird to Jimmy heart.

She would take the secret hiding place his father built many centuries ago with other congressmen that felt the same way about the leader. The leader was getting to powerful and to strong. He no longer wanted just power or wealth. But, complete control of people lives and their minds, it was just too unreal, to dangerous no one should have that much control. How many times had his own grandfather state that the leader should been dead, but he lived and never aged or gotten sick?

How can someone live that long and not or ever aged or die, it just can't be? A question that was on many lips and never spoken or breathed. The food again wanted to come up out of his stomach and his throat as he kept on driving toward another place that would be more private. A meeting place where people met in secret from the government that were also hunted by the government and yet had deluded the government every move. Now he had to get to his wife's cousin that was on a mission that might be a false one of hope. He was in danger and anyone that was with him. Things were getting to deep that Mr. Western feared worst for the fighters. It seemed that the leader had found a way to find anyone that worked for the fighters within the congress and senators house. Jim could feel his heart pound hard in his chest like someone hitting him hard. Sweat beamed down his face as the feel of drips falling down his nose. He was hot and nervous as hell with each wait, with each time passing. Was he out of danger or did they catch his family and Jeremy's family as well. He wanted to connect to his wife's mind again, but didn't want to chance anything that might find out about their mind to mind connection. The danger was real, death was now no penetrating time, and it was now. Someone had squealed about our connection with the fighters. But who and why? Then as I took a breath, I felt the deep pit of my stomach over turn. I walked toward a large tree that trunks hide in the darkness of the forest that covered the sunlight. A form lying on the ground, its head missing from its body, then more scattered around bushes and trees that lay down my feet. I step away slowly as I heard my feet break small twinges and old grass as I started toward my mobile. These were the ones I had to report to when I needed to contact Mary's cousin; they had the means to connect him without using computers or any methods that would trace them or each other. Now somehow the traitor had told the government where each meeting took place and when. Now how was he going to warn any one? Jim closed his eyes and quickly asked his wife if she and the children got out safe and that the place was being watch. No one was safe.

The feel of her mind racing through his heart took all his breath, her own warning shout out with one word. RUN. Jim didn't hesitate as his feet drove through trees, bushes, as he leaped high over small streams that bleed red from the heads that had fallen off those people that were killed close to his mobile. Jim didn't get in the mobile, but ran in forest like he owned the place. And yet, Jim really didn't know where he was going and how he was going find his family safe. He just knew that forest was not alive, but silent as he ran over tree roots and forest moist grounds that came up under each step he took. His shoes torn and lost rims of rubber sole open up to his naked feet bled with each landing. Jim ran and ran until he could not run any more. Somehow, Jim thought about sending some kind of message to his wife and then again he was afraid of what he might find when he sent out his mind to hers.

Jim need to know about his wife's condition and know that she was safe with their children. Sweat runny and salty, as it dripped down his face as he licked his lips, tasted the salt and dirt that mixed with sweat. His eyes started to burn as the dirt and sweat ran down his face. His left hand came up over his face to get the wetness off and then slowly sent out another word to his wife. *Are you alive? I don't know where I am or what is going on, but I need to know if you are safe with the children.* Jim sent out his mind, but found nothing in return. Silence was all he felt and heard. Not good, not good. His mind spinning with things that might have happen to his wife and children and not one of the thoughts were good. I got to do something? But what could I do? How can I get any word to her or even find out if she was alive? I can't believe any of this. Jim shook his head sadly, as wetness blurred his vision. Maybe his wife was playing it safe with the kids and Joan. She might be closing off all contact with him, maybe the government enforcers have someone who could receive their mind links. He inhaled a breath as he tried to stand straighter. The darkness seemed to close in around him tighter, wrapping him in a cover that pushed his breath harder to let go, push the air out of his lungs the sound came out in gasping noises when he coughed. His chest now painfully aware of another pain that spread down his arms and legs, Jim crumbled on the ground holding his chest with his hands and arms tightly. Jim shoulder shook hard as one loud sob made the animals shriek in fear, birds flew out of trees with a rush of feathers and sounds.

CHAPTER SEVEN

IM WOKEN UP AND found that he had slept on the cold moist ground and it had made his joints ache as he moved to get up. Insects silently chirping out in whispers of his present with the birds of night giving out their warnings to all that would listen. How did he get here? Why was he here? What happen? All ran through his mind as he shook his head and climb to get up off the ground. Jim felt his hands dirty then looked down at his clothes torn in places that he knew wasn't there before. Fog drift open and memories clouded now return with fear and recognition of those that died before he got to the place that was once the meeting place of the fighters and now, now, they were dead. Somehow, the meeting place had been breach. A traitor that had been involve with the other congress and senators must have waited, just waited for the right time to move and kill anyone that was part of the movement that focus on freedom for the people, the people that were both human and non-humans. But who was it and why would he or she wanted to just kill those that were friends or family for that matter. A puzzle and a something else that Jim could not say right now, he was tired and hungry again, but the emptiness was more than just those things that bother him. Jim lay his body and head down on a log at first, but the log was too hard for his head, he had to get up and look around for a safer place to rest. Jim feet hurt as he walked more toward the forest trees and followed the small stream that was more of a puddle. Then again Jim knew it had to lead him to some place safe. The star's glowing light shine brightly between the trees knitted growth, the moon somehow was high over the trees as its own rays bounced down to show Jim shadows of his surroundings. The sight gave way to another thought enter Jim mind as he took a breath then walked farther into the forest of the trees and bushes that were scattered in a path that he could not see. The stream led to another path of forest, something shrieked out like a wild bird or animal screaming out a painful fit. The sound startled Jim thoughts as he walked slowly in silence.

Marie had to do something fast as she kept on telling Joan not to stop running, but to keep on moving as fast as she could, they had to get out of the house that Marie and her husband Jim had taken as theirs after they had gotten married. It was part of the government homes that only married couples were given for their hard work with the congress. Now another secret that only her family knew and that of the freedom fighters, a tunnel that was built more than hundred years ago or more that had been dug underneath most of the homes in the neighborhood that belonged to those that were loyal to the freedom fighters, it was a way for those to escape from any threat. The tunnel was old and yet, very solid as most of the tunnels had been only used for certain times of their lives, the tunnels did not used any kind of electricity or any kind of water that would led the government to them. Instead of electric, there were rocks of many colors that glowed for different reason the red rock would only glow when any one that was not of the fighter's equal of holding a green rock, a sound would shriek out to warn anyone in the tunnel that enemies were there. The blue rocks that glowed would only glow when someone was close, its smoothing glow would give off a warm feel of sleepiness and calm. Green rocks were only use for two things, one to keep the red rocks from going off and two used as a weapon when combining it with a yellow rock together, it lets loose a laser like beam that would silently kill anyone in its path. Marie knew where the one green rock was she kept in her garden and now the green rock is in her hands would someday be used for a day like today. And then again she was hoping it would not bring any danger either. She had to get to the fighters gathering at the out skirts of the city fast. Her animal that hide inside of her wanted out as danger came fast. Her front door exploded open with smoke and dust fogging around them all as the children had almost screamed out as silent stretched across Joan red tear face. Joan heard Marie talking quietly to her as they grab the children and ran down the tunnel and hope that they had not been seen as they gotten in the hidden wall. The wall that had the stove top was hard and solid, but behind it was the tunnel that led to the path that only Marie knew and now Joan knew too.

Marie held out the green rock that glowed from her hands. Her own hand started to grow dark hair that covered arms. The rock that she held cancel out the ones the red rocks that grew warnings of any one that should not be in the tunnel stop its warnings. The blue rocks glowed brightly making everyone's face a light blue. Stairs were steep and unsure of each footing as they all climb slowly down until they came to another wall that was at the end of the steps. No turns that led down another path; just a wall with pictures of death and unknown that would scream out danger if anyone came down without the green rocks. Joan took out her green rock that was inside of her dark brown grown that gather around her ankles, it was one that showed off her feet; that had also brown shoes, flat and yet, womanly. Her hands nervous and shaking as she held the rock high over the picture, the children hung tight around her legs and hip as small wimping sounds were the only sound around them all. The wall opened to another path that led even farther down. Momma I counted hundred at least of steps from the house, are we going to get caught by the government people, is daddy coming home to. He wouldn't know where we are. Momma I don't want daddy to get caught by those bad people. Joan small little girl of four years old had just finished her last year of high school only two weeks ago and still she saw her small one as a child, her baby. A smile came across Joan red cheeks as the thought of her husband death that led to this flight of survival. Daddy is alright, he will not follow us. He is in a better place than we are right now. We need to stay alive for him, for the cause of the fighters that will make daddy a hero. Now come on sweetheart. Let's get down farther where we will be safe for him. Joan said as she kissed her daughter blonde hair. She looked so much like her husband that the pain of her lost torn her own heart. The wall behind closed with shush as darkness evades the small group of two women and five children. Darkness, no light and yet, each of them knew where their feet had to go on. Joan took the green rock out again and held it high over their heads for some kind of light that glowed green making their face a mask of ghostly green light. Shoes were silent as the feel of wetness drip down from a ceiling and fell on the ground as they kept on walking. Marie moved ahead of them as her eyes and that of her three children were more knee in the darkness as that of Joan and her two children. Marie oldest son, Markesan had changed his form from human to wolf in moments that no one realized he had done so. Markesan sniff the ground for anything that would help them down to the right path of the tunnels keeper. Somehow he had found link to another wolf that might be his mate, he had to get to that one thought, he was only fourteen years old, but already he was told he was too old for mating in wolf form and too young to mate in human form. Right now he felt the tug of the bond that was getting stronger as they kept on walking. *Mark, I can almost feel you, you need to get your family out of here. The government had found out about the tunnels and the red rocks and that of the green rocks canceling the warnings. Hurry, we need you and your family is unsafe.* The voice was smooth and tender like a stream bubbling up tickling his nose. The feel was gentle but still warning off his family's impending danger. Marie heard the warning too and changed her form in seconds before warning Joan to get on her back fast. Mark let Jolie ride him and his sister let small Christen on her back as Mark brother took up the back of them, his fur standing up as the feel of danger coming closer, more feet and shouts of stop or else. Dante would not let them get close to the group as he rose up on his hind legs to reach up to his ten feet of pure muscle, but that was not what scared the coming danger, they had not thought of Dante power of thought and commanding force of his will.

Their mother felt her husband thought of her and only one word she could send to him, to their bond link. RUN! RUN! DANGER!

CHAPTER EIGHT

S o how many do you think we killed back there? Max asked Mike lean back on the floor of the truck their had taken them out of the community where they all had lived all their lives, expect Mike, he had lived mostly with his Uncle some where they had called Scotland at one time, now it was just part of the vast continent that was connected to many other places and other people that speak different languages and their life style were even different. A small chuckle came out of Mike chest as he thought about those people. He had work with them and their animal hybrids. They were dangerous when angrier, but when not angry, they had a way of knowing things faster. Mike shook his head as heard Max shout at him and tug on his feet with his own feet. Max never wore shoes, but his feet were as hard as a shoe. Max feet callus and hard, they were dirty too, no light skin, but dark and firm.

I can't say if any of them were even killed. Can ye tell me ye had seen anything that loud survived? Mike asked Max as he looked at him squarely in the eyes.

No I—I don't think I have, well not like this. I mean, I had followed the tunnels that led under each house here –I mean back years ago when I was a kid. It was kind of strange. There were these round like metal things that if you turn one of them, some kind of leak of gas came out and it made me sick, so I thought it would make other people sick to. That was when I had to save my woman here, Susan, before she had the baby. One of those damn enforcers took a like to her and stole her from me. I had to do something fast or they would kill both of us. Susan was going to let them do whatever to her so I could live. I wasn't going to let her do that. We were just kids and it was not that long ago when I found all those metal things that turn, they had me in a room with bars and the floor had a round metal plate, it that plate I knew was under the building. Those damn things that would send up sick like smells that could make everyone sick. I was right of course, but I didn't know that it would also blow them up too. So Susan and I went down the metal plate thing on the floor and just disappeared. We heard them scream out a warning that they were after us. But by the time we got back to the community, the building just blew up. So, I knew that they had to be dead. We escape alive uncharm, but we swore that we would never left the community again! Max said as he leaned back down on the floor next to Susan and their baby asleep.

Maybe your right, too many houses blew up back there, so the fact is this, no one could survive any of those houses that blew-up. You did a good job of saving us all. Thank you, Max! Thank you very much. I owe you my life as well as many other lives for what you had done for the freedom fighters. Mike said with a small grin.

Max just looked at him with Susan and their baby girl in peace. A thought came and went as he thought of that word, peace. What was it like to be at peace, to have something that he never knew or felt? Then again it was a dream to have no more killing, no more wondering where the next meal was coming from. The truck jerked back and forth on the road that led to nowhere. The road uneven with a path that was full of trees and bushes that grew or broke through many paved roads that were pave in cement or concrete that was smooth and even. But now after centuries of unused or needed forest of trees and pathways now are only seen in roads with down bushes that lead to somewhere unknown to anyone to adventure out.

Steve got up off the floor of the truck back end, he need to see what was going on up front. A small space that was between the freezer that held their food supplies was a door that had a small window to see who was driving up front. Steve used the door to get in the seat that was next to Jack who was driving the truck. Jack, man, are we any closer to any place we are safe. I don't even know where we are going? Steve climb up front, then sat down next to him.

Bro, I got one of the disc it had some kind of GPS map thing, I put it in the computer in this big baby I built, well we built this machine. It will save us; no fucking enforcer knows about something like this moving on land. The enforcer might be looking for us, even thou we are right under their noses. Jack said as he pointed upward over their heads. Steve nodded as he agreed with Jack theory.

The sky looked dark again, but the threat was more rain, but ahead Steve could see sky painted blue with white clouds tinted with darkness. A threat and yet, the sight of blue sky took Steve breath. So how is this GPS and the computer in this old thing working to get us to safety? Steve asked as he looked around the truck front seats and the trucks panel was not like anything he had seen before, there were no bright lights flashing on and off, but he knew Jack had install a computer for a better way to drive or something like that. So how are you driving this thing? Steve asked AS HE looked around for something to help drive the truck.

A chuckle rose out Jack skinny body as he held his hands over the steering wheel steady. Steve we are like real brothers in many ways my man. But I got the brains to know how to work on machines that you cannot even dream about, and I know how to work on computers too. So let me just tell you that I figured out how to make this beauty work for our advantages on the ground. You don't worry about how to drive this until I tell you when. Then I will tell you how to use each device around in here to help with the driving. Man there are no lights to use to make this thing go. You use only your strength and your mind with this thing. You get me? Jack said with a chuckle.

Yeah I guess your right? I only know how to read and count good. I guess all of us have some sort of knowledge that might help. But —I —don't know? I'm just still a little confused about a lot of shit. Where you put the disc any ways? Steve asked him as he felt a jerk and then another tugged on his head.

Jack just smiled that sly smile of his to Steve. Steve knew somehow his best friend (Jack was more of a brother) had hide the disc in places that no one would suspect he would. That gave Steve some relief and yet, he was still uneasy about not knowing. Who put those toys we found in my parent's attic in the back of the truck with the freezers? Did the kids help? Or did Max and Mr. Farmer? Steve asked Jack as he patted the panel down like a drum.

We all did all the work while you were in town working or whatever. Mr. Farmer had feeling that shit was coming and somehow knew we need to get the food in the truck. But damn if I can figure that guy out? He told us to get the important food and the ones we need to eat fast inside of the back of this truck I was working on. You know Mr. Farmer, he got that sense we just don't know about and we all just did what we were told. We had been doing it for most of our lives. We may not be adults yet, but he sure does treat us like we are. So we did what he said for a long time. You remember when we found this and what my dad told us to do with it before he and my mom disappeared like your folks did? Both of been working on it night and day before you went to work, except for when Brook died. It was not good and it hasn't been that long ago either. But Max chill up with more brains than what I thought he had. He found five freezers that could hold more of the food in Mr. Farmer's basement and somehow they had put them in the back of the big truck. We both worked hard to get those freezers inside of the back of the truck and making it work. Then the kids brought the toys and the boxes of disc with them, put the things inside of here without any problem. Then we work on getting most of the food in the freezer and making weapons out of things that would shame a new born. Not saying that any new born would know much about what we know, and that isn't much because we haven't been to any kind of school, but what our parent taught us. But I think we done a good job. Jack said as his chest rose up with pride of what he had just said and done.

Steve agreed with him, then looked back through the door in hopes to see Mike and his motor bike. It was another strange thing that made him wonder how it could ride on land and not on air like so many other mobile cars do. It silent right now, Mr. Farmer was sitting his chair that someone had put in the back of the truck for him. Mr. Farmer looked like he was asleep with his head bent low against his shoulder in a strange way that look as if he was uncomfortable. The children each held one of the toys in their hands softly playing with the toys or just holding them tightly against their chest. Dirty faces and tangled hair with bits of dirt and bugs dead. The children clothes seemed tight around their bodies to be anything but torn and worn out to see any color or size. Their eyes were like glass, dull and unloving, but the toys gave them some life and maybe some reason to stay alive. Mike smiled at them with a wink to each of the children and wave to them to come closer to him.

Steve had to smile and yet, deep down he just hoped that they would have a better life. Steve thoughts of what was going to happen to them. How much violence or death would they or would they endure for the next year or more. Steve just hoped at the end of their trail no one would be left dead or dying. Somehow, Steve knew that would not happen, someone would die or just leave. Steve felt the community was his safe place, a place he called home, he never thought he would be gone from there, never sleeping in a building that was in his family forever, now that was gone and so was Brooke. Then again, his job was gone too, there was nothing too go back too! And no place would he ever call home. How could he think about hope for those children and Susan baby? But looking at their eyes had spoken many things that Steve never thought of, freedom.

Jack stop the truck with a jerk and pull, the sound of the stick that had been sitting between them made a sound like something chocking a throat held tight in a hold of some kind. It was Jack making the stick move hard, then everything stop. The computers mapping trail shriek out a loud forward, but Jack just jump out of the truck with me behind him. Mike stood over something that I could not see well at first, the ground rose up in large pieces of earth and black concrete rock. How in the hell are we going to over that with this big thing we are driving? I asked.

Hmmhmm. Tis a wonder how the forest grew around something like this. There is no pathway around it and no way can we go over it on ground level. We may need one night here until we can figure out a plan. No one leaves the truck, we sleep now, and I shall scout out for a path to see if the trail we are heading is the right path. Mike said as he jumped out of the truck.

I thought you just said no one leaves the truck. I asked him with a buff of air. I was a little upset that we were stuck.

The computer went off again with a swirl of sounds that was loud and made the truck shift backwards with a jerk then another sound of air shushing and jerks. Jack jump back in fast as he took hold of the door that swung open, Mike ran over to the passenger side and pushed me out of the way, I grab hold of the door, pushed myself up on the seat and watched the truck shift the stick back and forth without anyone touching it.

We are backing up, the path is hidden now, we will back up, turn left on the second road going east. We will be off course, but unable to venture forward. The computer seemed to just come alive with us inside of the truck. I looked back to see if the children and Max and Susan were alright. Max came running up against the doors window with a gasp of air. What the fuck is going on up front. Mike shot off the back like a rat racing for food.

Get on back there Max with your family. The computer is just fixing our course. We just came to a stop that tis blocked with earth. So we need to let the computer do its job. Mike said as he and I turn to look out the front window.

Max closed the window, went back to sit down with the children and listen to Susan story that Mike had started before the truck stopped. The story was about a forest of animals that were friendly and all protected each other from strange people that came in to take away their children. It was one story Max had never heard, but he enjoyed Susan's voice as she told her version of it.

I have no freaking knowledge on how that thing took control as if it did. I am not even driving it now. Shit fuck, computer you program you took turn the truck around and take over my job? Jack asked the computer directly, as Jack fist his hands together and hit the steering wheel. Jack face winced as the pain and sound of bone breaking in his hands were heard around the front seats. Shit damn that hurt. Fucking shit computer answer me. Jack asked again.

We are controlling a truck with a trailer that has four freezers full of human food. The trailer also has boxes hidden that have memories of the past, it is important to bring those to the fighters of this future time. I will not let no one in my protection be harmed. I will control the trucks function to keep all comfortable, safe. I am freedom; I am fighters past, the computer said with a soft tender voice that was female or a soft male. There was no sound of threats or fear. But I knew I had swallow hard, my throat dry and stomach aching from lack of food. I was getting hungry, but this was too much too even swallow. I felt my stomach making noise that was too familiar in many ways.

Free are ye knowledge of the fighter's homage state? Mike asked it.

Yes, I know of the past state that freedom fighter's headquarters had started. I am program to bring those that are holding my past to that point. I know your voice it is in my program memory. But you cannot be him, he has died many centuries ago, maybe more. I was program in the year 2034, the world had changed as more land started to connect with other parts of the world that was separate by water, and now I am not sure of the world condition. I know many countries had fought for control of many other countries that was once apart from them by water. Many deaths plagued the human world at the time of my creation, I am program to remember and repeat my memories to those that request my knowledge of the past. Now we are at our —there are trees—bushes—a forest is in the road that I must take all of you through. Where are the streets? –roads? The hard drive that was installed in my memory was never program wrong. All maps and area had been installed for future developments. Has the street been rerouted? My hard drive's has not been touched for centuries sense I had been program? I must find another path for us to use. The computer said as it shut down with a swish and sound of bleeps and burps.

Computer tell us exactly where we need to be and maybe we know a better route, tis our time and nae yours any more. Mike said as he looked down at the panel were the computer was put in. The trucks dashboard lit up as the computer came on again with a sign as if the computer was alive. I can give you a read out in a few minutes. The sound of beeps and shushing sound of the truck stalling in a path that was close off from anyone that wanted or need to go forth. I had scanned the area 10 miles and then again another 20 miles from where we are now. The area seems to be more forest, but I had found some odd metal things that seem to be deep within the grounds bushes and under the surface of grass. The computer said as more beeps, the truck jerk slowly back and sat there waiting for scanning of a larger areas that farther more than 30 miles.

Look I can find a path big enough for this thing better than you are scanning area's that ye don't know aboot. Mike said, as his slang got deeper with each word he spoke. He was getting madder as he thought about how the computer was putting him off. He had never argued with a computer but this was just too much. Mike shoved Steve over as he pushed his way out of the truck and went straight to the back of the trucks trailer, and found his bike leaning against the walls close to the large freezer that held their larger meats. Mike had pulled up himself up on the back of the trailer and pulled his bike out with a turn his face a mask of annoyed. Mike sat on the bike listening to the sounds of the bike engines roaring to life, vibrating his arms, his body. Mike had to find his helmet that had all his controls that was hidden inside. His voice and his eyes were the only way to operate the helmet and sometimes his bike.

One of the children, he thought it might have been one of the girls wearing his helmet as she listened to Susan stories.

Mike made his bike roar louder, the children turn in their sits to look at him. The girl got up and took off the helmet, then gave it to Mike. Her eyes dull and sad, hungrier hung in her eyes as she just looked at Mike. Mike pushed his hands inside of his pocket. He was hunting for that one thing that he had always put in his pocket before he left home. But he wasn't so sure if he had it still. Then he found the small red stick that tasted sweet. Mike realized that he had ten pieces of the stick, he handed the sticks to each of the children. The feel of their hands in his were cold and too fragile to keep in his hands. Mike slowly withdrew his hands and look at them with a sign, he got back on his bike, let the bike roar again as he drew his bike front wheels up in the air as he bounced off the back of the truck. The feel of the bike under Mike made him feel free, alive with the air whipping around his thin cloths. All thought put aside Mike pulled his own computer on as he spoke softly into his helmet. *I need scan of all area's that may have large paths that could hold a truck of this size. Analyzing area's contents surrounding truck. Area's forest growth, under bushes has some unknown objects I cannot define objects.* The computer in Mike helmet sound like his mother, but he knew she was dead; she died when he was just a boy of twelve years old and yet the sound gave him some comfort. His family had to escape the government in their reign. His father was part of the government in a small way. His part was only to report to both part of the world's congress families of how each part of the world government was working and how each of them were keeping the poor where they belong. His father barely got out of town with his family. The only safe place that his father knew was Mikes Uncle. He was old, but very powerful in many ways.

Their airmobile died before they got to the safe house and had to run through the thick forest that surround Mike uncle's estate. The darkness that now surround Mike as he sat on his bike looking inside of the forest, bought back his memory more apparent of the past. His feet bare as he scrambled with his mother hasting him to hurry fast toward the thickest of the forest. No light, only darkness blindness stretched out in front of them. His brother no older than five years old, but he ran as fast with his tiny legs could go following both his father and his mother. Mike felt his body breaking as it grew longer, stronger, a growl came out of his throat a scream of madness stopped him in his tracks. Both his father and mother had changed too, but his little brother had lain in a pool of blood behind their father. Mike couldn't understand his body changing to something he had never knew was possible? His hair changing to a white fur standing up along his back as he bent over and on to four muscular legs, his ears pointy up on top of his head, his eyes wide with more keen sight of the darkness that once blind him. His mouth growing longer with fangs that pierce his lower lip, the taste of his blood made him even angrier. His mother screamed out for him to leave to go to his uncle as fast as he could. You must leave Michael; you are more important to them alive; we cannot let them have you. You must leave. Our whole world depends on your strength and your reason you live. You are the one that will save many of the humans and those that are the guardians of the secret. You must go, do not come back, or turn to save us. We will always be a part of you my cub. Mike memory faded as his computer repeated its find. *I had found a path hidden beneath plants and trees that had fallen. Either by storms or by other possibly that one had taken the path as a blockage. Do you wish to continue riding closer to the path? I can scan longer for a larger pathway.* The computer asked Mike taking him out of his past memories. Mike shook his head as he tried to clear the thoughts of yesterday's past. Then he noticed the odd thing that was pointing out of the spot that the computer had just told him. Mike took a breath and let his visor that settle over his face as he had put his helmet on earlier and now he need to breathe in the forest air. He needed to let his smell, his sense of any kind of danger of any kind of smell to tell him what his computer could not tell him. A fade sound of birds shrieking around him woke his already keen sense to another height. Animals hunting in distance howling at something they must have cornered. A rush of birds and small animals scrambling out of bushes and trees seem to be running for their lives. Mike turned his handlebars in fast motion of his wrist and let the bike roar its own challenges at the sound of howls and then a growl that felt as if it was too close to Mike bike. He wasn't afraid or scared, Mike just chuckle with a shake of his head, and then did his own howling with a loud growl that came out deep from his heart and his stomach. The howling stop, all fell silent under his growl and his roaring. Another chuckle came out of his throat and went in the forest to look more at the pointing thing that was under the bushes. Mike got off his bike and park the bike against a tree, Mike put his helmet on the seat with care as he looked down and move the bushes away, the bushes were thorny and green with the hint of mildew that shot more so when Mike got even closer to the bushes. The thing he found was not what he would call anything he had ever seen before it was strange square like with rust that was deep within the metal it was made of. Touching the metal like square with his hands color it a dark black, that smell even more metallic than the years of rusting in the forest floor for more years than he would imagine. Flakes seem to fly off in hands as he rubbed hard on the thing. Words were old and dark to give any indication of what it said. *Computer, can you decipher these words on the thing I am holding?* Mike asked his computer that was in his helmet.

Deciphering now, cannot decipher too much damage to decipher one word or another. The computer told Mike as it scanned more over the metal thing in his hands. Mike lay it back down to see if he could find something else that might help them. Something somehow told him to look deep in the ground for clues. Mike pulled back his sleeves of his shirt he worn, he noticed that his shirt was torn at the end in many places. Another one he had to get. He worn out more shirts and pants that he had. That did not stop Mike in his quest to find out about this road that the main computer on the truck knew about. But he had to find a new way to get them off this road and onto another towards the area where the freedom fighters were supposed to them. Mike watched his hands change into claws that torn through his skin making his bones pop and crack as it grew with talons of sharp nails that could tear anything to shredded. Mike knew he had to listen to his instincts and his instincts told him to dig deep and hard under the bushes along this hidden path of the past. And then he found himself touching something hard, unable to dig anymore, Mike brush the rest of the dirt away from whatever he had found. A road of some kind was underneath the dirt and patches of bushes and trees that up level all the areas around him. *Computer, can you scan another 20 meters or more in the south direction of where we are at?* Mike asked as he looked around.

Scanning area for roads and any other paths that would lead out of area were we are now.

The computer said as another voice came over its controls in Mike helmet, he didn't reorganize the voice, it was different from his own computer controls in his helmet. Mike stood still as he listened to the voice coming over his computer. *Have you found anything that will able the truck to proceed its entrance to the freedom fighter's quarters. I have found a path that is blocked 20 meters north not south of where we are now. I am attempting to turn the truck in the direction north of our status. We will be leaving in 10 minutes. Are you coming or staying?* The computer that came over Mike own helmet computer was in fact the main computer in the truck. Mike was both relieve and shock that it was able to infiltrate his computer in his helmet. He thought his uncle had put some kind of safe guard so no one could penetrate its controls. But the computer in the truck had took over in a sense of his own computer in his helmet. Confusion set in as he walked over to his bike, then somehow he had to look back at what he had found out. Something tug at his sense, he had to go back on his back into the spot where he had found that strange thing under the bushes. *I am going to follow something in the forest.* Mike told the computer. *Affirmative, be aware of things that may not be and those that may be of kind. I feel a present that I cannot distinguish if it is human or animal. My sensory are old and may have some dysfunction in its memory.* Mike heard all he wanted to hear and left the sight of the truck and hope he could find it again soon. Right now he need to follow his instinct and it told him to go farther in the forest.

He wasn't going to complaint with a computer that he didn't understand or really wanted to. A shake of his head and he was off to his own adventure and he knew it would be somewhat strange as everything in his life was strange.

The light in the forest seem odd as it cast an eerie glow of orange and red that peek out of leaves of green and brown along the path Mike had taken. His skin didn't feel like his own skin that was human, but more fur and uneasiness that settle in his stomach like lead. His stomach aching a bit from not eating for a few days had caused him more grief than just leaving his mission undone. He need to shake the feeling of being watched and followed as he drove his bike through groves of wobble trees that strung out (it seem) from corners of his eyes and his paths. A bush of heavy spikes of green pointy out at every area he wanted to move around the bike with. The bush was larger than what Mike had thought it was, as he got closer to the area that a path that was hidden underneath his bike wheels. A path that had been hidden underneath the growth of vines and grass and trees that surround area's that might had been homes or stores at one time. When the houses had become abandon and the forest took over? How long had it been sense humans inhabit the area? Where had they gone too? What caused them too just disappear like this? Those thoughts made Mike stumble along the pathway with his bike moving side to side in a wavy as if he was trying to miss something he hadn't seen. Question that no one he knew could answer or did he knew? Maybe that strange computer that Jack built into the truck, that pulled them out of the community that they had lived for all their lives and now they are running from the government enforcers and the police. He had to help them get to the freedom fighters headquarters soon. The box that held the disc that was in Steve parent's home was a key to stop the government or more so to destroy the government and take them all down. It was strange just how things came about in just a few days. Mike thought about his uncle and those that were around him talking about something that the government had order.

After his uncle was finished talking to these men although Mike was not sure if he trusted those men that his Uncle was talking too. Mike had gone to his room so his Uncle had more time to speak freely from small ears. Mike was able to hear better than most humans and then some of the other kinds of half-breeds that were once humans and now he really couldn't tell what they wanted to be called. He knew he didn't like half breeds or any other name that some people would call his kind. Humans did not except those that were different from them and they teased and abuse that were different in many ways. As he grew up he watched his own parents died, but His Uncle had saved him that day, but he still had a nightmares of sorts. Other children (human children) were more uncaring and were more aggressive as well as their parents toward his parents. The sounds were more like whispers from a distance that would be or normally be hard for normal people could hear. But Mike heard voices that spoke of past lives that lived here with uncertainty. *He is here with us. Can't you smell him?* The voices said to one another as they echoed out their sounds back and forth. Mike chuckle as he thought about smells and tried to smell them, but came back with nothing. That was strange, he could not smell them or feel them, but he heard them. A tingle rode up his left arm that had a small tattoo of his mother form of animal with his father large massive mountain loin form standing up next to his mother's smaller form. It was the last thing he remembered from the attack. That form of their defense against the government attacking them. The sight of their death became imbedded like a bad dream for many years and still haunted him today. Mike closed his eyes to try to shake his memory away that somehow wanted to haunt him now.

With a deep breath inhale, Mike let it out slowly and let the thoughts of yesterday's back in its past. Trees' growing around him in different shapes, and sizes and yet they linger in an embrace of a family forgotten like a favorite toy. Grass tall as he was standing growing in a fast paste, he almost couldn't see what was in front of him or behind him, but the path was clear in his mind as he kept his bike on the track he found beneath the growing grass and bushes that spring up around him. Birds came back in swam of different kinds of feathers that Mike couldn't tell what kinds of birds any of them were. Sense of a present came close to his skin as felt something close, something he couldn't see in front of him, but he could feel them just the same. Shrieks of the bird's sounded like someone screaming, Silence was no longer around him, the forest came alive with shrieks and cries of living things that either moved under bushes to step in front of his bike as he tried to stop his bike from hitting each small animal that came in front of him. The ground uneven with rocks and large stone jumping in each corner of the path, Mike had curve his bike slowly at times and then fast when the path was even and clear. He kept on riding farther away from where the others had stop and were attempting to turn the large truck around. Then out of the trees something larger than his bike and heavier landed across his bike with a loud thud, Mike landed hard on the ground as his bike spun on its side against a tree. His head spinning around as he tried to clear his thoughts and worked on his head that pained him, his arms stretched over his head to get his helmet off. Leaning his head back down on the grounds hard surface still gave him pain as his wince and touched the top of his head to see if anything broke open. Nothing, he was safe, but the pain was still there. Turning over on his side, Mike tried to get up off the ground, but as soon as he moved again the large thing pounce on him heavier and meaner. Mike heard a deep growl and then a snarl that took his breath as he listened. Mike fell again down on the ground daze and a little upset. Slowly Mike tried to take off his helmet to both get air and to give some relief for his head. He moved very slowly as his vision blur from the pain and then cleared as he fought to keep conscious. The sight he saw made him panting, his heartbeat like a drum or thunder forced back in the clouds. His breath ragged in his lungs as he tried to control his heart. What the fuck are ye? Why did ye hit me so hard mate? I do nae ken you? Nevertheless, I am nae ye enemy, I could nae harm ye. So be ye still beast. Mike said as he stood up slowly, his feet a wee bit wobbly. The sight of the large furry animal took Mike breath and his heart beat hard in his chest as the sweat bleed down from hair down to eyes. Slowly Mike took off his shirt as he watched the dark wolf like animal that blend in with the forest rich darkness that surround them. The animal had some white and gray streaks that blend in with the black fur that rose up in a line of his back. The shoulder slump as it looked at Mike in readiness to jump him any moment. The wolf was going to bounce to attack him as he watched, his back legs spread out in a lower stance of ready, Mike just stood there watching him. Mentally Mike tried to speak to him, but the wolf just abed him. No thoughts, no feeling of anything. I am just taking off me shirt, I am too a hybrid of sorts. I have me sigil of me kind on me back, if ye would just look at it and well pre haps ye would just talk to me instead of attacking me without cause. Mike said as he let his shirt fall down to his feet. The wolf stopped as he heard in the distance a howl, then a he heard a growl that seem a little closer to where Mike and the wolf stood.

Both of them looked around to find who was growling at them. Then another wolf came out of the forest to stand next to the one that had. The new wolf had white fur with a silver streak at the tip of its tail, its eyes deep blue with a mix of silver swirling his gaze as the wolf look at Mike hard. The sternness of the new wolf stance, gave Mike fear that he thought he would never feel. He was one of the fiercest hybrid ever created. His uncle had taught him that he was never to let anyone (even other hybrids) know he was afraid for any reason for any time of anything. Mike took his fear shook it off and let his own stance show that he wasn't afraid and was surer of his strength and his abilities. Mike took a breath and let it out through his nose slowly. Mike slowly let his legs spread in a ready stance of fight. His body tense as the feel of his skin tingle, then fur slowly rose over his arms and chest. Golden fur with white tips over his body, His face stretched into a snout, whiskers growing out each side of his nose that was now long and black.

His mouth long with fangs pointy and sharp, a growl and loud made the wolves step back away from Mike. Mike felt his bones break and change form as he fell on all four. His hands stretch out with claws tapping the ground as Mike got ready to fight if they didn't back down. Mike felt his pants tear as his legs stretched out of them with his long blonde gold tail wipe out fast.

Mike sent out his thoughts again to the wolves and hope that they would respond to him. It was odd that he didn't even sense them when he riding his bike or right now. It was as if they thought on a level that Mike could not hear. Now in his form of Mountain lion, Mike that was a little smaller than the wolves, but he was better built. Mike growl louder with a loud roar that shook the leaves from the trees as if the wind had been blowing. The sky overhead started to grow dark as clouds covered the sun rays. Birds kept quiet as the three deadliest praetor face each other in a battle that wasn't sure of reasons. Mike again tried mentally to talk to them, but nothing came back. Mike didn't want to hurt them, he just wanted to know why they were attacking him and why would they not talk to him either. He felt as if some kind of magic or something blocking any form of communication. He had to keep his mind on the wolves in front of him. Not what was happening in front of him? Yes, it bothered him, but if he let them know it did, then they would be able to attack him off guard. They didn't even have a scent another thing that bothered him. They were able to track him now with his scent, but he couldn't sense them or smell them either. How did they do it, how did they hide their scent and how can they hide any form of thoughts from him. Surely they can read him if they could smell him then they could read his mind too. But how can they block their thoughts from him? He couldn't understand how any of these things could be happening.

And yet here he was with these wolves that had no scent and had capture him easily. Submit should he submit to them or would they just kill him. Mike back down without even fighting them. Mike thought about it and his only choice was to submit to them and wait for them to make some kind of move. Mike relaxed his form and let his human part start to take over. His fur and his body reform back to skin, his snout pulled back into his face, nose grew back small with its round point, his eyes wide with dark black eyes gone now as it too got smaller then a turn of color and mikes eyes now blue. His claws stretched back to fingers and hands. Then his tail fold back in his rear. He stood tall and straight, then, Mike just lowered his head with one blink he just closed his eyes and let his sense flow outward toward the two large wolves that waited in front of him.

Then a blur of fur swirl in a mist of wind that surround the two wolves as they too changed back into human form. They stood naked looking at Mike with blank stares and wonder. Their minds still blank and Mike still could not penetrate their minds. He was more puzzled and confused as he walked slowly toward his bike, and yet he didn't let his eyes leave them. His bare chest heaving fast as he felt his animal form trying to submerge again over his skin. But he held it back the best he could. The feel of danger hung around the two wolves as they watched him in their human form. One of them had long haggy brown hair that hung down his skinny back; they both looked as if they had not eaten for weeks. They look alike in some ways, their faces were round with a chin that was square, their eyes dark brown wide with noses that were not long, but not pointy. Mike noticed that they had streaks of white and black in different parts of their hair. Mike took a breath and let it out slowly as he bent low to touch his bike he wanted to bring the bike up off the ground. But stop as he heard a growl and then movement from the two mute twins that Mike decide to call them wordless and brainless. All he gotten from them was growls and barking sounds. It reminded Mike of the packs that was close to his Uncles home. He had let them live in the forest and even gone far to let them build homes around the forest of his Uncles estates. They were nice and help with anything that had to with the freedom fighters Mike had been friends with many of the young werewolves-boys, he had played with them and had been as far as a friend to have sleepovers at his uncle's home and then invited to theirs as well... But, these wolves were so different Mike couldn't make any sense into who or what they were, yeah they were wolves, and they were strangers too. Something was just not right. After looking at them closer I noticed that they had a partly cloth like wrapped around their middle to hide their private parts. At least I didn't need to look at something that was a bit obscene. I bent again low to touch my bike. Slowly I pulled my bike off the ground and let it lean back against my legs. The bike was more awkward than heavy. He needed them to speak and not just look at him as if he was either food or something they wanted to kill.

Bushes moved behind the two wolves that stood looking at Mike with a stance of readiness to strike any moment Mike would do something. The wolves stood there just looking at each other, their eyes still without a flutter of their lashes. Someone step out of the forest with a slim body that stopped Mike heart as he watched who it was. Her face came in view as Mike looked from bottom up. Her legs thick muscular hard with her steps coming closer to him. Then her body slim with muscles stretching farther up with her breast heaving with her breath coming out hard and fast, her body growing strong with strength. She look as if she came from heaven with her long white blonde hair flowing in a light breeze that kissed her face and hair. Her body curves that showed her muscle with in her belly and chest slowly Mike took a swallow of his salve that hadn't known that he was even feeling her effect on him. He wasn't one of her packs or one of her wolfs. Mike was not one of her pack wolves, but something totally different and more powerful than what they are. Slowly she walked toward Mike as she pushed the two larger men that stood in front of him back away from his sight. Silently she just looked at Mike with intendment that would have anyone thinking she was going to eat them alive. But Mike just stood there feeling his heart beating in his chest that was not from fear, but from this beauty, this strange animal that had made his blood flow hot and make his knees weak as a new born baby. Her torn gown was white as snow that sent shiver down Mike back; she was too beautiful for him to look at.

She was now close enough to Mike face and neck that Mike could smell her clearly, she smelled like woods, forest greens, moss new and fresh. She did not smell of wolves, but something he had not known about. Slowly Mike tried to touch her mind with his, but all he could feel was silent.

You are not one of us, we will not speak to you, you are one of the whiskers ones that climb trees and hunt down our young ones. You are one of our enemies that will die on our territory. Our hunting grounds that your kind has attack us many times. We. Will. Not. Share our grounds with no one. She said in Mike head as she smelled him again around his neck.

Peace; I am not one of the whiskers. I am called Mike; I am an outsider from a place that hunts all of our kinds. They are now hunting me and, those of humans that I promised to save, and keep safe within my powers. We are to go to the land of freedom fighters. We are looking for another way to enter a path that would lead us to the land of freedom fighters. Mike sent back to the woman that stood to close to his side that he almost could kiss her if he turned his head. But mike thought not to do so would be a bad thing if he did. Yeah, he would one dead hybrid and Steve would be one dead promise to the freedom, yeah that would just give the leader of the government right to continue to kill and take more lives from the poor. Mike just listened to your promise to defend the poor and protect those that promise to the freedom fighters. Yeah, don't screw up not now, not ever, Mike kept on reminding himself. With a deep breath inhale her scent in his memory as well as what she looked like.

Fighters of freedom! Is that who you are? Are you one of them that have been spying on us? I say again feline we do not share our territory. She said as she back away from me and looked at me with her hazel blue eyes that sent my body in chill mode. I need to get control of my body fast I thought silently.

She chuckled deep in her throat as she read my mind. I became so embarrassed that I knew anything I thought or felt she would know. *You like what you see, but we do not breed with anyone other than what we are that includes humans.* She said with a smile.

My bike fell away from my left side of my leg as I was being push toward where she had left. The other two were-wolves had moved behind me before I even noticed that they had done so. Their hands changed into claws that stretched out toward my back as I felt each talon of their claws scrape my back. As I followed her I left my shirt on the ground forgotten. I staggered behind her as I felt the grass thorns of its pebbles that were beneath the earth's forgotten path. I knew somehow that I would find that one place that would lead me easier back to the fighters. The forest scent gave way of how old the forest is, moss old with heavy scent mold mix with dirt and something else, wet wolves. Mike twitched his nose as the scents invaded his smell and his senses. The she –wolf walked with a silent step, Mike watched her just glide over the grounds foliage's and fallen trees scattered along the path. Her stride gliding over fallen trees and rocks, green grass tall and leaning down with each step she took. His own steps level with hers, as he knew that he could be just as soft and glide like her owe feet too. Mike took a soft breath and let the air out slowly as he took control of his cats. The damn thing wanted not just to be turn on by the female, but he wanted to fight too. The thought of getting capture by a pack of wolves was not good for his cat forms. They all wanted to come out to play tag and paw at the wild dogs in front and in the back of him too. Trees branches that were more of bites against his bare arms scrape him and they seem to just want to paw his arms up and down along his back side too. The pain was little compare to other tortures he had endure in his past. He was now more powerful than that one time; he was young and very much immature before all his forms came to his full power. Because of freedom fighters had worked hard to help him to archive his powers to its fullness. He knew if he wanted to he could do more than just damage to these wolves, even though it took him long hours and long days working each hour of day to form his body into all kinds of feline breeds and that of his human side too. Now he couldn't even use his powers without putting Steve and the others in danger. Mike knew they were not with him or around him, but there is always that one possibility that would sense where they were and who they were. Steve and the others had unknowingly left their scent on him. The air breeze ruffled his hair as he kept on walking or more following the female wolf into the forest. The smell of the forest tickled his nose that twitched as another smell came closer to him. At first he couldn't decide what the smell was, then again the smell felt or smell familiar. Human? No that wasn't it! Not human and not wolf either. The smell was harsh with a scent of hard mold and animal mix with human. But the animal was one part he could not tell what kind. No sound coming from behind him or in front of him and yet the forest noise was loud enough that he could tell something just came alive.

CHAPTER NINE

ANTE YOU DID A good job of those enforcers. But what did you do to those that were still above ground in our home? I know I heard something and the ground kind of shook underneath our feet. Wait a minute; did you get that damn thing to work? I thought I heard before the house explosive after we searched the bottom of the tunnels path? What did you blow up that shook the ground so bad? Come on Dante just don't be so silent and deadly walking like a freaking badass. Dante sister said as she walked beside him. Dante was walking like a stud peacock. His head high with his snout up high as if he was sniffing something in the air, He had used one of his powers to control to make the enforcers kill each other. Then he sent his power to where the other men were waiting for them in their home, the airmobile was still on with no one inside of the air mobile, so he sent the mobile against his family home hard and with one loud boom. That was when he knew that the remaining enforcers had died in a blasé of red and bright yellow explosive. The sound shook the ground hard and fast. Their feet stumbled a little, but their mother knew that the human could not run fast enough through the tunnel, so each took one of the humans on their backs as they thunder through the tunnels in blurs of black furs that stood high over their skin as caution stall their paths. They had to listen and smell for any kind of danger that was either behind them or in front of them.

Their claws scraping along the ground that was cover in hard smooth floor that made their feet sound like sharp nails being pull long the grounds in a rattle like chains, their nose twitching in all direction as their tongues hung out in gasp of air that came in fast as they flew out of danger that was once their home. No sound came from any of the humans that rode backs as they flew farther into darkness that was both their friend and their enemy.

Carrlynia head snapped as something around them seemed to come alive, a small light in a distance that she knew both of her family had to have seen it to. Somehow, she could not trust the light nor what was at the end of it. Had the tunnel ended or had they found others escaping under the tunnels passageways? She could not tell as her brothers slowed down and let their mother come in front of them slowly to watch and sniff the air for anything that could tell them what it was they were stopping.

What they had smell wasn't danger but something that told them that in a short distance a scent of familiar-that of one of their own hybrid breed.

Mark and his mother spoke with their minds, neither one of them wanted Joan and her daughter to hear what they were saying. Dante and Carrlynia listen silently as both spoke about the scent and what they may in counter at the end of the tunnel?

Mother we do not know if they are friends or foe. They may be enforcer's ears. We should be more careful around them. Cannot let anything happen to any of these humans or let them know about the freedom fighters where bout's. Mark sent his words of concern. He wasn't sure if those that were at the end would be the same ones that he was speaking too. All he knew is to be caution. He had to help his mother to protect those three humans that were with them.

Let's just be careful with what we say, they may be listening to us now. Maria said to her son. She could feel his hesitation to what is unknown about those at the end of the tunnel. Maria knew the fighters would not have known this fast about their flight, it was impossible. She had not sent out any warnings. She was too afraid that someone in the enforcers knew how to intervene her messages by thoughts. So who were those at the end? Joan husband had just died not too long ago and Maria husband is missing too. She knew the fighters had not been warned yet. They just could not have been at this time. Slowly Mark sent down his bundle next to Dante and Carrlynia. Maria looked at her son then felt her lungs grow heavy with air as fear stole her heart and body. The sight of Mark leaving her had made every nerve in her tingle with fear.

Mark I had been waiting for you. Come on we are friends of the fighters. I will not blame you for hesitating about us. I would be just as caution as you are. The voice said to Mark. The sound of her voice was calm and assured. No fear or waving that told him that there was danger. And yet, he felt the need to fight somehow the feeling was strong and sure something told him, but he could not figure out why or who it was that made him feel this way. Mark brother Dante held out his chest like he was a king and moved Mark away from him with ease, Dante smell the air and could not tell what the smell was or what he was smelling either. Mark somehow Dante was good at finding out danger at times faster than he can, especially when it came to heated wolves. He had to let Dante sense guide him and just follow his lead. Quietly they both step out of the tunnel and into the forest that was once a neighborhood that had homes of greatness, but the years and centuries that passed no one had ever lived or claimed any of the homes, now trees and forest alike of tall grass, marshes of all kinds inhabit, no homes standing tall, only sign was the knowledge of them being there. The sun was heavy in heat, light clouds covered patches of sky over the heads of trees. A small area spread out in a corner on the left side of Dante sight. There sitting in a pond of greenery and bushes, lay two female wolves buffing air out of their lungs in fits of exhaustion, Mark could not make out their furs strips to give him any indication of who they were and where they came from. He felt no danger, but sometimes that could not always be true. Dante stood there in front of those female wolves with his chest buff out in stance of pride. I stood beside him and tried to mimic his stance.

Come boys, you two have to be joking us. We saw more alpha male testosterone within our first year of mating season than both of you here. So please don't act so stupid. The two female wolves said as one.

Look, we don't know you, but how did you know we were inside that tunnel, and another thing how did you know to wait here for us? I asked them as Dante stood silence next to me.

One of the females had dark gray strips mixed with white deeply in her coat. Her scent was of mating. I had to shake my head within. I had fought the urge to mate with the female, but his brother was here and it would have resulted in a fight with him and Dante was stronger and younger than he is. Mark would had learned to fight, but his powers were still a little off track. Dante powers developed earlier than Mark had. Mark just hope Dante youth was his downfall and not ready to mate yet. Mark to a breath and sat down. *Who are you both and how do you know us?* Mark asked again.

Alright, first we are in legal with the enforcers or the leader.

Second: We were with the pack that was call the forgotten.

We work with the fighters from time to time. Our pack was attack six nights ago; we had met up with ten of the fighter's leaders in the forest north of here.

But, we were attack again and this time ten leaders and our last four sisters and two or our young cubs were killed at the edge of the forest. We were sent by the alpha leader Rossman of the freedom fighters. He had told us at his near death time. We also know that your father had tried to connect the leaders, but failed. He had escape the attack by going into the forest deep to hide. We saw him and tried to hide his scent by tracing his scent away from the attackers. We can't understand how our pack was found in the forest or the leaders either. We are confused, but we knew we had to get to Maria and her small pack fast. We are not enforcer's formats. My name is Olaya and this sister Oryeia. If we were part of the enforcer's we would have killed your pack by now. But we are not or would be. I rather kill the leader of these humans than be part of them. I am telling you the truth. The female said as she rose.

Mark hesitated as he thought about what she said... Mark could not sense anything about those females. Then again, he felt something that was wrong. He just couldn't pen point it. He needed more information, something that would tell him if they spoke truth or not. Something about Dad that he would have told them or tell something or us that would or might have been a clue. Mark thought about that very morning and what his father had said or worn to work. It all seem so long ago and not just a few hours or more. Think Mark! Remember school or what he learned in his computer modular of memories stored in the back of one's mind, any information that was stored would or could be used when needed. Then again, Mark tried to into that stored mind and found nothing. Maybe he was just working too hard to retrieve any memory of his father this morning. Mark looked at the female with more caution than he wanted to display.

Hmm, we don't blame you or any of you to be on guard. They said together.

How old is your pack? Maria said as she stepped out of the tunnel with grace of a cat.

The forgotten have been together as one for more than twelve centuries and had breed with other packs in the same area. Our father was grander the sighted one, and our mother the great feline Moller We were a pack of more than sixty, twelve of them were alpha warriors, we had 20 cubs that were counted last eve, twelve and ten female ready to be mated in the moon first turn for them. The rest of the packs were made-up of different kinds of wolves needs for the pack. Hunters, clothes makers, huts makers and so on. Sixty to be all and most of them now gone, we are the only ones living. It is our responsibility to rebirth our pack. We cannot trust other packs without our alpha to protect us. So we are here with the fighter's request. They said as one.

I feel that you may be telling us truth in your words. the feel of fear and horror that came to those that we called mate held memories of the freedom fighters that waited for anyone that needed or wanted to leave the city where the government hunted them. But my husband was too late and he saw many dead. Not one lived to give him direction to the outpost. He will might be lost; I just hope he will survive his fate. Maria said sadly. But how best that you said you had seen him and not spoke to him about what has happen in the outer world as this? Maria again asked in a confusion fashion.

We were uncertain of him until we had almost come upon his drive. The thing had many vision of what a fighters were. We know that no enforcers married hybrids and that many of the fighters in the outer world had taken hybrids as their own mate. This gave us the clue, and then we stumble upon your face and remember you when we were cubs and your Cousin Mike had taken one of our sister as mate for a short time. She had died at childbirth. It was a sad day. But rejoiced in the fact that both hybrid felines and canines has come together for the same reasons, to destroy the government and their controllers. We were but cubs and not ready for mates as we are now. They both said.

Another truth I feel deep sadness. I remember that day and that month of the birth and death. It was a sad day for Mike and his were-brothers and sisters. They too had felt the grief of Michael's lost. My heart wonders if he had ever mated again after that. I know he is on another mission of sorts for the freedom fighters. A mission will turn the tides of who will control the humans and the hybrids in a world of uncertainty.

Mark, Dante are my two sons that are alpha males, Dante holds more power than I never have known of one. Mark is my right hand in all that is hybrid, he much like his father and his grander. Mark has the ability to know of ones moves before his foes can justify his moves. It is unique and very handy when need for any unknown enemies think to attack beforehand. He is the one that warn us before the enforcers came to our home to try to capture us. We are very blessed with these alphas. How did the enforcer not sense either of you? Maria asked them.

A hint of giggles and lips smacking with a roar of both wolves, a spark of amusement in their eyes told them all what they had done or more what they ate.

We came in as humans of women innocents. We had told the first enforcers that we were lost and could not find our way back to our family. We had promised them enjoyment if they help us. So, we let them guide us behind a building and had what call sex, but as the men climax, well we were rather hungry and we had never had humans before. So, we took a bite and killed them with one bite. They tasted foul of evil. Our mouths taint with their blood gagged us. We did take their mobile drive though. That was how we got here. The thing had already been program to come here, we were very fortunate. They said with a smile of pure evil and mischief. Mark like them after that.

We are going to need the mobile to get out of here and back to the outpost Mother. We are not safe here. I can feel danger and not just in the air, but in my mouth and along my back. The enforcers are not too far away. Mark said to them.

Dante had blown them up hadn't he? Carrlynia asked as she came out of the tunnel with the humans behind her.

I had taken out those that were close or inside of the house. But, I didn't get those that were on their way to our homes. Therefore, if Mark sense them coming, then they are the ones that were call before I blow them up to pieces.

So you are telling us that we are still endanger. Where the mobile, I need to get these humans to safety. Carrlynia said as she turned back to push the children and Joan toward the center of the pack. One of the female's name Olaya stood over Jolie as she licked her lips to give her their scent and taste that would help her know when they were endanger or not. She then went over to Joan, her massive body tall and stronger than Joan human body that was brittle and fragile. I need to keep all of you here safe ma' am Olaya said as she spoke openly with her mouth and not her mind. Would you let me kiss your hand at least? She asked again.

Joan just knot yes as she extended her hand toward the large wolf. Joan knew what she was doing, her best friend was a hybrid wolf and sometimes even a cat, a very large cat. They shared many things growing up and the fact that just a lick from one of their kind would give them a scent of them deep in their make that would also give them the ability to find any one lost or killed or even tell them of danger. It was something that kept Joan safe with Maria for so long. Maria charged at the other hybrid. Maria just didn't trust this female. If a hybrid licked a human in any way, then that human could be tracked down to kill like a wolf to a deer. Maria had to stop that female before she claims Joan for her food.

Now we are one and we will get in that thing that we do not know how to control in order to drive. So we will let one of the hybrid of grey house do the driving. Olaya said as she knotted toward Mark and his mother. They both nodded to her.

I can drive the mobile and I know where the outpost is and how to get there –I just hope there is no tracer on that mobile that would bring the enforcers—I mean I don't want any tracers to give the enforcers any knowledge of our whereabouts. Maria said aloud with a sign.

As everyone, notice that the enforcer mobile was on top of another mobile that hood was cave in, the climb was hard on the children, but not on the hybrids that help them up slowly. The mobile (Maria notice) had three different drives or mobile boards. Maria smile at the thought that if something went wrong then her son could take one of them with the children and Joan. It was a good thing, but Maria still wasn't sure if there was a tracer on the mobile or not. Then it hit her as she thought about Mark ability to sense danger before it happens.

Mark can you find any tracer on the enforcer mobile that we need to—Maria couldn't finish her words as she watched Mark slowly walk around in silence. His hand waving for everyone else to be silent too, everyone stood still and silent as Mark steps became silent to each wall and board of the mobile he closed his eyes and let his sense of power out around the mobile in all directions. He felt hearts and lungs beating hard fast as he kept the sense outward. He also felt danger, but not from a tracer that was not in any metal inside of the mobile. He felt something that was more hybrid. Betrayer of some kind, a tracer of the human kind made. But which one had done the deed to let her pack die and others that were not part of them and yet, children, women, those that may have loved her and now are all dead in brutal maze of blood. How could anyone think about doing something like that and why for what reason did those innocents had to die mean? Mark shook his fury head and let his head lower to the floor as another sense rose over his nose and his heart. He smelled heat from one of the wolves that sat next to the wall. His eyes sharp and held tight as he looked up to them slowly with his fang showing over his lips, he felt the pinch of the sharp fangs cut his lower lips.

Something is under this panel near the board's main drive. I can't say what it is, but I feel danger. Mark said as he kept on pawing the panel floor. Then he just changed back to human form and tried to whip out his pocket knife from his torn pants that he still had under his fur body. Dante changed back too human also with some unpleasant words of how his bones hurt when he changed form.

I hate it when I have change back and forth from wolf to human to human to wolf. The bones bending and cracking, lengthening when I have to change is a pain in the freaking ass. Dante round face and blue eyes, his cheekbones higher than his brothers made him seem to have dimples as he smiled at the two female wolves still in their forms. Dante fought his long brown hair back away from his face as he tried to help his brother pull the floor up. The sound of metal scraping upward off the hinges came up loud. Beeps of all kinds with lights going off open up to the young boy's eyes as they watched the marvel of computers that was the main drive of the mobile ability to float. Maria moved the two aside as memories of what a tracer looked like. She knew her two sons would not know. Mark may be able to sense it. However, he would not know how to disable the tracers without letting a sound of distress to signal anyone close by that the tracers had been taken. Mark knew he had to destroy the tracer fast. But how one of the question he need was answered. How can he destroy something inside of a hard drive that was mix with the main motor of the mobile ability to keep up float and driven without making it enable? Carrlynia pushed her brother aside to look at the tracer's exact place. She had knowledge of computers, she also knew how some mobile are operated on a certain hard drive, and the crystals of the moon had powers to keep machines like the mobile cable of operating for a lifetime, (that is as long as the mobiles are not damage). Jolie knew some of icons of the mobiles operative components that were in tangle with the crystals. Mark sat back and let the two young girls work their magic. Mark started to sniff more over on the other side of the panels to search for more tracers hidden underneath the floors main drives. Mark knew that this Mobile was at least three parts of one air unit. That means that three people were able to drive the mobile in different section and the air unit could split in three halves' to be able to search as three units and not one. A good idea for them maybe, but for them it would mean a better set of ways to keep the humans safer if they had to split in three. The idea was good, first thing first, he needed to get these tracers out of the floor before they could do anything.

It didn't take the girls long to find the tracers that were square and part of the main computer, but not connected to the crystal that gave the mobile power to drive, Three small squares like blocks of wires and metal with a tiny red light in each square tracer. Jolie took out two out of the one that Carrlynia took out. Both girls wipe the sweat off their faces as they pulled the tracer out of its confinement.

Mark saw very little sweat coming down their face but let it be. He wanted to sneaker, but held back his laugh as he looked at his mother working the control in a speedy way. The sight of seeing her work, her stern face hard and unthinkable spellbound him with respect and admiration of who she is and why of it. The humans are becoming fewer as more scientist are determine to mix breeds that are not listed in their genealogy of species. That much Mark knew about what was going on. He had watched most of the splitting of genes and DNA's that would create other species he had learned in his classroom that he had watched on the vision con. In all government home's children bedrooms were also their classrooms that came on certain times during days. Mark and his siblings had their own teacher in each room they slept in. Teachers were more like computerize formats that only told what they were program to teach by the government control. Mark knew that he broke in something that only the government knew and not children or anyone that was not part of the government.

Mark had decided that if they really had any enemies it was more the scientist than the government or maybe it was both or the same. Mark told himself that he would not yet tell anyone his theory on the Scientist or the government. He first had to find out for sure if any of them were chasing them, or doing what he thinks they are doing to those who are missing. More answer too many questions and not enough time find answers. Mark knew it would plague him for some time until he found out one way or the other.

CHAPTER TEN

IM FOUND THAT RUNNING had taken more than just his will or his ability to live. It tore in his soul like something evil rip out his lungs as his legs finally gave out. He couldn't walk or run any farther. The forgotten should have been able to sense him by now. What had happened and why couldn't they contact him, they should have been able to contact him by now? No! He would not think about that, even though the sight at the meeting place had children laid dead around bushes. They had to be; no, he would not think that. No! No! He would find the forgotten and get help. He had to. He couldn't remember were the outpost of the freedom fighters was. He was too deep in the forest to even know where he was. He silently cried as he felt the air around him, then Jim looked down at the ground and found traces of blood dry and fur on the grounds around him. The moon's bright light shine down on each of the blood soak ground giving Jim sickness that he did not want to have. His friends, his family, his brother had been married to one of the wolves and promise that he would always be able to help the fighters with the pack behind him. But Jim had not seen his brother in years sense his own marriage to Maria of the house of grey. Slowly Jim walked slowly in area that he thought was near the forgotten packs huts. No sound of birds flying over his head, the winds seem to stand still with no air to breath. Silent of the forest made Jim hair on his arm stand up. Jim felt a sudden dread than anything he had ever felt. The taste of death reached his mouth, then his eyes as heat and bugs that gather around children, men, and women lying on the-ground in puddle of blood dry and wet around them. Jim saw small animals eating flesh off those that were farther away from his sight. Jim thought as he looked at the homes that was once alive with children running back and forth from one home to the next laughter filled those homes and the village. And now the homes and villages all burnt down only flames smothering out its after mass after all died within those piers. Yes, that's what it was, a massacre of innocent people that had nothing to do with the government. Although the government (he was sure) did not think that. Jim knew from years and had watch for years of how the government thinks from working for them and watching his father and grandfather working for them too. Jim knew no one cared within the government if it did not suit them or gave them what they wanted or need. What they wanted was not here, it was something he really didn't know for sure what it was. A rumor around the congress and senate house was that someone had found the proof that our history that was cover up for centuries. History was so miss sharp and deformed that no one knew what was true and what was false. Jim looked around more as tears fell down his cheeks, not knowing that he was even crying, but felt his heart beat fast in his chest like a speeding air in a storm, Jim fell to his knees. The smell of metallic harsh and hard drift in his nose with the pain in his heart he openly cried out loud. He couldn't figure out what he was going to do now, there was no one around now. Where was he going and how was he going to get to the fighter's headquarters? He can't remember where it was or how to get to it. Somehow, he also knew he had to look for his brother's body and bury him and his wife and children. Jim got up with a slip once on a small puddle of mud and blood and got up again with more mud on his hands and face, knees and body. Jim looked down at his clothes and found that there was not much left. His clothes dirty and smell of forest and death. Sweat beat down his face like water flowing down from the sky. Jim wiped the wetness off his face as he continued to look around at the place he had called his second home and his friends. His heart already in turmoil over all that went on the few hours or was it one day and one night. He couldn't decipher which. His confusion and his pain was just too much right now for him to think nothing. Bodies scattered around each part of the village like trash, litter. The smell of burnt flesh mixed with those that were laid in paths of blood and guts, gave Jim reason to let what he had still in his stomach out over around those that were gone. He could not stop or help what he did. Daniel, where are— no no? Jim ran as fast he could when he saw his favorite niece Rebba, she was laying on her back with a long sharp thing though her heart, her golden hair curled around her face with tints of redness sticking her hair together. Her body still, unmoving, it was as if she was asleep. Jim couldn't take his eyes off her without thinking of her laughter, her smile wide with those twinkling grey eyes shining at him with the mischief behind every smile, every twinkle in her eyes. Jim loved her as if she was his daughter. Then he found Daniel, his brother and his sister-in-law close by each other. Dead all of them dead, gone from his heart, from his soul! How can he bury his brother's family and still be able continue? Jim knew he should be thinking about his own, his wife Maria and their three kids or pups. If anything happened to any of them or all four of them —Jim thought nothing but his own death. Life would not be worth going on without his family. Jim took a breath and then coughed hard as Jim smelled thick with death deepen around him. Jim knew he had to find something to dig up the dirt and bury his brother and his family.

Four hours into the shoveling and burying his family, Jim was totally exhausted and ready to find a place safe to rest. But he didn't really want was not to stay in the village, he had to go on farther into the forest to hope to find someone out there that would know about the fighters. Even though his legs and body felt like dead lead. He had to keep on moving. Jim look inside of his brother's home that was nothing but sticks of wood smothered in ashes and smoke. Something kept on nagging him to look inside of the place. But why? Jim found his brother and his sister-in-law room that had a metal box almost sticking out from what was once his brother's bed. Maybe whoever killed these innocent hybrid wolves either had not notice the box or didn't know what it was or maybe they were not looking for the box. But Jim knew what it was that was he hope knew that it was the box that his brother had told him for so many years about. The box had important things that the government would have loved to have, but Jim guess the ones that were sent here didn't know about it. Things that would have gave the enforcer lee way of where the fighters had gone. Jim realized that enforcer would also have the name of those that worked for the government that helped the fighters too. Jim name and that of his friend that had died not long ago were the main body of fighter's contacts within the government. What was it that opened the metal box Jim knew it was made a certain way that no key or combination lock could open the metal. But, the contents were inside safely and only certain persons knew how to open the metal box. Jim knew how to open it up or at least he thought he knew. Jim couldn't see any kind of seams that would indicate any way of getting in, but he knew that his DNA was the same as his brothers Daniel DNA. So if he could just touch it in the right place the box would open up. Jim rubbed his hands(both) over the box slowly, the front of the box lit up red and then blue and again red with yellow beaming over the red light, a swish sound and the metal box open up. The metal box had information of the freedom fighter names and locations, with that information he knew the government would love to have that information. Relief washed over Jim in a small wave of knowing now he could find his way to the fighters without trouble. But then again, Jim thought of the villagers that had died and those at the meeting place of where the fighters were suppose too meet any one that needed them. Only certain people knew about the place and the forgotten packs. So, what if whoever knew about those places here and killed everyone here, what if they had done the same thing at the headquarters too. Jim had to find out and he needed help to sure the safety of the fighters. But how was he going to do that? He was one person with no if any kind of hybrid power. His only thought was he needed to go deep inside of himself to find that one percent of hybrid mix he was and tried to bring it out. Jim knew it was going to hurt as if no other pain had ever hurt before. But he needed to find his one percent of something to help him get to the headquarters before they got attack soon. Jim got up and started to walk away from a nightmare that would haunt him for a very long time. Jim knew that the faces he had seen back in the village, their eyes and the stillness of their body would haunt him for a very long time, or maybe he would never forget what he had seen. A chill seemed to come up his spine as he shivered as the nightmare of the village death took hold of his mind. He had to push the memory back as tried to concentrate on his wolf or was it feline? He could not remember right as he walked deeper in the forest and away from the village. Darkness covered the forest around him as the trees kept any light from coming down on him. Jim eyes had to adjust to any of the darkness that he approached in the forest. Jim heart broke slowly as he kept on thinking about the villages, but then his angrier rose over the nightmare and made his determination to fight those that killed everyone in that village. The government made the mistake of killing those innocents without a doubt many hybrids of all kinds would retaliate against any one or thing that would kill any hybrids without cause. And what had happened back there was no reason to kill innocents. Then again, the government had no guilt, no reasoning or understanding on killing anyone, not even their own.

A sound above Jim head made him stop as he realized that he had gone more than 50 miles from the village on foot, the sound came faster with a splash of wet dropping down from the leaves onto his face and body. The feel of the wet following down on him gave him both a relief from the heat he wore and that of the filth that covered his body.

Jim feet (he knew) had been bleeding from not wearing shoes that would have protecting his feet. But a few days or so his shoes lost its path on his feet. One had been stuck in a muck of mud and the other was lost during a night that was pure hell of heat and bugs biting him as he tried to sleep on the wet grass. Jim knew he had to endure what all had happened to him. Jim tried again to send a message to his wife with his mind. But nothing, the feel of his mind went silence as he tried to call her over and over again. No sound of her voice inside of his head or his heart, Maria please don't be dead too. I don't think I can take another blow. Jim bowed his head as he tried to ask someone that might hear him. Jim never knew how to pray, he wasn't one to believe in someone that he could not hear, or see would or could even be able to help him. But he had no other choice. Another try with his mind, but instead of asking for Maria, Jim sent out one message that was more of a song, but a signal to anyone that was with the freedom fighters.

Uh America uh America God's shines grace on thee from sea to shiny sea. Jim felt bad that he couldn't remember the song right, but he tried for the key words to get some kind of message to the fighters. Sea, a form of water that was unending from above to the bottom that as far as Jim knew had not known what was down there. And yet, Jim thought maybe the government knew. At least Jim knew that there were so many secrets kept from congress and the senate. The only government official knew anything about anything that might be important would have been those that were the ones that worked very close to the leader. Jim took a breath and sent out his song again with his mind.

Hours it seemed to pass as Jim kept on walking, but he started to sing our loud to just hear his voice. The sound of silent and his mind kept on trying to go back to the village and those that had died. Jim couldn't sing a note, but the song was old and the one his mother had sang to him as a little boy.

UH, AMERICA, AMERICA, GOD SHINE HIS GRACE ON THEE AND CROWN THY HOOD WITH BROTHERHOOD FROM SEA TO SHINY SEA. Jim kept on sing until he started to hate that song. Then he felt something—it was like a strange feeling of a tickle that went down his spine, his mind heard something soft. But the sound was familiar, it sounded like a song of some sort? The voice was soft, strong, and held authority. Jim listened as he walked faster toward the sound in his head.

The song went like this: God bless America Land that I love, stand beside her and guide her through night with light above from the mountain to prairie to ocean white with foam god bless America my home sweet home. Stand beside her and guide her to land that I love. The song ended with a giggle.

Jim knew he was getting closer to the headquarters of the fighters, (he hoped) it wasn't too soon he would see it. But that voice sound like someone he knew? Jim let the voice linger longer in his mind as he tried to put the face with the voice. Who was it? Jim just hoped it was one of the freedom fighters. And not someone in the enforcer that was able to receive links from those that can send out their thoughts to one or another, but they knew the song that was one of signals that told anyone that was listening or sending out their respond or signal that they were part of the fighters. Few Jim knew most of the songs and most knew just a few lines. So just listening to the song told Jim something about the singer. They knew more than two lines of the song that was a respond to his song. Yes, that was it, he knew at once he was closer than he thought he was to the headquarters that was in the forest where he was right now standing still, he knew who that singer was and why she was even giggling the song. Jim sent out one word to that mischief sister of his. Annie? Jim waited for her to giggle again.

But she sang another song. *Oh say can you see by my eyes if you can.* Another storm of giggles came to Jim mind. Oh she was Annie alright. She was all mischief and wonder. Jim knew his little sister that really wasn't his real sister, but his parents had taken the girl in when she was just an embryo waiting for someone to claim her. But no one had, so they took her and hide her with the fighter's hybrids. Annie was a hybrid feline with some bird of some kind that was large and built to kill anything in its path. Freedom fighters welcome her birth and her strength. She was still learning how to use her abilities. Jim was proud of her and just listening to sing gave Jim strength to know she was alive and not harm like his brother and his family back at the village.

Annie, can you tell the other fighters that the entrance to the forest had been breach and the village of the forgotten have been destroyed all has perished. Jim sent out his thoughts. Jim smile as he heard Annie sing song voice, it was soft, but held a lot of authority. She must have been training for high command position. She was always the show off and she was always the one to get into trouble and yet, knew how to get out of it fast. She had the ability to command an army of hybrids and humans too.

Jim took a breath and laughed as he thought about his sister the mess, mischievous, aggressive little mouse. And yet, Jim loved her.

Oh say can you see, by my eyes if you can. I need to know where my eyes should see. I sang while I walked faster toward that giggle I knew was my sister. My feet hurt, but I knew I was getting closer to them.

A breeze blew through the trees with a scent of forest mildew musky smell of trees green leaves new and fresh blowing in the breeze. The smell lingered hard in Jim nose as he took in the smell and let it fell up his lungs with the clean air. Jim felt good as he inhaled the air that came in his chest. The sound of his feet touching the grass and moss tickle and itch at the same time. Jim pants torn and almost off his legs made him feel naked and unclean. But he had to get to the headquarters that would both save him or he would be able to save them. Whichever the choice was to be, he just hoped he would make it there.

The sounds of birds screaming out warnings of pending alarm of what could happen to them, either that they were screaming out where to roost safely. Jim noticed to that the rain had pasted and only then, wet drops falling down on his head he could feel. The sky a shade of dark blue with clouds white with tint of gray casting its own shadow down on Jim form walking, Jim whistle a tune that he remembered as a young boy growing up around the government and their young people. His memories seem to laps in time, to a period that brought a smile and laughter to his face.

CHAPTER ELEVEN

IKE KNEW HE WAS in a pack of wolves that were not hybrids for some reason he felt something different from the start of the two that corner him back in the forest and now with the white she wolf, that was more girl right now. Her long legs muscular with light hair casting downward, her arms swaying with muscles that were taunt with firmness that spoke of strength. Her face was the only thing that was thin and feminine, and yet again her face wore the sight of authority and command. Mike step were silent and gentle as he thought of how he need to escape them and try to find that one path that would help the others get out fast. Somehow, Mike knew that his friends would be in trouble, even if they were in some kind of machine that had wheels and was very big too. But Mike could not get that nagging feeling of dread, danger somehow was close by them. Mike knew he had to do something fast.

A clearing came in Mike view as they all stop short in the center. There were trees of different kind in ring like circle around the clearing with bushes that had red and purple flowers on branches with thorns and green leaves. Along the circle path was small like huts made of mud and logs and some of them had stones along each wall of their huts. Small worn out fire pits were set close to each hut. Mike figure the pits had been use to cook meats or some food. Inside the huts there might be one or two rooms, no telling how many children or adults lived inside of the huts. Mike took a breath and clear his throat as he looked straight ahead and saw a tall man with straight long black and blonde hair that touched his back side that touched his ass. His face was round with muscle hard around his mouth his nose straight with a small round nob his eyes blue as the sky, but dark when Mike got closer to him. Mike could smell this alpha scent hard harsh and forest husky all that could spell out more danger than he wanted or need right now. Mike spine tingled down in a way of his cat's hidden need to fight this. Mike was alpha feline and wolf too. But, he hid his scent from any one that might be a hybrid or were-animal. It was just too dangerous for him or anyone around him to know of his higher breed. Mike pulled his chest back and held his head high and just looked at the man standing in front of him. Mike knew the danger of looking at an alpha in the eyes when a there might be a challenge when anyone looked into their eyes. Mike let his mind open up and let the alpha read what he was and who he was. He also let him know that he came in peace, but would fight to keep his friends safe. Mike had not shown any sign of emotion to anyone. Mike kept his face calm, flat face. Mike breath coming hard and fast, but not too fast that his animal part of his body would change. A chuckle came out of the alpha that stood close to face. The alpha breath harsh with stench of fresh meat uncooked, Mike own mouth wanted to water, but he held his needs back and just looked up in the alpha face and eyes. The challenge was there and yet, Mike pulled back a little his scent and let this large alpha male wolf think on who he was first and then maybe he will show him. But, he had to work fast, his friends might be in trouble, he had to think fast and his only thought was to either speak to this alpha or fight him. Either way, he needed information on how to get through a path that was gone or forgotten that would lead them to the freedom fighters.

Both men stood in silence no sound from anyone around them, all stood still as statues or trees.

I can feel your aura and see that it is red with fire and yellow with truth, blue with loyalty. Your pride and your true self I know of. If you challenge me to a fight, I will win. I am alpha omega. You are just a pup or should I say kitten in wolf clothing. (*Chuckle*) the alpha just shook slightly as he laughed at Mike standing in a position in front of him.

Mike knew that this alpha had more power than what he had thought. Something told him somehow this alpha was more. Mike had to slowly back down with his steps and not look at him in the eyes as of yet. He was not ready to challenge him. Mike needed to get information first and then kick ass. I am not here to fight or challenge your stand. sir. I am here in your territory only to find a way out. I am looking for the freedom fighter's headquarters. I apologize if you believe I am here to challenge you in any form. I am not here for that at all. Mike said out-loud, as he heard the alpha spoke to him in the same matter. Mike looked down at the ground, but stood his ground as he took small even breaths to calm his hybrid strength down to a control.

Fear of waiting if the alpha would fight or back down too. Mike hope the latter would be the decision. He didn't want to fight him. Mike didn't want to show him that he was more than alpha omega, he was the top of the line hybrid that had more than just alpha omega. But Mike didn't want to prove this alpha wrong. Mike knew if he would just show submission, maybe this alpha would show or tell him how to get to the right path toward the fighter's headquarters.

Freedom fighters, you are with those scared humans that can only stay hidden. They are scared to look at their own shadows. They cannot fight, that name is not for them. We call them fighters of none. We do know the path out of our territory, but we will not show you. The alpha said, as he sneered at Mike.

Mike could not tell him who he was again it was too dangerous and the fact that this alpha had called his brothers and sister cowards in a sort of way. Mike closed his eyes to calm his rage, his anger that was starting to boil. Mike had to remind himself of his responsibility. His breath coming slow, hard as his breath came through his nose steadily as Mike worked on calming his change. Mike knew he had to have control. Slowly Mike looked up at the alpha with reluctances to meet his eyes. Mike knew he didn't want to fight the alpha, but he may not have a choice. Mike shift to the right slowly and let his left leg stand firm in place as his right leg went stiff. Then slowly he let his shoulder crouch forward a little. He stood ready, but act as if he didn't know how to fight. The alpha laughed at Mike stance as he watched him stand in an odd way.

We will fight and see how you fair, I shall not kill you yet, but let you suffer cat and remember that this is the pack lone-wolves and not your feline nest. Then maybe I will spare your suffering and —kill you. The alpha laughed again. His head bent back as his stomach jingled as he laughed hard.

But Mike change within seconds as he launched upward with his change of bones shaping hard and faster as Mike decide on what animal he would become. Mike could not stop his change as he landed hard on the alpha omega. Mike skin stretched as bones lengthen and strengthen as he changed with less of a second of knowing what he decided to change too. Mike claws on each fingers rose out sharp deadly as he reached out to strike the Alpha leader down. The face of the omega gave off shock and surprise as he landed on his back still in human form. Blood gust out of the alpha throat and as Mike tasted the wolf blood, his skin grew long silky black fur that shine like blue in the sun rays, his form of cat was the jaguar. Mike was larger than normal Jaguars. Mike fangs drip with blood as he looked around him with a sneer and one loud growl. Mike watched every hybrid changed into their wolf form and growl back at him with sneer and howls. The white wolf step forward with a sneer and one loud howl, then she kneeled at Mike feet. Mike change back into human form panted hard, blood still drip off his mouth and teeth a shake of his head, then he wiped the blood off his mouth with the back of his hands and arms.

Who are you that you can be so large, I know what a jaguar is and how large it is? But your jaguar is larger than any cat I have ever seen. You have defeated our leader who was both Alpha and omega. He was bigger than any wolf! But not as big as you were! But he was strong than any of us. You are feline, we cannot take you as our leader and yet she watched Mike change again into a large coyote with dark blond fur that stood up, then he changed again into a larger black wolf with streaks of blond and black fur standing high over his back. Then Mike changed into a tiger, leopard, lion etc. Mike let all see who he really is and hope they would cooperate. Mike needed information and get Steve and the others out of where they were. Danger was too close to them and he need to work fast.

I am Alpha of old, I am King of all hybrids that were ever created.

I am Michael of the freedom fighter's heroic tribes, heroic pack of both wolf and cats of all kinds, unwanted, thought of them as un-needed. I have made them warriors to save those that are endanger from the government that rules the humans and takes children as slaves or as scientist used them for things that would kill them, but used to control all humans and hybrids. Freedom fighters have been working to find cures and find ways to topple the government and that of the leader who has been in control for more than twenty centuries. If you or any of your pack knows of a place that the fighter's has taken as a base, I need to know now. I do not know this place of paths that could take me there. But, I need to know now. I fear that my sense had told me of danger that perhaps come here soon. I cannot delay or many of you will die here, that of my friends also may be in danger as we speak now. So, I am asking you now again to tell me where the path lays so I can save all of you. Mike said as he watched the pack turn back into human form. The white wolf stood up on her hind legs and changed back to her woman form. She was still beauty and was as elegant as she was when she captured Mike back in the forest.

We will help you only if you can convince the pack of cats that keeps on attacking our pups and killing off our preys. She asked him.

Mike thought about that and the fact that he was the supreme king of all hybrids. He would have to challenge the alpha cat or the omega cat to make a point of who he is. I try to speak to them first. Mike said as looked back in the forest and hope he could do all this without the enforcers closing in on them all before he could get back.

Mike stroll out of the village and into the forest as the jaguar. Something told him that the cats were closer to the village than he thought Mike didn't have to go too far in the forest as he found a pond or something that looked like a pond. The sand around it was hard with stone pebble like floors. Mike shook his paws as some of the pebbles embed in his claws. The Mike looked down at the water that smell of mold and old water that stood to long. Bushes over grown around the ponds round form made it look like a circle or something? Mike couldn't image what it was at one time or another. The forest deep rich dark with secrets that no one but the forest knows and yet, Mike took a breath as he panted hard then looked back to where the wolf pack village stood farther away from this strange pond that was a circle with square blocks of stones that made its mark. The pack was too far from where he had walked from. A howl sound in the silence of the trees would make any human shake with fear, but it told Mike only that one of the packs scouts was watching him, he would be careful not to do or move back toward that village until he had things right with the pack of felines. Mike need to drink, but the smell of the water and told mike that the pond was poison. He growled loud and let his headrest, something told him to wait here. A feeling of eyes watching him and not the scout, but something other than those wolves. Mike lay silent still and let whoever come to him, it was the safe way. Mike knew to that only the strongest cat would try to fight him and let him try. Maybe if he just played stupid again, but then twice would be just luck, Mike had to do something fast, the feel of something big coming toward him with silent paws or feet, then it stopped right near Mike head. Slowly Mike looked up lazily at the new intruder. Mike yawn and then lick his lips as he watched his visitor watching him slowly get up. Their eyes meeting as Mike look straight at what he was looking at. A smile came across Mike as recognize who he was looking at.

Oi mate. I didn't think me seeing ye here. Are ye the one that is causing all this trouble with the pack of wolves back there? Mike said as he changed back to human and watch the other cat change too.

What are ye doin here in these woods. Ye were to work with the fighters as their general or something of that sort. Cousin we dona want to fight ye. Ye bein the king and all, we ken that ye would just look at us and we be wetin in our pants. So speak ye words now and be gone with ye now. The tall long blond man said that look a little like Mike.

Look mate, I do na want to fight ye either. But the wolves say that ye been hunting on their territory? And that many of their prey's had been disappearing with ye packs. I am only trien to find a path to the fighters and ken that the wolves may ken of it. So if you be willn to give me reason to nae fight ye for the territory I would be much oblige if ye would commit on it. Mike asked his cousin. Mike cousin had long blonde hair like him with blue eyes and wide smile that was straight white pointy teeth or fangs if you look at him the right way. Mike knew that his cousin nose was still broken from their ruff play at their great Uncle house. Now Michael, I dona know about ye speakin to those lads and lasses aboot me pack of cats and bein on their hunting grounds. We hunt were we feel the need to hunt our prey. We need to feed our kittens too. If they have a problem with us, then they can come and stop us. Mike cousin said as he looked straight in Mike eyes.

Ye ken who I am and I heard the trouble of all that is happen here. They too have pups that need to feed. So, I say this we go to the village with your council of elders and I will sit in the council to help with any decision ye make with the pack of wolves. Both of ye packs need to work together. We cannae need to fight over area's that may be taken soon by the enforcer soon, I cannae deny me sense that they are close and I need to get some folks that are verr import to the freedom fighters. They may have a solution to our troubles, but first I need to solve this first before I get them out of here. So are ye goin to help me or nae. Mike asked his cousin. Mike cousin name was Willie and he did not like to argue with Mike on anything. But his mind was always on his mate and his kittens that waited for him back in his village. Alright, if ye have a solution then we will obey by ye laws of ye rules. Willie walked slowly back in the forest then looked at Mike again. I can tell ye that we donae want to be in the wolf pack village, but if ye are willing to bring them here in the round pond that separate's our village and territory then I think me elders will agree to meet with the packs leader. Will said as he continued to walk away.

Agree, I will speak to the wolves' elders and bring them here, but I will over watch ye words and movements. Donae think that the enforcers or any of the government men would nae want ye to fight to the death for them. They will do something to make the other think they were the ones to start a fight and donae think that either one will survive. All of ye packs will die by their hands. I ken of this more than ye think. It would be something I would do if I were them, so listen to me aboot this. Mike said.

Mike went back to the wolf village and hope that he could convince the elders to come to the pond for the meeting with the feline's elders. A councils of odds will either put them at war and is what the government would want. Mike had to think again about other packs in other parts of the world. They might just be either, at war or one of them might understand that it was more than one or the other that started the territory war. It may figure out it was the government somehow had started the war with one of their moles. But then it may be too late. Mike will try at least see what he could do for these two packs and maybe they could help him. Mike had to try. Maybe there would be way to connect to other packs that no one but freedom fighters and those that are loyal to them. Damn it all, fuck shit. Mike kept on thinking of a way somehow to contact the fighters. But how without giving off his location to one of the enforcers that might be listening waiting for one thought sent out to someone? Mike could not chance any of his thoughts out right now. Mike let out huff of air that he had not unknown he had held it. The walk back to the village was no more than a few 50 miles or less to where he had left his cousin.

The white wolf moved slowly as if she was walking on air thin and graceful like his cat. She was beauty and deadly more so than the alpha wolf he had killed. Mike knew too that leader he killed was no Omega, but just a big ass wolf with attitude, now, this wolf, this female wolf was more than just wolf, she was omega with one big ass hint of evil behind her silent eyes. Mike knew he had to be careful if he wanted any of the elders here in the council to listen to him.

Have you spoken with the pack of cats? What did they say when you approach them about them hunting in our territory? She asked Mike as she circle Mike slowly with her hands resting on his shoulder.

Don't get to close little one. I might bite. Mike said with a smile that showed off his fangs. He didn't want to let them forget who he was. She walked away from him silently. I will assemble the council of elder at once if that is what you want. She said with a husky voice that spoke of sex and other things. Mike just smile with a small chuckle and a shake of his head he thought of how she looked. Her walk slowly and smooth as her hips swayed back and forth with her long white hair dancing along her back as she walked toward one of the huts in the distance. Mike whistles a tune as he watched her move.

Yeah, she was one bitch he would not kick out of his den. Mike walked toward the hut that the white wolf went in. Inside of the hut was dark and smell of animal musk with a hint of mold. Mike seen four men sitting down in a small like circle, they all had gray hair that was once dark and straight. Their clothes were like others that were in the pack, loose animal skin leggings with a parcel shirt that was open in the front. Their eyes were dark as their hair had once been with wise and understanding of knowledge that might have been forgotten. Now Mike knew that the elders had known about him without him even telling them, they would also know that he had killed their leader before he even came in the hut.

I am Michael of freedom fighter's warrior and I am the supreme king of the hybrids. I came here in peace and without cause to start any war. I wish only to find the right path that would lead me and those that I am vow to protect. I have spoken to the leader of the cats. He is speaking to his council; he is willing to bring them in a neutral ground to speak of the hunting ground. I will listen to cause and reason before any one takes any action to defend their clan or pack. Fear not of any harm to anyone that comes to the meeting. But be aware that I believe that both packs are being watched. You need to keep your strongest warriors close by the village and be ready for any interferes from anyone that is not with either pack. Have you agreed to find solution to this problem? Mike asked them.

Every one of the elders just looked at him with silent faces that showed no sign of any emotion. Faces blank and unmoving stared at nothing, they only breathed hard and fast. Their minds mingled together as they spoke in silent to each other. Mike heard them although some had spoken of how the cats stole some of their pups and found them dead a few days later. Mike thought about that then thought again with another question.

Were you sure that it was the cats, did the pups have cat fur on them or had their eyes been scratched out or how did you know it was the cats? What was the hint that said it was the cats had killed the pups? And why would they want to kill pups and not adults, why not attack the village instead of killing children? All of these scenarios are good question and I believe that the cats had nothing to do with your pup's death.

Let us ask the same question to the cats and see who is right and who is wrong. Give them and all of your clan a chance to find out who is on your territory. Mike asked the elders again.

Silent among the elders as one stood up and looked back at the others still sitting down on the ground.

I shall go and speak with the felines and see if they are lying or telling the truth. I do not remember our pup's death by any scratches that would show that it was a cat, but their necks were slice that I do remember, one of the pups was my greatest granddaughter. My heart is still broken from her death. I shall see if they were the ones that killed her. One of the elders that had long dark black hair with streaks of silver pulled back in a ponytail. His face square with a stern look of no emotion. But his dark eyes sunk deeply in his face with his nose that looked broke, but long with a small nob at the end showed Mike his true feelings of understanding and deep sorrow for a lose that grew deep in the man heart. Mike took a gulp of air and stood up next to the elder. The man turned to look at Mike.

I am called Moon wolf. We know who you are and why you had killed our alpha, he was not a good alpha. We think he may have something to do with the cats and our young pups. However, we do nay have proof of his doings. But I will show no decision on any matter until I have the proof. Moon wolf said. His voice deep and rich with wisdom and knowledge that Mike didn't realize this man had.

I shall also go with you Moon wolf. Another elder said. He had long white braid hair pull back in a ponytail. His face lean with fur growth around eyes that only show part of his skin, but more white fur of his wolf, his arms visible with the same white fur growing now faster than Mike seen before.

My name is Graymore. He said as he stood next to Mike. Then next two got up and agreed with both Graymore and Moon wolf. Mike smile as he knew he was on the right track.

Mike and the elders got to the pond with five large warriors from the packs hybrid wolves.

The cats were sitting on rocks and large square stones that moss and some grass grew along the path of stone and rock. Some of the cats had even sat on tree branch. The elders of the cats had long blonde hair that was wild and gather around their face's as it was a hat or halo. Their eyes slit like a cats with yellow or green tint. They were lean with muscles that covered their arms and chest with legs stiff with thick muscles that held them up. Mike knew that many of those elders were also alphas that were once leaders of their packs. Four packs of cats from regions of the forest had stood close by. Mike knew that those packs were part of the pack his cousin lead. Each pack of cats was only a small part of his cousin province and their leaders obey his cousin words that was and is law. Mike took in the sight of all the cats in different sizes of their cat's forms and strength. Mike counted twenty cats to nine hybrid wolves that came with Mike to the pond. Mike knew his cousin was fair in some lot things even though he took more cats with him compared to the small group of wolves that came with Mike. Something was not right and he would get to it fast.

CHAPTER TWELVE

ARIA-JANE WAS NERVOUS AND scared as she watched her children take out two tracers from the mobile that they had stolen from the enforcers. Her heart beat fast as her two oldest children took the tracers outside and placed them inside one of the other mobiles. Joan started one of the computers as she over roads its banks that only worked with the enforcers. Joan knew how to work the computers drives that were only used by the enforcer's special codes. The feel of the mobile rising higher over buildings; and going toward the north of the city, and forest that grew all around the city like a plague. The two large female wolves still in form, but talking to us with their minds gave me uneasiness of how they found us so fast. Something about them was giving off something I just could not shake the feelings. Mark had taken to one of the wolves like a fly to honey. It was dangerous that Mark had these feelings that may be false. Maria had to listen to her instinct that told her to watch those two wolves. They had not changed back in to human form and just sitting back against the walls. Something was wrong and Maria could not pin point the reason and the why of it? But it— then for some reason the thought just came to her. They were new to their hybrid skin and could not adjust to their human skin nor their wolf skin either. Confusion was common among the young and these young wolves were new to their skin of maybe two years or less. The mix blood and genes of the wolf and human sometimes fight for domination. In some cases, many young wolves or any kind of hybrid mix died. That was why children were considered treasure among the freedom fighters and hybrids in general. Maria took a breath and it out without even realizing that she had even held back. She was still nervous and unsure of them. Until they do something soon, Maria was just going to watch them very careful. Mark walked over to one of the panels that no one was using and placed his hands that were still in a claw like form. He was just as nervous as she was, that made things more terrible.

Whatever Mark was nervous about something it was not good. She knew her sons both of them very well. She also knew he was at an age that he could smell when it was time for a female wolf to go in heat for the first time before the full moon rose. The way Mark was acting, he had sense one of the young wolves had gone into heat and that just makes things more dangerous for all of them. Mark in a lot of ways he was still a child, but he also was going into adulthood by human standards, for hybrids he was already a man to be mated by now. Maria didn't like the thought of Mark tearing his brother apart just to prove himself worthy to mate with one of the wolves. Maria went to her son Mark and laid a hand on his shoulder carefully. One move would trigger his heated need to fight for the female. Mark I know that you might be fight an urge to fight or to even mate with one of those young wolves. I can tell that you are doing fine with the feel of mating scent. It is strong but we are family and those that are not we must resent what is around them or what they are sending you may be false scent. That is one scent I know about, sometimes are body can produce a scent that will confuse a male for one reason or another, it is call a false heat. Very confusing I know, but you need to fight it and remind yourself that we are family and family right now is more important than those that we do not know. Do you understand what I am telling you? I asked Mark. He looked at me then his hand changed back to human hand, his claws had disappeared with his nodded of his head. Maria watched his eyes turn back to human as he nodded again to her. Yes, he was fighting the smell and the feeling to mate with one of the females. But we as one are family that as that one is a pack that would endure all that is not welcome to us.

The feel of the mobile moving smooth and gentle across the air around them felt good, the mobile hummed softly and Maria had watched Jolie fall asleep in Joan arms as Carrlynia took over the other controls of the middle mobile. Mark and Carrlynia, and Maria were controlling the mobile. Jolie had sat in Joan arms, her mothers, Jolie thoughts travel down it seem to the hybrids that were still in their animal form. Yeah, she might be four years old in human age and should not be so intelligent, but her mother had said that all fetus that are created in tubes before they are put in the woman womb, they are tested for any damages to any of the brain or body that would enable the child's progress. Government scientist and healthcare physician have been able to keep healthy and intelligent child with higher ability with their brains that could do things that no one else could. Jolie knew she was reading at five months and walking at two months with words that would have shock more people. Jolie thought again about her brain power and how she could decipher if those Hybrids were true or foe. Jolie decide to use her brainpower that she trained to use with care. Jolie had only used that power once and it was only to find out about her father's work. Now she need it to find out about those hybrids sitting with their mouths open and tongue sticking out panting. She slowly lean back in her mother arms to rest her head and closed her eyes. A humming sound came in her mind as she let her mind, her brainwork over the hybrids body and their genes. Somehow, Jolie wasn't certain, but she didn't think they were fully hybrids or even friend. They seem more foe. Again Jolie thought about the hybrids, their abilities to do things, like change back to human and then again to some sort of animal. However, the one thing about hybrids is their ability to sense danger and mind link. Those things are rare with normal humans, but hybrids it was normal and all of them could it. It was simple to them and normal. Jolie took a breath and let it out as she studied hard over the both of the hybrids sitting still looking at Mark and Maria. A small smile came over Jolie as she felt a tingle of something that was a little more than she wanted to feel. Jolie felt a surge of heat that told her that both hybrids were in heat and they wanted Mark and Dante. That was just sick as she felt the need grow with musk and mold like smell from them. Jolie also felt something else, something not right, Jolie really couldn't say what it was or felt like, but it felt wrong, evil. A feeling she just couldn't describe right. Jolie shivered and let the feel of that evil go deep inside of her to let her know which one it was coming from or why. The feel gave a bitter taste of hard harsh rotted eggs. Jolie shook her as if she had something on her hair. She needed to tell Maria or Mark or one of them about the two female hybrids sitting still in their animal form. Jolie knew she couldn't send any thoughts to them without giving the female hybrids hearing her. She needed another way of telling them. Jolie looked around, then, she thought about that doll that Maria had given her.

It was pretty and felt good in her arms. Jolie knew that no she knew of had a doll before. A rare thing that held her heart and now it was gone. But she still could use that it had to work. Jolie started to cry like a child her age. Maria and Joan startled and surprise at the sound that Jolie was making, she never cried or screamed out about something. What was she saying? Joan move up from her lying position and sat up with Jolie still in her arms. Shsh sweet heart, what is it. Mommy is here, you can tell me what is wrong. Joan asked her. Jolie looked up to her mother and tears stream down her face.

I-I-I wwwant my baby doll. I wawant my babbby doll. Jolie cried out with a squeal that made her voice high.

What doll are you asking about? Joan asked her calmly as she thought about the fact that her daughter never played with toys. Toys were rare and unusual. So why was she crying about a doll. Wait a minute another thought came back to her. Maria had given her a doll not too long ago and Jolie had been holding that doll everyday with care and with something in her pretty eyes that said something that Joan knew she had not seen before. But they didn't bring the doll with them. Jolie had been watching another class of government control of science or math – she wasn't sure which. But that doll had been lying on the sitting area away from her.

Maria thought about that doll she had gave to Jolie and where the doll been when they left the house. The sitting room came back to her memory. Why did she want with that doll of all of a sudden? Maria let Mark take full control over the airmobile while she went to Jolie and Joan. Maria spread her arms out and let Jolie inside of her embrace, Maria smooth the child gently as she rocked her too.

Shsh. Sweetheart. Maria said. Then she heard a voice softer than any voice she ever heard, it was small like a child-like Jolie sweet sound. But the voice was in her mind, a mind link that no human can make, Maria had thought so, but then again, there were those human that could, very few, but still. Can Jolie link her mind with hers? Maria listen carefully as the sound was soft and silent.

Maria, the one hybrid on the left is not a good one. She is evil and has plans to kill us for the enforcers. I read her memories from the story she told us and not all of it is true. The one on the right is in heat and wants Mark, but wants to kill Dante and Carrlynia too. She is not all bad, but I don't know I think she is confused about her friend. I hope they can't read me. I am trying to block them from my thoughts I am sending you. Jolie said as she sniffles and cried a little with he-cups.

Maria took a breath and then with whispers of words she sent her thoughts back at Jolie.

Sweetheart how –no how do you know which one is evil and how can you read their past memories? How —? You got me to confused?

I taught my mind to bend at my brain and worked to be able send my thoughts and I can do more than just that. I can feel if someone is lying or there is something not right. I am working on other parts of my brain to make things move without touching it. I found out that if I let myself just concentrate on things or just well, it's hard to explain. I just know I can do many things with that one point in my brain that has not been use and use it to my best ways I can. Do you understand what I am saying? I cannot explain it any other way. But I need my doll. So let us just say I need my baby doll and not say any more to that. Jolie said to Maria in her mind link. Maria smiled as she rocked Jolie back and forth, as she too blocked her thoughts out to the other hybrids still in their animal form.

What is wrong with the human girl? Why is she in need of something called a doll? What is a doll? Said Olaya to them all. She could not hear what was being said to Maria in her thoughts so she had presumed that Maria was not speaking to her children and was to concern with the human girl to speak to them. Strange and yet, maybe she was concern with this doll or whatever it was upsetting the human girl.

Can I help the child with this doll? Olaya asked them.

No we left the doll back at the house and now the house that the enforcer had taken is gone with everything else that was ours. Mark said to them.

Girls, why don't you just turn back to human form and we could see what you look like in human form. We won't bite you we promise. Dante said with a smile and chuckle at them.

We do not have clothing to hide our bodies from human sights. We stay hybrid until we can find clothing. Oryeia said with a stern command that told them that she was in control, she was the lead of the two females. Mark had to stand back in his mind. Something told him that she was more dangerous than the enforcers they were running away.

Maria looked at her son Mark and saw the words that were unspoken by mouth out loud or with any kind of link. It was more their eyes that told both of them what was not said. Jolie had the gift that all humans had, but never had tried to use any of the gift that was inside of them. Maria was not surprise to find that Jolie had the gift, she was more intelligent than any of the other human children she had known. She was also wise for her age. Everything about Jolie was never a surprise.

Maria nodded her head to her son and asked him if he remember where they had put the doll.

I think I remember Mark putting the doll inside one of his hidden pockets of his backpack. Maria said out-loud. Mark, can you please check that backpack and see if you can find Mimi? I think we put that doll inside your backpack? Maria asked him with a wink.

Mark couldn't or didn't understand what she was talking about? He did have his backpack, but so did Dante and his sister. It was a habit that his mother had been certain they kept. Inside although had only cloths and shoes. Mark had not put any doll inside or did Dante put the doll in his backpack. Dante was good at putting things inside of his backpack that was not his or had taken out something that was. A joke that was not very funny. Mark had found his dad shoes in his backpack one time and another time Dante put his sister private things in his back pack. Mark didn't want to laugh but that was kind of funny. Mark shook his head and smile inside of his face.

The doll had long shaggy blonde hair and painted face that look really bad. Mark couldn't remember what color the eyes were, or did it have eyes? Mark open the pack that was close to the far wall and felt a block and then a small sound that was soft and smooth. It sounded like Jolie, but Jolie was a human child and had no animal genes that would make her a hybrid and yet, that voice was hers. The voice was coming in his head like a mind link, but she couldn't do that. She was human and human cannot mind link like hybrids or could she? Mark thought.

Mark the one that calls herself Oryeia is a traitor to her own kind. And the other one I think is in heat, but then something off about it. I don't think it is real although—I can't really explain it, it just feels wrong, not right. Jolie voice was smooth like whisper soft and quiet.

Mark sniff the air as if he was going to sneeze, but didn't. He smelled the scent that coming from one of the hybrids and knew that she was right. The scent of heat, of sex that was need by one of the hybrids females, but the scent was not real it had a hard musk that was not all heating scent. Mark shook his head clear as some how he felt another voice come in his head.

Mark what is wrong, have you found this doll thing that the little human girl is asking? Oryeia asked with a hint of curiosity and confusion.

A doll is something that a human child feels good holding when they are afraid. Jolie is her name and she is very afraid, she had just lost her father not too long ago. So yes, she is in need of that doll right now. So I think maybe we had put the doll in my back pack. So let me find it please. Mark told her with an uneasy feeling of betray and need to rip these women apart with his claws. Mark push all those thoughts and feelings back as far as he could in his mind. Mark didn't want them to know his suspect of them, at least not yet. Then he found something that felt like an arm and then a head with something wiry like. The damn doll was inside of his backpack, who the fuck put the shit thing in his back pack. No it was not someone, but his brother. Mark took a breath and let it out in one huff of air. His nose flared with the scent of one of the females that was in that fake heat. His body responded by getting hard and stiff. But he had to push that feeling back and battle the scent that was going to drive him mad with need to mate with the one hybrid wolf. But then again maybe that was it, maybe mating with that one female might be a question to the one answer that's if everyone has the same question as he has. It was a chance he needed to take. The doll was like a rag to him, not a real baby.

But Jolie seem to think that the doll was real. Mark could not deny the child that. Mark turn and looked down at the child that held out her arms to the doll he handed to her. Jolie eyes drip with sadness and then her eyes became happy with her arms and hands stretch out toward the doll that Mark had. Her tears slowed down as she wiped her face and tears away with a sniff and a smile.

Is that a doll? What does it do? I have never seen one before? The human child has stopped crying. Oryeia said as confusion and puzzlement came over her tone. Oryeia was astounded by how the child had stopped crying so fast. It seemed to her that the child was comforted by the strange thing that looked human, it was too small and had hair that was to shaggy to be even be human, it was smaller too than human. She wanted to touch the strange thing that looks so much like a human child, but smaller. Oryeia looked at Mark with stun confusion in her eyes.

Mark looked at her and knew the confusion in her eyes was real. She never seen a doll before or knew what it was for and why it was important to Jolie. So he just let it go with a smile and a hint to Jolie in a quiet way. The doll was more than just comfort to Jolie. Jolie knew something that had to with her ability to send her thoughts to him and maybe to his mother it seemed and something about the doll too. Mark walked back to the airmobile panels and started to put the thing on stall and let the thing just float in the air. Now he was more than upset and confused, need answers before he continued to find this freedom headquarters.

Oryeia looked at Jolie with interest and curiosity as she started to change her form from wolf to human. Oryeia body shivered with a blur and started to form long blonde hair that floated down her back and around her shoulder hiding her naked chest. Her eyes as dark brown as mud with lips small, but wide with dimples on each end of her cheeks, her eye lashes long white with thick white brows that rose up as she tried to reach up to touch the doll in Jolie hands. Jolie sniff then back away from Oryeia. Something about that move gave Mark a hint of who was the traitor and maybe was also sending out the false mating scent. Mark took another breath and let it out slowly with one huff of air, he went to Oryeia, and then kneel by Jolie. His look in his eyes was more of angrier and of control; he had to take in himself. Mark legs bent under his rear as he swung his arms down beside him as he thought of Jolie and Oryeia curiosity of the doll. Mark reached out toward Jolie and the doll. Jolie slowly gave Mark the doll with some hesitation and fear that was evident in her eyes as she looked up at Oryeia and that of the other wolf that was half-human form and that of its hybrid state.

Mark felt the tingle of the small soft voice that sound like Jolie in whispers that made his skin craw with fear of how powerful can this child be. Mark rub his hair and pulled his hair back away from his face as he rose to meet Oryeia and that of the hybrid still in mid form. This—this is called a doll and as you can see it kind of helped Jolie with her fear and her anxiety, its comfort, calms her down, gives –her calmness that no one can at times. Go ahead, you can touch the doll, it wouldn't hurt you I promise. Mark said as he handed the doll to her. Oryeia sniff the doll hair and body as she turned the doll repeatedly in her hands.

This feels strange, it has glass eyes, it cannot see can it? Oryeia asked both Mark and Jolie.

It is not real, it is something that is only for a little girl to use and play with as she pretends that the doll is real. It comforts many little girls. Mark said as he sniffed her scent close to his. He wanted to identify what she was thinking or what she was up too. Mark tried to get in her mind deeper than he should. But it was important to try to find out who she was working for.

With one breath Mark let it out it slowly and closed his eyes as if he was letting the smell of her scent (more over her mating scent) inside of him. His eyes tense with want, but knew he had to keep the deceptive of how he truly felt. Mark smack his dry lips and gave a snare with a low growl. Oryeia look surprise and a little shock as she heard Mark growl, Mark eyes stared straight toward her as she held the doll slowly in her hands. The feel was odd and not natural, something for humans not hybrids. Oryeia thought. Then the sight of Mark eyes just penetrating her own, a feeling of need of want with no feelings of love or anything she had ever thought was important to her and yet the feel of need to mate with him. Well the feelings were strong and maddening. Oryeia took a gulp of air, slowly gave the girl the doll back without moving her eyes away from Mark. The scent from her rose higher and stronger as her heart beat fast in her chest.

Mark had distracted and hoped his mother had enough hint that would get her inside Oryeia mind and maybe they could even invade her friend too. They need the information on who they were working for before they truly leave the city and the enforcers. Mark put his mind to work fast as he walked slowly toward, Dante just watched him with a smile that spread with his own growl. Mark nodded no to him as he looked up at his little brother that was old enough as a hybrid and not old enough as a human. He did not want to fight him. Dante stood back and let his big brother take the female first.

He had never mated before, but that smell that was coming from her was making him crazy. He was both hybrid and human with the need to mate and yet, he didn't know one thing about doing it. Was it like having sex with a girl? Dante took a breath then let it out though his nose. He had never had sex with a human girl or mate with another hybrid wolf. But he had imagined what it might be. He guessed his brother must have mated many times or at least had sex with human girls. He is of course a lot older than he was. Maybe Mark would tell him about the mating thing? Dante knew that his father had a hard time even talking about girls to him so he just said you will learn as you get older. That was one thing his father thought would happen, but they had no girls around (except for his sister and she did not count) to even meeting or knowing a girl. Now just seeing this strange female with that scent that was making want things he didn't understand crazy.

Right now he needed to keep track on the stupid airmobile. So far he hadn't seen or heard or even felt the fucking enforcers. But that didn't mean a damn thing. Dante knew that the enforcer had the invisible abilities implanted in them. A device that had been old, but still worked. Dante figured out how to over shadow their invisible cloak. Sense he is a hybrid and darkness is more of a friend than most days, he is able to see better in the dark. His eyes turn a reddish color that blends or bends light to his brains and turns darkness in a hazy like light, but he could see enough if not better in the dark. Right now his only concern was something was up and neither his mother nor his brother gave him any kind of hint why or maybe they have and he had not even noticed. Yeah that was it! His mother sent that one message to him about something he could not understand. Dante shook his head to clear anything that could make it more confusing. Then he let his mind just drift outward and something he heard or felt. It was soft like a child voice at first Dante thought it was his sister, but she was not even paying attention to anything around them. Hmm, didn't smell that strange smell coming from that hybrid bitch. Maybe not, she couldn't smell that mating smell, only male hybrid can smell. Dante listen again at the voice, and then he heard his mother voice softly whispering to him to back off away from Mark. She said she would explain things to him later. Dante nodded his head toward her and let the dog lay. He would ask question when the time is right. Dante pulled his attention back to the airmobile and the sight of all those buildings on each side of the cars movement. The building looked as it was dark outside in still. The sky had some light, but the buildings had hidden the sun from shining down on them. Dante could see some of the buildings tall and gray against the hidden sun rays. It looked more like darkness than early in the day. Dante had to swivel the airmobile around buildings that at one time housed many families on different levels of floors. Windows broken, shattered, and weather and years of small animals living now inside of the buildings homes, then there were homes that were built for the families that worked for the leader. Their homes were like his home, large with wide windows that worked to catch the rays of the sun for light during the night time, room's solid with large walls that had device that brought up pictures that change with human ages. It was like some pictures that came up at their home. Pictures that showed how Dante and family had grown from new born to childhood to now, the picture changed with each year that they had lived there. How did the pictures appear like magic on the walls was one mystery that Dante never really wanted or need (that is he felt he did need to know was important)?

Dante smile at himself as some memory stole his thoughts, Mark and his first changing into the hybrid wolf and again to human. A chuckle came out of Dante chest as his thoughts came out of how Mark became stuck between human legs and wolf face and arms. The sight of the hybrid was one of laughter and tears as Mark scream out that Dante would be next to learn to change. And that was true, but Dante was a better at changing and that made Mark mad. Dante smile as he watched the gray building rise like rocks on a mountain come closer to his vision. Airmobile made a silent swishing sound as he made sharp turns around each building he came upon.

The sun brightness made Dante eyes burn as he winched his eyes. He let the computer control the airmobile as he keyed in the direct path that he knew was at least close to where the freedom fighters would be waiting for them.

The sun was high over the buildings that started to look like small brick walls of sea with a blend of forest that broke between communities and roads that were once flat smooth paths. Dante could see many things, but hoped he could motivate any one that followed them out in the open. Any one of them that held the invisibility device that had been implanted in each enforcer within their induction might be just watching them. Dante studied the area with more intense, the sun blocked his hybrid eyes from seeing them. Darkness was his only hope that would let him be able to see any enforcer that held the invisibility device. Dante let his sense float around the outside of the airmobile. He trusted his sense more during the day than any other sense he had or has.

CHAPTER THIRTEEN

I CAN'T BELIEVE IT I think I finally got to the headquarters. But for what price, my best friend killed himself with the enforcers trying to arrest him, or were they going to kill him. All he knew was that when he sent out his message to his wife Maria and the kids to keep Joan and her daughter safe. Even thou the message he got from his mind link with his wife startle him as she seemed to scream out danger run. Those words made him pause in his step. Danger something stirred in his bones, a feeling that just came over him as he looked straight ahead. The scene was more forest with fallen bricks all around, forgotten poles rusted and half off its points. Things just didn't look right to him as he kept on looking at nothing, but thought about his brother and his brother's clan that had been ambush, everyone had died, men, women and children, old and new born, every single one of them dead. Then — this voice that sound like his— sister, she knew the code the one that told him that she was a freedom fighter. No one he knew had known knowledge of those words to a song that was a pledge, and part of the fighter's code. And he still got some kind of feelings, hesitation of sorts deep in his bone, but he could not figure out what was causing it. Another thought came to him as he stopped in his track, he knew that he had to send another signal that would tell her something different. Something that would only be known between him and his wife, a song. Something that was familiar and yet, not so, a signal of some sort, surely she would know the song for its true meaning.

Better not shout, better not pout, and better be good for goodness sake. Cause I am coming to town. I can see you if you'd been good, I see you if you'd been bad. So you better not shout, you better not pout, better be good for goodness sakes. Jim sang.

Silence, birds flew in a startling glance as Jim moved back away from the trees that stood close to him, the feel of the bird's flight gave him a feeling of dread and fear. Something told him to run back away from where he was heading. Danger, just that feel of death that he had left behind him was like following him now. A feeling of danger hung over his senses as he knew if he got closer the feeling of danger would only scream louder. Slowly Jim turn around walked slowly toward the forest then he stood there not far from where he had been. Birds shriek out protest through trees, toward a sky that had changed in a short time from morning to dawn. What is happening? Why was the sky changing so fast? Had the government went to that extreme to control day and night, weather? If they had, then freedom fighters were in more than just trouble, the world was in danger itself. No one should have that much control. Jim heard nothing, no buzz of airmobile or humming sounds from enforcer's storm mobile before it landed. Sounds gave way to anything or anyone that would intricate danger was close by. But as Jim listen to any sounds around him, leaves fluttered against the winds kissing around him in a silent whisper. Danger was closer than Jim thought as he watched his sister, his friend and now his enemy, stroll over toward him. Her long legs strong built muscular thick like a tree trunk. Her face round with a square like nose and wide lips, her teeth sharp pointy as she sneered at Jim.

He watched her move slow with each step firm and ready to charge him. Her eyes stern with fierce intent to fight him. She bent her form low with fur rising on her smooth dark skin. Her nose grew a snort with a square pink nose that seemed to flare in a scent she was hunting. Her head grew larger as bone crack and broke with each length and stretch of skin and bone popping in places where as human was not there.

Jim had seen many hybrids change many times in a rush of flesh and bones and it still astound to watch this woman change into her wolf.

I thought you would never get here? Jim West? I had been waiting too long, did you enjoy my little fun? Had do something while I was waiting for you. (Chuckle). You should have heard your brother growl as I cut down his mate and those brats that he called his kids. (Laugh). I did have some help if you please. They are rather well train and you might say well control by— (laugh) me. It's really funny how I can just say kill and well they just do it. Now, Jim is that child that has those infamous things that would destroy our homes. I need that information I know you have it. Give it up or well I can tell my minions to just kill your family now. Do you want that? One word just one word and their dead, can you live with that? She said as she showed off her fangs dripping with salve.

Jim stood there watching feeling the heat that blended with fear that coated his body. How was he going to fight her, why had she betrayed the freedom fighters this way? Annie was his sister and he cared for her, even though she was adopted, taken in as one of them at a young age. But she was close to him as if she was a sister. Now she stood with her hybrid form of were wolf and human stance waiting to kill him. she threatened his family lives as if she knew where they were and had the power to kill them if he did not produce any form of information about the child that held the government destruction. No he had to believe that his family would survive, they would find out about the traitor. Jim took a breath, held his head high and sent out his private message to Maria that Annie was the traitor and she had sent her own to kill them. Be save my heart.

Mike watch and listen to both packs argue about who killed who and why? Mike cousin stood up and yelled at the leader of the wolves that stood taller with his broad back and chest buff out as he yelled back at Mike cousin.

We had found your scent on the pups that had their necks torn out and their hearts too. It is your cat scent we had smell on them no other scent. Your pack can not deny the scent. The leader wolf said as he buffed out air from his nose that shift a little.

The scent is not from our pack of cats, it is not known to anyone, I had spoken before the grand king had come. I had told you then and I shall tell you again. The scent is not from my cats.

Do you want another war that would make the decision a little better? The wolf leader said with a sneer.

Mike had enough of them and wanted to get this finish.

Mike stood up as he let his full form of both cat and wolf take over his features, his body changed as a cat long face with whiskers long and pointy stood out, his neck formed with Grey like fur as his chest and legs shaped into muscular wolf back paws with sharp long talons that was ready to strike any who might oppose him. A roar silent all that stood around him he had enough of it. Mike had to make them listen to him. He was their king.

Everyone stood back as shock and fear rose through the air around them. Mike stood a good 10 ft. tall, his shoulder broad out like a branch strong with mix fur rolling down his arms. Mike no longer had hands but claws that were sharp as knives to a blade.

Mike looked at them and knew he had turn in his true form. The enforcer could have taken one of the cubs and killed them and used its scent over the pups as well. I need to know if any were cat or kittens had been killed before the pups were killed. When did this start and if not years ago but when did it start? I need to know now. Mike roared.

Mike cousin step closer toward him and yet, stood a few feet back from Mike. He bowed low and did not look at Mike eyes without knowing that would make Mike want to challenge him. He knew too that he could not win any fight with Mike beast.

So he bowed and looked down, the wolf leader had done the same thing as Mike cousin.

The killing started four or five weeks ago. We found the pups near the water lake here. Their necks torn with the scent of cat all over them, we—found them slaughter. The leader of the wolves hung his head low as grief tore into him in argue and in fear.

Mike took a breath and let it out slow, he signed out his growl as the pain enter him too. The loss of any type of children put his heart to pain. And yet, he knew it had to be the government that had struck the packs on both sides. A war that would start here and end all over the world.

Mike looked at his cousin for something he could say to ease the pain. But he too felt the loss of the young ones.

I cannot bring them back, but I swore to you that I would do all I can to find the cat that had killed your pups. I too lost kittens not long after your own pups died. It has to be what our king had said. The government wants us to war and bring all the hybrids and other folks like us to go to war against each other. Destroy us all.

We need to listen to one another and not in angrier or in pain. Nothing will solve this and no one can return from the dead. But to revenges the death of our pups and kittens, we must work together and find that traitor.

Someone outside of the meeting camp screamed out a warning of sorts as they tumble down a slope in the distance.

A wolf and a cat scramble down together in a fast motion of blurs as they pushed back trees and bushes that were in their ways. They had to do something fast. What they had found was more hideous than anything they had ever seen. Both them went together as a team. No one knew that they were even friends, they had even hunted together. Best friends that felt the pain of both kitten's death and that of the pups. They were the ones that went as far as to investigate the killings when everyone was just pointing fingers at other packs. No one wanted to listen to them, so they just took the investigation as a team hoping that with both of them they could find the right killer. But insisted they found more packs in villages farther away killed. Everyone in the village died. The wolf packs of the forgotten and the cat pack loin died. They even gotten so far as to find out who it was and knew neither packs would like it. James (wolf) saw a man standing close to a family that was dead. He was kneeling down next to the family in sobs and a growl that would have shaken even the king. Something said that the man was related to the family. Then they travel to the packs of cats that were not far from that village. What they saw made them run as far away as they could go. Now that man was in danger and those evil things might come here to their own packs. Jasper (cat) pulled his long blonde hair out of his face as he came to where both packs of wolves and cats had a meeting of sorts.

Father I am sorry for not— (Jasper father smack Jasper in the face). How dare you leave the pack when danger was around us? You frighten your mother and the other kittens. Jasper father said as he rose up off the floor with the other councilmen of the packs of cats.

James looked at Mike form with awe and felt bravo. Are you going to slap me too father? James asked his own father standing close to the king of all hybrids and were-animals.

No but I would get some answers why you scare us thus. You could have been killed. What is wrong with you? He asked.

James long brown hair had streaks of red and white, which would make him someday an alpha of the pack. Mike recognized the fact that both James and Jasper had come together from where? Mike thought about them for a few minutes and then came to a conclusion they must be friends.

But what have they found that they had left both packs during the danger that surrounds both packs.

Stop with yelling at the pups and listen to them. Mike said as he turned to them.

What have you found that you had to team up together? Mike asked them still in his animal form. His voice course and hard to form with his snout long; and gray with long white whiskers, that twitched when he talked. His eyes not blue, but green like a cat long and not round like a wolf. Yet, his eyes spoke more intelligent.

Jasper and I tried to tell our folks about what we found by the pups that died here four weeks ago. The kittens died the same way almost the same week. We decide that if no one was going to listen to us. We wanted to do the investigation ourselves. So we found that both pups and kittens were slaughter the same way and the killing did not have teeth marks, but had been slashed with something sharp. No one searched in the water or around bushes, everyone was too upset to think straight or make the right decision. So Jasper and I did the looking during the night with a low crystal rock. We hunted the next day until we found the sharp thing in the water with parts of fur still on it. Then we tried to tell someone, but no one listen to us, we both asked our pack leaders, but they just patted our heads and told us to go. So we just followed our instinct and our noses that told us that the smell was strange, we could smell some of the pup's litters death scent but the scents were mixed with something else? The scent really didn't come from either village's not cat not wolf either, but something else. It—it was different scent I had never smelled before. So we just followed the smell and left our packs to find the killers and try to stop this stupid war. We were friends for so long, so many centuries and never felt fear of one another. We even had trades from one of the larger villages. And that village was and I say was forgotten pack.

The village has been attack as well as the village of cats everyone in both villages were dead. They are gone, villages became a lake of blood, nothing no one alive. But –but at the forgotten village a man, a human different but human, he cried and so loud with pain that made us stand back. We had seen the attack on the cat village. But we were only two pups not grown up with a large pack behind us. We just watched those things, those strange things that looked human, but they couldn't be. They were wicked with long arms that were like sharp swords or knives. Their faces hidden with a mask of something I never saw let alone could even describe. It –it was a black or dark metal face that covered their eyes and nose. Their mouths were nothing but wide red like grill that lit up with each kill. The cloths –well the clothes I could not even tell you it was nothing but metal like plates kissing legs and arms of each strange human or thing body. But—I think I saw a were-shifter or was she a hybrid—I can't tell from where we were hiding. Only that we could hear only some of the cats and wolves screaming thoughts of death and dying and watching just watching them dying for no reason we could not do anything, we were only pups not grownups with enough strength to fight them. I know we couldn't sleep sense we got back, we only saw that shifter that traitor that order those enforcers to kill everyone in those innocent villages. But I can take you to where the shifter is now, I think she is going to kill that man. He sent a message to someone name Maria and her kids. That was why I said I don't think he's all human. James and Jasper said in unison.

Mike smile at them and knew who they were talking about on both accounts. The shifter had to be Annie, she was the one who left on many days when they need her help at the fighter's headquarters on the east side of the planets coast. She had the abilities to shifter into cat or wolf, but not both at the same time like he could. And the man, it had to be his cousin Maria who was a hybrid wolf. And this hybrid the boys said was nothing but trouble and his cousin sister in law. Made it worse if he told his cousin of his suspects. He had to get to Jim. If what the two pups said was true about those strange things, then Annie was involve with the enforcers. She's out in the open and just waiting for a show down a clash of all other folks that are like us, but are not and yet we all will go to war hybrids against each other, a diversion for the government to attack the headquarter or to get to Steve? Fuck shit, a divide diversion. To separate both clans for the attack! Mike looked at both clans of were-animals and hybrids then the idea came to him fast. I need to know how many cats you can assembly together right now. These two pups had done what none of you would even try. They worked together and not accuse, but hunted for the truth and found more than just these poor children death as the only end, but a more horrible act. So again I ask you how many can you bring to me cousin. Mike asked him first.

We have a hundred in our pack of warriors and more hidden away in caves. They are alphas that will not be part of our clan or pack. They are loners and will fight only if it endangers them or their kind. I believe I can sway them to our cause. I go now to bring them to this place that is equal to our kind and the wolves. We will work together and kill those that killed our kindred.

Mike turn to the wolves and ask the same question to them.

We have a hundred warriors in our packs and we too have alphas that have become elusive, but will fight with us. I will send the warning that will bring them here.

The leader howled with the woman that had brought Mike to the packs hidden village in woods. She was there with her white hair hanging low down her spine. Her dress white and sheer as if she wasn't wearing any clothes.

I need five of each pack strongest warriors, I need to send them to a large metal thing that has packs of none-were-animals, and they are not humans, but not quite hybrids either. They hold the key to destroy the government control over all that we know. We need to get them to the headquarters of the freedom fighters. Right now I can only think that we will be divide as packs and as hybrids and I do not like it one bit. Mike stomp down bushes that hide pockets of rocks and square bricks that lay at the bottom of the lake that flowed low at the edges. Then he looked up at the sky its blend of night and day gave way of the eclipse that he knew would be coming soon. But he could not phantom how the eclipses happen so soon. It had to be at noon and not so late. Time was running out and Steve was in endangered or had he already been attack by now. He promised him and the others that he would protect them. Had Jack realized who he was, it was one thing that he knew about Jack and his family, memories were good like cameras in a mind that could not forget things. Mr. Farmer mind had to be alter to keep Steve safe and what he had hidden up in that attic of his parents.

Now they are in a thing that had wheels and a metal like body that could keep him safe. But for how long, can they stay safe inside that big thing? Another thought came to Mike as he thought about the computer, can that thing have any weapons hidden inside that Jack had not known about. He did put the hard drive together when his father was alive – Mike thinks so. But does it have weapons to keep the others inside safe. Mike could not take the chance that the thing didn't have weapons. They were endangered and he and the other packs had to keep them safe. Five of each pack of cats and wolves would work. Now he had to wait for all the packs to come together for the fight of their lives. Then another thought the packs mates and the children? If they left them the enforcers would be able to come and kill them while they are fighting them somewhere else. This was getting more and more complicated with each thought. Another worry for him and now he had to figure out how he would protect and fight at the same time.

The five warriors from each pack came to him as well as all the packs wolves and cats of all shapes and sizes. They all stood around the lake and trees and large rocks that hid some of them, but Mike could feel them there.

We have two hundred hybrids and were animals. We need to have a plan to fight the enforcers attack and protect my charges.

Our packs need to gather as one, Mike explained and then said, but our mates will be without protection, so I need them to gather things and go within the mountains as cats and as wolves, hide within caves take only what you need. Then mix your scents with other creatures that linger here in the forest with your scent.

Do not let any scent linger that is one of yours behind and led the enforcers to any of the packs. If you know of a cave that lead up to the mountain side if you find this stay inside of the cave beware that water can hide better your scent if all of you wash with some other scent. That will keep any scent from spreading out. Do what you can to keep safe. Twelve mountain lions and twelve alpha wolves would keep all of you safe within the mountain. Can we do this? Mike said.

Second the five hybrid cats and five hybrid wolves are going to retrace my path that led me here. I want you all to find a strange looking metal box with wheels; it is very large with a window that is in the front. You need to say that I send you. Michael. They would listen and know they are endangered. Be aware of all your surroundings and listen very carefully at silent of the birds. Then look upward and if you see the birds shriek up in a fast motion from trees or bushes, and then get to the truck the large metal thing that Steve and his friends are in. Do not engage in any fight unless you know you can win the fight. The enforcers are built different; they are more machine none human and are more dangerous. Now leave and be safe. Michael said with a huff.

But if we do not engage in the fight or any fight that had or has put those in the metal machine endanger, how are we going to keep those you want us to protect, be safe? Asked One of the Were-wolf.

That was a very good question. Look at your surroundings and use your mind before you engage. Be sure of your flight to attack. Do not let them harm or kill any one of you. Mike said as he walked away from them.

Then Mike looked at the alphas from the mountain ranges, the alpha hybrid cats and wolves stood away from each other with sneers and ready to change into their hybrid form within a few minutes of their sight of each other.

Stand down all of you, keep your alpha intact within range, the enforcers may be more powerful then we may think. Their body is not human as you may or should say not sense their human parts.

Be of care. Then in the distance Mike saw her, Annie was just hunching low in her hybrid form of wolf and that of cat in other ways. Her long snout had whiskers long and twitching as she bared her fangs that were also longer than most hybrids. Her fangs dripped with salves.

So she has learned how to mix her wolf and cat now, how interesting and how dangerous this is now. Mike knew he had to move if he was going to save that man he had suspect was Jim, his cousin husband. He looked at the sight of all the packs of cats and wolves running into the forest that was hiding the enforcers. A roar and a warning to those below him that they were endanger if they went in without sensing the enforcers. But then he could only sense very little of the enforcers himself.

They were not human but something else that he could not sense. His wings spread out flat in the air as he flew downward straight on Annie back, but she jumped up toward the man at the same time.

The feel of something hard fall against her side took her breath out as she also felt the feel of the ground coming toward her was even harder. Annie teeth gritted as the feel of her teeth clenching together as she felt the ground under body. The hardness of that body against her made her even madder as she struggled to fight this hybrid of sort off of her.

Mike had her down her body was in full form of hybrid mix. Something he never knew about her. For so long, Mike thought she was just wolf, but somehow she is a mix hybrid. But how could he had ever not sense her hybrids mix, how could he have not known of her traitorous ways. Right now it did not matter, he had to stop her and save Jim. Mike could see Jim standing close to one of the trees that stood at the edge of the field. Mike knew that he had to save Jim. Jim had married his cousin Maria and they had pups.

The enforcers came out of hiding and started toward Jim, but then he saw the packs of cats and wolves tearing off the forcers heads with ease, but the enforcers body was metal than human skin. The taste of blood mixed with metal like lead leaking out of some forcers that two wolves attacked before the enforcers was even out of the trees. But the enforcers still were coming out in hundreds. Mike had to concentrate on Annie and nothing else. She was the traitor to the freedom fighters and those innocents' people and children that were killed for no reason. There was another fact about Annie betrayal that she was Jim sister adopted. That fact made Mike scream more at how this woman had deceived everyone around her with her lies and her deception of her true self. She had killed those that would welcome her in as their own. Mike would make sure that this would be her last thing in her lying life. No longer would she kill anyone or deceive anyone any more. Mike sank his fangs into her side as he fought to tear her side apart to get to her heart. The taste of blood spill into his mouth made his hybrid state more wild untamed as the feel of her body screamed out.

Annie felt the pain of fangs sinking deep on her side as she tore into the ground dirt and old moldy grass, her head turned around to see what had taken her attention, it was bigger and stranger than her mix hybrid state had landed on her with the body of both cat and wolf and yet there was wings on the side fluttering high over her head. No was her only thought that came out of her mouth. It could not be him. He was killed months ago. That was what she was told months ago and they even had funeral for him. No it could not be him. Did they suspect her as the traitor and thought to play this game? No they would not let her kill so many villages of hybrids and those innocent humans. But how did he live? She need to fight hard and live to be one of the enforcer's true commanders. She would be next to the leader of the world. A commander that would only serve the leader directly, she would not die, not today or any day. Annie turn her hind legs out from under and strike Mike on his stomach hard as her claws dug in his stomach with fierce need to survive.

NO you don't little one. I am your nightmare and will be forever more. Mike said as he ripped her side off with one tug of his strong long snout that had more teeth and longer fangs than hers. She could feel her skin changing as furs rip off her, pain stole her sense as rage made her fierce against this so called King that was suppose be dead rose up inside of her, she wanted him dead, she needed him dead, but he wasn't and she was going to finish him now. Her claws took hold of Mike's fur, then rip off a piece of his wing. The feel of her claws ripping fur gave her more strength to keep on fighting. She flipped Mike off her side as she pushed her hind legs up over under her enemy and found that her side was bleeding faster as Mike fangs pulled more skin off. Slowly Annie faced him as she changed within moments to stop the bleeding and then back again. Her side still bled, but as much the tear seemed to be healing it still was there. Too much blood too much loss of it that it made her weak a shake of her head to clear any thoughts of passing out help her with a growl and show of her fangs in a sneer. Mike had to step back a few paces, but circled her with the same sneer of fangs that drip with her blood still in his mouth. The taste was bitter, but then again it was sweet as he knew that she was going to die and her own hybrid mix will not save her. He watched her change back and forth from one form to another form it was would still make her weak and maybe even weaker. Changing back and forth was more adrenalin and used more energy than what she had lost.

Your weak Annie, give it up. You're not going to win this time. I finally found you and your treason ways had got up. I will kill you with pleasure as you have killed those innocent people and children you killed them with pleasure. Mike said with husky greed of knowing he would finally kill something that has disguise him profoundly.

Mike roared as Mike spring upward on Annie again, but this time he pounced on her neck.

Annie knew what he was going to do and moved fast away from him before he tore into her neck. Her sight for a landing came fast as both of her hind legs struck out toward Mike face hard. Blood pour out of his nose as Annie hind claws tore Mike face. Annie roared out her strike as she swirled around and landed farther away. She was ready to strike again, as she looked for the best spot to strike again. Mike knew she was looking for an opening and an open she would get. Mike just let her think that the wound she inflicted on him was enough for him to change form to heal faster. As Mike made the change slowly, he watched her in the corner of his eyes.

Yes, she was waiting for the one moment of the change when hybrid became weaker, but Mike didn't make the change to human, but to a larger cat mix, large tiger and a lion with the long snout of a wolf. He caught her off guard as she leaped toward him in the air and slice her stomach in two. Her body landed in two pieces as Mike roared his victory as he watched Annie lifeless body parts separate and fall down near his feet.

Mike looked around him with keen sight of all the other packs still fighting the enforcers, but sense Annie died, the enforcers stop as the feel of her death sent them in their tracks and turn to look at Mike. Mike knew they would attack him. Mike sent out a mental message to all the packs, *attack now that they are seeing me only. Attack and destroy all of the enforcers now.* Mike roared loud his command.

Jim was shock and happy to see the packs coming together as one attacking the enforcers. Jim noticed Annie had been busy fighting the biggest hybrid—but what kind of hybrid was it. A mix of sorts of cats and wolf, but it had wings. Jim shook his head to clear what he was seeing. His mind was or is playing tricks, it couldn't be—no—it is? That big hybrid mix was the King of the hybrids and he was alive and well and for god's sake fighting with all the other hybrids packs. Somehow he had gotten them all to work together. Now Jim saw that Annie was defeated and dead. The enforcers were still fighting, but had turned their attention toward Mike. The packs form one long circular line, together cats and wolves side by side attack enforcers. Destroying every enforcer within range of claws and fangs. Jim could feel his heart pound hard in his chest making his lungs take in heavy air that would not release its breath.

CHAPTER FOURTEEN

J IM LEAN BACK AGAINST the tree as things all came to a silence of nothing. Mike had walked with pride as he looked down at Jim. My people, our people the freedom fighters are here in a matter of speaking. Why are you here? What has happened to you and where is my cousin Maria? Mike asked Jim as mike stood with his legs firm and spread ready for anything off.

Jim had to shake his head slowly as his mind swerved to all that had happened within the few days or more sense he had gotten up with his wife. I –don't know where Maria is or the kids. But Mr. Righteous died and I had sent a message to Maria to get Joan and her little girl out of their home fast. So if they are safe –I just—hope so. I can't contact them and they can't contact me either. And if I am right that –that so call sister of mine was the one that had told any of the leader or his enforcers commanders about any of the senators and congressman that was or is still with the freedom fighters. She knew who each and every one of the senators that were involved with the freedom fighters and where they lived. So we are in shit big. I need to get in touch with one of the head leaders of the fighters. Everyone is in danger. Jim said as he reached up to grab part of the tree he was leaning against. His legs weak as his body finally gave way to the darkness he had been fighting for the past few day's sense he left the restaurant after his friend killed himself. He was hungry and tired, he also missed his family and hope they are still alive and safe. Jim felt his eyes close heavy and thick as everything went black.

Mike watched Jim pass out; he knew Jim had to be exhausted from all the running and was properly hungry too. Mike told two other cats and one wolf to help take Jim back to one of their camps and feed him and let him rest. They now need to get to his other distance, his biggest responsibility. He hoped Steve and the others were alright. But he needed to get to them fast. His wings could work, but only for one more flight. After that he needed to rest his other hybrid mix. The run would help him keep his mind clear and focus on Steve and the others in that strange thing they were driving. At least the thing was big enough for them to stay safe in for a while or so, that is he hoped. Jim would be alright now, the traitor is dead and so is those evil enforcers all gone now, no more worrying about villages being attacked or children dying. And if what Jim had said was true and Mike was sure that Jim was right, the leader and enforcers know each and everyone in the senate that is involve with the freedom fighters and their families too, there is or will be a blood bath. No one is safe from the government. Mike had to get Steve to the headquarters in the country of Dover Ridge. The place was more than year from where they now, that is if they had to walk? Mike had passed four large cats and five large wolves that smelled danger that blend with blood and something more strangely, the smell was strong and made him cough as he got closer. The blood gave them all a taste of rage that put their hybrid mix wild with need to kill.

Trees, bushes and logs fallen from old trees, rocks hard long flat on the ground help them launch their hind legs upward and on top of the long square like metal roof. The sound from all their legs landing hard on top of the thing shook with steel screeching as talon and claws touching the metal roof. Around them below around the metal thing was a pool of blood and four of the five packs of wolves and cats were looking up at them with pride and knowledge that they had been successful in getting to the point where their king had told them to be. The enforcers had been attacking the thing with laser like weapons that were part of their body (arms-hands.). Mike look more around him and knew where the all the smell of blood was coming from and all he saw was one of his wolves had died. From all five packs only one had died from five each cat and wolves, one just one. That was sad, but good. And yet, they had killed the enforcers that attack the metal thing that had Steve inside was all gone. Destroyed by those he sent. The packs might be ready if they could get more packs in other villages that were not attack by Annie. May be he would get an army together and fight the enforcers. Yeah, that might be a good idea. But first thing first he had to get Steve and the others to a safe place and the headquarters in this region has been compromised or destroyed all together. Mike jump off the metal hood of the long thing that Steve and the others were in. The ground wet with both blood and something more strange in smell, a metal like liquid that made his feet wet dark mud like coat around each of the enforcers that laid on the ground dead. Mike walked behind the thing that had a door the open up in the middle, and yet it was wide enough for him to see that everyone was safe.

Steve saw Mike form of both human and wolf, his face was more human with fur around his cheeks, and his mouth was long with fangs growing back in his mouth as his snout growing back in his round face as his eyes large with catlike yellow split shining right at him. Steve had to take a breath that shook his body.

WHERE IN THE HELL WERE YOU? FUCKING SHIT MAN, THOSE ENFORCER, DID YOU SEND THEM? CAUSE IT SURE IN HELL LOOKED LIKE YOU DID? FUCKING SHIT MAN, WE WERE ATTACK AND THE SHIT COMPUTER WENT ON SOME KIND OF LOCK DOWN. IT CLOSED ALL DOORS—put some kind of shield that enforcer could not penetrate. But—but the sounds outside and the feel of the truck being hit over and over again, Fucking shit-fucking shit. Steve said as he rubbed his head and pulled back his hair that was a mess. Sweat pour down everyone inside as it was hot and they were both hungry and thirsty as Mike looked at each one around. Max and Susan sat close to the large boxes that held their food. Max just looked at him in that silly looking dress, his legs spread out close to Susan own legs that were long and skinny. Susan owned dress was torn and dirty, with rips on the arms and a tear on the side under her arms. Her hair dark with dirt and tangled over her head, Yet, Max had always thought her beautiful.

Jack was standing in a corner with his own long legs set in black pants and torn yellow shirt. His face stern with eyes that were upset as he kept on looking at Mike! So Jeanie let you in and let you're what-ever packs on top of us. I think you're a little too late to join any party that was here. We just enjoyed the noise and all the rattling and shaking. It brought back memories of shake and roll. If –you know what I mean. Jack said as he walked over toward Mike and his packs that came with him. The doors swung open wide to show how many enforcers were on the ground around the truck and that of the packs hybrids of different sizes and different kinds.

Jack moved away from the side of the trucks inside corner and walked toward Mike. Steve asked you question Mike? Are you going to answer him or are you just going to stand there looking at us like we're something strange? Jack asked Mike as he spoke slowly to him.

Mike just looked at them all, the children were safe as they say as far in the back of the truck with the toys. He took a breath and let his final human form come over him. Mike human form made snaps in his bones pop in places that would make him more human looking than hybrid. He couldn't answer them in a language they would understand yet. His snout had finally gone back enough with his fangs that he could at least speak a little bit. I was unable to contact you. As you see Jack and Steve, I had run into trouble. Look I don't have time to explain everything that occur within the few days that just pasted. I can't believe that all of you are alright. All I can say is trust me, trust my hybrids. They will not harm you. I sent them here to protect all if you. We need to get the truck to back toward the first strip of road it can use and turn right away from the forest a mile or two from here. There will be two large cats standing on the right side with their paws reach high. They are statue made out of trees. On the left will be two large wolves doing the same thing generally. They are also made out of trees. Stay there until I get there with two of the leaders of the packs here. I need to know if you are not harmed. Mike asked Steve and the others.

Steve looked at Mike with unsureness if he did or could trust Mike. He had abandoned them without even trying contacted them. Steve just looked at Mike with a frown and grinded his teeth that was loose again. He didn't have many teeth left.

Are you going to send your pack here with us for safety? Or are we going alone as—well as we felt like not too long ago. Steve said as he moved lower to the metal floor edge that met Mike's shoulder. Steve wanted to meet Mike eyes and his face. Truth was what he wanted from this strange man they had met a few days ago on that old bus into the city. Yeah, they had escape the enforcer back there when the enforcers invaded Steve website news building, they had ridden that strange thing that Mike called a motorbike of some kind. But still, Steve could not trust someone that really didn't explain how he knew him or Steve friends. Steve had to many question that he thought about with those question none of them were ever answered. Mike would not tell him a damn thing. Answers Steve needed answers and he was going to get it. One way or another Steve knew he would get it out of Mike.

Steve just stared at Mike as he chewed on his lips. Well, are you going to answer me or what? I got a lot of question running through my head and you haven't really answer any of them sense we meet. Don't even go there with Mr. Farmer and the others. They really could not answer me either. So come on and answer me. Steve asked again.

Mike looked back at his packs that came with him from the fight with Annie. Someone Steve would not know or that of Jim.

Freedom fighter's headquarters here might have been compromised by a traitor that was once part of a family of mixed human and hybrids, she gave them information about important people that work for the freedom fighters for centuries and they also work for the government too. The traitor has given the government everybody's name that works for the government and the freedom fighters they are endanger. So we either go to the headquarters here or find out how bad or we go on and find the main headquarters in the country Dover Ridge. Mike said as he looked straight at Steve. Look I can't answer your entire question right now. But your question will be answered in due time. Mike said again after a few moments of silence between them.

Steve took a breath and let it out with a huff. Steve put his hand on his long shaggy hair and rubbed. Look I never heard of Dover Ridge and I only left my community to go to work in the city other than that I had never been outside of it. All this is new to me and the others too, we are just people that just lived and died in a world-a-a government-a world that don't care about who lives or dies for that matter. We don't have any kind of money or ways to learn to read write, do math or anything like that, we are nothing important-until now. We—don't fight—we don't know anything about fighting anyone, but I (Steve looked around him before he could finish his sentence) thhhhhhink we would fight to stay alive. Steve said quietly as he turned back to Mike.

Mike nodded his head and agreed with Steve. Steve had the right not to trust him, they had just meet and both his parents and Steve parents had done something to secure a memory that was so deep in

Steve and Jack mind that somehow the death of his sister triggered the memory and slowly some of the things that their parents imbedded in Steve mind was unfolding, coming together.

What are you asking me? Who am I? I will tell you this much, I am very important to the freedom fighters. I told you that much, but I guess I should tell you that these packs listen to me as one title, one true leader to them and lead justice as one ruler. Now is that what you want. Is that want you wanted, is that what you want to know. If it isn't what you –then what is it? Mike said almost yelling at Steve as he walked enough away from Steve sitting on the edges of the open back trucks.

Steve just looked at Mike with shock and surprise in his eyes. Did Mike just tell him that he is some king of the hybrids, is that his secret? Steve looked down and took a breath as he got up off the edge of the trucks open door and pointed to Jack. We need to get back on the road and follow this king of hybrids. Steve said as he walked toward the front of the trucks driving part. Jack moved in front of Steve to sit in the driver's seat. The computer came on with a roar and a switch of gears as Jack watch the panel that explored in bright colors of yellow and red with blue that shine inside of the cabin of the trucks front driving area. *All shields are down, government enforcers have been defeated. We are now in progress of finding road. Do you need me to reinforce the shield in any way?* The computer responded to them.

No shields as of now, we need to back up and turn back to the cross roads and turn right a few miles from the forest and stay on that strip of road until we find those trees that looked like hybrids on each side. Jack said as he leaned back in his seat.

The drive was quiet, both Jack and Steve sat in silence, trees large with large bushes some with white flowers and some with red like round cherry like buds. The scenery was beautiful and yet, the large scene made them winch with fright. The events of the past few days took total on their trust of Mike, but they need to get away from the enforcers or more likely the government. They did not have a choice. Steve thought about the disc that he had hidden in the back of the trucks trailer. If it were so important to the government? Then why didn't they look for it before now? Why use something that could be duplicated or changed for any ones uses for the good or worse for any ones need to control for power over the world. What if those discs had the wrong information, what if the information had been compromised? Proof, proof of what these things are holding inside of them, something that can be seen and not listening too. But where was the proof and who had the proof and why? Why didn't it show up before now and why now? Steve had to do something to block out more question that plagued him with every moment he thought about those damn discs.

I am bored which normal, I can't stop thinking Jack? Steve said as he looked outside the side window with his legs sticking out the window. The air was fresh crisp with scent of green grass and trees, mold and musk heavy filled around the inside of the cabin that they were driving. Steve nodded his head as he looked at Jack for some words or something. Jack just drove, his hands over the wheel, turning here and there, but never leaving the wheel in front of him. Jack just stared out straight ahead not showing if he was even listening to Steve. Jack face blank and chewing on something other than his lips, Jack moved the wheel to the left as came to the cross roads and looked at Steve with a shake of his head, Jack smiled at Steve. I know what you're thinking, and (silence for a while) you may have a point. I mean I was thinking that those discs are not the only thing that would proof something to—too I—I don't know –maybe I am just rambling on. The government can do whatever they want with those damn discs. Then just tell those around them that they are lies and no proof that those things are true. What can those discs do to make the government fall apart and how can they? Jack said as he waved his left hand up and down on the wheel he was using to steer the truck into the path that Mike told them to take.

Large trees with wide trunks bursting out of the greenery around them on each side of the ruff path that was paved with grass and rocks on uneven cemented road, silence was the only answer as both of them thought about what was just said.

Steve then moved his legs from the window and shifted in his seat as another thought came over him. A clue or something that would be inside of one of the discs that they did not know about—might have something in it that would be the alternant destruction of the government. But what would that be? Hey Jack what would happen if we found something that would destroy the government? You know something inside of the discs that would tell us where or how to use it or something like that. I think there might be something hidden inside one of the discs that we did not yet find? Steve said as he looked nervous and anxious as he moved around in his seat.

Maybe you're right and maybe not. But who's to say if Mike knows and will not even tell us about it. Can we trust him? Or do we just wait for the right moment, the right time? Steve said as he looked at Jack with excitement and hope, then again he thought about all those children in the back of the truck and the joy they were having playing with those ancient toys. How can he think about hope when they may die by Mikes hands or not? Either way of Mike's hybrid packs or those of the enforcers! Damn do and a damn don't. Tell me Jack can we live with ourselves if those innocent children either get caught by the government or die? Steve asked as he looked at Jack and at the scenery around him.

Hmm. Maybe you're right again. I don't think I can live with anyone death and even Susan or her baby or those children in the back. But here we are going into a flame that we have no control over. So what do we do? Jack asked as he stop close to where they were supposed to be.

I guess we all have to just be—well we just got to be careful around Mike or anyone else we come in contact.

Yeah I think your right. More careful around any one we do not know, especially Mike and his hybrids. Steve agreed.

Mike went back to the packs village with most of the packs that went with him to fight Annie and save Jim. He only sent twenty-ten of each packs, ten wolves and ten cats twenty in all to with Steve for safety reason. Jim was unconscious, under nourished and exhausted. He might know something other than what he had told them before he passed out. Mike had question for him and hoped Jim was feed and slept enough to answer his question.

Jim woke up weak and felt dizzy. His stomach ached from little food that was in his stomach. Maria and Joan with kids were in danger. Annie sent someone to kill them, he has to do something fast. But wait a minute, his memory came back slowly like a fog in his mind. Annie is dead, she fought with Mike, his wife cousin, the King of the hybrids and one of most important freedom fighter warriors. He came, he actual came to save him. But—Jim thought again as he just stared at all the wolves and cats that sat around him. They were panting like they were hot, the air or weather was too hot, not really. But even Jim felt some heat too. Jim shook his head again as he remembered Mike fighting with Annie and then killing her. He figured that the other hybrids probably killed all the other enforcers that he saw back in the forest. He was saved when he thought he would've been or should have been dead. Maria, she was still in danger. Annie said that she had someone or something that was with Maria and Joan and the kids. Did she send a message to them to kill my family?

Jim needed to find out if his family is safe? But how-who would be able to find them or sense them? Mike, yeah! Mike would be able to, he is the strongest hybrid that ever lived. He had a connection with Maria. Yeah, Mike would do it for him. Another thought came over Jim. What happen to the headquarters? What happen to the freedom fighters? To many question and no one around to answer him right now. Food, Jim smelled food, Meat roasted with thick gravy and wild potatoes and some kind of green vegetable. One of the wolves put a plate down in front of Jim bed he was sitting on. Jim guessed that one of them had laid him on the bed. The bed was not much, but the bed seemed to be made of logs from fallen trees and there was some kind of fur from some kind of animal to make the bed soft and warm. The bed wasn't that far from the floor. The ground under Jim feet was cool against his skin. The food was set on a table made from something round and black, strange he had never seen it before. The thing was round and there were four of them underneath a flat rock that was used as a table. Jim took a taste of the food as the smell rose in his lungs and made his mouth water and his stomach growl. Jim grab the meat and swallowed the meat with fast chews and swallows as each piece of meat and potatoes and greens stuff in Jim mouth so fast that he had a hard time swallowing, he coughed, but would not let the food go. Slowly Jim sat down on the bed and let the food settle down in his stomach. His head stop spinning, his weak legs felt better they were not as weak. Jim grabbed a metal like cup that had water. And swallow the clear clean water. The taste wet as his throat was dry. Jim lips chap and dry from not drinking any clean water for days. Just the taste now set his stomach and body calm, a cool tingle settle through his body, from his chest down to his toes. Jim closed his eyes as he leaned his head back down on the bed. The feel of the pillows under his head soft and warm, his body relaxed again and started to drift off as his body was finally satisfied and yet, his mind went back to his wife and kids. Annie is dead and he would never know who had his family and if they were safe. Darkness clouded his head again as sleep settle in his mind and his body. The sound of voices soft and quiet spoke of other villages attacked by Annie enforcers gone now. Fear of more enforcers coming after the attack of Annie death. Jim went to sleep as their voices silence his mind.

Mike came in the villages of the both pack now coming together after the fight they had with the enforcers and Annie who betray them all. Mike needed to speak to Jim and find out what he knew or what he didn't know. Then maybe share some Intel of what he knew back at him. But when Mike went the small cabin that was made out of old fallen logs and hay that covered the roofs flat wood to keep the cabin warm. Jim was asleep, a tray of food eaten and a cup empty was near Jim bed. Mike just shook his head slowly and walked out with a sign. Mike thought it was best let Jim sleep for right now. His question will be answered due time, if Jim could. Annie was dead and gone, and yet the facts still stand like a nightmare. Mike was glad that Jim got food and drink, he had to be starving and thirsty sense he left his family. Mike just look at nothing but the ground, his thoughts gone to all those that were around him, but his mind spinning with too many question that seemed to have no answers, well there were answers but—were the answers in front of him and he just don't see it. Mike looked back at Jim and then at his packs of cats and wolves. One of the elders step closer to Mike with a blank stare of no emotion of thought. The elder stood there in front of Mike with his arms crossed over his chest that was wide and broad. The elders long braid black hair hung behind his back with feathers entwine with each turn of his braid. His face round with wrinkles at the edge of his eyes, dark and mysterious as he looked at Mike with those intent dark eyes!

It is more-wise for you my king to send your cousin a warning of Annie and that of Jim survival. They are in route am I right?

Yes, they are and they are headed toward us. But – Mike took a breath and let his mind outward to Maria Jane. He knew he had to tell her about Jim and the fact that they might be endanger. So he told her everything. His mind sent out toward Maria mind that link them as kin of what had happen and that Jim her husband is well. But they were in danger.

CHAPTER FIFTEEN

ORYEIA LOOKED AT THE doll with both curiosity and wonder and nonchalant attitude. Something came over her mind; a thought of some kind telling her something half said with a link that she hoped was lost. The voice that sink in Oryeia and her friends head became silent with a low scream of terror that stole her thoughts for a short time. Silence, nothing but silence now! The only word she heard before the scream was death to the family of Westerners. But that was more gribbles than what she could understand. Oryeia stood back as her fur stood up on her back.

Mark recalled what Jolie had said about her. She was the traitor they needed to be careful around her. Then as the air mobile found the wide open sky of dark blue and tint of night sky, the sun was setting somewhere beyond the clouds where they were fling. Under them were the abandon homes that were now forest and shattered humans living inside those homes. No heat or food nothing that Mark would be able to understand why the government let these people live like this. No one should be hungry or cold. Especially the children that hunt the streets and forest just to survive! Oryeia looked at Mark with shock as something seemed to just strike her mentally down. Oryeia's body crumbled down on all fours legs, her body turning back to the wolf she was. Fangs long ready to strike them down. She was looking back at Jolie and her mother, she was human and killed many of her cubs. Maria face shimmed with hesitation as she tried not to change with the child in her arms.

Mark and Carrlynia fur rose as they stood between Maria and the other two hybrids that had bare their fangs with salvia dripping from their fangs.

Mark growled as Carrlynia howled her protest. No one attacks or threatens their family they both said.

A part of me wanted death of your family and still does—but—I-don't want to kill anyone here. Oryeia said as she shook her head clear as a fog that seemed to deem her thoughts and feelings took control that made her want to kill something or someone. But a part of her didn't want to that. It was not them that killed her cubs and her new mate. No it was not them, her sister felt the same strange things inside of them that made them want blood, which spoke to them, controlling them when they spoke to the family here. Annie, no she was to be the queen of all hybrids, a leader of humans too. Yes, she was the one that told them that the humans killed her family. The humans have control over hybrids. They want to kill them all. That was what she said, Annie said that. Oryeia shook her head to clear more of the fog. She started to feel weak and dizzy. Her eyes closed as the floor met her body and head.

Mark watched Oryeia faint and became confused. Mark sniffed the ground around them and then looked at Dante for some kind of answer, but Dante was too busy keeping the mobile air born.

Mother what has just happen? Who was she talking about? Mark asked his mother as he sniffed Oryeia body for any sign that could tell him something. Mark just didn't know what that something was.

Mother did father speak to you? Mark asked as he back away from Oryeia, he noticed that Olaya had stayed away from them, she had back up against the wall of the mobile with her tail in between her legs. Her head low with a whiny and yelp as she looked at Mark. Her eyes glisten with tears that no hybrids shed. Mark heart stop as the smell of mating stop, but the smell of something else. The smell of piss and fear rose around her.

I don't know what is going on, but we need to know now. Mark said as he walked closer to Olaya.

I am afraid to – I can't feel that horrible voice in my head any more. But –something confusing, I –I – am confused it's too much. Olaya said as she lowered her body down to the floor. Her submission was clear to Mark and the others as she had been telling the truth. Mark took a breath and let it out with a huff. Mark walked over to his mother and his sister who was still in wolf form. S—oo what now? Mark asked as his mother changed back into human form.

Mike had sent me a signal that told me that he had Jim your father. He is safe, but these two had been controlled by your aunt Annie. She was the traitor, the betrayal of our kind and that of the human kind too. We need to know now about the headquarters. Mike is now going to Dover Ridge, where the main freedom fighters live with many of our kind and humans too in peace and freedom. We need to meet them close to the boarders if we can make it that far. These two females will be judge by our courts of hybrids and not humans of the government. So let's see if this tub has a holding cell for them. Maria said as she put Jolie down from her arms.

Jolie listen to them all as they circled the two hybrids that lay coral against the mobile wall.

Something still is not right. I just can't say what it is. But something is off. Dante said as he still drove with a shake of his head and fur standing along his arms up in a feebler way. Dante decide to be the one to be on guard. Mark maybe the strongest in strength, and Carrlynia had that way with words that made everyone think. But his mother was both the smartest, strongest and the wisest of them. She knew a lot more than they did. Mike is alive and doing what again? Dante asked as he turned the mobile toward the setting sun. The cast of the sun going down behind trees and forgotten homes that were now just rumbles. Still there were people living in them.

Dante knew he could sense lies and sense danger. He had to depend on those sense to help them all. A breath and a swipe of his hands across his face wetness sweat soaking his long blonde hair that was streak with brown and gray. His eyes brown with tint of black, they were odd large for a hybrid-human. The way the mobile was operated or control was by way of color a light that was a board or panel like. The only way to make the mobile work was to use his hands or fingers to touch each color lights to make it either go up or backwards or even do some other things. Dante knew which light makes the mobile raise up over the trees and which one will make it move on ground. But which light would make any weapons that should be on the mobile work? Dante studied the controls and looked for some sigh or something that would tell him which one would be the weapons. The sun was forgotten now as the stars lit up the sky like a blanket of silk with diamonds twinkling the night as a beckon for all below.

Dante listen too at his brother and mother questioning Olaya and Oryeia. Their voice blend in with the sounds of the lights soft glows as he touched each color light! Dante concentrate on both the voices and the sky.

So tell us what you know and we will make a decision if we believe you or not? Mark said as he crossed his arms over his chest.

We told you that our village had been captured and destroyed that is true. But we left out that we did not really see who done it. We thought we found out it was humans. Every one of the packs bodies had the smell of humans on them. We had just gotten back from a hunt and we had visited our sister pack twenty legends away from home. It took us at least two days and one day to get back home. But we didn't get to far into our sister pack when we noticed something that was not right. The village had been torn apart with everyone dead too. We knew we need to get back home fast. So we ran through the day and nights until we got home. That was when we saw them killing our family, I mean we really just found our families dead, but the smell was new and death was fresh. Bodies shattered around in a fighting stance but torn apart like a blade cutting right through bone and skin. No one had changed into their hybrid form of wolf. If–if they did, or tried to changed back into wolf that would have heal them fast or death would have let them die in their half form. But no one had done so. It–was very confusing.

We don't remember what happen after that, except—except that voice and a—a face foggy, gray I think? I-I can only recall that the face was a female. She was wild looking; I can't tell you if she had color in her hair or eyes. But only the voice was female. She said she had full control of our hybrid forms, she also said that she would kill us and all those around us too. We were told who to retrieve and bring them to a point that she was supposed to tell us when we get closer to that point. She also told us where the tunnels were and to wait for our preys. So we did what we were told even if we were frighten and scared for anyone that got in our way, we did what we were told only because we had no choice. We were being controlled and had no control over any other actions. We don't really want to hurt anyone. We were control. It is painful to fight the mental control, we tried. But it is useless. We lost all of our family and friends on both villages. That is the truth. Please believe us. The voice is gone, there is no more control as you see. We have the ability to turn all human form and not half way. Please believe us. Oryeia said as she backed up more against the walls.

Are they telling the truth? Dante we need to know? Mark asked him.

Ask Carrlynia? She has the more abilities to find out who can lie and ask mom to! They are stronger in that ability than I am. Dante said as he kept his attention on the sky.

Mark turn to his mother and sister as they had already read both of the female hybrids that cowed in a far wall of the mobile.

Mark I know one thing I can tell they are scared to death of us. I can also say that they are telling the truth, Olaya is grieving a lost as well as Oryeia. Said both Maria and her daughter Carrlynia together!

So lets' see? What are we going to do with them now? Mark asked his mother and sister.

Joan got up as she took hold of Jolie from Maria arms. Jolie looked at both of the hybrid females. They are telling the truth. Oryeia has lost her husband and little ones. Olaya has lost her parents and brothers and sisters. That is why they are both grieving. Jolie said as she put her arms around her mothers' neck.

Alright then, we will just keep watching them until we get to the hybrid king and let him judge them. Mark said as he turned to look at Dante. Are we getting any closer to where we are supposed to be?

CHAPTER SIXTEEN

IKE RAN FAST TO where Steve and the others were waiting for him. He knew Steve had question that he just pushed aside for later. But he also knew that he would have to answer Steve sooner and not later. But how can he explain how his parents and Steve parents have been working for the freedom fighters for years. How could he tell Steve about hybrids genes that they have. Yes, Steve and his sister had the genes. But sense they had little food to keep the genes intact and would have been able to grow stronger in their body. The genes grew weak and almost gone, well Steve sister died because of some other disease that she should not have gotten. But she died of it. It had to be a flute of some kind. She had the genes, but –again she must not have eaten enough to grow and let the gene get stronger.

Now how in the fuck was he, king of the fucking hybrids going tell someone that has no idea of their strength, their—he just didn't know how he was going to answer any of those question that Steve had for him. For all Mike knew Steve might get mad or angry or even leave with the disc and then what was Mike going to do. Mike needed both the disc and Steve and the others in order to defend the government the freedom fighter government.

Mike rubbed his face and let the late noon air kiss his face, birds sung in tall trees that gather around the village he stood in. Air blowing hard as it wiped around his curly blonde hair as it rose up in a dance. Mike stood ready to leap up ahead of four of his hybrids he had chosen to company him in the meeting with Steve at the gate of the ancient. It had been something else at one time, but Mike never knew what it was or why the large trees were carved like wolves and cats that were half human and half hybrids. But Mike took the sight and what knowledge other hybrids told in his heart for truth. A tale of the first hybrid, a human that mated with a wolf and a cat, the children became our mothers and fathers of many hybrid tribes. But was that the truth or something that was just made up to explain how they were created? Mike started to run faster as he found the trail widening to where the hybrid knew a short cut to the statues.

Trees, bushes and old rumble crumbled along the path that was scattered with vines and greenery that covered the crumbled rocks that circle or squared like in places. Mike could see an outline of uneven grass that tilt upward and down at points. Must have been roads or something of that kind? Mike figured as he ran through the forest. The skies darken more as noon became part of the night. Star twinkled like diamonds he had once seen against the black silk cloth. The sight took his breath as he recalled his wife before she died. That was one day he could not forget. They were married under the skies bright lights of the stars like she always wanted, then the next day after all the feast of the many freedom fighters and hybrids packs, a great calamity of those running from weapons that no one could see, but felt as many fires brought out around them setting innocents on fire, death was all around Mike as another thought of his parents and that of his brother death years before. She had been caught with her sister in one of the homes that burnt down fast. Mike was a mess after that. He swore under oath before the fires of the freedom fighters and then he made another oath that he would not stop killing or hunting down the leader's death men until they were all gone. It has been to many years sense he thought of her, but the pain was still in his heart. He could never speak her name without roaring out death to anyone around him. Mike took a deep chilling breath and let out his roar that tighten his heart. He would more than just avenge his wife and parents; he would do it for all innocents that were lost to the government. His hybrid wolf legs thick and muscular torn into the ground deep as his claws and talons rip the soil apart as it gripped hard underneath him. His long snout with its whiskers white and tangling on its side of his nose twitching as the feel of the forest animals heard him approach. Mike fangs hung long and sharp on both upper and lower jars of his mouth. His breath taken in hard air that made his own heart beat fast in his chest. He had to get to Steve before more enforcers found out their leader Annie was killed. Jim was still back at the village recouping from his long walks and travels through the forest edges. He had seen too much and felt too many pains. Jim told him that the village where his brother had lived was gone. All were dead, torn apart like sticks to a match. He had buried his brother and his family there at the village. He could not bury any more than what he had done in a short time. His strength was weak and need the right food to restore his body back to strength. Water was little along the way to where he was now. So Mike let Jim rest until his family came for him. They all needed to be together it was too much too little time to lose to be apart like this. The statue came in view to Mike sight as another view came to him. The truck was parked along the side of the path. Mike could see the back of the trucks doors, as it swung open. He did not see anyone inside of the doors that showed where his friends had to be. They were all gone. A scent of something strange hunted around the truck. Mike heard alarm screaming out from the trucks from the computer that was put in the front of the trucks panel. The sound screamed out danger, do not leave the vehicle. All weapons stand by. The computer shouted out.

Mike and his packs of mixed wolves and cats waited a few yards away from the trucks back.

Where was Steve and the others? It was odd not to see them and just let the computer go off like this? What happen? Where are they? Mike thought about what he saw and knew that something was wrong. Mike sniff the air again, the scent was new and fresh.

Enforcers, men, mostly human, maybe twenty or more came closer enough to fight them or take them or something. Mike couldn't tell how many of them were here. But the fact was they had Steve and the others. Then another thought, did they have the disc? Did Steve tell them where the disc was? Mike had to check out the truck and look at where the disc was hiding inside. The door slammed open a sound of a sharp bang that slammed into metal against metal frame. Mike held back a breath as he went straight to where the disc was supposed to be. Mike knew where the metal box was stored behind the large freezers. He knew that the no one could find the box if they even tried to hunt for it. The walls behind the freezers were solid and smooth. There was no indication that there was something hidden behind them.

Mike touched the walls slowly with his human hands to find that one spot that he had made. The feel of warmth around the dull flat smooth scratching told him that the box was still inside. No one but he and Mr. Farmer knew how to get the boxes out. Steve knew it was there, but he could not open the wall. Mike took a breath as he moved his hands around the spot, then let the feel heat up more around his hands and wall. The feel tingled against his palms of his hands as the scratch grew bright and then moved with a thud of metal against metal. The box blended in with the wall easy. The feel of the cool box in mike hands and fingers as he moved his hands and fingers across each tips of the corners of the box felt good. The disc was safe. No one took them. But still what had happened to Steve and the others.

Mike had the feeling that the enforcers had more traitors working for them than Annie. She was just one pawn, one message to let them know they were being watched carefully. It was also a warning that the senators were also being watch more carefully. Their families were watched. Too much twist in this power struggle and that was what Mike called it. Power struggle of a world that has gone mad as hybrids and with few human beings struggled to survive in this world that only wants them gone. Mike said as sweat beamed down his human face. How was he going to solve this one? How was he going to save Steve and the others at the same time try to find the traitors too? There were too many obstacles that were in the way, but Mike knew he had to try. Mike took off in the direction of where the main scent of the enforcers and changed into a long lean golden feline of part lion and part tiger with white stripes against the blonde golden fur of his body. His head round with a mass of furry white mane and a long snout that held his sharp fangs that drip with angrier and with hungrier for its prey had hidden the main course. Steve disc were safe for right now. Mike had to put them back inside of the secret wall that only he and Mr. Farmer knew about. Mike had left two of his packs best computer programmers to reinstall the trucks computers in a way that only his voice would be able to command the truck to do what he wanted like activating the shield to keep others out of the trucks and to warn anyone of danger. It only took a few hours for them to finish. And then I decide to leave them at the truck to help guard the thing that was too large, but right for all it had in it at one time and now.

CHAPTER SEVENTEEN

ANTE SHRUGGED AS HE listened to Mark tell his mother that they had to trust them (that was or is the two female hybrid wolves). He still wasn't sure if he trusted them. Yes, they did tell the truth about their village being attack by something or someone. But he and his family knew that humans would not attack them unless they were one of the enforcers. With that thought, Dante took a breath and let it out with a buff of air. His mind on the sky and everything around them as he drove the mobile out toward the heavens and beyond in a funny way of things, Dover ridge country was one place he had not been but knew little of too. One word his cousin said about the place was it was beautiful and felt free. Uh, like yeah. There is no freedom, every one answered to someone. So where is the freedom, or what do they define freedom? Dante smiled as he thought about freedom on his own definition. His define would be to just run with other wolves that were not hybrids or were-wolves. To run would be in the forest and streams. Mountains would be great to, and to hunt deer or something. Yeah that would be even greater. Maybe everyone idea of freedom is different. Dante smile as he turned to his brother and let his smile turn to a frown. Mark was standing in his underwear and his only pants and shirt hanging over both of his arms. He had his arms on his hips as he just looked down at the two females sitting in a corner cowing at him. Yeah, he could tell they were scared. But for some reason he felt he should not trust them. Something, just something told him not to.

Mark could feel Dante warning in his head as his mother creep in thoughts too. Her words smooth, but firm. We may know now something's about them and their reason, but something was still off. She had told Mark. He put his pants on first and then his shirt. His feet free of any kind of restraints, he could feel the cool metal vibrate under his toes as he walked back to other panel of the mobile and watched the sky turn a deeper purple in the distance. Silence was in the mobile as they all kept quiet.

Only breathing and hush sounds of their breath coming and going out of their lungs were heard, Mark sat close to where the control panel was then thought about his family then his father came up. Mark was worried about his fathers and where he was at. His father was not a strong hybrid or anything. He was mostly a business man for the government like his fathers was before him.

The congressmen and women came from a history of family involvement throughout the centuries and maybe farther than that too. After someone in the family dies that has worked for the government in ways that helped the freedom fighters dies then someone else takes over the place of the other they have to be part of the decent family. That made Mark chuckle as he thought he was in line to take his father place in the government. But does he even have that job? Mark knew that was impossible that the government would even think about the giving him that proposition not with what had happen and the fact that the government has found all or most of the congressmen and women that are alliance to the freedom fighters cause. That thought stopped Mark thinking, they were more endanger than he thought. The government might know where all the places where the alliances were. They might be right now being killed by the government the enforcers were probably there already that had to be cause his family and that of Joan's family was attacked her husband died at a meeting with his father by the enforcers. Damn it, all of this was either a set up to find the other alliances or kill all of the ones they found out that worked in the congress that were alliance with the fighters. This was not good. Dante we need to separate and go in different direction to get the enforcers off our tracks. These women might have lost family and been compromised by someone and died or something but we cannot trust them. We need to leave them some where they would be picked up by the government enforcers. We need to do it fast.

Dante heard his brother's word and agreed with the plan, but something was close on their tails. In coming Mark, south side of the mobile, two crafts closing in we can get rid of them through the city of mountains. It's not that far from where we are. We can separate at that point to confuse them in their pursuit. Dante said as he swung the mobile over tall trees that reached high over any buildings he ever knew. The sight of the city that forest grew over 100's of years of forgotten buildings that became part of the mountains seemed to blend deeply and were forgotten of what they were at one time. His words were one that should not be spoken as their mother yelled back at them.

No streets or other homes were comparable to the cities abandonment of these homes that lay within buildings that still dwell people live in. These were once a wonderment to see and be in, but now forest just took over as people were forced to live outside of the grand cities and live in homes that were given by the government only.

Dante knew too that in each mountain lays a cave of some sort that echoes out the other side of it. But to find it may be a problem. Dante could only make out what the screen of the mobiles front glass could show him. He knew there might be a switch that would put out more lights for him to see along his path toward the dark and unknown city of mountains. If he was not careful everyone inside would be dead. He had to use caution at every turn.

Can you hide us within those trees ahead of us?

Mark asked his brother as he went to the other controls that would separate them.

We could but I can't see in this dense darkness. No stars out-no lights at all to see what's in the path of us. I mean what is in the trees that might kill us. We need to caution our steps. I am driving this thing without any focal lights that would give us away, but it's preventing us from seeing around us too. So I am putting out the distance lights that would echoed off other parts of the mountains making the enforcers that are targeting us now to think we are over there. So I will get at least a little bit of light to guide us over in that part of the forest. I think I found a cave, but I am not sure if we are still safe. I can see one of the enforcers scrambled over to where the light echoed off some of the trees. But where's the other enforcers. I know they are somewhere around here. I found them on our scanner beam. The scanner located the enforcers behind us, but I don't see them now. Dante said as he turned the mobile toward the darkness in the forest ahead of them. The mobile jerked upward with a feel of someone striking them hard behind them. The sound of metal striking metal bending inward made Dante hesitate in his effort to out run the enforcers. Mark took over the steering of the mobile as Dante stood back away from the Mark, his mind was running as he looked around the mobiles area. His mother stood in human fully with Jolie still in her arms and Ms. Joan holding on to Carrlynia arm. She was trembling like a cold leaf.

We need to stop the enforcers I got a plan but I need you three to move toward the far corner on my left. NO you two stay right there. I got plans for you both. So don't move until I say so. Is that clear girls? The two girls knotted as they sat right back down.

Another hit was aimed right at where Dante was standing the feel of the mobile moving back and forth felt as if they were on water mobile. The swaying was getting to Mark as he fought to stand where he was and not fall down. Mark had to make a decision fast, then he realized that if they separate within the cave one of them could go through the back of the cave, he knew there was another entrance and exit to the caves around here. These mountains were once tall buildings, but are now part of the mountain terrains. Another blast silently hit the mobile, the blasts was enough for the mobile to split in small places that Mark face shown fear and concern of what to do. He wanted to call out to his mother, but he knew that was cowardly. With a deep breath he jumped over to where his mother was holding Jolie and his sister was close to one of the hybrids that was huddling under an extended table from the mobile outer walls. The walls white as the panels with the controls were different colors bright and dark for some reason.

Dante knotted but looked at his sister and the two females. You take one of them and I will take Carrlynia-you take mother and Ms. Joan and Jolie. We will be find! I can still control your part of the mobile. But we are going to act as if they hit enough that we had crashed. All of our power will be shut off and I will put a tracker blast in the third part of the mobile and crash enough that they might think we had died in them. Unless they have a body scanner or one of those fancy guns that can find our DNA among the crash. We got to be lucky if they are one of those enforcers that are real dumb and not have one or other. Dante said as he looked at his brother with a smile. I may be younger than you but I can think like dad taught us too. Think like one of your enemies. And what would you do if you were in their shoes. So I figured that if those guns that are inside of this thing then they might have it too. Dante said as he motioned toward the floor.

Mark bent down close to one of the holders that were used as storage for weapons and mobiles engineers. Mark thought about what Dante said about DNA, he saw the guns there that were more like lasers than heat guns. Strange it was just strange. But DNA was blood and bones and hair. How were they going to get away with it? One thing was for sure, those two females had to have a tracking device that they could not find. That had to be how they were found this fast. I got another idea, female Olaya I need to see you now. Come with me, mother give the child to her mother. I need you too. Sister, watch that one until I return. A door slide opened in the middle of the wall of the mobile and Mark and his mother step in the room with Olaya walking behind them. Her fear of what was or might happen to her and her friend was evidence on her face and her walk. She was in half form as her wolf would not let her completely change back to human. She still had the legs of were-wolf but her upper body was human. Standing there watching them move closer to the back wall, the room was smaller than they thought. Not enough room for the three of them to talk.

Mother I need something that would make them I mean the enforcers think we had died in the crash. They might have those DNA heat guns that would tell them we had escaped and was not killed in the crash so. Mark waited as his mother thought about what he said. Let me see this right, you want me or us to cut our arms and let blood flow around the mobile to trick the enforcers? I think there is a better and safer plan. You need hybrid blood that is mixed with human blood and we need to do this fast. The mobile is going to crash and the third part of this will be the one to impact the crash. Hmm. Maria looked at Olaya and took her arm in her hands. When do you need the blood and DNA I can cut my hair and that of your sister's too. Matter of fact you need a haircut too. And so does Dante. Hmm. Let me see your arm son. Mark knew what his mother was thinking and planning. The plan was better and no one will die for it. When is the impact son? Maria asked as she let her claws grow sharp. Maria looked at the female that was in a state of mixed parts of human and wolf. Bones they need bones and time before the enforcers find the crashed mobiles. Hmm.

Mark went back to Dante and the partly part mobile that was starting to close partly to make it two mobiles. Dante how long to impact? Mark asked his brother.

I would estimate 30 minutes no longer than that I can fight the enforcer by flying over the tree tops I know maneuvers that might well might lose them for a time. Just watch and get ready to crash. Dante said as he turned the mobile around toward the enforcers and smack right through them with strikes on each side of the enforcer's mobiles. Mark took the vantage of the situation and took out one of the laser guns that was stored with the DNA heaters. His aim missed as he pulled the gun out of one of the open stale windows that was hidden behind a wall. Dante slide the mobile back pass the enforcers again as he flew a few yards away. Everyone in their mobile slid back and forth across the floor of the mobile. Jolie was laughing as she slid on the floor as if she was going down a slid. Joan tried to catch Jolie but the girl was having too much fun. Mark slid against one of the walls that were close to the window. Carrlynia took another gun and went to the other side of Marks window and started to point at the mobiles as they went by again through the enforcers mobile. Mark wait just wait for it. Get them right now. Carrlynia said as her gun beamed straight at the enforcer's window. Mark shot at the other mobile at the same time Carrlynia did. The shot was right at a spot where the enforcers use to plug in their energy fuel. The shot was intense enough to blast it to pieces. The feel of the blast was felt by everyone in the mobile. The mobile separated more as the blast kept on coming, one of the metal walls hit the other mobile were Carrlynia shot. With that sight of the two mobiles gone, Mark still wanted to crash one part of the mobile but seeing that the other two mobiles were landing in many different parts on the forest ground, he had to go to plan two. Land the mobile close or inside of that cave. Mark said as he moved closer to Dante.

We still need to do something with the DNA heaters. One of the mobile would be able to use theirs to search for us. We need those bodies inside of this mobile, Mother can you manipulate their DNA to match us? Mark asked her.

A nodded from their mother's head and Carrlynia was ready to jump out of the dividing part of the mobile. She knew where the mobiles crashed and how badly the bodies became. Her stance in readiness was a sight that made Maria proud of her daughter's lean muscular body that showed how lethal she could be. Carrlynia changed into her wolf and jumped as the wall that was coming up to close the mobiles separation to make two mobiles. Mark grabbed Olaya and dragged his mother closer to his side. He had to get to the controls to maneuver down closer in the caves mouth as he watched his brother control the mobile with ease. He was too good and to young as far as Mark was concern. But he knew how to think more like a man than most kids his age. Maybe Mark was getting to old maybe that was a problem or was it. The cave seemed to swallow them up hole as darkness ate their only light from the stars and moon. Mark turn his beam from the mobile on they were safe right now, no one was around but them. The sounds of bugs whispering to each other made Mark think creepy and good. Danger was only present or coming when bugs and small animals become silent.

Mark listened closely to all of the animals around him as he landed the mobile intact inside of the cave floor. The floor was covered with dirt and dust as webs decorated the walls inside of the cave. Mark grew still as heard his sister howl in the distances the sound was a signal that they all knew told them she found them safe. Which in this case the mobiles were intact enough for her to drag one or two of the enforcers back to where they were, then Dante sprung out of the other mobile in his wolf form and followed his sister to where she was with the other enforcers!

Mark looked at the two females and knew they had to somehow leave them. One thing was for sure they either would not make it when the enforcers get to them or they might try to run for it, another course would be they would tell the enforcers about them. That would not be good if they were caught by the enforcers. With a deep breath Mark went over to his brother and silently spoke to him of his plan. *Sister is bringing the enforcers bodies and getting them inside of this mobile, we need to change their DNA and hope the other enforcers who are probably close by searching for them. We will let them think these enforcers are us and they may leave us alone. We need to work fast. Dante can you get this beast down inside of that caves main entrance first.*

Dante sat the mobile inside of the cave dark mouth as it settled on the dirt floor that was full of moister and the smell of thick mold. Mark I am turning a light on one of the beams should give us some light. We need to see what we are doing and how are we going to change their DNA?

I mean we don't have anything to do it. I think big brother you're in lala land. Dante said as he turned the beam light on. The caves walls were covered in mud with webs decorating each corner of the caves outlets to the other side. Dante looked at each web and then looked at his brother. Uh, I think we are in trouble look at those webs. Dante said as he pointed them out. Joan walked out of the mobile slowly as she noticed the webs delicate design. This is beautiful. I never been this close to a giant black and brown widow it's in the recluses something family. I just know they are most deadly spiders here in the world. We got to be careful not to move the webs. If you do the webs act like a homing device for them and get here fast, their teeth are large and they well they can and will kill you. So be careful. Joan said as she pushed her daughter back in the mobile.

What does the spider look like again? Mark asked as he noticed bright green eyes staring at him. Mark back up and went inside, while Dante ease back in the mobile with Mark. Alright this is bad. Mark closed the mobile that was separated from Dante and they both became two separate mobile. The feel of the mobile engine under Mark feet rumbled with vibration as he walked barefoot, his shoes were torn off when he changed into his wolf form. His feet sticking to the floor as he walked over to the control panels. Then as he tried to leave the caves entrance something fell on top of the craft.

The fell of something hard and heavy landed on top of the mobile head. Mark felt the shake of the mobiles body swung back and forth with metal sounding like it was creaking apart. Dante watched as his brother's mobile fight off a large spider that Joan said was called brown black widow recluse. The strange looking spider was larger than the mobile maybe even larger than any buildings he ever seen. Dante could see the many green eyes that looked at Marks mobile like it was food escaping from its webs. The mouth was dripping salvia that Dante suspect might be poison. The sight of the spider gave Dante a shake of fear, but he had to take that fear and bury it back in his mind and let the fear just fall off. He had to something fast or he would lose his brother and his mother. Then he saw someone get out of the mobile from behind the craft. Dante couldn't tell who it was, but knew that whomever was trying to distract the spider away. Then there was another person that came out a smaller person. That told Dante it must be Jolie, she was special with a gift of truth and knowledge but she was human. That in itself was special. She was running toward one of the webs. Her small feet were small in her steps and slow. The spider came off the mobile, but Jolie and her mother would be in danger if the spider gets to them. Dante didn't want to see them killed they were humans and friends. Dante studied the panel looking for something some kind of weapon that would stun the spider at least. It would be enough for them to get out of the cave. On panel in front of Dante was a bright clear light that glowed as he touched the panel gently to see if there was any indication of what it was. The feel of runes of sun and light told him it was a stun gun. He could stun the spider enough that it would leave Joan and her daughter alone. May be he could get them inside of his mobile. Then he saw it another spider larger than the other with brown stripes and black legs with grey stripes too. Its fangs dripped with brown venom its eyes many but all green, the spider went forward toward the other spider. The sound of clicking noise and chirps was heard echoing though the caves wall.

Dante had to think fast. The stun was alright, but he had to have something stronger and better. Then he heard the mobiles swish of the door open on the side of the mobiles back. He saw one of the females that were inside of this mobile with his brother and sister and mother. She was a liars and enemy to the freedom fighters. He didn't care what she said or did. It's just facts the enforcers had been following them sense they left their home. It seemed that enforcers knew where they been sense then. It's seemed funny that they had said that their family was killed by the fighters when he knew and his family knew that was a lie. Freedom fighters did not attack innocent hybrid villages and killed all the people in them. Then they changed their story fast when they used someone or act like someone was controlling them. His mother did get a message from her cousin the King of hybrids and he said that their Aunt was the traitor and she is dead now. So was it her that controlled the other two females? Maybe or maybe not they could just be acting. Even though Jolie and his mother said they were telling the truth. Right now one of them had just escape from him and is heading toward the spiders. Dante made the mobile raise upward toward the ceiling as he floated above the spider's head. He could see Joan trapped in one of the webs her eyes wide as she struggled to get free. The other spider had attacked again the one that was close to Joan. Jolie was screaming Dante could hear her voice echoed in his ear. Something was pounding against his chest it was causing him to sweat and feel pain that went through his body. He had to get to them or else they would die. He would be both a coward and something he was fighting against not to be. No one leaves humans behind his breed protects all that are innocent. He is going to use the mobile to stop the spiders he has to. But how would he be able to protect Joan and Jolie if he dies. There has to be a way. Yeah! The other mobile that they separated from! It crashed its where? Without thought Dante touched a red button that flashed bright in his face. The red flash beamed out a bright white light that blasted the first spider back tail. The spider then turned around to attack Dante's mobile with a hiss of venom the spider started to climb the mobiles roof, but Dante pushed the button again and the second spider came after the first one. Both spiders fighting now each other trying to get on top of the mobiles roof, but the mobile sent out another blast that sent the spiders flying against the walls. Joan was stuck in the web and Jolie was working hard to get her mother out of it. Olaya was working hard to getting Joan out of the web. She had to do something. Her half human part was no way in her way, it was more right now her wolf that was in the way. She could not work being stuck with both hybrids. The task was getting on her nerves. Joan screamed when she saw the two spiders decide to come back at them again. Jolie screamed as she took a rock she found on the ground and hit the web as hard as she could. The web just bounced like springs but didn't break. The spiders fought as they tried to get close to Joan and the other victims that were standing close to their web.

Dante was stun with fear as he watched the spiders fighting. Dante felt his heart pounding hard in his chest his beast wanted out it wanted blood. The feeling grew as Dante watched the spiders cast their legs against each other's body. The fight escalated as fangs reached out toward parts of their bodies. Blood dripped out of legs and then one of the spiders bit the lower part of the other spiders large behind. The one screamed out its mercy that turned into rage. Dante had to work fast but waited as he watched the female cut the webs that tangled around Joan waist and legs. They worked fast as the hybrid talons sharp and ready to cut the webs that seemed more rope than lava that spun out of the spiders' ass. The web was thick as rope as her talons cut loose one of the webs then another one by her legs, the spiders screamed out their protest when Joan finally got loose, she grabbed Jolie and ran toward the mobile that was still hovering over their heads ad that of the spiders too. Joan didn't know if Dante knew how to get them inside of the mobile without bring the mobile down for them. One of the spiders got loose from the fight then headed toward them as Joan and Jolie got close to the entrance of the cave.

Dante saw them escaping toward the entrance of the cave. He knew there was a control that would that get them up in the mobile. But he could not concentrate on what was what on the panel. His mind went to Joan and Jolie. He really didn't care about the prisoner that was out there saving the two humans that was more important than his own life. Why was she doing this? She no reason too, she was nothing but a traitor to all that are innocent. His brother and he had agreed with their mother that these females were not to be trusted if they were controlled then they were used as tracking devices. No he would just let the female be there with the spiders. Right now he had to save Joan and Jolie.

Both girls ran out to the edge of the caves mouth, a small cliff hung over the mouth that they didn't realized was there when they came in the first time. Mark mobile was not in sight. He must've had fallen down in the forest floor around the trees. Joan saw Dante turn on one of the beams must have been a laser high intense the spider that was in front of her turned around and saw the mobile hanging over its head. It tried to stand on its back legs, but two of the legs were bitten off by the other spider in the fight. The spider tumbled off on its back, the sight of the spider now in its position gave everyone the ability to kill the spider easier as the back. The female was behind the second spider, her stance was ready as she went into her full wolf form and let her hybrid go. She was larger than a normal wolf and stronger than a human with muscles bulging out her arms and legs to make her stronger than anything that Dante had ever seen. The female ran straight toward the spider legs underneath its belly. With her talon sharp as blades pointy as a needle started to tear into the belly like a zipper on a coat. The spider stopped as the other bulge his fangs into the second spiders head and body. The sound of the spider killing the other and started to eat the other spider, spiders are known to be cannibals. Dante had to get to Joan and Jolie. A new spider was standing close to where Joan and her child were standing. They were too close to the edge. Dante drove the mobile straight to the head of the new spiders that was a dark black stripe maybe a black widow of some kind hybrid like the others they had seen. No spider can be that big and not be a hybrid. A mix of other spiders but grew to be so big that scientist could not hold them. That had to be why these were monster in size. Dante aim his beams that injured one of the spiders. Dante aim as he took a breath and scream out die monster. The spider turned to see who was coming toward him, the sound of the mobile humming in his sensitive ears made it stop and look up at something small, but the feel of that bright light hurt it enough that the spider's snappers clink together as the mobile flew over his head. The bottom of the spider's belly was soft and easy to split with talons sharp as blades. The female saw her mark again, she ran in wolf form under the black spider and scratched the belly with her claws and teeth. The spider fell down on top of the other spiders backwards. Its legs moving fast as he tried to get up, the blood that dripped down its side flowed down like a small water fall. But the spider did not want to die, it kept on trying to get up, but was too weak so it spits out its venom toward the mobile. Dante had to dodge the venom fast he didn't want the humans to touch the mobile with venom all over it. Then he saw the female in wolf form looking at Joan and Jolie, they step farther away from her and fell off the cliff. The female ran down its path toward the forest. Dante cursed as he followed where Joan and Jolie fell off.

Their screams echoed through the forest full of darkness. Dante heart beat fast it felt as if the heart was coming out of Dante chest. His sight was good in the dark, better than humans' sight at night. But right now he could not see a thing in this darkness; the darkness looked like a piece of black coal. Trees arms spread out toward the sky reaching out toward the mobile like they were going to grab hold of the mobile with arms.

Mark had just flew out like a rocket of some kind out of that cave. He could not believe what he saw; giant spiders that he knew had to be poisonous. Where was he was one thought as he tried to look back at the cave. But Mark realized that he was farther away than he thought he was.

The trees tall and graceful touched the mobiles bottom with scratches to claim the mobile as theirs. Mark had to be careful as he realized the darkness was getting worse. His sight was no longer good as his sight was becoming one with the darkness. He had to land and rest, maybe wait for his sister and mother they had left the mobile as it landed close to the cave. But that spider that monster landed on top of his mobile and it shook hard then spin out of the cave like a rocket. It was incredible and scary as shit to see it.

But his brother his little brother, he-he was in that cave, no Mark thought he was not going to think about. Dante was not dead nor was Joan and little Jolie. They were alive he had to believe that. Mark turned his around to look at the traitor cowing in a corner. Her face in a form of a wolf but he still could tell she was afraid of the same thing. How far did they fly out from the cave? How far was his sister and mother? He hoped they were alright. With a breath Mark set the mobile on what he thought was a lake. The moonshine down on the lake to make it look like they were landing on the sky's velvet cloth of diamonds and crystals shining down on them, the sight was more beautiful than he would ever see again.

Mark stood quiet to think what to do next. He was alone sort of but alone in his thoughts and his soul. His family was more than family they were important than his breath. Now Dante maybe gone with the two humans they were supposed to protect. Maybe to be safe maybe he could or should try to send out a message to someone out there that might be his family? Hmm. *Can anyone hear me? I am lost and I cannot find my dog.* Mark said as he stood there with his eyes closed. He tried hard to listen for anyone who knew the answers. It was one of his mother's idea that they remember and that the question was also the answers too. If anyone had tap in to their mind link, then they would be in trouble. No one but the family knew the answer. The female walked slowly toward the door of the mobile. Maybe he should get of the mobile and see if the other creatures around the forest knew how to speak to a hybrid. His mother had said that the forest animals knew all creatures that live in the forest. They were very territorial when it came to anyone that are not welcome.

That was a chance Mark had to take. He opened the door and went out into the forest. Night creatures with wings large fling over his head screeching out.

Their calls to anyone who would listen, their words only known to those that of their kind. But yet, Mark understood each phrase each word. Hunt a great hunt was coming to the evil ones. But who was the evil ones? Mark couldn't speak to them ask them questions. But he didn't want to step away from the mobile either. He didn't trust the female. She was a tracker and the enforcer was not that far. Yeah, they got two of the enforcer's mobiles and some of enforcers too. But the tracker was the one way the enforcers were able to find and this female has the tracker. He knows he couldn't let her take the mobile or take her with him either. He had to do something but what? He had decided it was better to have her in front of him than have her take off with the mobile. The trees green leaves shadowed by the night sky blew through the trees making the leaves dance slowly to a silent sound that only they could hear it. Insects gathering around under bushes and small trees singing songs that would tell other insects were to find the food. Mark walked slowly watching the female and keeping his eyes on everything around him. His feet wet and moist as the ground underneath him, his feet felt twinges and wet leaves with dirt wet and muddy. Slowly over larger twinges he tried not to break one so he could be silent in his steps as he walked. The female was in her wolf form and walking as slowly as he was. Caution was all around him. No light, darkness was thick, sight was limited, and Mark could make out trees, but limbs and fallen trees bushes larger than the height of his knees. Mark stumbled a few times as he watched the female jump over limbs and fallen trees as if she could see better than he could. Wait a minute that's it, their eye sight I mean when they turn into a wolf or cat are better than our eye sight. Hmm, that might work.

Mark change as he walked behind the female. The feel of the hybrid changing his human skin to the wolf felt good, bones breaking as each part bent to form each part of the wolf. The trail would be a lot better now. His sight is much better and the sticks don't hurt him now.

CHAPTER EIGHTEEN

TEVE LAY ON THE ground controlling his breathing and his heartbeat. Staying calm and not letting any negative thought making his heart rate go higher. Steve knew that these hybrids could hear his lungs take in air and that his heart was pretty much noisy when it came to the hybrids hearing. The feel of heavy hands grabbing Steve shoulders and hauling him up over someone shoulder made Steve huff air he didn't want to let out. He was grateful that the hybrid that carried him didn't say or do anything. The feel of the ground coming up and down from where Steve was at was getting to his stomach and his head. His head bounced against the hybrids back side making his head hurt. Jack and Mr. Farmer was close by he could hear them mumble as they went by.

Jack had to do something to get these total ass holes to let Steve down and leave him. But they don't believe he is dead. Maybe they could hear Steve heart beat slowed down to a point that most people would think he was dead. That was the only reason they were taking Steve with them. Steve had to escape and get back to the truck. The disc was unguarded and someone could get to the disc like the government. Those things are great resources and history. Jack needed to find a way for Steve to get out. Jack walked in a wide and wiggle line, he kept on bumping against Mr. Farmer, then he tripped against Max, they fell on the ground together and Jack grabbed Max neck and yelled at him. Don't do that shit ass. You hear me boy. I don't give a shit who you think you are. Now move away from me jackass. Jack said as he shoved Max against Mr. Farmer. That was then he got the idea. A fight with Max and Mr. Farmer maybe the fight would get that hybrid to put Steve down. They had to fight like they mean it. Mr. Farmer got the same idea and bunched Max in the face hard, Max nose bled as his head spin around. Susan whipped around and bunched Jack in his nose and then went straight to his groin. Jack bent over holding his manhood. The pain made him want to scream, but he just got madder. Grinding his teeth (or what was left of his teeth) and tried to get up with all his might. Jack to his fist and hit Susan in the face, her face turned around as she fell down on the ground. Max and Mr. Farmer fought hard. Their fists swinging at each other's face and stomach, Mr. Farmer eyes swollen as Max kept on hitting Mr. Farmer's face.

The children looked at us and started to argue first then hitting each other. The hybrids just looked at us and stopped in their tracks as they noticed that their prisoners did not follow them. As this was going on, Susan took her baby and put her close to a bush to be hidden from the fight she knew was coming. If they lose the fight the baby would die and if they win the fight the baby would live, but only if she herself would live through the fight itself.

The sight of all those people fighting among themselves was unusual to them. They had never seen so many humans fight for no reason, especially children. The children were or are the weakness of humans. They do not hunt like the hybrids or their children either. This was a sight.

Jack shoved Max and his woman against one of the hybrids, the children followed Jack lead as Max and Susan grabbed a rock from the ground where they were landed under feet of one of the hybrids. Susan laid the rock on the hybrids open feet that was bare. Max did the same on the opposite feet of the same hybrid. His howl lit up the other hybrids angrier. One of the hybrid grabbed Susan by the hair, but Susan still had the rock in her hands, she pushed her arm back as far as she could and smacked the hybrid nose hard. The hybrid let Susan fall from his hands. The children ran up Max back with long thick sticks and heavy rocks and started to hit the hybrid hard on his face. Then they tumble down as the hybrid screamed out his pain, he fell backward with the other hybrids running a small hill that they had taken away from the captives. The hybrids fell back as the one that was attacked by the children fell to his back. The other hybrids scrambled underneath the one hybrid that was still on the ground. The children looked at each other and at the sight of the hybrids getting up from the fallen hybrid. Slowly they backed away and then let their weapons fly that they found around the ground. The weapons went flying over

Max and Susan head, the hybrids fell as marks took from what the children threw. The ones that did not fall Max and Susan with Jack and Mr. Farmer stood in ready stance their arms on their sides, clinching their fists ready to fight. Max and Susan were in running stance with their arms touching the ground ready to do injuries. Her flips went high over the heads of the hybrids in surprise and shock as she came down on the hybrids heads and one by one they fell as her strike went true as a marker.

The robed hybrid took off his robe and was in his hybrid form. The sight of the ground trembled as the hybrids injured and all were ready to fight the children and Jack, Mr. Farmer and Max with Susan. Susan had to look around before she took off, her sight was on a blanket that her baby was wrapped in, and she was close to a large bush that was farther away from the fight. Somehow they all knew this was going to happen. It was talked about in whispers, but the signal was there when Jack shoved Mr. Farmer back. Her face was bloody, her eye black swollen already, a scar sharp on the side of her good eyes bled as she looked again at her baby by the bush. Hybrids started to charge as they ran up to Max and Susan as they were in front. The children stood next with more limbs from fallen trees that were around them, Jack and Mr. Farmer were behind them all. The sight of this did not make the hybrids scared, it made them laugh. The sound of chuckles burst out in laughter among the hybrids. But they were ready to tear those humans apart. With another howl the hybrids spring up in the air and landed in front of each children and Jack. Steve was laying down close to Susan baby by the bush. Susan jump up and ran toward Steve, the baby was alright, but Steve was playing dead a game they all played when they were children. It always helped them when they got caught by the enforcers at times. Now it is used for times like this. Steve started to breath, his breath coming in slowly, a cough and shout as the one hybrid that wore a rob came over fast with his claws sharp and deadly, his mouth full of sharp fangs that dripped with saliva. Steve had hold of something sharp by his side, he pulled it without thinking and struck the hybrid right in the chest. Susan was on the ground with injuries that made her bleed out all over the ground close to her baby. She was unconsciousness as she laid close to her baby. Her face was pale and she was not moving.

Steve looked up and found that he was getting to mad right now, no he wasn't mad he was going into a rage, no one hurts his friends. Steve felt his arms making noise that sounded like breaking bones, the feel of his bones stretching and breaking growing into something that Steve wasn't sure of scared him and yet the pain felt both good and bad, but Steve felt as if he was getting to out of control. His arms getting longer looking like legs more, his face growing fur as his nose and mouth grew long like a snout with fangs breaking though his gums that were missing teeth. Steve had to roll over as the smell of blood made him raged at those that hurt his friends. As Steve felt the change in him the robed hybrid came back up and attacked Steve before he could finish his formation. Steve could feel the pain of bones breaking but the strength was wonderful. The robed hybrid attacked hard with his own claws. But Steve still had that sharp thing that he used to stab the hybrid the first time. Now seeing blood was all he wanted. Steve grab his weapon and started at the rob hybrid. Steve fur was a dark black with a white line that came from the top of his head to his back. His eyes changed into a red ball of hate. Steve slashed the robe hybrid on the arm then again close to the hybrids head. But at that point the robe hybrid grabbed the sharp thing with his claws and pulled it close to him. Steve knew what was going to happen, so with his other claws Steve let his talons grab the hybrids face as he bitten the robe hybrids snout. The hybrid screamed out as he felt the pain of his nose rip off his snout. He stumbled back then fell to the ground. Steve jumped on the hybrid with all his body. The feel of skin peeling off with his teeth and claws, felt too good. But Steve wanted to do more damage, his friends need him. With a jump in the air, Steve landed on another hybrid that was beating a child that was smaller and weaker than that big hybrid. Steve rip the hybrids neck off with his powerful fangs that went longer than his mouth could hold it in. The taste of the hybrid blood dripping in his mouth didn't quench his thirst. He wanted more, and with that Steve started again until all of the hybrids either stopped fighting them or died at his attack. Steve stood there not able to understand what happen to him, but only knew it saved his friends lives. Max ran to check on Susan and the baby. But when he got there by the large bush that had the blanket that Susan used for the baby they were gone. The body of the hybrid that wore the robe was still there lying in his own life blood.

The ground around them was soaked with blood from the children that did not survive the battle and of those hybrids that died at Steve hands. His breath was coming fast as his chest wet with sweat went bare. Steve form of wolf passed over his body and Steve became human again. But he did not have any cloths as he realized that he was naked standing around children and that of his friends.

Mr. Farmer looked around for something that Steve could use to hide his bare body.

Max came back in tears as he held the blanket close to his chest. She's gone my little girl and my mate. Their gone I can't I can't find them. Max said as his tears fell.

Steve was unsure if something got to them before they could. Look I didn't know what happen to me. But I am grateful for it. Maybe it's another secret my parents and everyone else's parents kept. I might be able to sniff anyone that might have taken them, but we need answer from those two that are partly dead. Steve said as he went close to the two hybrids that could not escape like the others did.

Their injuries were bad, Steve had bitten off one of the hybrids leg and the other his front legs. He didn't want to kill them yet, he needed answer of who and why they attack them back at the truck.

The hybrids changed back to human forms as they lay there waiting to die.

Now you can tell us why you all attack us and took us as prisoners and who told you to do this. Steve asked one of them as he bent low in the man face.

Our families are being held by the government and we were told to get any one that is in a strange mobile. We were only following our leader. The man said as he took breath that was painful.

Government got all of your family in their holding area. Damn it if you all need help why you should have just call your King. I am sure he will help your village to save your families. But what you all did was just suicide. I killed most of your warriors. What now, if your families are being held by the government then they would be killed because you all failed your mission, so they died and you all died too. What have you all accomplished by that? Shit stupid hybrids. Steve said as he watched the hybrid man die. The other hybrid laughed at Steve as he pointed to him.

You are a traitor to our kind. We had sent messages to the King he is too busy and has no time for a small village like ours. Kill me now traitor so I can know if my family lives. He said as he laid back on the ground. His leg bled fussily on the ground. His laugh was weak as his life seemed to leaving him slowly.

I am not a traitor I didn't know I was a hybrid. My parents died before I could even remember them. My sister took care of me until I got a job and took care of her. But she is dead and so is my parents'. So I had no one to tell me that I was a hybrid. So you all thought you could just –Steve had to stop talking the man died too. There was no one to answer his question. Now he wanted to know where was their village and how did they get the information about their families. Those question would never be answered until he finds some of the ones that escape. If their families were captured by the government. They might be killed if they got capture by the government no matter either way the hybrids and the villages were doomed. If one of the hybrids were able to bring someone to the sight of the government hide out Steve wasn't sure if either hybrids would be able to live if they thought the government would let them go. Steve thought as he looked at the forest that was in front of them. They had to get back to the truck. But how? No one here knew the forest well not this one. Mr. Farmer had found the robe that the hybrid taken off he put it on Steve and looked back at Max who was on the ground crying.

Max we will find them we promise. I think we need to look close to the bushes and trees that were in lineament of where Susan and the baby were. There has to be some sort of clue. Steve said as he walked back over to where all of this started.

We need to bury our dead. I don't want any one eaten my sister. One of the kids said.

We are not burying anyone, not yet, I think it is safe if we just find a hole somewhere close by and put the bodies in them and then burn the bodies. It well be the best we can do right now. So send two or three of your scouts and find a hole. I know this place had to have one there are many outposts that always told people that holes opened up many centuries ago and left the wide hole open under camouflage. So look with caution. Steve said as he looked at his best friend Jack standing over two little ones that were almost gone to us. His tears falling down with his sweat from the battle was making his skin shine like a star on the night sky dark cloth. Then Jack got up and walked over to Steve. So you think now you're the leader and telling us what to do? Jack asked Steve as he looked straight in his best friends' eyes. Steve just winked at him. I don't see you doing or saying anything? So what's the story then? Steve asked as he stood there with the robe blowing around his angle. He still felt as if he had no clothes on, but again it did feel good.

Jack kicked a rock that was underneath his feet, his shoes had worn out to its limit back at the truck. He was used to the feel of the rocks and grass under his feet. But the smell of dead bodies of all those that fought not long ago made him wanted to vomit. Jack took a breath and let it out slowly, his stance was relaxed again as he looked at his friend's eyes. Well I guess I would split up one group to try to get back to the truck. And the other group to help find Susan and her baby!

Jack said as he rubbed his face with his left hand and had his right hand hanging down to his sides.

And who will protect these groups if they get attack before they reach the truck or find those who will find Susan? Steve asked him. You know I just found this hybrid in me. It kind of feels good in a way then again it feels really bad like it hurts when my bones break and start growing in a fast speed that really hurts. So I don't know how you think I could help both groups. I can't be at the groups at the same time. Steve said as he walked over to where the children were gathering the dead children in pile close to the bushes where Susan and her baby were taken. The sight of the dead made Steve hurt inside. They the children should have never fought. The fight was for the grown up and not the children. But there was only ten in the pile and they had left with at least twenty or less, but he figured ten or did he miss count? Steve saw one little girl with dirty red hair with her neck ripped out, two small boys with blonde hair and the leader of the group of children's all had died in the fighting. He wasn't sure right now if it was a boy or girl but that three. Another child with streaks of black with blonde mix that makes it four, wait a minute, Steve started to count the children that were standing around the pile. One –two –three-four-five-six-ten children he had counted in all. But he thought there was twenty or Steve didn't know, maybe he just didn't pay attention and didn't bother to count before they got in the back of the truck. They had fourteen in all and now ten. Still too many died and too many living to see all the death of their friends and him, changing into a hybrid.

That he never thought or image that he could do that. Steve thought hybrids were born and raised hybrids. But he wasn't, he was raised human with a sister that died human and he remembered his parents that were humans. So how did he become hybrid and be human too. It just didn't make sense. Steve looked back at Jack as he walked over to Steve side. So what is it? Steve asked.

I think your right you can't be at the same time with two different groups. And we really don't know where either one is. Jack said as he patted Steve back.

Yeah, well I am not sure either. But I know that we came from that way south, and I could smell Susan now, that is her blood. She went into the forest straight ahead. I might be able to track her now. I am able to distinguish which is her blood and the children too. Steve said as he looked straight at the forest and all its darkness and unknown to them. He wasn't sure if there might be more of those hybrids that capture them back at the truck out there. They had to try at least. Mr. Farmer step over and looked with Steve then smiled at him. We did a good job in communicating you know. I had to work on what Jack was doing or what he wanted us to do. But I guess I knew when he pushed me and make like I did it. Then he hit Max and Susan went off like a mad hatter in a market place. So yeah we think together like glue to paper. Mr. Farmer said.

So when are we goin to get my wife and baby. Max said as he started into the forest.

Steve and the others walked behind Max and into the unknown of the forest.

CHAPTER NINETEEN

JIM HAD TO LEAVE the village no matter what the problem is. Its night time and the forest is full of hunters. But Jim needed to find his wife and get to the freedom fighters. After Anne lies, he thought about the other hybrids that might be traitors. Jim Stood there looking at the forest and back at the village. His mind went to his family, and he missed his wife and all three of his children. He knew his son Mark would act like the leader that he was. He knew when to talk and when not to but listen and when to ask question. His daughter Carrie was he called her was like that too a leader by nature. But then again she like to watch and listen more and show how to get out of trouble. Jim chuckled at that thought of both of his older kids. How many times had he stepped back to see how his two son got out of trouble? His wife would just tell Jim, that it is god to let them get into trouble and watch how they get out of it. This is how they learn things on their own someday. It was hard not to help them, but it was lessons that they had to learn and make decision on too. They had to grow-up and now they were out there with his wife and in endanger from the government. That scared Jim more as he thought about it. Jim mind wonder about where are they and are they alright are they safe or are they dead too. Maybe that is why he could not mind link with his wife. How would they find each other if they were alive? Jim rubbed his neck and slapped his hands together as if he was getting ready to spring up from the ground and change into a wolf or cat. But his blood didn't have much hybrid blood that would make him change not like his brother or adopted sister. His brother had more than he had. Jim had watched his brother change into a wolf he had the more of the genes than he was able too. But –But Jim was just human and that was it, he could not change like his brother or sister for that much was true and he had taken it as is or as he should. Even though his wife was hybrid at birth and so were his children he loved them. It was a fact that she was more animal than she was human although they married out of pure love that grew stronger with each day that passed. It was her that taught the children to hunt and fight as he watched them grow up. She had taught them the way of hybrid wolf. Jim thought about how she hunted outside of the city at times and brought food home from her kills, she had to do this in order to keep her hybrid from going wild. Jim shook his head and chuckled as he thought of his family and how things just got out of hand now. They were in danger and choice were made that he did not like or could control. Jims feet were bare and his shirt was made of some kind of animal skin with his pants shorter than what he liked showed off his legs that were full of scratches and cuts from his escape from the Government. His legs were scratchy and felt odd but bare.

Another hybrid was getting closer to Jim as Jim notice that he was watching Jim make a decision. Jim could not tell what the hybrid was feeling as it was apparent to see that the hybrid had a mask of non-emotion on his face and stance. His face a blank stare that show nothing to see what was being felt.

The large hybrid thought about Jim as he noticed how Jim eyes tense with concern for someone the hybrid thought might be his mate, it would be hard on anyone if his mate would be missing. Damn government assholes, Jim was and is a good man he helped save the villages from those traitors who attacked them last night. He wanted to help Jim but the King asked him personally to protect this man that had save the villages of wolves and cats. And with that also saved his own family. It was clear that at one point that they were told not to interfere with human matters, but this became both human and hybrid cause and right now this hybrid alpha was worried too about Jim family safety.

Jim was total into the forest, no sound seemed to come out of the forest, bird's he noticed was silent in branches. Bugs that lived high into the grass were even silent too. It was not normal. Something was coming, but what? The hybrid that stood next to Jim had left him and walked behind Jim. What is going on? Everyone in the village seemed not to notice the sounds around them. Jim walked a small distance in the forest, Mike was in flight with the other hybrids looking for that boy that had the information that would destroy the government fast. But where was the boy and why was it taking his wife's cousin this long to find that boy? But right now no sounds mean that something is coming in bad. Jim slowly looked up at the trees hoping to hear or see a bird. But nothing, it was not good. Jim slowly walked back to the forest he had a feeling of being watched it was strange a feeling of evil or something that wanted to eat him. His feet stepped on something sharp that was laid against a small branch of a tree. His feet hurt, blood spotted the ground as he hopped toward the field that lead to the village he just came from. He knew that the blood would be its lead into the village death was behind him. He had to get away fast.

One of the hybrids saw Jim running from the forest with a hop, he could almost smell blood. He was injured. The hybrid ran toward Jim and picked him up in his arms like bag of heavy potatoes. The hybrid swing Jim over his shoulder and took Jim foot that was injured in his mouth the blood sipped into the hybrids mouth and added fuel to his fire that was stirring with what had happen to the one he was to protect. He knew that the king would do something to him. He really didn't what to know what or anything. He just wanted to be safe, let Jim be safe. The hybrid took Jim to the hut where he laid last night and had eaten too. Jim need to heal and this was it. Jim found himself back at the hut with the big hybrid that carried him back into the village again. His foot didn't feel hurt anymore, it had to be the hybrids salvia that healed it. Jim rubbed his foot again the blood stopped, but he was more concern with the blood that he spilled in the forest and back to the village right now rather than later, Jim got off his bed and back out to the village edge to look at the forest and tell someone there about his feelings. The air was still, someone or something was getting ready to attack. Jim ran to the big hybrid that had taken him back to his hut. He was not out of it long to know they must have felt it too by now. Twelve large hybrid wolves stood next to twelve hybrid cats, they stood as still as ice on a lake, the sight was impressive. Jim had to get a weapon of some kind, one of the wolves had two long sharp pole that had a hole through it.

It had to be one of the shooters that bleed out a poison dart of some kind. It would work if he knew how to use it. It had to be simple to use he guessed. Jim went over to the hybrid and asked him about the poles.

These poles are not toys Jim, these could kill you if you use them the wrong way. He got to listen to me if you want to learn fast. I can teach you how to use them, but you got to be careful not to let the darts go now your throat. Understand me Jim. The hybrid said as he showed Jim how to use the poles correctly. Jim had a knack for learning things fast if he wanted to. This was one of the things he need to learn if he was to live and protect these hybrids too. The training was fast and he learn to fast and too careful with the pole. Take a breath and let it out slowly before you put the dart in the pole, then take a deep breath and hold it as you put the mouth piece to your lips, point the pole toward your victim and let your breath out fast, but do not take a breath when the pole is still over your mouth, wait for the pole to be taken down for the next darts. There are five darts to each pole and one blow in each part of the mouth peace. So five darts are let loose at one time. Not good when you got to cough. Jim thought.

Jim something is moving through the trees, they are not in direct sight, but we feel them strongly. The hybrid said as he pulled his back away from his face. The hybrid had long brown hair that hung mostly in his lean face.

Jim noticed that every one of the hybrids that were standing there had some kind of weapon in their hands. An ancient bow and arrow metal with wire strings tight and ready to use. They stood there like statues, no feelings of fear showed in their eyes or in their stand. The only thing that Jim saw was readiness to fight. But how many was out there in the forest? If there are more than what he thinks they have the battle would be lost. There has to be something better they could do? Another plan that would increase their odds? Jim thought. Jim went back into the elder's hut. Jim knew that they would still be there. Jim had to ask if they had tunnels like some villages do, but not all of them can have a tunnel. So he had to ask them. Jim put his weapon down outside of the huts entrance.

I am called Jim, I am with the freedom fighters for many years I cannot remember when I was not, not even when I was a child, and I was with the fighters. I am asked these question in peace. I do not wish to see any of your villages destroyed by these rogues. I need to know if you have a tunnel underneath the village that would come out away from the forest. Can you tell me this? Jim asked them as he noticed that every one of the elders were sitting in a semi-circle. They stood up and showed in silence the tunnel. None of them would answer his second question. But somehow he knew the answers before he even asked them.

As Jim went down the tunnel that was set in the middle of the huts floor, Jim heard children running down a path in the tunnel. Another plan came to him. If it leads out like it leads in, then the attackers would be able to see them or find the entrance this way. Hmm. We may have the enemies getting in here as we speak. But I got an idea, it may work or it may not. Jim said to the elders that we standing around the entrance of the tunnel. Jim could not tell what they were thinking, their faces were blank without any feelings that Jim could see. Jim stood there waiting for an answer or question or something. One of the elder that had a long brown hair with streaks of grey through it more toward his seat as the others seemed to follow him back down on the ground. He took out a long white form from his out pocket bag that sat close to him, then he brought something out of the bag. It was long white leaf, something Jim knew or thought was a white pen-rose panel leaf. The leaf was found on a strange planet in the northern part of the universe. Sometimes Jim got a little confused when it came to the north or south part of the universe. The outside of Earth always looked the same all around. But he did know this planet had some glowing effect when it came to darkness. Jim looked at as the elder handed the leaf back to Jim to study.

Jim took the leaf and then looked at the others sitting down.

We have many of these plants growing around the village. If you think that our enemies will attack us by way of the tunnels. I think you may think again. The plants protect our places of darkness. We only use the darkness of the tunnels for hunting and a faster way of getting home. Sometimes-the elder stop in his track of words and looked at Jim smiling.

How far do the tunnels go and where does the tunnel end? Do they get us out of the village far enough for us to get the enemies from behind or is it enough to hind the children in them? Jim asked him as he watched the elder eyes that understood what Jim was trying to tell them.

Hmm, the tunnels are deep and have many different places to go each one of the tunnels are hidden inside of the villager's huts. They all connect to one large tunnel and hall that we use for food storage during the winter months. The large tunnel the main one that all connect to goes out side of the forest close to edge of the pine mountains. That is where we hunt for food. The elder said with a smile. He understood what Jim was thinking. It was both a good idea and a scary one. If they didn't win this battle? Then everyone's that had fought would had fought for nothing.

Let me get the leader right now, he is at the hybrid wolves hut. I will also find Mies and he will get the hybrid cat leader. The elder said as he slapped his hands together. One small child dress in old rags that looked like it might have been a sack of something she was wearing. Her hair was dirty and tangled, Jim couldn't tell what color it was, the dirt looked like mud and grass. Her face brown with scratches coming across the cheeks to show how dirty she was. She was small but Jim could tell she was feisty, her smile showed sharp teeth like razors or needles pointing straight down ready to slice anyone to bits. Her nails were like daggers that had mud or was it blood dry mixed with mud at edges of her fingers. Jim watched her leave fast on all fours as she changed quickly into a black badger. She wasn't a child she was a Were-animal. Strange that all the scientist work hard to change human DNA for the good, but the government took the scientist find their work their knowledge and used it for other things.

Uh, maybe humans are none exist maybe we are all hybrids of some sort and Jim shook his thought he was getting nowhere with this. He knew he couldn't change into anything he tried but he just couldn't. He was human and his wife was or is hybrid. Even his kids are hybrids.

The two leaders of the hybrid cat and wolves came in huffs of air. Their nose growing long and ready to fight. Jim noticed the two had salvia dripping out of their mouths as they grin at the elder.

Now sit young ones. Jim has an idea that will save us! Yes? The elder said as he looked at all the other elders that were sitting on soft pillows that Jim had not notice before. His mind went to the two leaders of the hybrid villages he was staying. They looked at him and waited for Jim to say something.

I got an idea but I am not sure if it would work or not. Jim said as he started to sit down in front of the elders. Then a group of three cats came in the hut their tails swing fast as if they were upset about something. Jim watched them sit on the opposite side of the wolf's elders, their form still in cat roared their protest.

Jim knew that was a yell in cat language. Jim stood up off the floor and looked straight at the cats. But it was the elder wolves that spoke first.

We were not informed of your arrival as of yet, so forgive us for this meeting. This meeting of both felines and wolves would help with this battle that is coming to us all. Let Jim the human hybrid tells us of his plans. We can listen, but we can devise our own plans too. The elder said as all of the others agreed with him.

Alright, then this is one scenario I thought of.

: first we need to know how many children do with you all have here in the villages between the cats and the wolves. My plan is to hide the children there if we need to.

: second thought if we could lure some of the enemies down in the tunnels, we could use something to kill them with as they run through the tunnels.

: third thought we could get them from behind or we could escape out of the tunnels and burn the village as we leave. The tunnels could be set on fire too.

Well what do you all think? I know I am just a human, but my brother was a hybrid and my wife is one too. So are my children.

Jim said as the room became silent all around him. The cats changed form back to human and sat down with covers over their laps to hide anything that is private. Jim walked out of the hut as he was motioned to leave them. No words were spoken only hands were pointed toward the huts opening.

Outside Jim felt the air stir something moved across his vision. Jim started to move toward the thing he thought he saw, but stopped as he realized that thing did not see him.

It was a hybrid with brown streaks blended with black fur, a hybrid wolf, but then the wolf was speaking to someone or something that sat close to the forest shadows. The huts were surrounded with the forest, Jim couldn't decide which was front of the village and which was the back. Jim listen to them talk. The wolf knew about the tunnels, but not the plan Jim told the elders.

They were in danger if the enemies come from the tunnels now. They had to think fast, Jim ran from the sight and went straight to the hybrids who were guarding the front of the village. Jim pulled on the one hybrid that stayed with Jim when he was brought here by his wife cousin the hybrid King.

We are in danger big man. I just heard – listen to me, Jim started to yell. The hybrid kept on telling Jim to go back to him hut. He should not be out here with them, this hybrid battles not humans. They hybrid said as he turned back to the area he was standing.

Jim took his pole and smack at least four hybrids on their heads and another four on their legs. Jim had to do something to get their attention. With the pole still in Jim hands he took off with eight hybrid mixes of wolves and cats following him toward where the traitor was still talking to someone.

Jim stopped and threw the pole out toward the forest shadow that had that one person the traitor was talking to.

The shadow moved with speed as the pole reached out toward him. The miss was enough that they all saw who it was.

The sight of a large white tiger with a black streak running down its back. It was Larvie, the one hybrid that everyone knew to be with the President. Jim remembered him from all the meetings with the President during his time as a Senator but Jim shook his head and knew the others had the traitor in their claws. Jim could hear the traitor scream his protest, but the one that protected Jim did not listen to the traitor. Jim noticed that they had taken the traitor to the elders, but he had to stop the battle from coming from the tunnels. The fight is getting close. The enemies were making plans and one was to get in the tunnels and come out fighting with death as their intent.

Jim took two of the hybrids that were still standing close to him. Jim had to do some yelling if he was going to save this village, he didn't what it to look like the one his brother died in.

Jim marched in the hut as they were being told of what the traitor had done. But it was Jim voice that shook the hut and brought attention to what he was trying to tell them.

STOP LISTEN TO ME NOW. THAT THING HAD JUST TOLD LARVIA ABOUT THE TUNNELS. I KNOW THIS BECAUSE I USE

TOO BE A SENATOR AND THAT THING THAT WHITE TIGER IS ONE OF THE PRESIDENTS THE LEADER THAT IS TRYING TO WIPE OUT THE HUMAN AND THE HYBRIDS EXIST ion. IF YOU KEEP ON TALKING AND THAT IS WHAT HE WANTS YOU ALL TO DO, EVERYONE HERE WILL BE DEAD. WE NEED TO ACT NOW. GET TO THE TUNNELS WITH SOME KIND OF WEAPON THAT WOULD FOLLOW THE ATTACKERS AND KILL THEM. Jim said as he yelled his protest of what the elders where not doing.

The elders stood can about the tunnels and our weapons. He is related up and motion to all the other hybrids to get ready and listen to Jim give him what knowledge you to the King we must listen to him. He knows of the white death beast. The elders as he left in his wolf form with the other hybrids changing into their form of animal, they were preparing to go to battle with the other hybrids that were at the front of the villages.

We need enough hybrids at the front to make them think we have an army, but we need at least ten or more inside of the village to fight any of the enemies that might escape from the huts. Maybe some of the females could help us and the children.

They could hide in the huts with hammers or fire to send down the tunnels path. We need everyone to help. I know Larvia ways of getting what he wants and his only thought is to kill in order to get what he wants. So stop talking and let's get in the tunnels fast. Jim said as he ran out of the huts with all the hybrids changing into their form. Each went in huts and rip out the families as they told them what was to happen. The families were willing to help. The flame sticks shined its light as the sky grew dark as the sun came down behind the forest. Each child each female of all kinds of hybrid form took hold of the flame sticks with long knives and arrows of metal tint came back into their huts ready to strike anything that came out of the tunnels path.

Then as silent as the night fell around the village, Jim stood close watching carefully at the forest and at the huts behind him. A divergent was setting around him the forest was being watched as well as the huts. But the sky was another thing. What if Larvia had taken a nest of the hybrid hawks? Maybe they would be attack above them. That thought made Jim hope he was wrong. His chest heaving heavy out of his chest, he almost thought he was having an attack of some kind. His head swam with heat and wetness that dripped off his forehead in waves as he wiped his head off. The feel of wetness dripping down his back and face and now his nose, became annoyance to him. Jim shook his body like a wet dog. Jim look up to see if was under a tree or something? The sky was clear o tree or birds in sight, he was just hot. Females with long knives tilt their heads close to the huts entrance listening for sounds.

Slowly movement started coming out of the huts tunnels. was ready, weapons raised high over the openings a cry was let out from the front line a distraction to the ones that were waiting close to their huts for the ones that were coming out of the tunnels. Slowly the screams came out of each huts as the attackers came out charging but never coming out completely. Their heads rolling off their neck-shoulders as they step out with one foot out the door. Children were able to get the huts and send flames down the entrance of the tunnels in their huts. The sight made Jim wonder if the flames would set the huts on fire. But none of that happen. The front became a mass of death, but the hybrids that were on Jim side of the battle had been able to fight in both teams and individually. The battle was strong to many to count that were fighting against us, but as Jim fought alongside them the battle seemed to be on their side. But the turn came fast as two of their sixteen hybrids were killed right beside Jim legs. Jim's pole did little as the attackers came close to his face. But he used the pole on both side to hit and strike each attacker that wore military clothes. They were not hybrids, but human hybrids of different kind. Their strength was unbelievable. But another thought came, it was two or four months past that the leader ask the Senators to agree to let him continue on with the military's new projects. They did not have a choice in the matter. The leader had enough power that anything they decide would either not be what the leader wanted or it just didn't matter what they said the leader would always get what he wanted because he lived for thousands of years, his words were final. These were the leader's project, he made humans into some kind of hybrid strength.

No matter what they did to these attackers they would not die. Jim had another thought, he remembered his friend that had died after they had dinner that day when he had no choice but to run. He told him not that day but a few days before that he accidently found out what the leader had been doing with the military humans. He heard the only way to kill these humans were to strike at the base of the neck and into the heart of the humans. Jim knew nothing about any of it, but he had to try to kill to strike right at the neck. Then he tried to send the message on how to kill these guys by way of his mind. He was after all a hybrid of sorts too.

The only way to kill these hybrids that was not of the villages he stayed in had only one way to kill them was to strike their neck and strike at the chest take out the heart of these humans' animals. Jim said as he took aim at the neck of one of the attackers running toward him.

The neck split the human into. Jim remember at the huts the women and children had killed the attackers by cutting their necks off as they came out of the huts. This was the same they need to kill these strange people. The wolf hybrid that was one of the elders had been in his wolf form, but let out a cry with his claws the elder strike two humans down. He was fast, but there more of the attackers than there was of the hybrids in the village. The fighting became so intense that Jim was pushed and shove against either one of the hybrids that was part of the village or the attacker. That was both good and bad for Jim. He used the pole end to jam hard at the attacker's chest, he need to burst that heart in order to kill him. It was one of the only alternative he had at the moment. The hybrid that was close to Jim help him by pushing the attacker against the poles edge. The attacker heart burst blood spill out of him like a gust of wind through the trees. The feel of the wetness striking Jim's face made him flinch back, but the sight was good. Jim turned to the hybrid and told him to change into the wolf. So together they fought side by side one forcing the attackers against the poles edge. The hybrid sent a command towards the cats, telling them to form a line of claws talons to point outward. Then he told the wolves to push the attacker against the cat's claws. The wolves changed within moments of the command as well as the cats, the charge went fast as a large group of twenty or more were shoved hard against the daggers that awaited them. The attacker's chest burst as the claws strike the death. The other attackers moved closer toward them as the cat's claws rip out the hearts of the attackers that slam into them. The wolf's claws were as sharp as the cat's talons, so they started to rip out the hearts of the attackers fast and swift. Jim head was wet with sweat as the fighting got worst. The attackers marched closer to the hybrids to stop them from killing their brothers in the fight. But the attackers got a surprise the children got involve in the battle with long daggers that they could hold tightly in their hands. The children went underneath legs and hind legs to get to the attacker from underneath. Their daggers were not as good, but the sight of them was enough to scare Jim to death. He didn't want these children to die or get hurt. But they were doing it as if they done it before. The daggers were long enough for the daggers to reach the heart from below. One of the children had sliced one of the attacker's legs off hard and smooth while another put his dagger straight through the back to the chest heart. The blood flowed outward and landed on the children head as they continued to crawl around the battles legs. Jim worked fast and hard as one after another attacker came at him thinking that they would be the one to kill the only human in the fighting with the hybrids. But the pole became sharp and Jim held it in his hands tightly. The pole acted like a spear and the aim was always right. Then everyone stopped fighting the attacker pulled back away from the village and hybrids. Jim saw them run back into the forest. The white tiger stood outside of the forest watching the battle and not becoming part of it. Jim looked at him with angry and hope of killing that hybrid that traitor to all hybrids that lived.

The elders called everyone back inside of the village middle hut for a meeting of how many hybrids were killed and how many were injured. The counts of dead hybrids were small, four, children were the ones hurt. Jim listen to the elders tell everyone they did good. But Jim had to walk away, somehow he knew Larvia was planning something more definite more deadly. Slowly Jim thought as he walked through the village waste of huts that were partly burnt from the children that threw the flame down the tunnels. Attacker's headless bodies scattered along his walk. Jim stumble over one of the bodies. Jim stop his fall with his pole that he still had in his hands.

Jim looked down and found one of the attacker still alive but injured enough that he was unconscious. Jim slowly send out a message to a hybrid that had protected him when he first came to the village with his wife's cousin. Jim bent down looking at the attacker face, smooth with round cheeks and stern nose that had a small dip, the eyes were closed, but the attacker's mouth was wide with fat lips. The hair was blonde with brown streaks along the blonde stem of hair. The man had to be at least 5"6. Jim looked up at the hybrid that was standing close by Jim side. He is still alive; I don't know if he has a tracker on him or not. Some trackers have senders on them. What I mean is they the leaders like Larvia can hear us through this attacker. I don't have the ability to find out? Jim said as he looked up again at the hybrid.

You may not but I know what you are talking about we do not need the device for us to hear what is heard from another. Our healer has the means to find this device on this man. We will kill him after we are done. He will not harm or kill anyone.

CHAPTER TWENTY

TEVE LOOKED AROUND MORE, his eyes seemed to adjust better now that he had changed into something he really does not want to think about. But he noticed that there are something's he is glade happen he could see a lot better than before. His eyes sight was alright, he could see alright, but now he seemed to be able to see bugs on limbs and bushes. And his hearing it magnified, Steve could hear Jack heart beat pound in his chest like a drum of some kind. Steve smiled at the thought and kept on walking. They all decide that it would be better if they just stayed together and not wander off trying to find that damn truck jack drove. He sky was starting to get dark as they marched through the forest, branches and limbs were scattered around like a blockage of some sort. Steve feet didn't hurt as he knew his shoes or what was left of them were gone now, the ground was scattered rocks and sticks that melted with the grass to hide anything that would tell them where or what it was at one time.

Jack was hitting bugs as they flew over his chest that was open with sores and cuts from the battle. Children followed him like ants following their leader. Jack didn't mind much the kids were gifts he would say, the children were the future and the gift from God. Jack scratched one of the kids head as he went by. Max was still crying and whaling about his Susan his daughter. They were gone and he didn't think they were even alive. Max skinny form dressed up in an old dress that was once some young girls play dress swag roughly through the ground as Max march hard and desperate to find his mate Susan. Mr. Farmer took hold of a long twinge that grew high over some rocks close to where Susan and her baby had disappeared. As Mr. Farmer chewed on a small grass that moved around his mouth like a cow's mouth and thought about what happen to Steve.

Steve wasn't or was suppose too change into a hybrid or was it a were? Mr. Farmer was getting to old for this, his mind was not cable of keeping up with all the changes. When he saw Steve change into that – damn it was a hybrid. Half human and half something else. He could change into either form fully or partly it didn't matter.

That scared Mr. Farmer as he thought again o the why and how of Steve. Maybe he should just wait the answer was there right in his face, but he couldn't see it because he was searching for answer that was there and well he could see it, this was really bothering him.

The stem he was chewing on broke in his mouth leaving the remaining of the stem rough and unappealing. Mr. Farmer threw the stem down and rubbed his dirty hands together as if he was cleaning them.

Mr. Farmer kept his eyes on both the ground and o Steve, he wasn't sure if they were safe from what Steve became. A hybrid was born and grew up with its packs and learn how to control his nature of killing. That was the trouble its killings or hunting. Sometimes Were-animals or hybrid hunted. Would they become the hunted or prey? Would Steve learn how control his hybrids needs or its control to change into a hybrid permanently. The only cases Mr. Farmer has known were the ones that died and many died at their first changes. He guessed that the changes in form was hard on the bones as it required them to break and stretch to the point of pain that would make anyone scream out hard and fast, Mr. Farmer has never witness any of it before, but just listen to many others talk about throughout the years sense he visited on many times his friends outside of the community. They were quiet group of people that came from the freedom city of Detroit State country. It was strange, the name and country like so many of them separate from the main body of this country this place that he and the others only knew as home. Detroit was not very big, mountains dry air, with buildings that half fallen like here too. Abandoned with people living in those abandoned homes. Distance memories from a past that told them that every one of the state countries were one country and not divided. One country that was a faded world of destruction and isolation of people that could not get along or even cared. But isn't it like this here? He couldn't even understand why the fighters even wanted to fight the government any ways. The why was not really answered, it wasn't really even thought of. Mr. Farmer kept on walking and listening to anything that was around him. He had to keep his ears open for anything. Silent rose around Mr. Farmer, it was a sign that told him that something was coming, when the animals became silent it rose like a scream that woke him up to tell him that they were going to be attacked. He noticed that Steve stop in his track fast and sniffed the air like he knew what he was doing. No one taught him that. So how did he know what to do? Was it something he knew naturally? Right now Steve was the only defense they had against any attackers.

One word came out of Steve mouth. Climb. climb fast. Steve shouted at his friends. Everyone ran up trees, some of the children were too small to climb their legs just couldn't get hold in order for them to climb. Steve grab the kids by their hair and threw them upward. He hoped one of the guys would grabbed one of the two smaller children that were too small to climb. Steve looked up and found that Jack had grab both of the kids and was handing one to Max to hang onto. Everyone was as high as they could go with the small ones hanging on Jacks and Maxes necks and backs. Steve stood his ground, the wind took up over the bushes and leaves, the hood flew over his face to hide it from any of the attackers.

First Steve thought that maybe he should try to change into his animal form the wolf, but with this robe maybe these were part of the group of wolves that capture them back at the truck. He will wait and see who these people are first then take it from there. His eyes hidden from anyone's view as three hybrids came trotting toward Steve, they were still in their wolf form, but slowly changed back into human partly. It was enough for Steve to understand what they were talking about.

We are here Master Lone. They said and bowed a little.

Steve knotted his head yes to them, but did not want to say a word. He was afraid that they would know this Lone and his voice. Steve watched them look around for someone or something. But then he noticed that they were sniffing like he did earlier. It was the smell that made his nose wiggle as the scent came closer to him. He knew at once it wasn't coming from his friends or the children. It was the hybrids that they had killed back in the meadow. Steve stood there waiting for them to do or say something. It would tell him he had to move fast in order to kill them. This new skin made him feel strong more confident in what happen to him and his friends.

Where is your men they were to march with you to find those captives we need to bring to the tiger by night fall? Our families are in danger if we do not obey him. Said one of the hybrids that were in both forms.

Steve thought of what the hybrid had just said. The tiger who was the tiger? And why did he have these hybrids families?

Steve took a breath and let it out as he slowly whispered his thoughts.

I had been in battle, my head took wound, my thoughts are faded, and I cannot recall my name or who you are. I know only that I woke not long ago. The attack from something large took us by surprise. Many of those that went with us have been killed. I know not if anyone but I have survived the battle. Steve said as he held his head as if he was in pain. Steve slowly took hold of the tree's trunk and let himself lower slowly downward to the grounds floor. The two hybrids grab hold of Steve arms and sat down with him. How many came with you who is expecting us back at the village I can't remember. It is very foggy in my head. Steve whispered to them as he shook his slowly and put his head down on his lap. Steve waited for them to say something. It worked.

There is only us, the village is bare the tiger has taken hold of the families that are ours. We go home to nothing. But if you did not capture the ones the tiger has told us too. Then our families are doom. We are without families and homes. The hybrids both said. Does-does the tiger know of you coming to see me? Steve asked them.

No he did not see us nor his attackers they are with him at the dark mountain village, the dead village on the north side. That is where he told us to take those you had capture. But you have none here that we can negotiate for our families' release. The one hybrid said as he lowered his head.

Steve thought for a minute and came to conclusion of all that has happened. They capture them only because of the tiger that has some kind of power or something took their families away. He made them capture him and his friends. Steve felt sick as he remembered that he killed many of the hybrids that capture him and his friends. They went into battle with the hybrids they didn't know about the tiger and their village families. No words were spoken on the why of things only hints now that Steve remembered. They had to survive somehow, those hybrids had captured them with false words and then took them out into the forest like prisoners. They had to fight them. There was no choice.

With that Steve got up and whistle upward towards the trees. Then he let his hood fall back away from his face. The others skinned down the tree and gathered around the two hybrids that sat next to Steve. The hybrids got up fast and almost hit Mr. Farmer as they watched each child and the three adult humans. The sight shock them as they knew they were outnumbered.

Steve face blank with no emotion or thought step closer to the hybrids.

Tell me if it is true. Two of our close friends are missing had been sense we killed your friends and Lone I suppose was the leader, he is dead I took his robe for my clothing. I am a hybrid. I never knew I could do this, but it came to me like grass to dirt. I was not born hybrid or taught hybrid change. But I can feel the change come to me when I feel danger. So tell me if I am in the right. And tell me where my two friends are. Steve said as he stood with his feet spread apart.

You are hybrid you killed all of our brothers in battle alone? The hybrids said as he stepped back again. He was afraid of Steve. Something told them that Steve was more than just a hybrid. Something was different.

Jack stood next to Steve and spoke. No Steve didn't fight them alone, we all help in fighting them and they had to die no choice. He just helped us do it. So tell us were the two friends are and maybe we will let you go free. Jack said as he looked at the two hybrids.

We don't know of two people that you speak of. We only spoke of our families and that of our brothers that went with Lone to capture those that were spoken by the tiger.

Steve looked at them, he felt they were speaking the truth. They didn't even mention any one new. They only spoke about their family capture and being held by some tiger. Would you know who might tell us where the two friends might be held? Steve asked them.

No we cannot think of who would take them. We only know of the tiger that took our families. And now our families are being killed our children like yours dead as we speak. We cannot go home and know that the village is dead like the one on the mountain.

We need to get back to the truck and we might be able to get the computer to tell us about any villages that might have them. Mr. Farmer said as he motioned in the opposite direction.

Steve thought about that for a moment then said to Mr. Farmer. We need food, we need to rest and we need to hide. The truck would be the right place for this tiger to get us. We don't know if anyone is even watching it. We don't know if the King is even a where of us missing. So right now night is coming in fast we need to get inside of something to stay safe. We can't go looking for them if we get captured again or killed. So what are your names? Steve said as he turned to look at the hybrids.

I am called Loo and this is my brother Woo bear. We are all brothers.

Steve waited to make another decision, these hybrids are more scared of them right now. But they are talking and maybe willing to help us if he helped them.

Do you know of any place we could hide for a time? We need food as the elder man asked.

We may know of a place but we do not know if we could trust you. You killed our brothers and now our families will die too. We do not have the decision of elders. They are all dead by the tiger's attackers. We have no leaders but the robed ones of the temples. Now they are dead too. The hybrid complained.

Yes, we killed them too. But we did not know about the tiger that took your families as captives we know only that we need to escape and when we got the chance we fought our way out of the plot.

But that does not mean would not help them or you. We know how one feels about families. I had at once a sister that I cared for and tried to help. But she died one day when I need to go to the great city to work. We need food and that was the only way I knew to get food was to work hard and help her as much as I could. But she died and she will not come back. It pains me to think about her that way. But I must. It will be a reminder of how our government tents to those that need them. So we will take our justices and help you get your families back. Steve said. The others agreed with a shake of his head.

The two hybrids looked at all the children and the adults. Their minds racing with indecision on what to do. And knowing that these children and these people would not be enough to fight the tiger and his men.

We are not sure of your strength. We know what we see and know that these children cannot fight what we have seen and had already fought. Our families are dead, Lone did not get the ones in that strange thing by the road. We know that, Lone had to bring those people to the tiger by dawn, but he was not at the place last dawn when he was supposed to. So our families are dead we are no longer part of that dead village. It is doom as we speak. The hybrid said that had the streak in his hair.

May be not. Didn't you think I was Lone? Do you think I could pass for him? Steve asked them.

We do not know if they would know of him but the robe has tricked us. May hap they would be tricked too. But the people that were from that truck? How would you explain to them what happen? The hybrid said that was holding his arms around his stomach.

Are you in pain? Did one of the tigers put something in you to hear or see what has happened? Jack asked as he went toward the hybrid. It was not that Jack was afraid of the hybrid, but what the government might have done to them. Anything could have happened to them a possible scenario would be an implant of some sort that would give the government a way to hear and see whatever they wanted from these hybrids. It just wasn't save to be with them! Jack thought as he studied the hybrid still holding on to his arm and stomach. How can we know if you don't have something planted in you somehow? Jack asked them.

Steve knotted in agreement as he walked close to the two hybrids. How was he going to help find these people for them and save these two hybrids that seem honesty innocent?

Max asked them one question. Where is my wife and baby?

The hybrids looked at Max like he was something strange. The sight of seeing a man in an old robe that looked like one of the robes that the females wear.

You female? Or may haps you want to be female? They said.

I am a man and this—this is my—my robe to do—to do, I like this alright. It lets me move faster and get into place better. So shut up and tell me where my family is? Max said as he huffed out his words in one breath. He was excited and upset at the same time.

We know not of your family, only the ones that were taken from us by the tiger. He is sly and fast and he knows how to kill without sound. He has our families or maybe he had them once. Now we know they are dead. The hybrid said.

Max put his arm across each other as he looked into the forest. He couldn't think right now. His mind was on Susan and the baby.

Maybe that tiger has Susan and the baby. I think we should take a chance on finding out. But we need a plan first. Mr. Farmer said as he bent down to the ground. But Farmer they may have something in them look at that one he is still holding his stomach. We just can't take any chance that the tiger would come down here fast. I think he is just waiting just waiting for someone to say something and then pounce on us. Jack said as he whispered next to Mr. Farmer. Mr. Farmer lowered his head and shook his head. The thought of what Jack said about that tiger coming to get them waiting just for the right time to get them. That scared Mr. Farmer and started to think. Mr. Farmer got and off the ground and slowly looked at Steve, with a knot of his head, Mr. Farmer knew Steve understood, but he looked at all of the people that went with him. Everyone including the children. Mr. Farmer walked away toward a tree that was farther enough that they could watch the two hybrids carefully. Mr. Farmer wasn't sure if he should trust them or not. The one hybrid was still holding his arm across his stomach. Something was not right.

Mr. Farmer thought it best to talk to everyone and make a decision on the two hybrids. And what to do with this tiger that took the families from the village that these two hybrids claim, something was just not right.

Look Jack has some concerns that maybe warrant. We need to be more cautious with those two. Jack why don't you tell them what you seem to notice with them. Mr. Farmer said as he listened carefully. No one put in until Jack started to talk.

Those two well the one that was holding his stomach for a while. He doesn't seem to be hurting, I don't see any pain in his face or eyes. There's got to be a reason why he is doing that? Jack said again.

We don't know them or those guys that we fought back there. But we do know that we got to get back to the truck fast. Something tells me that we are in danger. And if we don't get out of here we are going to fry big time. Mr. Farmer said as he the touched the hat he wore from yesterday.

Max really didn't care about what they said, all he wanted was his Susan and his baby. They were the most important people to him and nothing else matter.

But then if that thing they said might have his Susan and baby, then maybe they should do something it was a chance.

If we help them then maybe, we would be able to find Susan and baby too. Max said.

I really don't think she is there. But –Steve stopped talking he had a feeling that someone was watching them and it wasn't the hybrids that were standing farther enough away that they could not hear them. Slowly Steve motion everyone to move into the forest and away from the two hybrids. The forest became to quite, birds sat on their branches watching them in silent. Bugs stopped their chirping as the ground felt still. The air it seemed to know what was going on the wind stop blowing against the leaves. The night sun fell behind trees in the distance. Steve could feel something he wasn't sure what it was, but his wolf growl and his hair on his body rose up.

Steve stay calm, we need to get as far from those two hybrid. You can't fight and win all the time. We don't know for sure, but I can figure this there might be more than what you fought back there where we lost Susan and her baby. So come on, we need to stay alive and not be dead. Jack said as he pulled on Steve robe. They ran into the forest until they came to an open meadow. The place was not like the one they had been with the hybrids they fought, there was no lake or water of any kind close, only long stems of wild wheat with long grass flowing with a dance that they only knew and hear the sounds that sip through a breeze kissing everyone faces and hair. Steve still didn't feel right, but the sounds of the birds and bugs made it good. The warning he knew came from them, it was common knowledge that animals could sense danger. Steve listen carefully around them, his eyes keen, seeing things he normal as a human not be able to see, but he could see now better. All he could see around him was small bugs running up the tall stock of wheat. The smell of new grass mix with barks from trees drew Steve breath I clean. He didn't cough, it felt good not to cough. Steve thought about his sister Brook. She would love it here. Steve knew her enough that he could see her running through the tall stock of weeds, her hair blonde blowing though the breeze. That smile of hers made Steve laugh. She would always melt his heart and he never could say no to her. She was his life, but with life he knew she was sick and would die. That hurt, he didn't get to say good bye to her or watch her die. She was alone in that house and no one came to be with her as she faded away. Steve became quite as the rest of the gang came marching in the meadow. Their mouths open to the sight of all the beauty that was around them.

The sky was giving the meadow a shadow of forgotten life as they call knew it would be night soon and they all need to be safe. At that point Steve had to get up off the ground and make them sleep in the trees. Steve looked up at two trees and found something big nestled up on four branches with a long robe bridge that came over to each tree.

Jack-Mr. Farmer-Max we need to get up into those trees over there soon. Night is coming and so is something else. I can't really say what it is, but we need to be safe. Get the kids and come on. Steve said as he walked over toward the forest that was ahead of them. He got there and found a ladder of vines climbing up toward where the nest like home was. Jack climb up first and then the children went up behind him. Max and Mr. Farmer climbed behind them. Steve looked around and this was strange, no movement or sounds were coming from up in the trees. Steve just hoped the children would be alright up there. Steve grab the vine and started to go up. In the forest was darkness that seemed to swallow the trees and bushes that spread over the forest ground. Steve thought he would be able to see better with the hybrid that settle inside of him. But his sight was limited just like it was when he didn't realize that he had hybrid blood in him. Steve wondered about that, was his parent's hybrids but only stayed in human form to hide from the government or what. Was his sister a hybrid-no she wasn't or she would still be alive? Her body would have healed when she got sick. So why him why did he changed to a wolf?

With a shake of his head Steve went up the rope. The nest he thought was not a nest on the branches of the trees that were connected by a bridges were actually huts made from straws that grew in the meadow below. Steve sniffed the air to see if he could find out who build these huts up here in the trees.

But Steve smelled nothing but stale air mixed with tree mold another smell came to him, it smelled like old grass. Then Steve stood still and listen to the sounds. Night birds sent off their calls to each to know where the hunts were and where they were. Bugs chirped loudly as the night grew deeper within the hours. Steve felt safe right now. The others had already settled down in one of the huts. Steve noticed that they were all together, Max and Jack bed down close to the door and the children were sleeping across from them-Mr. Farmer found a chair in the far corner of the hut and fell asleep. Steve knew his place was outside guarding them as they sleep.

The air was cool, not cold or hot, or even warm, but cool.

Steve sat down next to the door way. His robe covered his body and kept him warm against any wind that might come through. He tried to stay awake, but dose off as soon as silent came to him.

Morning-Steve rose up as he realized that he over slept and been in a fetal position on the floor. The children came out with Max being pulled by their small hands. Max hair was in tangles as bugs and dirt covered his hair. Steve swore he could see more than just bugs in Max hair. Jack came out next as he stretched over his head and outward.

Where's Mr. Farmer? I thought he slept with all of you? Steve asked them.

Well I thought you saw him when he came out of the hut. He said he had to take a leak somewhere. So he left a few hours ago. Jack said as the children argued over the same problem. They all had to relief themselves. Steve couldn't remember if he saw them do it while they were captured or after they fought. But knew they had of do so sometimes! Steve thought.

I guess I fell asleep. Steve said as he scratched his head. Yeah guys come on over here, I got food for us and a place where you all can relief yourselves. Mr. Farmer said as he motioned to everyone still close to the hut where they slept.

Someone was standing next to him as they watched Mr. Farmer move away toward another area of the trees of huts leaving the others to wonder what happen?

Steve went over to where Mr. Farmer had gone to, the others followed with reluctance.

The birds of the day flew high in the morning light as new morning bugs flew over their heads, fly-bees with colors of rainbows buzzing over flowers that they had not notice last night were hugging walls of each hut that stood on large branches of trees.

Steve took in the fresh smell of flowers he had never seen. Living in the community for all his life they had never grew or knew how to grow flowers. All that he ever saw was grass or trees or burnt out homes. But then he remembered one day when his sister and him sat on the back porch looking at the night sky. They were talking and holding hands like lovers would. Neither one had ever thought about other people in their lives, they just wanted each other and that was all. Having sex was not thought of, that was just too much Steve thought. He never touched her that way, but he had thoughts for one minute of it. And yet, they never did it. Only kissed and held each other at night. A flower that one beauty took him back to the one person he loved and she was gone. She would not see this flower that reminded him of her. Steve heart hurt at that thought. He missed her, but he had to push his feelings back. She was gone and he could not bring her back. Steve shrugged off the thoughts the memories that should not come right now.

As soon as they all got there to where Mr. Farmer was sitting everyone saw that he was not alone.

There were twelve people of different sizes sitting around a small table that was close to the ground. Mr. Farmer sat close to a corner of the area where they were to eat. The smell of food made everyone's stomach growl loudly. The children were told to sit by the other table where the children from the tree huts were sitting down and ready to eat. Max had straightened his dress/robe out when he first got up, his hair was tangled and flies seem to want to nest in it. He sat down close to Jack as they all sat around the table. But as soon as Steve bent to sit down, one of the older hut people moved him away.

You are hybrid blood Priest; we do not feed dogs of their kind. You sit away from us. The older man said with the balding white hair and round face. His body was round as a jar and short in size. His face was a mask of knowledge as he kept on looking at Steve with gray eyes that seemed to look at Steve stern. Steve nodded alright and moved away, he was hungry but knew he wasn't going to eat no matter what.

Steve is a friend. Steve just found out that he has hybrid blood. His turn was when we had to battle with the hybrids that captured us. Steve was or is no has never been brought up as a hybrid pup. He doesn't know how to turn on a dime or how to use his hybrid power. Steve is just a child-his age is less than most hybrids that are concerned children by their standards. Steve is fourteen years old, but took care of all of us by getting a job at 9 years old, he looked older and was reading and writing and doing math at four years old. So you see he is not a hybrid by birth but human and a child too. Mr. Farmer said as he looked straight in the elder's eyes.

The children need to eat and so does Steve. We all hadn't had real food in a few days or so. I –I really don't remember when we did or not. I just want my Susan and our baby. Max said almost in tears as he fell to his seat with a lump. His hands covered his face as he cried hard again like he did last night. Everyone in the hut heard his tears as he called out for Susan and their baby.

Jack looked at the food and saw only leafs and vegetables of wild greens and tall wild corn with strawberries that were large and fat with juices he thought. It all looked good, there were no cooked meat. Only vegetables that grew wild, with some fruits that were wild too. Jack picked up a strawberry he could not resist. But knew that they all need to eat. Steve need to eat more than they did, Jack knew that hybrids ate a lot more meat and high proteins that most humans. Looking at all of this would not keep Steve full and his ability to change would not happen again.

We do not know much about hybrids only they had taken our children and wives. Not good not good. We are cautious about any one that is hybrid that comes to our village. We had built it up in the trees because of them many years ago. This is the only safe place that we are not hunted down by them. The man said as he shook his head back and forth. He nodded no and walked away toward the table that had all the food. Vegetables line up along the table with mixes of something different that neither one knew what it was for sure. The smell lingered though the air setting off Steve hybrid hungrier.

Steve noticed a woman that looked to be at least in her 50's, she was short with black hair that hung low over her shoulder in braids with colorful strings dancing through her braids. Her eyes were the same color as the old man's eyes, but sad as she looked closely at Steve face. Her hands gentle but old wrinkle with standing skin that rose with each movement of her finger and hands. She had a gentle touch as she rubbed slowly on Steve face. She wanted to know what his face felt like, she acted as if she never touched a hybrid before. It made Steve cautious as the feel of human hands on his face made want to move away. But Steve stood there letting the woman touch him.

Max moved closer to where the food was and started to eat the fruit and carrots that were larger than his own hands. Hmmm. This is good, come on guys Steve won't hurt you all. He is just a big puppy with a big appetite.

Max said as he started to stuff his mouth with the food.

The old man watch the woman turn away from Steve and looked at him with those pleading eyes. The man nodded no but then open his arms wide and let everyone eat. His people were small they were not animals or hybrids. They were just small people with large hearts. Children were important to them and any death was a start to the end of their lives.

Steve sat down close to Jack and Mr. Farmer who sat at the end of the table toward the back of the small space that was used to eat food.

All of our lives we were hunted by those that feel that we are nothing but food and to be used as slaves.

We are people-we live here within the trees. If you are innocent of hybrid birth then I will let you eat our food, but stay close to your friends and do not touch our children. The man said as he sat down across from them.

Max stuff food in his mouth, but looked straight at a girl that was holding a new baby in her arms. The baby had dark brown hair that curled and bounced as the girl moved her arms to reach the food for her. Baby had to be around his little girl's age. She was still too young to walk or talk, she was in diapers and innocent to the core. The sight made Max sad again. He stopped eating and took a large cup of water to his lips and gulp the drink down. He wanted to ask the man again about his wife his little girl. They had to know something shouldn't they? Max sat the drink down with a start. The sound of the cup slamming on the wooden table made others winch as he stood up and made his remark clear.

I know you all has to know about Susan and our baby. They are my life my only life. Without them I am nothing but dirt. So where are they? Who has them? Why were they being taken? Max asked them as he looked at all of the people around the table.

We do not know of your wife or child. We are innocent of that. We do not take those that are not ours. We protect children if they are being held by the hybrids for food or slavery. If your family has been taken and we cannot be sure of it. We think now that they might be at village that is called death. I cannot say if that is for sure. We know that many of our children had been taken and we followed the path that lead us to that village that is death. We found some of our children but we cannot fight them. We are little with no weapons like theirs that could be defended. So we are here with little of our young men and women. We have children, but not many as before. I am sorry for your lost. The old man said as he picked up a large orange stick that looked like a carrot, but smelled like a cumber. The end of it was flat but orange? Whatever it was Max went to try it too, the taste was good and watered his mouth for more.

How far is this place, we were told that they held other hybrids from another village that-well two other hybrids thought we were from that village too. They told us that if they could not get those people that were in the truck their families were dead. That was why they sent a small pack to help look and capture any one that road in the truck. So we played along for a little while and they said that the families were being held at the dead village with a white tiger or something like that. We were at one point going to go there, but there was something not right when that hybrid held his stomach. We think they had a tracker in their stomachs. We also think that whatever was tracking them were not far from their sight. We had into ran back into the forest as fast as our weak bodies could take us. Some of us climbed trees and went to each tree that was close to us as we ran through the forest. I didn't sense any one following us or seen anyone either. But we found this meadow not far just right over there in that opening in the trees. Steve said as he pointed toward where they found themselves after they escaped from the two hybrids.

You did not fight them? The woman asked as she stop in her tracks to get more water.

No we didn't we are going to pick a fight first. I rather fight if we are forced. But just to fight no way. Steve said as he chewed on carcum. It was part carrot and part cumber. The sight was orange shaped like a cumber but tasted like both together. Steve just looked and waited for someone to answer his statement.

We do not fight either, but will if we need to. This is your way too and it is good. The man said as he drank his water.

I think we need to visit that place just to see what is going on. We can't let them have Susan and her baby either. We just can't let it go and think she will be alright. So tomorrow we get up early and start to climb down to find this place. If we can devise a plan to get their children, then we might be able to get Susan too. Mr. Farmer said as wipe his hands clean with his pants legs.

CHAPTER TWENTY-ONE

ARK FELT THE STING of twinges pointing down his back as he got up off the ground. It was morning the night seemed to be fading away as a fog of memories flowed down his mind. What happen last night became a blur after he sense someone in the forest. Olaya was sitting close to a large fallen tree that was close to where Mark had fell from something. His head started to hurt as he shook it clear of any thoughts of where he was and how he got there. Mark sniff the air trying to smell anything that would tell him if there is bad coming his way. Mark had to get off the ground, but his head was still foggy. Did this female hit him over his thick skull? His legs bent as he realized he was in wolf form and his head still hurt. Slowly Mark crept over to the female. Her form white fur with a streak of gray standing on edge. Her ears twinkled as she sensed Mark coming around, his wolf in full form coming close to her. What was he thinking? He couldn't fight all those enforcers that the government sent. She knew they were close now that the hunt was found. Hmm, if he tries anything she was going to do it again. She couldn't do it when she was inside of that mobile with all those losers. They would know she was the traitor. But now she was outside with this loser of a hybrid, his face wasn't even form like the wolf he was, no his short nose and round chin made his look more human. Olaya look at Mark closely as she went over on all four legs around Mark, the man child was not so fierce now was he. A smile came over Olaya face as knew she had him. Yeah she had the loser. The forest was dark as night, birds echoed their songs in a distance, the sound of chirps from bugs that crawl around Marks feet tickled him as he shook them off and started to walk closer to Olaya. His thoughts were only of how he would kill this traitor of hybrids and humans. She was nothing but poison. Somehow she had done something to the mobile and now he just couldn't trust the mobile to take him to the freedom fighters headquarters.

I am not sure if it is a good idea that you are still here with me. I might not let you live you know that don't you little pup. Mark said as he moved around Olaya slowly. He was in full form of the wolf, but his mind was still human. His eyes stern as he watched Olaya moves that he was not trusting. She was one of the traitors that his mother had scent. Something else he was not sure of but knew Olaya and her friend had tried to convince his family that they were need of help and that they were in heat and one of the males were their mate. But that was a lie, a lie that they bought and felt true. The sound of his paws touching the ground around them was wet with moister from the late day of the forest night. A light breeze felt like heaven to Mark as it touched and kissed his fur that was standing up and ready for a fight. He was ready to get this over with this wolf would not make it back to her master not today not now or ever. He knew too that he could not make any connect with anyone in his family, something told him that he was too close to where the enemies were waiting for a signal or something from this wolf. Slowly his pace stopped as another smell came toward him from the south of where he was standing. The smell was fear and he like it. She was afraid of him and what he would do to her. This was good, Mark kept on walking around her until he was on top of a log that once was behind her back. Her hair standing up in her rear as she took the fighting stance against a tree ready to fight him if she had too. Mark knew he was bigger and had fought before in the forest with his uncle and his mother cousin that was king of the hybrids. This was nothing to him.

Mark took flight in the air as he sent out a warning to anyone of his family to beware that he had blood in his mouth and body that was not his. One leap against her neck was all he took as her neck broke easily with his jaws that snap it fast. Now as he took a deep breath of anxiety from the kill and his heart rate that came with it took hold of his eyes. Everything went from red when he leaped on her to a dark red almost purple in sight of everything around him. His mouth tasted salted blood that had something else a taste of sweetness of death. His kill his first bride death.

He sat there looking at her as he licked off the blood from his snout, the taste was good, he wanted more, but stop himself. It was wrong to eat the flesh of one's own people.

But the taste was good, the feel of death to his own control was good. He had to shake the feeling off or he would let it control him and his own family would have to hunt him down. That was not good that was not what his family would want. Mark went back to where his air ship landed and hunt around for something to eat fast before the kill takes control over him. Mark walked over the dead hybrid and found where the ship had landed and went inside as a human not a wolf. His feet sound naked as he had no shoes now his clothes off and torn from his change, he had to find something to wear too.

Mark found food in a hidden door that was sealed by panels that once held two of the three parts of the air ship. His mind going to packages of meat first and then to whatever he found next. Clothes scattered in piles in a corner seemed strange as he went to them to see if he could use them. Old they were old as dirt, but uniforms of the government enforcers that might have used them at one point or another. One of the uniforms fit perfect on him. White although with patches of blood and smeared dirt. He did not mind one bit. He need shoes and found nothing to wear around, but then he remembered that his mother had thrown the bags of clothes and shoes she took with her every day of his life in the side area of the mobile. Mark open the bag up and too see if she bought his shoes, he knew that his brother had took his own that sat on his back every day, he only took it off when they went to bed, but it was always close to his hands if they had to move quickly. His sister had one too. But he kept on forgetting where he put his and he would never put enough in the bag for this situation. Now he hoped his mother remember how he packed things or more how he did not pack. As he pulled out two pants and two shirts with no buttons and shoes that did not have shoestrings. They were hers as he looked into the size of shoes, but then he found another sets of cloths sweat cloths that were loose and not her size. Another pair of slide on shoes that were too big for her feet and he knew at once the clothes and shoes were his. She remembered how he was. Mark put all the clothes back in the bag that had zipper and handle so he could hold on to it. The shoes fit perfect on his feet. Now he could go and find out where his family is. First he had to destroy this mobile or ship he would call it sometimes. Mark check out the panel and found the destruction trigger that would blow the mobile up.

He had only a few minutes to get out, the counting started at ten and Mark grabbed more food and water bottles into the bag fast and ran out the mobile with leaps that came from his hybrid side. He made it and disappeared into the forest as the mobile burst into flames.

CHAPTER TWENTY-TWO

S TEVE WAITED BELOW ONE of the trees that his friends where eating and sleeping in. Steve kept on thinking about Max and what those people had told him. The hybrid stole women and children from this village and they really don't trust any hybrids (laugh) Steve thought he would not trust any hybrids either if one of them stole his sister. Brooke his sister that stayed up late waiting for him to get home, her laughter when he was able to find some insulin for her. Her face round with tangles of red and blonde hair that fell down her back like rivers of long smooth soft water fall. Steve miss her and his head fell as he thought about her and then again a little angry that she did not tell him about his hybrid blood. She had to know about it, she was years older than he was. Yeah, it was strange that he never got sick, but still, hybrid blood is important and the family secret that he and the others found in the attic that day.

Too many secrets and no one is willing to tell him any more than what is necessary he guessed. A bird flew over his head and landed close to his shoulder, the sight was strange too, birds never come close to anyone in the community or in the city. The bird was big with large blue wings and a red head, its body was yellow, almost like looking at rainbows, but feathers not the sky. The bird peak was white and long. Hybrid of some kind. Steve thought as he looked around his surrounding, the trees were thick and the smell of fresh green grass tickle his nose, Steve started to sneeze, but caught himself with his hand and found something interesting around a bush that was close to the edge of the forest and the field that they were at yesterday. The bush had red berries and blue flowers, the smell of sweet made his mouth water. He was hungry and thirsty. But were the berries poison or could he eat them. A look back up the tree where his friends were and then again at the bush, he wanted those berries. Steve some of the berries in his pockets that he hoped would hold the berries until he got some answers about them.

The climb was easy now that he knew where the ladder was and he went up. Slowly he moved toward the tree hut where his were staying. A knock with his fist, and a whisper of his words.

food. Steve said as he waited for them to open the door.

Mr. Farmer was the one that open the door and he let Steve in the hut. One of the villagers was sitting next Jack and Max.

You know of why we do not trust you half breed. If you want our help you must bring our children and women back to us. We cannot fight the large hybrids that came here four moons ago. We do know where they took our family. But we cannot go there without our own safety. Do you understand what I am saying to all of you?

Steve understood to well what this villager was saying. The villager had long shaggy hair like Max unruly hair that still stood out like a rag in tangles. But this villager was a small woman with black dark hair that was held down with a band of some sort around her head. Her dress was brown with spots of redness that might have been blood or something that was red stain, the dress ragged and torn with rough edges that touched the ground as she moved from one spot to another on the floor.

Steve watched her with his sharp eyes that now did not miss any kind of movement.

Can you take us there tomorrow and maybe we can save them if we just could see the area and find out if my wife is there with our baby girl? Max asked her as he worried sense Susan was taken.

Max face showed anxiety and nervousness that took away more of his sadness, he was anxious to get his wife and baby back with him. As long as Steve remember Susan and Max they were always together and always had done things as one. But the new baby Susan had made it even tighter and stronger as he could remember how happy Max had been when the baby was born and had kept the two important people in his life as close to him as he could.

Mr. Farmer stood up off his chair as he thought about what to do. He knew they needed Susan and the baby was important too. One cannot function without the other. Another little antidote he heard as a child.

But if this villager takes them to where these villagers that were captured and maybe even Susan, there might be a chance they could get out of here and back to the truck and the secret. Mr. Farmer looked at Steve and wondered if he thought about Brooke and how she played a part in his life secret of how he became a hybrid.

If you take us there and we need prove of what you said first before we even go there, I do not what my small army to be captured either so we will stay here until then. Mr. Farmer said as he went over to Steve side.

You have your hybrid protector and we do not have anyone to protect us so how can we show you any prove. She said as she went over to Mr. Farmer face. She was a lot smaller in size maybe 4" ft. or smaller. But she was as tough as they were.

What name do have? We need your name villager? Max asked as he went over to stand behind the woman.

I am called Corinna and I am the healer of the village, but without my daughters and my sister we cannot do well with healing. My powers and knowledge can only do good with my family. She said as she stood tall for her statue.

I folded my arms across my chest and looked down at her. I was still hungry and food was all around me. My nose flared out as I spoke to her carefully.

I am just one hybrid and I am new at what I can do, so if you think I can defect those that capture your family and bring them back, I am sorry. I may not be able to so if the threat looks too high for me. I can tell you that I will try and I might scare them or maybe save them. But I cannot say either way until we see prove that what you say is true. We were miss judged before and will not happen again. Steve said as he unfolded his arms and let the rest on his sides.

The villager Corina had left the hut in angrier, her angrier could be heard as she slammed the huts door. She was so angry that the children that were with them jump.

Look we can't trust these people, if they were hiding something don't you think they would take us to their boss or something and just hand us over to them? Steve said as he took an apple that he found on the table that was close to a far wall. The apple was red in color and made Steve mouth water.

Go ahead Steve, we saved the apple for you. We know you got to be hungry and a new hybrid needs to eat as much as possible. Mr. Farmer said as he took out more food that was hidden from the villager and stored underneath on one of the make shift beds on the floor.

Steve took the food and just ate like a mad starving person he was. Pears and apples with green leafs that looked like spinach and lattice with tomatoes too. No meat as far as he could tell. But the taste was good and it made him feel good. And yet, Steve wanted and need some meat. After swallowing the food and drinking the water that Jack gave him, Steve had no words to say to anyone. He just wanted to be alone for right now. There was just too much to think about. For one thing he knew that he need to help them save Susan and her baby. But how was he going to battle all those other hybrids and save all those other people that these people here at this village has lost. How can he save them all? Steve knew he couldn't do it alone. Steve took a breath and coughed as looked around him. The others were all sitting down talking in small whispers, the children were listening as Mr. Farmer spoke slowly to them. Steve got up and went over to him.

Look we all know that Steve is a new hybrid and he really can't fight all those other hybrids that have Susan, we need to save her, but we also need to find our truck and get out of here. Mr. Farmer said as he took something off the floor.

So I am I going to do all this? Steve asked him as he sat next to Mr. Farmer.

Mr. Farmer looked at Steve as he settled down next him.

Do you even hear me son? I told them that you cannot fight these hybrids alone. We need to have a plan and an escape too. Mr. Farmer said as he unfolded his hands that were resting on his lap. Mr. Farmer's pants looked worn out from the battle they had fought back where they lost Susan and he found out that he was a hybrid.

Well I guess I came in at the wrong time, sorry. But how are we going to do this? Steve asked him again.

I don't know right now. I was hoping that someone would have great idea, but it seems that everyone wants me to come up with it and I don't have right now. But I think if we look at the possibilities of both sides.

We know we need to get back to the truck, but we also know that we need to save Susan and her baby too. We cannot be at both places at the same time. We need a plan, may two plans just to think if one does not work maybe another one would something to fall back on. The battle was a good plan, but it too was dangerous we lost some of the children at the battle, but fighting back was good. And using signals to tell each other what was going to happen was a good one. We need to keep that signal going for back up when and if that happens again. Mr. Farmer said as he looked at everyone around him. Max got up and walked around in his dress that was torn from the fighting too. The dirt and mud clung to his dress as he walked around rubbing his face and hair. His feet bare as Steve feet had been made thump noises as he walked. Steve could tell he was nervous and anxious as he moved back and forth.

I know Susan would not leave our baby so she has the baby right now. And if there are any children that she could see or be around she would protect them too. We can't leave children when they need help. Children are special and they need help when we could help. So maybe if I know Susan well she would do something to protect them but I don't know what the area would look like. I think she would find a place to hide them and keep them safe. But what if just think what if there are trees like these or houses that are so badly fallen, maybe there is a hidden way we could get in and out fast? Max said slowly as he thought.

Hmmm, you talking about tunnels? Jack asked him as he started to think about the possibilities.

We need to find out now before we continue with a plan of any sorts. Mr. Farmer said as he got up and went out of the house to ask one of the villagers.

The one villager that Mr. Farmer came to was the one that was in their hut or house not too long ago and went out of the room fast. But this was important if these villagers want their people back safely.

Excuse me, but we have a question to ask about tunnels? I know back where we came from are tunnels that lead us to sewers that come from houses and they help some people to hide from the enforcers when it is necessary. So we need to know if there is one here in the forest. Mr. Farmer asked her.

Tunnels we have many, but some of the tunnels are dangerous to be in. To many of the tunnels fall down and we have holes in the ground from them. Our leader believes that the weight of those that walk along the ground has made the ground weak and then the tunnels fall in and a hole is made.

Then do you think there might be one that would lead us to where these hybrids are holding your people and our Susan? Mr. Farmer asked her.

Maybe or maybe not. I do not know if there is or not. We do not go through the tunnels we stay here in the trees it is safe. But I know someone that has gone through the tunnels many times and he too says it unsafe to go through, but he knows all the tunnels and where they lead too. I can set a meeting with him to come to the place where we have ground people and he will come to speak to you. The villager said as she left Mr. Farmer and went toward the crowd of her people standing close to a hut in the distances.

Mr. Farmer stood there watching her leave, his mind coming up with a plan, but they could not leave yet and just go through the tunnels without knowing which one is which.

Steve went back down to the ground level and knew that Mr. Farmer would find out where the tunnels were, but it would be Max to know how to make those tunnels work for them. Steve knew Max well enough that Max would find a way to make a bomb or something that would help with the fight or battle. The children were another story, what could those small innocent children do to help them? Steve moved around the trees and let his hybrid take over, he started to strip off his clothes and change into his hybrid. The feel of the beast coming out and taking over was painful as his bones pop and stretched out and made him scream out his pain from the changing. But the change stopped as he heard voices coming from behind him. Steve body was in-between both human and wolf. But he was a hybrid so it was natural. He stood taller than he usually stood, but the sight of him made his seem scary as his body hair took over and grew over his arms and legs, nose and mouth grew too as a snout long and pointy with fangs sharp grew out of his mouth. Steve eyes changing from small human like to large wide eyes that focus into the dark forest that hid its secrets. The smell of wet grass and mold stung his nose, but the sharp smell went farther to who was talking in whispers. Steve had to move slowly and out of the reach of those that are here.

Steve noticed that branches and bushes moved slowly with the wind. The wind had bought a scent that Steve felt was not part the villagers scent. Steve stop in a hidden patches of large leaves that hid his body in darkness, only his eyes glowed as it watched carefully of what was happening.

Two large hybrid cats silently walked close to where the village was under their hidden trees. Their voices smooth and in silent mask of whispers.

We need to get the rest of those humans the master had asked us too. We need the young ones. Those humans will not listen to our master so we need to make them listen. One of the cats said to the other that was looking upward at the tree.

Are going to wait for Mull, he has one of the hostages, if we kill the pup then the other humans will listen to us this we know. Our master had said to do so. Make those weak things suffer and listen to him. This is true yes? Said the other cat.

Steve listen careful and knew the wind was not blowing at his back, but blowing their scents toward him. Those cats did not know he was even there waiting for them. His mouth closed but the taste of cats growing strong in his mouth started to make him drool, water drip off his mouth as he snarled at the sight of them, but he had to wait, someone else was coming and they might have Susan or one of the villagers with them.

Someone was pushing someone else through the forest, the sound of tears and fears rose over Steve bones as it got closer.

Fear tasted good and he like that Steve thought as he hutched in attack mode.

Move human, your weakness stinks and is making me sick. If you do not stop crying I will eat you now and not later. The one cat said that had a small child with blonde hair and her eyes were so red that Steve could not tell what color they were. The child as afraid and that just made him want more of that fear. Steve heart beat rose in his chest making it hard to not to move. The feel of the heart moving fast and painful in his chest gave him a rush of adrenalin throughout his body. He was ready to fight, but the child had to move away from those cats, he did not want to hurt the child by accident, he still was not sure of his hybrid body and what it could do and what it could not do. The one cat that had the child snarl at the child and shoved her up against one of the trees that lead to the villages. The child started to climb and that was Steve clue to attack now. His body flew out of the bushes that hid him and the other cats did not know what had hit them. Steve fangs rip off one of the cats tail off as he used his whole body as a tool to fight with. A weapon that was going wrong as his claws and talon rip skin and fur off two of the cats. The other cat sprung up behind him and started to claw at his back, but Steve turned so fast that the head of the cat came off with a twist of Steve claws. All three cats gone dead as dead could be. Steve chest rose fast as the adrenalin rush pour out of body and made his head spin. He had to work it off, the taste of fear from the child was making want to take her down and eat her. But he had to control that urge to kill others that he was suppose too protect not harm. His voice harsh as he tried to tell the child to run up the ladder that grew in the tree trunk.

Go up and tell the others what happen child, do not be afraid of me, I will not hurt you or anyone else. I am friend and will only hurt those that will harm you and your people I promise. Steve said in voice that he did not recognize.

The child got up to the village and found that she was in front of her grandmother the village healer. She ran to her with open arms and cried hard as she put her small arms around her grandmother waist.

Manny, what is it, how did you get here? I thought those bad hybrids took you, where is your mother and the others that were capture? The grandmother asked her as she patted the child's head.

They were going to kill me in front of all of you, but another hybrid wolf I think attack the cat hybrids and killed them, he said that he would not hurt me, but protect me and the village too. He killed the three cats, I saw him rip their heads off. The child said as she wiped her tears off her face with the back of her hands.

He did uh? That is good to have a protector and he will be here soon. I think I know this protector. The grandmother said as she looked at Mr. Farmer and the others that stood behind him.

She started to understand and looked back her own leader and told him straight out of what she thought.

That boy that came here with these humans are innocent, but the boy is hybrid and is good, he did not harm our child here and did say that he is here to protect us and he will bring the rest of our family here. They will be home too. We should help them with the fight and not let them go without our help. We need them, but they need us too. So we will fight by their side or die trying. She said as she stood high in her small statue.

The leader looked around and saw someone coming up the ladder with thick black hair and grey sleeves and stood there looking at him. It was the hybrid that came with the other humans. He stood silent as he walked over to the older man that wore strange looking cloths.

Farmer there were three cats down there and I had to change into my wolf to attack them before they came up here to do more harm. They had that child and was going to use her to make these people do what they want them to do. I think these people have secrets that they are not telling us, and I am not sure if those other capture people they have were forced so much. Steve said as he pointed to the leader.

The old woman that was the healer and grandmother to the child looked down at the child for answers.

Is this true, are the ones that we thought were capture are not captured? She asked her.

No we were capture and held as hostage, but we were forced to work on a tunnel at the edge of the forest large hill. We were taken at night and I did not see him, but I heard his voice that told the hybrids to take us and leave. He told them that they would get more of the village a little at a time. The child said.

Will he now, leader we need to find who the traitor is and send him off with the wild animal in the forest. We need to protect our people. The healer said as she pulled the child close to her side.

Steve hunched low as he felt something in the air tell him danger was close. As fast as he could Steve pulled both of the child and old woman away from sight. The leader threw a spear at the two standing there, but the spear struck Steve instead. Steve pulled the spear out of his back with ease, and he walked over to the leader as the villagers gather around the leader with their own spear over their head ready to strike their leader dead.

Why did you sell your family and these villagers family to those hybrids and what are they digging up there? Steve asked him as he went over to stand tall over the man body.

The other villagers held their spears and were ready to strike, but it was the healer that told them not to strike yet, we need answers first and then kill him. She said.

You will obey me as your leader. The small man said with short black hair that gathered around his head like a nest. His clothing was a tan like leather skirt that went around his fat waist and his legs bow with rings of gold and twigs circled his ankle and bare feet. The skin of the leader of the village was a light brown, but Steve looked at the skin more careful and he saw the scales laid against the leaders skin.

The girl said something again. Our leader I heard his voice, he told the hybrids that he wanted them to only bring the people back after they were broken, I don't know what he meant by that, but the others were digging something and I was pulled away from the dig. I saw a new girl and she had a baby.

At that point Max grabbed the girl away from the girl's grandmother, the face was shocked and fear at the same time. Her eyes wide as she looked at Max crazy hair that went all over his head like a nest of fleas.

Where is she is she alright, tell me is she alright. Tell me tell me I need to tell me now tell me. Max shook the girl hard, but pulled her close to his chest as he asked over and over tell me. He was both scared and nervous on top he was worried about both of his family.

I-I don't know for sure where they are, those hybrids took her away from the dig and went back into the forest with some men that were dress weird like. They had gray suits with a blue stripe around their middle. I don't know where they went I just know about my people and the leader that sold us to those hybrids. The girls said.

Max let go and silently cried as he realized that those that wore gray suits were enforcers and they had just captured his woman and child. They were dead as far as he knew. This is the end for him. He could not live if she died. He had to leave his friends and find his Susan and their baby girl. Max went back in the hut that they had just left. Max looked around the hut for something that he could use, pipe and rope with something to use as a bomb or something. Max toss blankets and cups and chairs around, tables and anything he could find to uncover whatever he could find and use.

I think I believe this child rather than you, leader. She does not lie or speak out about are people. The grandmother said as she walked closer to the leader of the village.

You are old woman and I am the leader. If you do not listen to me then you will die. The leader said.

Die? You say that you will order my death? I do not think these people are stupid, but you are another story. You are no longer our leader. The grandmother said as she pointed her finger.

The villagers held their weapons high over their heads. The leader flinched and stood away as they seemed to be waiting for some kind of signal.

Steve walked closer to the leader, he could see better than anyone here that stood looking at the leader. Steve saw the scales that seemed to blend with the leader's light brown skin. Something was not right, everyone else it seemed did not have scales. Something told him that this is not their leader, but some kind of mask or something he just could not put his word right. What is he? Steve thought as he slowly walked over to stand over the man.

The leader looked up at Steve, his fear tried to come up from his hidden place. But he couldn't hold it back long. The leader step back and looked around, he pointed to each member of his villager and said. Every one of you know that my own child and wife is missing also and you want to blame me for this. I do not think it is my fault I did not make any kind of deal or what this child claims I did. I do know that this hybrid is one of them and he may be the one that bought those hybrids to our village. We need to kill him and not me. I will not harm you or lie to you why would I do that? Think I have lost my family too in this. So there is your answer. The leader said as he puffed his chest out.

Steve stood still and smell the leaders scent and found it strange as it smelled like fish and taint with moldy grass. Fish? That was strange as any kind of water was a little bit away from the village, but that was not just it. Scales, brown scales. Steve went backwards and thought about those creatures his sister told him about back when she was alive and he was just a kid looking up at his sister like she was the most important person in the world to him. But was this man a chameleon of some sort. Wait a minute, if he was a hybrid wolf then it is possible for this man to be a chameleon. Even if this is too much to believe. But he had to find out, a colored blanket and something else would show if he was a chameleon or not.

Max can you help me really quick like. Steve asked his friend who walked out of the hut with something in his hands. What do you need me do Steve? Max said and knew his friend was trying to tell him something, it was in Steve eyes that said for Max to wait.

Look I need that red blanket that one of the children had, I think I am getting real cold right now. I feel as if my cough is getting worse. Can you just throw it to me? Steve asked him as Steve walked over to the leader and stood behind him.

Max came out with the blanket and threw over to Steve but it landed on the leaders left shoulder and the floor. The leader foot went over the blanket as he turned around to see Steve face. But the leader was not paying attention and his skin turned to red like the blanket. Someone else threw a green blanket at him and he turned that color too. Everyone stood in shock as they all see what the leader really was a chameleon. The villagers with the weapon stood back and put their weapon at their side as shock took them by surprise.

Chameleon, a hybrid chameleon, who sent you and why did you lie to these people? Steve said with his teeth bared and ready to strike the man down. But question need to be answered by this liar. Steve looked at Mr. Farmer as he heard knocks that sounded like codes he grew up with, the codes were a way for Jack and him and that of their small group be able to communicate without words. They had used it many times when it came to the enforcers stopping them for one thing or another. Steve listen carefully to each letter that would make out a word, IDEA-no Plan-ASK HIM WHERE THE PEOPLE ARE AT IF HE SPEAKS TRUTH. Hmm Steve thought as he looked back at the leader and then started to ask him a few question.

Tell me if you did not take the villager to the hybrids, then you would tell us where they are or better take us to them. Steve asked him.

You bought them here, you take us to the hybrid nest. The leader said as he stepped away from the blankets.

If I did and you did not, why did I protect that child and not just change into my new skin and eat every one of you. I would not do that, I did although, fought for that child life and the lives of your villagers if I did not stop those hybrids from coming up here. Steve said as he listened to the knocks and scraps Mr. Farmer was doing or making.

I don't know I think you plan this and told us lies, those hybrids were only a few and not important. They were your way to talk yourself in this village. We do not believe you are friend, but traitor to us. The leader said as he spits on the ground at Steve and the others.

Steve heard the words that Mr. Farmer had told him with the scraps and hitting on the villages handrails.

Jack was out of sight and was getting information about a fight or something.

Steve had to keep the leader busy and find something a trick to get him to say who he really is.

I may not know if you are truly the leader, but tell me do you change color like that a lot, does others here in the village do the same? Steve asked carefully. Steve walked slowly back and forth in front of the leader. His eyes not wavering from the leader's movements.

I do not know what you are accusing me of I am not a changer of skin. The leader said as moved away from the blankets.

The leader was small in height, but had a stomach that was almost round, his hair black as coal with eyes that were not human looking at Steve with the same suspicion in his own eyes.

Steve stop moving and just stared at the leader as if he would challenge the man. But he man was had grey hair that blended in with the black dark hair he had.

Steve wondered how old the man was or is. This is not good, if the man was what Mr. Farmer had said in his knocks and scraps the man would be tricky and dangerous.

Steve asked another question that had every one waiting for the answer.

So you believe you really believe that those that are with me are traitors as well as myself. Tell me why I did not already have all of you in the hybrid camp? Why would I not attack all of you and eat each of you, or why did I even let those children that went me and my friends not eat them either. Tell me or I can say that you are lying about all of this and you are using us as a way of getting out of stealing the villages children and families? Am I right? Steve asked.

The leader snared at Steve and walked closer to where the villagers had been standing. His stance was in check as Steve noticed that he was ready to pounce. But is that what a chameleon does? Do they pounce like hybrid cats or do they attack like hybrid wolves?

At then Jack came over with a box that looked like it had been buried deep in the ground. Jack had his shirt open as Steve noticed Jack had been sweating, his face shine as drips of sweat came down his face. His open shirt showed off the sweat in ripples. But Jack was skinny with bones peeking out, his frame was small, but that did not make him incapable of fighting. Jack had moves like no one, he was fast and knew what his opponent would do next by just watching the person eyes. That was one thing Jack had taught Steve about fighting. Steve own sister had her own moves too and had gave lessons to Steve and Jack. She was the one that said to watch your opponent's moves and their eyes it would let you know what they are going to do next.

Eyes, watch their eyes and then move to the opposite side and they will fail and you will be alright. Brooke would tell them. Steve started to grin, but watched Jack instead.

Hey is anybody hungry? I found some good stuff, been hunting for these bugs for a long time. If I may just look inside of this box? I might find what I am hunting for. Let's see here, oh man oh man my favorite, grasshoppers and here some beetles too. Looks good does anybody else want some beside me? Jack ask no one.

The leader licked his lips as he watched Jack pull out a large grasshopper it looked to good, his tongue went out fast before he realized what he had just done. The grasshopper tasted good as well as the beetle Jack took out too.

Tell me leader if these are the best? Does all chameleon here like these? Jack asked,

No I am the only chameleon here and these are the best. The leader said as he ate them slowly after what he had just said.

His eyes moving from one villager to the healer as he swallowed the bugs. Jack just stood there looking at him.

I will challenge you, on grounds that you are a liar and false person to this village. Spears and knifes will do us. Jack said as he threw the box of bugs down at the leader's feet.

I am not the liar here false human. I am the leader and I will prove to my people who I am.

So tell me if you are the only one here then that is a chameleon or not. You seem to say no, but something else is strange. How did you get to be the leader as far as I had found out the leader is not a hybrid? He is a leader that lost both of his family to something in the forest. So tell me if I am right or wrong? Jack him again.

I am not a hybrid you mistaken my words I said that you and your friends are traitors and chameleons too. The leader said as he tried to reframe his words earlier.

I don't think so if I am correct and I know what we all heard, you are the only one here that is a chameleon, but chameleon are loners and they do not mate for life as humans do. So where are the villagers that you took and gave to the hybrids? Jack asked him as he stood with both of his feet apart. The leader licked his lips as he realized that he had shown his tongue to the villagers and they may not believe him now. He had to do something to make them know he was on their side. But how? This human is doing something to trick no he wants a fight and that will be his down fall. He is skinny and will be easy to kill. The leader smile at Jack as he waited to hear the challenge.

What's wrong leader, you look like you have eaten more of the bugs I brought you? Jack had a feeling the leader knew what he was up to and the challenge would be the bait.

The leader stood quite as he waited for the human to do or say something.

Jack looked at him and decide that he would make the move first. If you are telling the truth, then why not just tell us about the villagers that are missing? That should not be bad if you tell us? Jack said as he moved slowly into another stance with his legs more together.

I said human I do not know anything about the hybrids kidnapping our villagers. So you think to trick me with moving your words to make it look like I had something to do with the hybrids. I know tricks and humans are good with tricks. Look at the other villages that use too be here, they are gone, it was the humans that trick them into believing that they are smarter and can be the leader. No I will not give in to my leads. This is my village and you are the traitor. You that come here without our permission and bring nothing but fear to my people. The leader said as he too stood in a fighting stance.

Jack smiled at him with his missing teeth. Jack thought about how to trick him, but that was already going.

Do you really think we were in on the villager's disappearance after the hybrids took them? Hmm you are going to have to come up with more prove, because we got here way after your people were taken. Jack said as thought again what to do to get that leader to show his colors.

Then the little girl that Steve saved from the hybrids came from behind her grandmothers back to look at the leader.

I heard your voice when you were talking to the hybrids after we were captured. My mother is still out there with them, I hope you did not let them know that I lived and their hybrids mates did not. The little girl said as she twisted her grandmother's hands in hers.

If it be true and I believe my granddaughter words to be that then our families that are still out there with the hybrids are no longer alive because of you. The healer said as she pointed her finger at the leader.

Huff, you are child and do not know truth from lies that are in your own mind. Children are known to hear words that are spoken. The leader said as he looked down at the healer's feet and spit at her. I am your leader and you will obey my words.

My child does not lie, but we will as not children but adults with minds of that. But because of our laws you will fight this man and prove to us that you tell truth to us. If he wins, then you die. The healer said in a more claim words.

Jack stood there as he spoke again. Well it is up to us to see who is and who is not a traitor. Knives and spears would make the decision for truth. Jack walked backwards and stood waiting for someone to tell him where to go.

We have round fighting area in a meadow of open woods. There we fight to the death. The healer said as she motioned for Jack and the leader to follow. Four village warriors stood behind the leaders back as they all agree it would be safer to so, with another four in front of the leader it became even more safer. But the leader thought again, if he need to escape from these humans that think they are better than hybrids. The leader knew where they were going but he also knew that he would win this fight. He was after all a hybrid and a chameleon and these humans here were weak and useless. He had sent off many of the humans that would help with the fight against the so called freedom fighters. They will be a shield and a weapon against them. After this he will send the rest of the villagers and continue in the next villages that will follow.

A smile came over the leader as he walked to the ground and toward the place they called the cove of trees. There the fight will start.

Jack knew the chameleon is fast and his tongue may be one of his weapon. But that will show that he is not human or like them, another sight that would be against him. The villagers do not like chameleon they are traitors to their own kind. Jack can be faster if he watched the leader's eyes closely. He had been in fights before and he knew how to just watch the eyes closely as they could tell what would come next. The eyes and the movement of each body parts can be the one way of knowing what the opponent would do next. Jack took a look at the place they were at, the cove of trees was a good name. They got to the place where they were fighting and found that trees where growing around a circle like grass arena like fighting place. Grass tall hid places to sit, as only the feel of hard blocks felled with wild like flowers and grass as tall as Jack hips, but it was clear enough to fight without bushes or trees to stop the fight. The sight of the place was beautiful, but it was where they made decision with fights to the death. Jack was not afraid and knew what to do. It was mostly the leader that would make the first move. Jack went over the round blocks that were covered in grass and wild flowers. Someone gave Jack a spear and a knife. The knife Jack put at his front pants belt slit. His shirt came off as he weighed the spear in his hands, Jack felt his feet against the rocks that were hidden underneath the grass and the weeds. Jack kept his thought on the ground as he wanted to feel the grounds make so he could know where to step and where not to walk. The ground was uneven and more rocks that were large and stones that had some sharp edges. The leader held his spear high over his head and found the weigh to be good and where Jack was too much into his thoughts, the spear sailed over his head and almost hit Jack as he stepped away fast.

Jack heard the spear released in the air, as soon as he counted to five he knew where to step back and how far to keep the spear from hitting him. Jack picked the leaders spear and knew now he had two spears to use. Nice, but that was not how the game will play. Jack step back with both spears in his two hands and pulled them back, but that was when he saw the leader pull his knife out and started to come after Jack. Jack just lowered his spears and pointed the spears at the leader, the leader almost stopped, but he felt the pain of the spears penetrated his stomach. A small wound the leader said as he pulled himself out of the spears marks. His wounds healing like magic, made Jack step back. He knew there were some chameleon that could heal faster than normal, but he never met one. This was amazing, but it was a distraction he could not take. Jack knife flew out of his front as the spears went in the leader and as if by its own choice Jack sliced the leader's neck. He did not slice it off and that was a mistake. Jack had to take the leaders head off in order to kill him. The fight went on as Jack danced his way from the leaders own knife. The spears lay in the grass with blood still dripping on the ground. Trees blew leaves and made beds out of the grounds Jack had been fighting. Birds were flying overhead as they screamed out their protest of how the fight was effecting their way of life. Some looked up for a sign, but the sun was bright as it fell slowly down behind the trees, and yet they still could see who was fighting and how the fight was won.

Jack watched as the leader bounce backwards away for a second as Jack grab one of the spears and threw it over the leader's head, the leader looked up as if the spear was going to land on him. But it was jack fast thinking as he found his knife and held it in a way that it sliced the leader's neck to a point that the blood vessel in his neck spit out blood in pools of wet sticky red rivers of blood. The leader's eyes went still it was too late for the leader to do anything. His breath coming in gasp of air that was not coming in his lungs. His heart pounding hard and fast to keep up with the loss of blood. Then the leader fell as his head was sliced more as he changed into his true self a chameleon and his head fell beside his own body. It was over and he could not heal from a decapitated head.

Jack stood there looking down at the leader's body that has changed into the chameleon. His body shine with wetness as sweat beamed down his chest and face. Jack face round with a chin that was square and a nose that was not big, but a mouth that not big or little but wide enough for everyone to see his smile as he turned to look at the villagers that were sitting down watching.

No one said anything, the villagers were silent as they watched their leader change into chameleon creature, the body turning green with purple streaks. The head not far from the body also changed in color of purple and black.

The sun was almost gone as the sky own light beaming in a fade of blue and black. Stars peeking out as it became their turn to light the sky.

Jack stood there as sweat shined his body in wetness, his face dripping and stinging his eyes. Jack wiped his face with the back of his left hand as he dropped his knife and let it fall away from his hands.

Steve and Mr. Farmer went down to meet Jack as they grabbed a shirt that was tucked in Mr. Farmers back pocket. The shirt belonged to Jack, it was torn and dirty, but Jack wore the shirt every day, it was one of his best shirts and his only shirt he owned.

The healer and the granddaughter walked over to Jack with a large pitcher of water. The pitcher was made out of a round wood that was cut out of a log or big branch, it was deep. The feel of it was rough and yet it held the water in place. Jack looked at the pitcher of water and his lips smack together as his tongue licked his lips again. The feel of his tongue was nothing to the water he was allowed to drink. The sound came out of nowhere as the villagers started to shout out Jacks name.

Your skin is as dark as the starless nights we have seen and yet the memories of those that are like you have always been of strength and wisdom. Your fighting stance is like watching wild birds dancing when it rains.

We can see your thoughts move to one and then to another as if you cannot make up your mind. You are smart and know much of fighting those that are not of our kind. You Jack hybrid friend you will be our new leader we will listen to you and obey you. The healer said as she poured the rest of the water from the pitcher out over Jack head and body. With the water we cleanse your soul and give a new life that will be part of our tribe.

Jack shook his head as he felt the water cool his body and head down, but he heard something he was not sure of. Did they say that he was the new leader? Jack stop in his thoughts to look at the healer. She was not tall or too small either, but she was old with grey hair that showed that she lived very long. Jack noticed her smile and her bowed head as everyone around them had bent knee and bowed head. You are our leader now and you are the one that has been spoken of from the start of our flight here in the forest that is our home. She said.

Jack wipe his face off with his hands as he tried to speak clearly. Did you say something about me being a leader? Jack asked her. A smile came over the healer mouth and eyes as she knotted yes.

Jack looked up at the villagers and wonder about his friends. Jack didn't know what to do with what he had just heard.

Steve heard the news and smile at his best friend and brother. Steve always thought of Jack as a brother than anything else or anyone else. They grew up in the community hunting for food like the children they bought with them. Mr. Farmer had always looked out for them after their parents died, food clothes and a bed at times. But this was more than what Steve would call good thing. Jack leader of the tree villagers. Brooke would laugh her head off at that. Jack was strong even though he was skinny and his bones seemed to stick out. Jack would be a good leader, but really now? Steve thought as he started to follow Mr. Farmer down to see Jack.

I don't know what to say, I never thought about being a leader? Can I talk it over with my friends and get back to you all in a few hours? I got to let this sink in. Jack said as he went over to his best friend Steve.

Look we need to talk fast and I need answers too. Where is Max? Jack said as he noticed that Max was missing out of this circle of friends.

I don't know? Steve said as he looked at Mr. Farmer and Jack. Some of the kids were missing too? Steve was getting a little nervous as remember seeing Max go back into the hut that they were all sharing.

That is strange. Maybe he is still there I hope. I got a bad feeling about him missing like this and where are the four children that went with us. I only counted two here right now. Jack said as he went passed everyone and almost ran back to the tree that had the ladder.

But where is the ladder? Max, he had something to do with this? Jack thought.

Steve and Mr. Farmer were right behind Jack and the villagers were behind them as they all reach the tree that had the ladder. Everyone was looking up at the village thinking someone has to be up there to send the ladder back down. But no one was there and no one sent any ladders down for them.

Jack asked for the healer and asked her if there were another tree ladder close by?

Yes, we have another one, but it is old and we do not use that ladder any more. The healer said.

Take us to it, because it may be the only way up and maybe another clue to where your village people are hidden. Jack said as his mind came up with more questions.

CHAPTER TWENTY-THREE

AX HAD LOOKED AROUND in the hut as Jack annoyed the leader into a fight that would either get them killed or save them. Max really did not want to find out either way. If anything he wanted to find his Susan and his baby girl. They were out there somewhere and he was going to find them if it means his own death he would find them.

Max knew what he was looking for and slowly the things started to come to him.

Four small knives sharp and deadly with blades that would kill with the first strike. Ropes that would help if he need to climb down or use for something else. Clothes he need clothes for both of his family.

Max turned a flat like mattress around on its opposite side and found a small box. The box was old as the sides seem to be peeling off. But Max found that underneath the peels of some kind was another part of the box, Max peel the paper away from the box and found there were words on the side. Max could not read or write, but he knew tunnels and pipes and wires that connected to things. Max could not count either, but he knew when a few minutes was up. The only one that knew how to read was his Susan, she worked hard to learn how to read with Steve and Jack. Mr. Farmer was the one to teach them, but Max just didn't want to learn words he was more interested in wires and tunnels and water pipes. He had learned a lot on his own and that was more of a prize than any words he could learn.

Right now he was getting curious about the box and what was in the thing.

Max turned the box in his hands and looked for something to open the box up. Was it like the box that they found in Steve parent's attic?

Does it have another clue about the past that would save the human world? Wasn't that what Mr. Farmer said they were? Max found a knob that had something hard and metal like connected with the knob. The box was not big, but it was the size of shoes. The box paper was too hard to make out what color it was, the paper had black and yellow that crumbles when Max touched it. The feel of the one metal part of the box was cool and rusty as he took his hand away and looked at his hands. Max hands had looked brown and red. Max wiped his hands on his dress that he was still wearing from Steve parent's attic. The dress helped Max move faster as he had no pants to hold his legs tight and his family jewels (that was what his father called it). The feel of freedom to move his legs from one place to another a lot easier and faster. It was something Max like about this dress, he was more to call the dress a robe than that-dress.

Right now he was trying to figure out how to open the box that was when he saw a rope and a long stick with a pointy sharp end. That was when he dropped the box and ran to the stick and the rope. Max wrapped the rope around his waist and shoulder, the rope was long and thick. The stick was big too, but he could not figure out how he was going to wear it so he could move around with both of the things he found.

The box laid on the ground open as Max looked down at the box, he put the stick down next to his feet as he bent down to sit down close to the box. Max pick the open box and looked inside of the box.

What is it? The thing was small but had a round metal base to it. Max could not tell what it was, but something told him that it was important and he would need it. Eventually he was going to find out what it was and how to use it. Max looked back in the box and found something that looked like yellow faded out paper. Max picked it up and looked at it, it had pictures he figure out but he could not read it.

The paper started to crumble in his hands and Max just threw the paper down. Max found a bag made out of grey material that had a long handle that he was able to put over his shoulder. Then he grabbed some fruit that was on top of a table that wobbled.

Max started to pick whatever food he could find into the bag that was wrapped around his shoulder.

When Max was finished he found that he could put the stick behind his back in between the ropes that made it tight enough to hold it in place.

Max looked around again to make sure he did not leave anything important behind. Nothing was forgotten and Max left the small place where he and his friends had slept and eat in.

When Max went out of the place he found that there were still some children sitting down close to where the ladder is.

Max sat down next the two children. Uh? I thought you all had gone to the fight? Max asked them.

We don't want to see them fighting.

We don't like the leader but he is the head of our village. Both of children said as they sat down eating a yellow round fruit that smelled good.

Max watched them and rubbed his head that was a mess of tingles and knots.

Max rub his hands together and smacked his dry lips. Do you two know where that tunnel everyone was talking about is? Max asked them.

We know someone that can take you there if that is why you are asking us this question.

Max looked at them and knotted yes and smile at them. The air was clear with the sun bright and ready to leave over the trees and let the night come in fast. Max knew how dangerous it was at night, but he wanted his Susan and baby girl. They were all he lived for and all he thought.

All right can you take me to him or did he go with the others to the fight too. Max asked them.

The children got up and motion for Max to follow them. Max followed them down through the bridges that connected each part of the village's home on the trees. The bridges Max found out were made out of old wood that fallen from old trees and they found how to take vines and make ropes that were mixed with animal hair. After a few more feet of village huts the children stop and went down another ladder that took them downward and on another part of the village. A tree large around the truck and tall that seem to go so high that Max could not see the end of it. They landed on top of another part of the village, but where they were had been blocked by the bridges and the huts that connected each part of the trees that held the villages as far as Max could see. Max found a hut that seemed small and abandon of other huts and that of any villagers. The only sound that Max could hear came from birds that nested close by on small branches that came from trees that stretched out toward the heavens. Max followed the children and stood there not knowing what to do next. Inside of the hut Max found were scattered food that had been eaten on the floor and a small table that stood in front of Max and the children. A shadow of something large sat against the wall, Max stood not knowing what to do next, he had to calm his nerves as his hands showed how nervous and how scared he was. But it wasn't of this creature that he was scared, it was the fact that this creature may not help him in finding his Susan.

Sit man, I do not know you, but these small ones do know that you seek a way to get your mate out of the hybrids nest? The voice was rough and soft as it spoke to Max. He could not see where the voice was coming from, but knew it was a man that was all Max knew.

Yes, I know that your villagers have lost your own family members too. I also know that you can lead me to a tunnel that would show me where the families are kept hidden by the hybrids. I might be able to save them if you can help me? Max asked him. Silence for a few minutes was all Max heard as well as the children beating heart.

Do you think you can fight those hybrids alone? The voice said with no emotion but the words were strong.

Max thought about the man statement and knew he was right. He could not fight them alone and he was not that good in a fight, but he knew traps and how to capture the bad guys. He was always good at that. He did blow up his old community after they left the place. But on his own like this he may not come out of this alive.

I think I can find a way to get them out without any blood spill, but if I need help I think those that are captured might help fight back. Max said as he thought of how his woman fights. Susan would kill anyone that harms a child, her own fighting skill matched his as they fought many times with John the cannibal back at the community. John had always heisted when it came to Susan and Max. John knew he would never win if he fought those two.

That may happen, but these are children and cannot leave the village now. They are unable to fight those that are larger than them. I can and I will assist you in this adventure. I am not what you think I am. Yes, at one time I was part of this village and now I am only called upon when danger has been present. The leader is not who he really is and our true leader is dead that I know and that is what I tried to tell Mocala, but she is does not believe me and I will not fight the leader. It would be unwise to do so. The voice as Max heard the voice standing up off the floor of the hut.

A light glowed from a window shining down on a figure that was too tall to be one of the villagers, they were short people with dark skin, but not as dark as Jack.

Then as Max back up against the door of the hut,

Max saw what he could not believe. The man was as tall as a tree, but he sat more on the hutches of his back legs, his face was wide with fur and nose that was more snout and teeth sharp and pointy as he smiled at Max.

Max step out of the hut as he felt his legs tremble and his face felt as if all the blood went out. Max took a gulp of air and his throat felt dry.

The man came out of the hut and stood over Max like a tree that held the village up over the ground. The bridge and hut shook as the man came out.

He stood with fur that was as dark as the night, his eyes black as the night had begun stood there looking down at Max making Max shake more.

You are small for a human. I am called Wild one protector of the tree villages that are here in the forest. He was born here and raised as one of the villagers. But he knew he was not one when he found that he was taller than they were and he was stronger they were. He decided that he needed to go away to find out who he is or was. But all he knew he had the strength to move trees that need to be moved. As he grew he found that he could fly and turn into a creature that he has never seen or knew of nor has the villagers. But they do not fear him, they know to keep his secret as long as he could protect them and this time they would not let him find the villagers that were stolen. He had to obey their choice or was it the leader command? He knew he had to wait for this moment.

I am protector of tree villages here in the forest. I will not harm you, but I will harm those that have taken my people away. We will bring your own family back too. Max stood there in silence as he thought about his Susan and his baby.

CHAPTER TWENTY-FOUR

IM WOKE UP WITH a head ache, his stomach started to make noises as he knew he was getting hungry and it was time to eat. The sun seemed too bright as it came over the trees, yesterday was a nightmare the fighting was intense as the hybrid village were attacked by enforcers that were built to kill and not to be killed.

But there was a way to kill those enforcers that seemed impossible to kill Jim had found the way. Jim clothes were shattered and torn, his pants were almost gone, he couldn't tell what color they were anymore, his shirt, well he did not have one, his bare chest smeared with blood that was not his covered his most of his chest hairs, he need a shirt and he need to clear his body. A basin full of water was at the table that had food on it when he came in the village before the battle started. A cloth brown and unsure of it cleaning Jim took as it is and washed his chest and face off until he was clear of blood and dirt. He couldn't do anything with his pants so he just kept it on.

But there is something out there that is bigger than those enforcers. That thought shook Jim as he knew they had to fight whatever the creature is. The device that they found inside of the enforcer may have a clue to what they are fighting. Jim walked through the village noticing the people picking up the dead and putting those that are injured close to the healer huts. Jim decide to go over to where the one hybrid that stood close to him and shield him from harm as they fought together in the battle last night.

Jim saw him as he passed a hut that had smoke coming from somewhere close to the huts opening.

A hybrid caster (who are priest like monks) holding a pole with feathers of different colors and round flat cloth with white bird holding a golden leaf in its peak. Jim knew the sign meant two or three things, one peace or the son of peace second prayers are needed, or forgive them. Third would be lord of high take those that are not heal. Either one, Jim like the meanings. Jim stop and looked up at the sky and said a small prayer to the one that created them.

I know I do not need to say a word, but there is so much I want to pray for and one is my wife and my three kid's safety with our family friends and my brother and his family keep them safe with you too. And thank you for all you had done for these hybrids and keep them safe too.

Jim went over to where the elders had their meeting hut and where he had to convince them to fight yesterday. There at the huts entrance was the small hybrid that was a badger, the white streak going down the small person back with black hard hair that waved in the wind as it blew in the early morning day. Jim took a breath as he started to remember he had not eaten and his stomach was empty the pain of not having food grew as he got closer to the hut. The smell of food cooking rose in the wind and caught Jim nose. His mouth watering as he walked blindly toward the hut with the food. He pasted the meeting hut. The badger stood up as he was leaning against the hut and followed Jim down to the hut that was cooking the food.

Jim and the badger stop at a large hut that was bigger than the meeting hut that was round and tall with large door flap that was easy to get and out of. But this one was bigger with hole at the top of the hut that looked like something that Jim swore he knew what it was, but he could not think what it was called.

But the smell was too good and he was hungry. His stomach was making louder noise as he started to open the flap of the hut. The badger was a little faster than Jim was and the flap went open to kiss Jim face as he felt the leather touch him hard. As Jim went in the hut he heard voices talking with deep rich baritone and one high voice that he knew it had to belong to a woman.

The badger was standing close to the large pot that was over a fireplace built with stones and bricks around it. Above the fireplace was the great hole and some kind of vent that was blowing the smoke outside was hanging on two sides of the hut hole. The hut had little smoke inside as the meal cooked giving off the smell of fresh food.

Maggie what are you cooking, the food is good yes? The badger asked the woman talking to someone else that sat by a table. The table was in the center of the hut it seemed that it was the cooking hut and no one slept there. That was what Jim thought, but then he found in a corner a large bed. Jim went to sit down on the seat next to the hybrid man. He was tall with shaggy brown hair and a large flat face with a nose that almost looked like a snout of a wolf, he was half form into his hybrid state and the sight was alright Jim thought. His brother had done the same at one time.

The flap went open again as the hybrid that was sitting next to Jim rose and waved his hands in a salute to another hybrid that came in.

I was just wondering Maggie where is the food for the elders, they are waiting at the meeting hut for the meal too began their talks with the cats. They are coming fast with other cats to help in this battle. So where is the food woman?

I have told you once, here I will give you this pot so they can take whatever food is needed. Here are the plates if they feel to eat like humans and not animals as the humans call us. The woman said as she pulled the pot from the fireplace and gave the pot to the other hybrid. Jim wanted to eat and he did not see any food over the fireplace any more. So he went out with an empty stomach and started to wonder out to find his hybrid protector. But the hybrid that went in the hut was calling Jim by name and Jim knew he had to follow this hybrid with the pot of food.

The meeting in the largest hut was round in size. There were many different hybrids that waited around one small table, another hybrid carried a pot that had something hot that steam and carried aroma of food on the table that had plates. Jim you will seat with me as you are the one that had warned us of this fight. Said one of the elder's. we wait for our healer to come as well as cat's healer that has joined fight and healing of all hybrids of all kinds with ours. There is no destination of any hybrids that are wounded and fight among each other as one toward those that fight against us all. We know that you have fought with the traitor Annie and our King has out witted her in her own fight. We also know that our own warrior wolves and that of the cats have helped with the fight as it became opened to our Kings flight and that of our warriors. We also know that you may know more about the resent fight we had with the enforcers, yes? The elder one said as he sat back down. Jim sat next to him on a small stool that had a back for Jim's back to rest. One of the plates was covered with eggs and bacon that still sizzler as the plate was given to Jim. Jim looked at the plate and wondered if he was seeing things. Food, real food. Two breads toasted with jam and butter. Jim stomach screamed out as everyone looked at him. A smile came from all of the elders and a laugh as they all heard Jim stomach. Jim ate as they were all given food from the pot that had separate sections for each food that was cooked. They all ate at first in silence as Jim stomach started to feel relief from hungry.

How is it that you have some knowledge of these enforcers Jim? One of the feline asked Jim.

I worked for the government as a senator and we get these meetings about what the leader has us to get him and why of it. I remember that one of the meetings was about these enforcers that was being some sort of unbreakable. We really didn't know much about this super enforcers, but the cost was more than what we had in the special bank that only we could give out to the leader when it was important. But somehow without our permission the leader took the bank on without us and took out the money for the scientist to make these enforcers. We got more information after we ask the leader to give that money back, but he just laughed and left us without enough money to pay for other things that were more important like our salary and food for the first family. We were screwed and the leader knew it. We all left the great city to find a better place for our families. I think everyone in the senate knew the leader was going to kill us all and take what he wanted and well we were not important any more. When I went to see one of my friends that was also with the freedom fighters he told me what he found out. He was with the scientist Max Turner and they talked and in turn my friend relayed the message back to me about the enforcer's enable of dying. But this scientist and two others had put a flaw in the plans for a reason. They did not want the enforcers to live a longer life. It would be a death of all mankind. It was already in trouble as is. But they did not tell the leader about that it was their result and their trigger if things got out of hand. So here I am and I am telling you all of what I know. I am also telling you that I believe that they are not done yet and the fight has just started. We need another plan to defeat them before they get here to kill us first? Jim said as he finished his meal.

They all agreed about a plan that would defeat the attackers. But how?

They must know that they cannot go through the tunnels we fought them at their entrance to our huts. So what is next? The elders asked as they finished eating.

Jim stop eating and drank his water that he got later from a female cat. Her lean legs tone with muscles and fur smooth and firm downward toward her feet that were claws thick and sharp.

Her face was had little fur I places were her cheek and neck were, she was a teenager just learning how to change shape from cat to human and now she is hybrid both human and cat together as one. It was hard to image how the pain of the bones breaking each time as they changed shape and how her face was more of cat with whiskers long blonde pointing outward from her nose. Her eyes blue as ice and not round like humans but slanted like a cat eyes. Jim watched her move with ease of a cat and silent as nothing. Her legs and feet moved silently against the floor, as the air seem to glide her path to each elder's open cups. Jim was impress with how the hybrid cat can move so quietly and yet they can kill with ease and fierce. Hmm that was thought tunnels-forest-trees-ponds-silence, but deadly. Hmm Jim thought again for answer, but first he need to know what the healer found out from that enforcer they found half dead and half alive? His mind running now with option of how to get to the enemies before they get here would be the best plan. He need to know where they are at and know the ground area and what is there that they could use. Jim put his plate and cup down and walked over to the center of the room. His mind he knew he had to talk fast and again convince these people to listen.

I got some plans, but I need to know what the healer has found out, so when is he coming? Jim asked as he walked around to loosen up his joints that seem to get stiffen up at his seat.

The elders moved in their seats as if their own body need to make room for something else.

One of the largest feline cats rose up and went out to get the healer and bring him in the meeting hut.

We shall have the healer tell us what he has found out and then we will discuss the matter of a plan to get rid of the enforcers that are invading our homes and our lands. The elders said as they all took turns with each word. It made Jim dizzy as he listened to them talk. In a few minutes Jim found himself in front of a large white coyote (they were rare in the wild) he was tall with ice blue eyes that almost looked to be white.

I am healer Matthew of Moon-shire village and I am the one that attended the enforcer's wounds and found the device and decipher the code inside of the human. If you would hear me and listen carefully, for there are things that you may not understand. I have deciphered the code, but there are confusing words that do not make sense. Let me tell you what I have first and then maybe we all could find the words. The healer said as he took out a large flat board that looked like some kind of screen device that is metal with something else that Jim could not make out what it is?

Jim went over to the healer and made a strange face as he waited for the healer to open the flat screen.

The healer opened the screen that was also a computer he stole from another human healer when he was at the great city. He also took other medical things that would have help the hybrids. He had been an assistant to human healers. And learned how he could help his hybrids to survive.

The healer opened the screen and let the computer open up as it went straight to the enforcers body was open by the chest all of his inside was pulled out and laid on a table, blood was spill on the floor and on the table. The sight was like looking at some kind of food frizzing mad wolves and cats.

These are the enforcer's body parts, but what we found under the heart was a device that looked like a box, you see it now.

The screen changed with a small box that had a red light with wires that looked like it was connected to the enforcer's heart. Another wire was longer and with something on the end of it.

Jim wanted to ask where the wire came from but was sure he knew. Then something else the healer showed everyone again with the body. The bones were not all human bones, there were some kind of metal and chemical that showed that the blood they were seeing was something else and not human.

These enforcers are not human, not completely. The enforcers are half machines or something like that we really don't know for sure. We do know that the box had a voice that controlled the enforcer. The long wire was connected to the brain that we also open up and found that the brain had another small wires that connected to the brain waves and made the enforcer enable to move or make any decision on their own. These are not humans. They are controlled androids with only one mission that is to kill us all. The healer said as he opened up another part of the computer and heard what was in the box relay words that sound like a computer or something with digital active words that made small sentences. But numbers were mixed in with the words and this made it confusing.

Hmm Jim thought as he thought about what the machine was saying. 35 longitudes and 40 latitudes are the areas sequences of arrival, be at 35 longitude 1300 hours. 1400 35 40 south head north 40 degrees east. Extinguish all that comes in connect with 35 longitudes that are not within the 40 area circular sight. Contain eliminate retain status and report.

That was when the healer closed the screen and looked at everyone in the meeting hut. 35 40 coordinate to a place a meeting place that was where they were meeting with someone that was giving the coordination and contain eliminate was anyone that was not with their cause. Jim said as he studied the sight of the box. It brought memories to when he had talked and was shown one of the boxes that were was the controller and it kept the enforcer alive as long as his head stayed on his body. And that was his friend told him and how he told the others to cut off the enforcers head off. There was nothing else his friend had said before he died.

Jim listen to all that was said by the healer and the screen computer. Hmm, Jim thought again about the coordinates it has to be close. But how could he find it out he has to fly or have someone with—wait a minutes. 35 longitudes that is horizontal and 40 latitudes-that is not it not really something was missing, but he had to look first in the sky and go from the village point 35 miles straight up and then go 40 miles go either to the right or to the left and he thinks may be he could figure it out then.

Jim looked at the elders and then took the lead as he stood up and started to talk.

I think I know what they are saying, but I need to look in the air. The fact is longitude and latitude are used to point out certain areas. We might be able to find them before they come back to kill us. We need to find this place. I think I know how if I can just get up there in the sky I mean fly like a bird. Do you understand what I am talking about? Jim said as he tried to get them to understand what he was trying to tell them. Jim felt frustrated and upset as he tried to tell them again.

Alright if we could find a way for you to fly how would this help us? One of feline elder ask.

I could see where the longitude is started and then look to see the latitude next at the one point of the two that meets in the middle would be where we would find that enforcers campsite is. We could find a weak spot and then we attack quietly. Jim said as he motioned his hands in ways that showed how long and latitude are shown in the air.

Silently fighting how would that be? Another elder feline asked.

Well we could talk about it but first we need to look at the 35 longitude and the 40 latitude first and find that point. We need to go in as quiet as we could and not let the other enforcers wake up. If I am right, then there might be at least a thousand of them waiting in that camp. But we need to kill them all and not let one live if we can help it. I think I got a good plan and how we can fight them. But there is another problem I just thought about, they have to have someone watching the village and everyone here move around. The tunnels still are one of the weakness we have here and that would still make the enforcers try again to get in the village at night or now. Jim felt his skin started to crawl. Someone was in the tunnels, he felt them running and getting out of one hut. Jim move as he grabbed one of the healer's long needles that had something in it. One look at the healer was all he had to know what was in the needle. A war cry came out of Jim as he ran through the village and opened up the one hut that made his skin go cold.

The hut had children sleeping in it. Jim had to do something first and it was not what he really like to do. Fire he needed to put in the tunnels. One of the elders had followed Jim. We need to put the flames in the tunnels now. Jim said as he looked at a large wolf as he grabbed one of the fire stick that stood close the huts door.

Jim ran in found the children dead with three adult hybrids that looked to strange. They almost didn't look like hybrids they looked to strange some kind of abnormality to their faces and bodies.

Their faces were cut up with eyes that looked like the enforcers they had killed. Did someone do the same thing to them as they done to the enforcers. Jim did not have time to think, his hands shot out and the needle stick went flying out of his hand and landed in one of the hybrids neck. The others came running after Jim, but he was faster, he took one of the fire sticks from the elder that stood behind him and threw it at the hybrids that fought with the enforcers. The hybrids screamed as the flames kissed his body. Jim watched then at someone that threw some kind of liquid at the hybrids the liquid caught with the flame that Jim had threw at them sent them up in a gulf of flames. But still they came after Jim and the others their bodies scored and smelled of burning flesh and fur stood as if they did not feel the pain of death that threaten. Two of the hybrids came out from behind Jim back they were the good guys and they had some wicked long swords that was pretty pointy. The swords went through the flames and their heads came off easy as the smell of flesh and fur mix in with the fire burnt Jim nose. No screams no cries, but just snapping of jaws that was pointing at Jim and the others. Their heads lay at the foot of their bodies as all fell into the flames.

Jim came out and wiped some of the blood off his face and arms. Many of the huts were in flames and that was what the enforcers wanted. For them not to have a place to rest but open for a finally attack.

The healer then came over to each of the huts people and told them that they would be alright.

I have a place and my tunnels do not connect to yours but they do connect to another place that is far from here and they would be safe. The healer said as he motioned for everyone to follow him.

You will take the children and all that cannot fight. The injured from last night will be help in the tunnels. The wolf elder said as he looked at Jim.

Hmm. We need to make sure that those tunnels are closed for good. Jim said as he was the badger come up with weapons that had once belong to the enforcers. Each weapon had a power mix that could be used as a bomb inside of the tunnels.

Jim asked the badger how many does he have. We need to work fast. Do we have a large pot to put the powder in first? Jim looked around and waited for the badger to come back with the large pot. One of the long poles with the hole inside would work too. How many tunnels are there in the village and which one is the center and which one is the first of the tunnels? Jim asked the elder. The elder took hold of what Jim was going to do with the powder that made things blow up. Gun powder was what some called it, but they had something even more deadly. A large laser like weapon they took months passed before their cubs and litters were attacked and killed. That would do it. The elder told Jim about the laser and Jim just laughed his head off like a mad man. He asked for the fastest runners from each hybrid tribe and give them parts of the string he found around each hut and started to tie them together. The elder gave Jim a larger piece of thread and they both mixed the powder and a string like thread but it was part of the laser that would help lit up the tunnel and blow their safe heaven up. For right now that safe heaven is not safe anymore.

Four cats and four wolves had step up and said that they would help with the cause. As it is their home and this was their war.

The first two was one wolf and one cat and they ran as fast as they could. The wait was unsure as Jim and the elder waited for the tug on the string, then another two went down just like the first one and they waited again for the tug then the last two went down and the tug was short and fast as the four that was down had helped with the last two that put their powder downs then followed by two string that laid along the trail down the tunnels connecting to each other.

Alright we are going to wait outside of the tunnels that are connect and the ones that follow those that are not located to this village we are going to set the first group off and then the second one and the last one will happen here at each of the huts in the village. We will close them off. Jim said as he moved to where the forest laid. Jim found that there were other tunnels that lead to different direction from the villages huts. Those tunnels lead each occupied hut down to safety from any intruders. The elders showed Jim where the tunnels began and how far they had to go in order to blow up the main tunnels to the village. The one tunnel lean back against a large tree that fell in a hole that Jim and the others had to jump down. One of the cats were spreading over their tracks with pepper that smell strong and made the overgrowth more mildew and mold like. But their scent was not there anymore.

A large bolder covered a path that Jim thought was to the opening of the tunnel, but he was fooled by the elder's smile. The tunnel door was not blocked, but open as the elder tap the side of the bolder close behind everyone that followed them, two hybrid hunters and two guards to help fight off any enforcers that were or might be at the end of the tunnels door.

The tunnels were dark and Jim could not see like the hybrids keen eyes at night. So one of the guards took out something small and round that glowed, he had it in his pocket of his pants that were torn at the bottom and on the inside of the seam.

It is one of my favorite toys when I was a pup. My papa had found it in a cave on one of his hunting for the village, it is a glowing rock. I give it to you as a gift you had help us many of our families and warn us before it began. We are most grateful for that. The one of the guards said to Jim. Jim lost his voice as he recalled his part of the battle and hoped that not many of the children suffered in the battle. It was war and many will suffer and die before they could stop the war. They got to where the tunnel ended and found a tree roots that collected down ward and blocked their path. But again the elder touched one side of the roots and they found another path that lead to a tunnels opening, it was the one that the enforcers used to get in the huts in the villages last night. But this time they stood back as they put out any light that might show where they were. Jim had to put the glowing rock back in his pants pocket and hoped that the glow would not be seen. Then the guard gave Jim a black bag to put the rock in for safety. Jim put the glow rock inside of the black bag and let his breath out. Nothing happen yet, but then four of the enforcers and six large hybrids came down the tunnel where they had been watching and waited silently until the last hybrid passed them. Jim set the fire on the long string that was planted on the side of the tunnels path and not the one that had been on the ground. Jim lit the thread that was not laser and ran into the other tunnel and back up to where they were at first.

The sound was large and made everything around them move like an earthquake. Jim and the elders moved down the line where another path that lead to the second part of the exploration would take place.

They waited again as the bush hided their place that led down ward to the top of the tunnel where it led to the village, but the hole was underneath a bush and a tree that has fallen. This time the line was closer than what Jim would have thought of. The thread that was on the top of the tunnel close to where they were looking down at the passing enforcers that were scared by now to where to go, but their minds were programed to follow orders and the order was to destroy the villages. So they keep on fighting the mind control and the fear of blowing up down in a dark tunnel. Jim could see it in their walk and in their running and knew it would not be the blowing up that would kill them, it would be the fighting the controller in their minds.

The second one went off without any problems and the sound made the first even worst. Jim needed to up in the air to find this 35 point to 45 latitude point. It had to connect to where their camp was and they could blow it up. That would get these out of the way, but not completely as the government it seems to be getting closer to in the forest that was not their land so it became the hybrids country.

Out of the village was a small meadow like the one that was used when the king got there to settle a fight before it got bad. A large bird with wings span of 80 to 80. The bird was brown with white tips and white head his eyes keen and strong stern as serious but knew what Jim need to see. The bird was big enough to hold Jim up in the air for long periods of time. He was alone and no other birds flew in his path.

How can I tell the bird where I need to be? Jim asked the elder as he got on.

You need only to touch the birds body and he can talk to you with a mind link. It is his only gift that he has from the created.

Jim touch the bird and told him of the 35 longitude and 45 latitudes and the point to where the enforcers are.

The birds told him that he had seen that place that had many humans in a camp with hybrids. It is strange to see as it is rare for hybrids and humans to be together without fighting. Jim was not all human. The bird had sense that. He had also found that Jim was one of freedom fighters that has been helping his kind to survive in peace. He will let this strange man to ride his back and take him to where the enemies were at.

Jim was relieved and scared to death as the bird flew up over clouds and trees that seem to jump out of the clouds in height.

CHAPTER TWENTY-FIVE

ARK WONDERED AROUND THE forest not knowing what to do next. He had just killed another hybrid that might have been his mate, but he was too young to have a mate, at least not now. The forest seemed to get dark as he walked through the bushes and tree stumps that were in his path. The sounds of forest animals running through the forest grounds and flying outward toward the trees and the sky that Mark could not see but the trees that hidden the moon and stars. Slowly Mark frozen in mid turn as he heard something running through the forest, his breath hard and heavy as he tried to control his heart beat. The sound of his heart would tell other hybrids where he was. He wasn't sure if that was a good thing or not. Wild hybrids may not understand him Mark thought.

Mark cleared his mind as he only wanted to hear who was running his way. A small step backward and one turn of his head, Mark noticed a large bush that had blue berries of some kind growing on it. The smell was sweet and it was just what he need to hide his scent. Mark figured the runner was at least five miles from where he was, then the runner stopped. That was when Mark stop rubbing the berries on his face and feet. He had to be silent and hoped the any wind coming in the forest would not send his scent toward the runner. Mark step behind the bush and kneeled down slowly as he waited for the runner to get near. The sound again came, a small creep of the floor of the forest ground. Heavy breathing and a cough that was familiar to Mark ears.

Slowly Mark got up and noticed that he did not smell who was behind the bush. So he got up slowly and carefully to see who it was. His eye sight was good in the dark as he was more hybrid than human. The sight that Mark saw was more of a surprise and something he thought he would not see any more.

Dante stood looking at his big brother and was in complete shock.

He had to land the mobile down below the cave where the spider had attack them. Joan and her daughter were safe with the mobile. He had set the mobile in flight if any attack struck the mobile. The mobile setting was straight to a place that his father had always said to go and it was outside and as far from the area and country that no one would even know about. But it was a secret that only he and brother know about, he wasn't sure if his sister knew about although. Dante knew he had to find some of the fighters here, but where? Dante thought about his scent as both of his parents told him that a hybrids smell and eye sights were one of the gifts that came with being a hybrid. Dante took that as he looked around the mobile for something to hide his scent, but only found food and some kind of green stuff that he was not sure of. The smell was like grass, but stronger than that. Dante cough as the smell made him gag. He had taken all of his clothes off, he thought it would be a better way of changing into his animal form if he needed to fight anyone. He went in the forest with just his bare body and nothing else. His skin turned a lime green to blend in with the forest vegetables that were growing fast around where he had landed the mobile. He was not embarrassed to show off his body, he did not have much to show as he was still considered a child and he felt good doing it. Now he looked at his big brother face to face and thought he was dead.

Mark knew his brother like to go around in the nude, but bugs and lice and ticks would have a time of him as food on the run. What is wrong with you man? Mark said as he looked shock but more surprise than shock.

Dante smile and chuckled at the sight of his brothers' face. It was the kind of face you just wish you could show off to others. Mark I thought you might be dead by now. You just disappeared like the wind. What happen bro? Dante said as he laughed a little at his brother.

Uh, well that one hybrid bitch that was still in my mobile part I killed. She is the traitor and well her body is a few miles south of here. I —don't want to show off my kill right now. Mark said as he started to laugh at his little brother body that was as bare as a new born baby.

Well the other bitch was not a traitor, she lost her life when she fought a spider off so Joan and her daughter would be safe. Mom and Carrie had been lost somewhere around here. I don't know where although I think they might be close by. The hair on my arms are standing up and I feel something watching us. Dante said as he turned around to see what his brother was looking at. Mark send his mind link and stop talking.

Dante you need to be quiet someone behind you is watching us and it is not Mom or sis. There are more of them standing there too. Slowly move around me and start to change your form. I am half naked myself. But my pants are going to rip in a few moments. Mark said to him with their mind links.

Friends or foe bro? We don't need to fight them if they are friend right? Dante said as his bones form muscles and strength got longer and stronger with each wolf form started to come forth. Within a few minutes Mark and Dante became wolf and moved into the darkness that was behind them. A large bush that covered their bodies shed their sight from anyone that was out there hunting them.

A large skunk with white tail and large ears seem to jump out from behind Mark and Dante starling them as they sat in waiting. But Mark nudging the skunk a little rough and the skunk sprayed them. That was what Mark and Dante needed to get rid of their scent. Mark move farther back into the bush, there had to be a place in here for them to hide even farther. He could smell the hybrids that were coming closer to where they had been. But then they heard a scream and shout as the skunk must be still upset and sprayed them too. The sound of the hybrids running toward the opposite of where they were seemed kind of funny as Mark and Dante rose partly up as they half form into their true hybrid form. They looked both human and wolf in this form that is both before either form of human or wolf.

They watch the small hunting party of eight wolf hybrids running so fast that one or two had hit a tree and hit each other as they were running away from the skunk that was still following them with hisses. Mark and Dante laughed, but not too loud. We need to find DAD, I got some messages that I think was dad. But I am not sure, I heard him singing a song that sounded like American I think? I am not sure, but it sounded like him. Dante said.

I didn't hear him? Mark said as he looked at his brother half green wolf.

You didn't? Look I think we need to go that way north about 20 miles and turn south another 10 miles. I saw a village that looked like they were being attacked by the enforcers. We need to get there I think that is where I heard him sing. Dante said as he pointed in that direction.

Mark was not sure of this. But it was the only way to find out where their father is and hope that their mother and sister had found each other and dad too.

They took off wondering where and how did those hybrids find them. But then again they were not caught.

Maria and Carrie woke up in a cage somewhere high over a camp full of enforcers. They were hanging over a pit of fire that was tickling their bodies and feet as they felt the heat rising toward them.

They were caught and this might be the end, but where is Mark and Dante and that of Joan and her daughter? Right now they had to stay calm or they would be dead and no use to anyone that might be alive.

Maria had to keep them in silence as she watched how the enforcers were moving like robots and strangeness. There were hybrids there too and that was not good not good at all. *Carrie, we need to use our mind link, it is the only way we will be able to talk. Any noise of any kind will just get their attention and it may not be good. Do you understand me?*

Mom what wwhat are they? They don't look like they are even alive? Carrie said as she looked scared.

They are human and some are hybrids, but they are also robots too. I think this was your father had tried to tell me one night after all of you went to bed. They have some kind of brain control and I think those hybrids have the same thing. None of them can think on their own. Some kind of device is inside of their heads that are telling them what to do.

Carrie looked down and watched the hybrids shake their heads as if something is bothering them.

Mom do you think some of them are good and were forced into this mind control thing? Carrie said.

Maybe you're right or maybe you are not. But we need to be careful. Because we don't know how dangerous they are. This mind control will make them do things that they may not do either way. Maria said as she looked hard at all of the enforcers below.

One of the men below came out of a large tent like building, the canvas of the tent was a deep green that blended with the forest. Maria keen eye sight could see as far as she needs to see. The man she noticed with blond hair and wearing a blue suit uniform almost like the enforcers uniforms, but the badges on his suite made it clear he was important, then she noticed someone else that was walking next to him in white coat and black with grey streaks. The man look upset and nervous as he walked with the other man dress in enforcer's uniform.

That man looks familiar Carrie? I know him but I can't remember his name. He looks like one of the scientist at the capital? Was not is he one of the scientist came over to our home for the celebration of new day? Maria asked mostly to herself than to her daughter. This would bug her no she knows who he is. That's Jeff Michaels, he is the one that made something that would make the enforcers immortals. Well that is what she thought he said. But he never told anyone how he would come up with the immortal device. Mind control might be one of his discovery, but that was discovered over 500 years ago and it did not work to will. But why? Why was he here? and why are they waiting to kill her and her daughter. She guessed that they might figure out that her husband and his family were part of the freedom fighter spies!

Carrie looked around them and up at how the cage was hanging down over the fire. The rope that was connected to cages hook was connected to a large bolder that she didn't realized that they were so close to the mountain side. Some kind of metal rod that was inside of the bolder with a pulling that was connected to the rope that had the cage. All of this is great, and her mind was spinning with ideas of how to get out of this mess.

But her idea went out as she saw who was at the top of the bolder. Another very large hybrid with muscles that seem look like mountains on a large tree branch thick and solid. His head was round with fur covering his facial features. But the eyes were so intense and scary as Carrie back away in the cage, her idea failed before she could even start it in motion. Carrie touched her mothers' arm as she kept her sight on the hybrid on top of the bolder. Watching him standing there looking down at them was making Carrie more nervous and scared, she saw the strange hybrid grin with his long snout showing off his fangs sharp and scary as far as Carrie was at the time.

Maria stop looking at the scientist and looked up at her daughter. In whispers that no one could hear, Maria asked her what was wrong?

Carrie spoke to her mother with her mind as it was safer that way. They were the only ones that could hear each other's thoughts. *Mom there is a big a very big hybrid over there on the bolder. He is looking down at us. I had an idea, but that is cancel now because of that thing up there.*

Carrie he is nothing! I can handle him if I have to. So what is your plan?

I need to get the cage to swing back and forth I am going to grab the rope, you grab my legs and the cage should break, the metal feels weak I know that we cannot get out of here like this not without falling in that flame. So I think that we might be able to grab the rope and climb up. But that thing may stop us. Before we get there or when we get up there. Carrie said as she leaned back and forth making the cage swing hard against the bolder. The cage made a sound and the hybrid jump down on top of the cage.

The ground shook hard, trees and bushes shook as they lean back and forth from the ground shaking. The sound of the ground opening up and hybrids falling down in the earth holes that sprout flames and hot air.

The hybrid fell off the cage as the cage broke and fell off the rope line that still was connected to the bolder. Maria grab her daughters leg and climb up to the top of the bolder then she grabbed her daughters hand pulled her up. The sight of the camp was like looking at something from the outside world, where many of the poor and needy are fighting just to survive. It hurt heart as she found many close to the great city. Now she had to get her daughter out of here fast before they recover and go after them. The sight of how the forest seem to clasp inward was a reminder of how weak the planet was getting. We need to be careful where we go, the ground is getting weak and we might be part of the planets craters. Maria told her daughter and messed up her hair.

You are too smart and too quick for this old wolf. Maria said as they walked on top of the bolder and down a path that lead them into the forest.

Steve and the others walked back to the village, but Jack kept on asking question about the tunnel and the place where the hybrids were holding the village people.

What does the tunnel look like it? Is it under the trees or under something else? How low is the ceiling? How did you all find the tunnel? How many of us can get through the tunnel? How big I the tunnel? How far is the tunnel and is there any hiding place on the outside? Where does it come out of? Jack kept on asking as they walked back to the tree village. As they went along the path back to the tree village, Steve just happen to look up and find that the village was a lot bigger than he thought it was. It was just the first tree after the meadow they had found after running from the hybrids and enforcers that they found these villages up in the trees that Steve really did notice any else. Now he sees the village in the dark as his hybrids sight starts to focus better. He could see the detail outline of the huts and the walk ways that connected each tree and each hut.

Steve noticed that his hearing was stronger now too, the sounds of bugs crawling on the trucks of trees as night birds scream out there hunting calls outward on the path of the breeze. The feel of the sticks and rocks under his feet did not hurt as much as it did before he could change into the wolf he was or was he a cat. Does it matter any ways which one he was, all he knew he could change into a hybrid?

Something big flew over their heads, Steve could hear the sound of wings big flapping against the wind as it blew heavy around the trees. Another sound caught Steve ears, children talking to someone, but they were going in the opposite direction of where Steve and the others were going. Then another voice was heard, a deep voice that Steve knew very well, Max.

Steve did not remember seeing Max at the fight back in the circle of stones, he was not around when Jack threaten the leader or showed everyone the leaders true colors. No Max was not in sight. Now Steve was getting worried. Max might have gone ahead to find the tunnel that would lead them to Max Susan and daughter. Max was crazy when it came to Susan and the baby of theirs. Steve could understand that. Steve missed his sister Brooke. She was all he had left after their parents died. Now she is dead and he has to keep on going. Maybe just maybe he would find his own mate, his own wife now that he was free and outside of the community and the city that seemed to hold him back.

Brook smile at Steve as she ate an apple that Steve gave her. Then the memory changed into a fight that bought outside of the community and Brooke was pulled into the fight as a group of young men and women came over to where she and Steve had found some woods for their fire inside of the community. The people wanted the wood. But Brooke told them to look somewhere else, there is plenty of wood around us, just look around and they would find all the wood they would want. But that was not all they wanted. They wanted me Steve too, but Brooke knew why they did and she would not let Steve out of her sight. The fight went on and she kicked them so bad that they did not know what was coming at them. Her legs flew high over their heads coming downward into their faces as her legs kept one hitting more places on their bodies that they ran fast back into their own neighborhood.

She was great and she taught both of Steve and his best friend Jack and Max and Susan at the time. We even learn how to communicate with out words. Blinking was another way of getting messages to each other and moving hands and tapping feet were communication between them. Brooke was and always be more than just his sister. Steve had to clear his mind as his senses went to the sounds of the birds and bugs moving along the forest. Steve body changed without Steve even knowing it as it felt something moving along the ground. One word came out of Steve mouth. Take cover, the ground is—. Steve stop talking as the ground moved fast, the sound of trees breaking and falling around them made everyone move out of the forest and back to where the fighting had been between Jack and the leader of the village. The ground crumbled underneath their feet as they ran through bushes and trees. Some screamed out as bodies disappeared under their feet. Steve grabbed some of the children that were with them and went through the forest like a cannonball-jet. He found a settle ground that was at least 10 miles from the sight of the fallen ground. Others were seen running but screaming for help. Steve felt his body change again into something else and he ran as fast as he could to get the others to the safe place he found. Jack had grabbed the healer and another man as he dragged them farther away from the forest path. Mr. Farmer had also grabbed two people that were fighting him to get away. But he would not let them go. This is not normal earthquake something has triggered the quake and we are in trouble it is a ripple effect that whoever done this will destroy everyone around this forest and mountains.

Jim was getting a little upset as he realized that the explosive they set off had made the ground unstable, an earthquake or craters made from unstable ground. Something that he was not aware of and if he knew he would not have done it this way. Now he could hear the screams coming from the villages around them. Many hybrids running like a large animal stampede.

The large bird he was on flew over the forest and away from all that was under Jim. The king may not be able to get out of this. Jim just hope his family was safe. He thought he saw Maria and Carrie. But the boys were not in sight. The camp of the enforcers gone as the quake took all that was in it way. That threat is not important now or even matters it was or is the fact that the ground is caving in fast. He had to go back and see if he could see if for sure that it was Maria and their daughter. He had to know if they were safe.

Steve ran fast as he could with the children in his arms and on his back. The fact that steve had thought something large something big that would fly on the wings of air and the ability to hold the children safely, his body stretched longer than he should, but a light a bright light blinded the children's sight as Steve felt something strange something hot come over his body and he found that what he had changed into was neither bird or bat, but something that he has never seen or heard of. He had been change into a creature that had the ability to carry more than five children in his arms and hold at least eight more on his back and tail. His long snout had bumps that were sharp and his legs were two with scales of dark green to blend into the forest greenery. He didn't notice, but the children did, he had wings long and black with a wing span that were like two long corn fields. The children kept on telling him to fly, but Steve was unsure if he could do it. The wings came out and took him up over the sight of the ground craving in around the forest. The sight was horrible, but ground stop crumbling down into craters. The forest stood still, birds started to come back. But Steve did not trust the ground and all those craters that were made somehow triggered by something Steve figured. Another open meadow that did not have a crater or anything. But as Steve got closer he noticed that the meadow was not what he thought, and flew upward, he did not want the children even touching the ground, it was a swamp full of green giants of monsters that were jumping out of its spots to grab one of the children. Steve flew higher and hit one of the monster in the snout hard that the thing fell back down in the swamp with a large splash that struck Steve legs. Steve long tail hit another monster on the head hard that the sound of something cracking underneath Steve tail. He knew it was not his tail that cracked, but the monster head, looking downward Steve saw the thing falling hard back into the swamp. Amazing Steve thought as he watched the other monster feed off the dead monster. At least those things would leave them alone. His wings took him even farther as he watched closely at the ground. That was when he saw the truck that took them here. There was something on the top of the truck and it was fighting off another hybrid that looked strangely as it fought.

Steve landed on top of the truck and stood still with the children behind his wings.

His mind sent off messages that he could not speak out loud. He was afraid his words would come out to loud. But he had to speak.

The hybrid turned around as he watched a giant dragon with children land on the truck he was to protect. His other hybrids had closed the back doors of the truck to keep the secret safe. But this is not real. A dragon is extinct and there are none hybrid-dragon alive.

The dragon got smaller and turned into a young human. That was even more-strange. Normal hybrids had always had some of the animal genes outside like wolf hybrids have more hair or fur on arms and legs with not round ears and not actually on the side of the head either. The ears of all hybrids were closer to the top of the head and had fur around the ear to hide them from humans. Cats had whiskers coming out the side of their noses as well as wolves and most hybrids too. Our eyes are round with no white showing, a dark blue or black solid eye. This man this hybrid looks more like a human, he did not have any of the traits that other hybrids have. He was small for one thing, but he looks like he needs to eat more, his face was getting white like he was going to faint or something.

The hybrid stood there just looking at Steve like he was from some other planets or something. Steve shook his head as he worked on clearing his mind.

Who are you? Steve asked him.

I am from the village of the canine forgotten. We were part of the Kings guards to protect all of you that have from this strange thing, two of our hybrids that are technology knowledge of this device have closed themselves in the front of the truck. Now it is my turn to ask who you are? Am I right to say that you are part of the trucks companions? The hybrid asked Steve.

Steve looked at the hybrid and noticed that his face was sort of round with a longer snout like mouth. That was strange?

What is the Kings name? I am not sure if his name is what? Steve asked as if he hope that the hybrid would know for sure what the Kings name is.

Everyone knows that the King name is Michael, but he goes by other names that other knows of him also. Here it is Michael. What name do you recall of him? Again the hybrid asked.

Mike is all I know I think? His hair is black as nights in a hidden cave? Steve asked again.

No our King has hair of gold when he is a feline and any other animal his hair becomes of dark fur, but black hair is not true! The hybrid said.

So where is his fling blanket? Steve asked the hybrid as another question that would reveal who this really is?

He does not have such thing as a fling blanket that is impossible to use. He usually rides something he calls motorcycle it is his favorite when he does not use his powers of the hybrid. The hybrid said as he came finally to this conclusion of why this man had asked him about his King's ways. He was trying to find if he was a traitor or not. This is a good way, but he should know many hybrids know of the King looks and his way of travel. All of this not new or different to any hybrids that live throughout the world. The hybrid told Steve.

Hmm is that so, but can you tell me why this truck is so important to him and the Government? Steve asked him.

Government? The truck has something in it that is important? We were told only to protect any of the ones that have been part of the truck? Is that what it is called truck? The hybrid asked slowly as he tried to understand this strange man that can change into a dragon.

Alright, but why is it important to the government? Steve asked him.

I cannot say, because hybrid I do not know why only it is a command from my King.

Then turn the computer on in the truck and we could see what it has to say. It would let you know who I am and maybe where the others are. Did you feel the ground shake like an earth quakes? Where are they now or had they died from the quake? Steve asked the hybrid.

You can call me Thero. My village is called the lost hybrids. We had blended with the other hybrid wolf village to give more mates to those that do not have one. It is a good plan, many of us are hunters for the villages and bring trades to all that need the food we hunt.

I will tell the ones that are in the front of the truck to turn the computer on for you. Unless you can command this computer then I know you are part the trucks companions. The hybrid said as he stumped his feet hard against the trucks roof where they were standing.

The truck started to make some loud sound that woke the birds up and many of the birds scream their protest. The trees shook as the birds took flight over their heads. The sky went from night to early morning. Because of hybrids eye sights was better during the night time as well as the daytime, but the sight at night gave them enough sight as if the night had more light like the daytime.

Steve took the children down slowly after he turned back into a dragon. It felt good to just change into anything he thought of and not feel any pain, but he was so hungry that he wanted eat something, but what? Food was inside of the truck back and that was where he need to be right now. But it would wait after he talked to the computer.

Steve stood close to the open door of the truck front part. His voice calm, but worried about his friends that he left behind.

Computer where is my friends Jack and Mr. Farmer as well as Max and the children? Steve asked the computer.

The voice that came out was not a woman's voice, but a child's voice, small and calm as it heard its command from Steve.

Searching now, perimeter is clear of all danger, searching for Jack and Farmer and those that are part of my process code.

20-mile radius no life form that is human or hybrid,

30-miles radius no life form found that is human or hybrid.

40-miles radius no life form found that is human or hybrid.

50-miles radius no life form found that is human or hybrid.

60-miles radius some life forms are found, ten hybrids small with twenty other hybrids large in size. One human that is not human but not hybrid either.

No Jack no Farmer no children of the streets are found.

Do you want me to continue to search within 70 to 100-miles radius? The computer said.

Steve listen and wonder who the non-human is. Was he an enforcer?

Computer is the non-human an enforcer? Steve asked.

No, form of body is human, but there is two hearts and brain waves are human with taint of hybrid blood.

Tell me computer can you tell me if any villages survived the quake?

Quake was triggered by explosive that were buried inside of tunnels many of the surrounding village from the tunnels explosive first charge. There are little survivors and those that are coming toward us now are the only survivors. The computer said.

Hmm, we need to search farther? Do a 100 to 200-mile radius north by southwest. Steve told the computer.

The computer search and found four movements that were getting close, but no Jack and no Mr. Farmer either. The four are hybrids. Two are females and two are male. They are less than 50-miles radius. I have concluded that their arrival would be in one hour and ten minutes.

I need to eat and I figure out what to do with the children and those that are coming. They may need to eat too. We have a long day and night ahead of us. We need to be prepared for anything now. The enforcers might think right if they believe we were the ones to make the quake happen. Steve said out loud as he turned to look at the hybrids waiting for someone or something. They had been looking toward the forest as if they could hear the ones coming close to them. Who were they and what had caused the quake to happen. Was the ground that unstable? Are any of the people that were coming friends or were they enemies? That would one question that they would not know until whoever has gotten here. Steve thought.

Printed in the United States
By Bookmasters